the Lake

LOUISE SHARLAND

avon.

Published by AVON
A division of HarperCollins*Publishers* Ltd
1 London Bridge Street
London SE1 9GF

www.harpercollins.co.uk

HarperCollins*Publishers*
1st Floor, Watermarque Building, Ringsend Road
Dublin 4, Ireland
This trade paperback edition 2021

1

First published in Great Britain by HarperCollins*Publishers* 2021

A catalogue copy of this book is available from the British Library.

ISBN: 978-0-00-846580-3

Typeset in Sabon Lt Std by Palimpsest Book Production Limited,
Falkirk, Stirlingshire
Printed and bound in UK by CPI Group (UK) Ltd, Croydon CR0 4YY

MIX
Paper from
responsible sources
FSC™ C007454

This book is produced from independently certified FSC™ paper
to ensure responsible forest management.

For more information visit: www.harpercollins.co.uk/green

For my family

He that studieth revenge keepeth his own wounds green, which otherwise would heal and do well.

– John Milton

1

The small patch of sand and scrubland that borders the lake is nearly empty; just a woman and her young son skipping stones. A few metres out, a paddleboarder has paused his journey to take in the view. I try my best to appreciate the beauty, but everything about this place is shrouded in pain. I distract myself by unwrapping the spray of white lilies I have brought, leaning them against the small wooden bench that overlooks the water. I could leave it of course – not return every year as I do – *move on* – but Michael was my son; my only child. He deserves to be remembered.

Nearby, the child's giggles drift on the breeze as he runs from his mother's outstretched hand. 'Sweetheart,' she calls, now breathless and unable to keep up. 'Don't get your new trainers wet!'

On the water the paddleboarder resumes his tour, his long rhythmic strokes hypnotic, enticing. The mother stumbles. In the time it takes to right herself, her little boy has wandered knee-deep into the water. The sound of rotors calls my attention, and I look up, following the path of a grey bug across the sky. A military helicopter from the nearby Royal Navy air station.

'Danny?' The woman's voice sounds frightened, far away. I scan the shore. Only she and I remain. Out on the lake, a piece of driftwood bobs and sinks. '*Danny!*' Fear transforms into frenzy as she charges into the water. Her dungarees, soaked and weighted, pull her to her knees. Hearing her hysterical screams, the paddleboarder moves forward, searching the water for any sign of the child. I freeze; do nothing. I desperately want to lift my feet from where they're weighted into the sand – run into the water and help – but some immense terror holds me back. Ever since Michael drowned I can't even step into a bath.

'I've found him!' someone cries, and suddenly I am free. The paddleboarder races towards the shore, the boy's frail, limp body draped across his arms.

'Put him down,' I yell, stripping off my jacket and throwing it on the grass. The woman regards me suspiciously. 'I'm a nurse!' And within seconds I'm forcing air into the little boy's waterlogged lungs, and gently kneading his small, immobile heart.

2

It's always the same: first the darkness, the struggle; and then the unbearable choking feeling as I desperately try to kick my way through fetid water towards that tiny pinprick of light. Something keeps dragging me down: two iron fists, clamped around my ankles, pulling hard. When I look back into the muddy depths, I see a face: bleak, death-vacant eyes staring back up at me.

'Kate, are you all right?' I feel someone tugging at my shoulder. 'Kate!'

I turn to see my husband Adam sitting up in bed beside me, the soft glow of a Kindle illuminating his handsome features. 'You've been sitting there staring at nothing for the last twenty minutes.'

'Have I?'

He reaches over and turns on the bedside lamp. 'Are you upset with me?'

'Upset?' It takes a few seconds to reset myself. 'Why would I be upset?'

'About cancelling our plans.'

'Of course not. It wasn't your fault there was a major RTA on the motorway.'

'I mean, I know how much you wanted to see that play.'

I take a shaky breath and reach for a tissue from the bedside table. 'It wasn't that, Adam. Yesterday was the anniversary.'

'What?'

'Michael's anniversary.'

'Oh, shit!'

'For some stupid reason I thought going out might help.'

Adam slips his arm around my shoulders and pulls me in close. 'I'm so sorry.' The bristles on his chin rub against my cheek. 'I should have remembered.'

'You were in A&E until midnight.'

'I still should have remembered.' He turns to me, his expression earnest. 'If you like, I can take you to the cemetery tomorrow?'

'I've been.'

His fingers tighten on my arm. 'The lake then?' I bow my head. 'You've been there too? You know how I feel about you going to the lake on your own. It's not good for you.' There is concern in his voice. Or is it disapproval?

'I just went to lay some flowers, that's all.'

'That's not the point. You know what your therapist said—'

'Please, Adam, just leave it.'

Adam pulls away slightly, surprised at my resolve.

It's not often that I disagree with him, but I'm tired. Tired of being managed and mollycoddled, and tired of being treated as if I were a child – or, even worse, a patient. Surely I have the right to remember my son in the way *I* see fit?

'How was it?' he asks finally. 'At the lake I mean.'

'Fine. Absolutely fine.'

I decide not to tell him about the little boy, or my sobs of relief as after nearly three minutes of CPR he mercifully began to breathe. Instead, I think of Michael's memorial bench; of the pale, weather-worn oak, and the brass plaque glinting in the early morning sun.

In memory of Michael David Penrose (2000–2015)
One word frees us of all the weight and pain of life: that word is love

Adam had disapproved, thought the quote morbid, but I had insisted.

'Why don't we go out for lunch tomorrow?' Adam's voice is firm, persuasive. 'We could try that new tapas place on Fore Street.'

'I'm not really sure . . .'

'*Kate.*' Adam runs his hand up along my arm to my shoulder, before slowly letting it slide down to my breast. 'We've talked about this before, haven't we? It's been six years now. Don't you think it's time for us to move on?'

'Move on?' I reply immediately, automatically. 'Yes, of course.' And although my voice rises in agreement, inside I am screaming.

When Adam is finally asleep, I creep downstairs

and pour myself a glass of wine. Reaching into the pocket of my dressing gown, I search for the small blue pill I hid there earlier. I welcome the sensation of the sugary coating dissolving on my tongue, before washing it down with a slug of Pinot.

I won't have any trouble getting back to sleep tonight.

After a lunch of zamburiñas and San Miguel, Adam and I browse the antique shops that are dotted along the Exeter quayside. By the time we make our way back to the car, the sun is sinking behind the cathedral, the cream-coloured stonework a jagged silhouette against darkening skies. For the first time in months I feel lighter; more myself.

We return home to the unremitting blink of the answerphone light.

'Just leave it,' I say, as I slide our takeaways into the oven. 'I'll check the messages later.' I'm looking forward to my squid in black bean sauce when the telephone rings. 'Can't we just leave it?' I ask again, but Adam is already lifting the receiver to his ear.

'Hullo?' He has his consultant's voice on, no doubt anticipating another call about an A&E emergency.

'Who is it?' I whisper.

'Not sure – they're asking for you,' says Adam, handing me the phone and taking a sip of wine.

'Hello?' I can hear someone clearing their throat, and then a soft female voice.

'Katie?'

'Doris, is that you?' Doris Livingstone is my

6

mother's next-door neighbour. 'What is it? Are you okay?'

There's a pause, and the older woman seems to be struggling with what to say next. 'Katie, your mother has had an accident. I've been trying to ring you all day.'

I think of my mobile phone lying dead at the bottom of my bag. 'Is she all right?'

'I'm not sure.' Doris makes a small hiccupping sound. 'I found her at the bottom of the stairs. She was barely breathing. The paramedics came and took her away.'

'Where did they take her? Which hospital?'

'The big one,' she replies. 'Plymouth.' There's another pause, this time longer. 'The way she looked when I found her – so pale – I thought . . .'

'Thank you, Doris. I'd better ring the hospital.'

'Yes, of course.'

'I'll ring you back as soon as I know anything. Speak then.' I carefully place the phone back into its cradle before turning and vomiting into the sink.

It takes nearly half an hour to get through to Plymouth A&E. I insist Adam eat his stir fry, but I can't bear to touch my squid: the thin, rubbery circles remind me now of the transplant valves I handled in my days as a cardiac nurse, in that happier past when Michael was alive and my world was still hopeful. I glance at the refrigerator door. Preserved within a small magnetic picture frame is a photograph I took of him the morning he left for boarding school. Gorgeous, chocolate-coloured curls frame a strong

7

brow and determined chin; but his deep brown eyes are uncertain, his smile hesitant. I feel Adam's hand on my shoulder.

'What did the hospital say?'

'They think it was a stroke.' My voice wavers, but I am determined not to cry. 'Ischemic, but they won't know for sure until they do more tests.'

'Oh, Kate.'

I turn and touch his cheek. 'I have to go.'

'Yes, of course.'

'I mean tonight – now.'

'What?'

'I could tell by the nurse's tone it's serious.' I recall the expression of benign neutrality I'd always adopted before breaking bad news on the ward. Adam pours his wine down the sink and reaches for the car keys.

'You get your coat. I'll drive.'

I point to the calendar stuck to the refrigerator door. 'You're on call.'

'Damn. Maybe—'

'You can't, Adam. You know you need to be within at least a forty-five-minute drive to the hospital.'

'I'll ring Sue, she might—'

'Really, sweetheart, I'll be fine. It's probably better if I go on my own anyway. You know what my mother's like.'

'But that's the hospital where—'

I lay my hand on his. 'I'll be fine. The nurse said she's stabilised, but you know, these things can change in a heartbeat.'

'But if you waited until tomorrow—'

8

'She could be dead by tomorrow.'

Adam takes off his glasses and rubs his eyes. 'Well, I suppose we've got no choice, but I'm really not happy about you driving all that way on your own, especially at this time of night. You're not planning to stay there, are you?'

I try to appear confident, to contain the panic that is threatening to overwhelm me. As much as I love my husband, I wish he would stop asking me all these questions. 'Depends on her status really. I've still got my keys to Mum's house, and there's Tam to see to.'

'That bloody cat,' Adam grumbles. 'Are you sure you don't want me to call the department? Maybe they can find someone to cover for me.'

'It's a Saturday night, darling. They won't be able to find cover at this short notice.'

'I know, but—'

'Adam, trust me, I'll be fine.'

My husband looks uncertain, as if trusting me is something he hasn't been able to do in a while. I'm not sure I blame him.

'I'm coming up first thing tomorrow,' he says. 'No arguments.'

'Okay,' I whisper, and let him envelop me in his strong, secure embrace.

The car's headlights bathe Adam in an eerie glow as I reverse out of the drive. I pull away, grateful to at last be on the road, but still wondering if I should have let him come with me. It isn't that I'm ashamed of my family, it's just that they're so damned hard to explain. A long-absent father, a rebellious older sister, and a fundamentalist Christian mother aren't exactly the ideal in-laws.

I glance at the clock on the dashboard. Eight fifteen. If traffic is good, I can make it to the hospital by ten. I put my foot down, head south. A sudden gust buffets the car, and my knuckles whiten as I grip the steering wheel. It takes a few seconds before I feel steady enough to reach over and turn on the radio. I'm grateful for the solid monotony of the weather forecast easing me on my way.

I haven't long exited the dual carriageway and am just merging onto a poorly lit B-road, when from out of the gloom appear half a dozen small shapes. Without warning, the figures dash across the road directly in front of me, glowing in my headlights. I slam on the brakes and feel the Mini snake as I struggle to manoeuvre it onto the soft verge. Heart pounding, I watch as the creatures flee into the bushes across the road.

'Bloody hell!'

Then I catch sight of it: just to my right stands a single roe deer. No larger than an Alsatian, the tiny creature stands frozen in fear. I ease open the door and manoeuvre my way out of the car. In the headlights' glare, the animal's eyes are huge golden orbs. If it wasn't for its gently heaving lungs it could be made of stone.

'I won't hurt you,' I whisper, edging my way forwards. Somewhere in my peripheral vision I register approaching headlights. As if waking from a trance, the animal blinks, flicks its ears and tears across the road – directly into the path of the oncoming car.

It's just after ten when I finally reach the hospital. The main corridor is quiet, apart from a security guard and two cleaners leaning on their brooms. I ignore the lifts, choosing instead the concrete solitude of the stairwell. At the top I pause before pushing my way through the swinging doors. Ahead of me the green-grey hallway is empty apart from a metal trolley loaded with medical waste bins, and the neon light hanging above hisses and spits. From nearby drifts the unmistakable stench of *hospital*: a nauseating blend of antiseptic, old food and sick. I swallow hard. I can feel the bile rising at the back of my throat, can taste it in my mouth.

The memory comes to me then: sudden and unexpected, like a knife blade in the gut.

I am in a small white room. In front of me is a window into another, smaller room. The grey curtains that frame the window are drawn shut. Next to me stands a police officer. She's dressed in a black uniform with bold white lettering on the back of her flak jacket.

White wall, grey curtains, black uniform. It seems strangely suitable that my world is now devoid of colour. The officer is speaking. I glance towards her. I can see her lips moving, but I can hear no sound. It's as if my world is on mute.

11

The door opens and a man in a white coat enters. He stinks of cheap aftershave. The policewoman touches me on the elbow and nods to him. I watch as he steps forward and pulls on the cord to open the curtains. At first, they jam, and the man tugs impatiently at the mechanism, his pale cheeks reddening. I want to call to him; to scream *don't open them! If you don't open them, I won't have to see!* But it's too late. The curtains are sliding open and I can't look away. Lying on a metal mortuary table in the room beyond the window is my fifteen-year-old son Michael.

3

Making my way into the Intensive Care Unit, my eyes fall to the white line painted on the floor, dividing the rectangular room into two. As I raise my gaze, I can see rows of patients on either side, some hidden behind tightly pulled curtains, all with cotton blankets forming peaks over their feet like tiny holiday park tents.

'Can I help you?'

I find myself looking into the smiling face of a young nurse. 'I'm trying to find my mother.'

'Okay, what's her name?'

'Rebecca Penrose.' It's as if uttering my mother's name has opened a well of despair. I begin to feel the room spinning.

'Oh dear,' says the nurse. 'Are you all right?'

'I'm fine,' I whisper, but my lips have gone numb. The nurse leads me to a chair. 'I'm sorry,' I mumble. 'I feel so silly.'

13

'No need,' replies the nurse. 'It happens all the time. You sit here, and I'll get you a drink of water.'

I close my eyes and force myself to remain calm. Who would have believed that I had once worked in a hospital almost exactly like this? Then Michael died and I found I could no longer bear the frightened looks of the patients, or the uncertain faces of their loved ones, so instead I took a part-time job as a practice nurse: blood tests, cervical smears, nicotine patches. In and out; minimal interaction. Just the way I like it.

'Here you are,' says the nurse, handing me a cup of water. 'Your mother is stabilised but heavily sedated.' She glances at her watch. 'I'm afraid there's not a lot I can tell you until the consultant comes back to review her test results in the morning. Rounds are at eleven. I can arrange for you to speak with him afterwards if that's convenient?' She gives my arm a gentle squeeze. 'Why don't you have a quick visit and then go and get some rest? Do you have someplace to stay?' I nod. 'Leave your number with the nurse at the desk. We'll call you if anything changes.'

I edge my way towards a bed in the far corner of the room. My mother is intubated, a ventilator doing her breathing for her. Her face is pale, her skin rice-paper thin. A blush of broken capillaries on her cheek hints at the drinking problem that has plagued her for most of her life; a dependency that escalated after she was cast out of her beloved Plymouth Brethren because of her younger daughter's sin. A tiny vein in her neck pulsates rhythmically. Everybody wants to live.

'Mum?' I lean forward to whisper. This place is too eerie, too quiet, for normal conversation. 'It's me, Katie.' Her eyelids flicker but there's no response. I check her stats. Decent oxygen, steady heart rate, blood pressure good. I reach forward and take her hand – something I haven't done for many years. 'Mum, it's Katie. I'm here.' I think I feel her hand grip mine, but reason that it's probably an involuntary motor response. Her perpetual pinched expression is gone, and she looks almost pretty. Was she ever pretty? On the mantel at our house in Cornwall is a family photo from when I was small and we were all still a family. My father, large, imposing but still with a sense of playfulness around the eyes, rests a hand on my shoulder. My mother, the stern matriarch, stares resolute into the camera. My sister Grace and I, pale and blank faced, are clearly doing exactly as we are told.

'I'm going to go now, Mum. I expect Tam needs feeding.' My throat feels tight and I'm having trouble swallowing. 'I'll be back tomorrow.'

It takes less than an hour to reach the bridge and cross into Cornwall. Following the road that echoes the curves of the River Tamar, I arrive in Calstock just after midnight. I park my Mini in the shadow of a railway viaduct that arches high above my mother's terraced cottage, and, for the first time in hours, I relax. Moonlight shimmers on the river opposite, and the cloying scent of honeysuckle drifts in through the half-open car window. Forcing myself from the car, I head towards the house. The wrought-iron gate gives a familiar whine as I pull it shut and make my way into the tiny front courtyard. The wisteria, which has framed the doorway for as long as I can remember, is now overgrown, the gnarled branches jealously entwining themselves amongst my mother's prize-winning climbing roses. The door itself, once a bright periwinkle blue, is chipped and faded; the wall lantern which hangs in the alcove, dark. I fumble for the front door key, grateful for the glow of a nearby streetlight. My hand trembles as I slip it into the lock and push open the door.

'Give me strength,' I mutter, before crossing the threshold into the gloom. I grope for the light switch, jumping back when my fingertips graze something slick and furry. Switching on the light, I find it's the fur collar of my mother's old winter coat hanging on the rack. I slip my hand into the pocket to check for a spare key for Adam, and my knuckles disappear deep into the thick wool. I can feel coins, a sweet wrapped in sticky paper, and something rectangular, smooth, and shiny; paper. Or is it cardboard? Holding it up to the light, I see that it's a photograph of my sister, Grace, and me, taken many years before, when I was nine and Grace nearly thirteen. It's a series of photo booth shots of the two of us smiling, posing, sucking our cheeks in like models. Grace, as always, is in the foreground, dwarfing me – I'm little more than one eye and half a cheekbone.

16

I slip the photos into my pocket and glance into the front room. The old settee is still there, now covered with a throw, as well as the two high-backed Queen Anne chairs that we were forbidden from sitting on as children. Behind that lies a small display cabinet of glass animals my mother started collecting not long after she had been ostracised by her fellow Brethren; forcibly cut off from all communication with former church members, family and friends because of the scandal of my teenage pregnancy.

I carry on into the kitchen, a narrow strip of white that hums in the fluorescent light. As I near the back door, the room widens out just enough to allow for a small expandable table. Once there had been room for four chairs, enough to suit a small family, but time and circumstance mean that only a single chair remains. I run my fingertips along the faded Formica countertop. There is no well-used spice rack or matching tea and coffee canisters, only a single jar of decaf and a stack of yellowing newsletters from the local community centre. The sound of a cat's high-pitched whine draws me to the back door.

'Tam,' I call to my mother's bad-tempered tabby, 'is that you?' I slip off the safety chain and turn the latch. The rusty lock groans in protest and from somewhere in the past comes the sound of voices.

'Open the door, Kat.'

I am twelve and Grace has just turned sixteen. It is two in the morning and I have been awoken by the sound of pebbles hitting my bedroom window. I come downstairs, push aside the net curtain on the back door and see her. Grace is wearing a black miniskirt and lace vest, her neon-pink bra straps just visible on her narrow shoulders.

'Grace?' My eyes widen as I open the door. 'Where have you been? Mum's been going mental.'

'Let me in.' My sister's voice is tight. 'There isn't much time.'

'You are going to be in so much trouble,' I whisper, sneaking two biscuits from my mother's hiding place in the pantry.

'Does it look like I give a shit?' Grace reaches past me and grabs a handful of custard creams. 'Donna-Marie and me have got ourselves jobs at a hotel in St Ives. Live in.'

'But what about—'

'There's no bloody way I'm going to work for one of Mum's nutty church friends. I'm sick to death of Brethren rules! No telly, no music, no books, no friends except Brethren, no college.' Grace ticks off the indignities one by one. 'I don't know about you, but I'm fucking suffocating.' Opening the utility drawer, she reaches in, tears two large bin bags from the roll and hands them to me. 'Now be a good little sister – go upstairs and fill these with my things.'

The faint chiming of the mantel clock reminds me of just how late it is. If I'm going to make it back to the hospital for the consultant's rounds at eleven, I'd better get some sleep. But first, I must ring Adam.

'How is she?'

'Intubated, but with good stats.'

There's a long pause before he speaks again. 'The longer she's on life support—'

'I know, honey. I know.'

'Raj has agreed to swap shifts with me tomorrow so I should be able to get to the hospital by eleven.'

'That would be great; really great.'

'If you speak to the consultant before I get there you need to ask about scans. Have they decided on CT or MRI? Will they be doing an echo and a CA? Don't let them fob you off.'

'Yes, Adam. I will ask all those things.'

'I know how much you don't like to cause a fuss, Kate, but this is important.' He sounds slightly irritated that I'm not embracing his proactive approach, but I'm tired. Every thought, every word seems to take enormous effort. It's as if my brain is slowly and methodically shutting down. I need to sleep.

'Have you rung Grace yet?'

'It's late. I'll ring her first thing in the morning.'

'*Kate*.'

'There's nothing she'll be able to do tonight anyway.'

'Promise you'll ring her first thing?'

'Yes, of course.'

Adam clears his throat as if preparing to say something difficult. 'Have you taken your medication?'

'What?'

'Your meds. Have you taken them?'

I try not to let the irritation creep into my voice. 'Yes, of course.'

19

'Just make sure you do.'

Once again, I am the naughty child. 'I'm going to get some sleep, Adam. You should as well.' My mobile feels as if it's stinging my cheek. 'I'll see you tomorrow at eleven. Love you.' I put the phone down before he can question me any further. I realise he's only looking out for me, but sometimes I just want to be left alone.

I make my way upstairs, passing my mother's bedroom and not even daring to glance into the gloomy space beyond the door. I go into the second bedroom. Once it had been painted bright pink, an indulgence my father had agreed to shortly before he left us. Twin beds had sat at either end of the small room, both dotted with stuffed animals that Grace and I had squirrelled away from church jumble sales. After Grace left for St Ives, it changed to a single, and when I was fifteen, there came the sudden addition of a second-hand cot for Michael. Now, however, there is just a single guest bed stacked high with old clothes and half-filled charity shop donation bags. Books dot the floor and, abandoned in the corner next to the wardrobe, there is a small mountain of battered suitcases. I catch sight of something on the bed and float, ghost-like, towards it. I feel my stomach lurch and then, almost collapsing onto the mattress, pull the bundle of soft fabric towards me. It's a grey hoodie with the words *Edgecombe Hall Swim Team* emblazoned across the front in white lettering. Michael often stayed with his grandmother on weekend breaks from boarding school. 'Too far to travel' was his excuse for not coming home, though I sometimes wondered if it was because he didn't want to be around his stepfather. Lifting the hoodie to my face, I breathe in deeply, desperate for a whiff of Cool Water – or even Lynx – body spray.

'He wasn't happy at *that school*, you know,' my mother had declared on the afternoon of Michael's wake. 'He would have come back home but for Adam.' She had refused a glass of sherry, but was somehow managing to slide a third slice of chocolate gateau through her rigid lips.

'Do we have to talk about this now?'

'You spoiled him,' my mother muttered, before turning to make her way back to the buffet table.

'What did you say?'

'Every whim, every impulse,' she turned, her voice cutting through the low-level hum of conversation, 'you pandered to. If you hadn't allowed him to go to that school, he wouldn't have gone swimming that night and wouldn't have—'

'How can you say that?' I remember feeling furious beyond belief. 'He wanted to go! He won that scholarship.' I felt an overpowering need to justify myself. 'All I ever tried to do was the right thing by him.'

'The right thing!' My mother's eyes were two dark pits. 'How would you know what the right thing is? You've never repented for your sins.'

'MICHAEL WAS NOT A SIN!'

I felt heads turning, an awkward hush descending. Before she could speak again, Adam was beside me.

'Grace is going to drive you home, Rebecca.' His voice rang with the authority of his years as an A&E consultant. 'Perhaps it might be best if you don't get in touch for a few days.'

Those few days lasted for nearly a year. If I hadn't made the first move – a colossal effort – I doubt I would have ever heard from my mother again.

4

I wake early, Michael's hoodie still clutched against my chest. The morning is grey and overcast, filling the room with a thick, sludgy light. It takes a few seconds for me to remember where I am. I switch on the bedside lamp, and its soft glow momentarily forces away the gloom.

After a quick shower I wander down to the kitchen. Tam is waiting for me by his food bowl. I scan through the pantry for cat food, to find only a single remaining tin. As I struggle with the ring pull, the cat's hungry cries fill the room.

'Okay, okay,' I empty the contents into his bowl. I even dare to give his tortoiseshell-coloured head a gentle stroke. 'I guess it's just you and me for now.'

I take my cup of black tea – given that there's no milk, bread or even crackers in the house I have to wonder what she lived on – and finally get down to what I've been putting off since last night. I ring Grace.

'Hi, Kat!' Grace is her usual breezy self, probably relaxing in bed while Simon makes a full English for her and Ellie.

'Grace, it's about Mum.'

Time seems to suspend itself in her silence.

'What's happened?'

'She's had a stroke. She's in hospital.'

'What?'

'Deep breaths, Grace. Long and slow.'

In the background I can hear her daughter asking what's wrong.

'Everything's fine, Ellie. Go downstairs and eat your breakfast.' Grace exhales deeply and I hear a door click shut in the background. 'It's not fine though, is it, Kat.'

'She's on a ventilator.'

'Shit.'

'Her stats were good when I saw her last night.'

'I should come.' Grace's voice is beginning to sound panicky. 'Simon's leaving on a business trip tonight and won't be back until Tuesday. I'll have to arrange cover at work. Maybe Ellie can stay with friends, but I'm not sure—'

'Easy, Grace.' It's hard to believe I'm giving the advice for once. 'The MRI and the other tests this morning should indicate what the . . .' I pause, uncertain of how to phrase the next statement, then realise there's no point in holding back, 'what the damage is.'

My sister begins to cry.

I force my own emotions deep inside, into that

24

place I rarely choose to go. 'Adam and I are meeting with the consultant this morning. I'll let you know everything as soon as I can.'

'I'll get to Devon as soon as possible. I just need to sort out teaching cover.'

'Don't worry, Grace.' Then, lying with an ease that surprises me, I add, 'Everything will be fine.'

It's still an hour before it's time to leave for the hospital. I decide that if I'm going to be sleeping in the guest room for the next few nights, I might as well make myself useful and tidy up a bit. I pick through the donation bags by the bed: motheaten cardigans, old slippers, some faded pillowcases. The books on the floor are more surprising: romance and historical fiction; clearly charity shop finds, as scribbled in pencil on the yellowing first pages are various prices, ranging from ten to fifty pence. My mother was always a stickler for a bargain, but *romance*? As Brethren, her reading material would have been censored. Just authorised scriptures and an approved version of the Bible. Novels, magazines, and newspapers would have been strictly forbidden. And even after the Brethren had withdrawn from us, essentially excommunicating us at every level, my mother would still follow church customs and practices, including only reading the approved texts. As a die-hard fundamentalist, she even insisted that I kept all my university Biology and Chemistry books out of her sight. Evolution was heresy after all. Now, spread out before me on the worn carpet were Rosamunde

25

Pilcher, Barbara Cartland, Catherine Cookson, and novels from other authors with titles like *Lord of the Scoundrels* that I had never heard of before. When did all this happen?

I tidy the donation bags away in the corner and stack the paperbacks next to the bed. The suitcases are odd; out of place. My mother never left Cornwall. She didn't even come to Exeter to attend my wedding to Adam. Why on earth would she have a collection of suitcases? I begin sorting through them, deciding to stack two smaller ones, Russian doll-like, inside the largest. I flick the latches and dust fills the air. Tam, who has been watching my efforts from the windowsill, lets out a sneeze, and I jump.

I look inside the suitcase. My eyes register it, but my brain can't compute. A familiar, desperate panic floods my brain. The suitcase isn't empty. Inside sits a black rucksack, the words *Animal* stitched across the front in grey lettering. I feel my heart rate quicken and force myself to take a few calming breaths. The last time I saw this rucksack it was in the box of Michael's things I had collected from Edgecombe Hall after his death. Unable to face dealing with it at the time, I had left it at my mother's house for nearly six months. Could she have taken it during that time as some sort of keepsake?

I carefully remove the artefact from its hiding place and lay it on the bed in front of me. As I try to open it, the zip seizes, and for a moment I wonder if the water rusted the metal.

Then I remember.

It wasn't on the lakeside with Michael the night he drowned. The few things he did leave behind – t-shirt and jeans, his wallet still in the back pocket – had been carefully folded and placed on a rock by the water's edge. His new Vans, tied together, had dangled from a nearby branch, and his iPhone was in the back pocket of his jeans.

This is all beginning to feel like too much, but I push back the pain and carry on. I reach inside the bag, curious, fearful of what I might find. My hand grasps something. I pull it out into the light. It's a sweet wrapper. I smile and shake my head. Michael's swimming coach was always strict about healthy eating for her athletes, forbidding junk food of any kind. I would often sneak a Mars bar or two into his things before I drove him back to school. Our little secret.

I tip the rucksack over and shake it with a fervour that surprises me. A pencil and paperclip emerge; nothing else.

'What the hell?' I scream. What was the backpack doing here, hidden away?

Stay calm. Keep it together.

I fetch a damp flannel from the bathroom and carefully wipe away all the dirt, dust and grime before laying the rucksack on the desk next to Michael's hoodie and an old swimming medal of his I'd found in the desk drawer. My personal shrine.

Nearby, church bells chime ten o'clock. I jump up as if stung. I'm going to be late meeting Adam.

* * *

27

It's after eleven by the time I finally arrive at the hospital. I park near the maternity ward entrance and watch a steady stream of tired, yet elated faces pass me on their way to visit the new arrivals. An elderly couple emerge from a silver Honda Jazz, flowers and pink balloons in tow. A young man, no older than sixteen, stands hunched in the smoking shelter taking a slow drag of a cigarette. The smell of smoke lingers just long enough for me to be reminded of the guilty pleasure. I haven't smoked in over eight years, ever since Adam and I made our first and only attempt at IVF.

As I get out of the car, I spot a dark-haired man with glasses, attractive in a greying-around-the-edges sort of a way, strolling towards me. It takes me a minute to realise that it's my husband. Jesus, I must be tired. Closing the car door, I smile and walk towards him.

'You're late.' Pushing back my fringe, he kisses me gently on the forehead. 'You look exhausted. Did you get any sleep?'

I stifle a yawn. 'A bit.'

'I was hoping to catch Mr Emery before he starts his rounds in ICU,' Adam gives me a look I know well, 'but we've probably missed him now.'

'I'm sorry honey. Traffic was terrible.'

'No matter,' he says, brightly. 'I rang the head nurse this morning. It looks like they're going to take her off ventilation this afternoon.'

I try not to think about the ramifications of that statement. Depending on the level of brain injury caused by the stroke, my mother may not be able to breathe unaided.

Adam hands me a small holdall. 'I brought those things you asked for. You're not planning to stay long, are you?'

'Hopefully just a few days.' I don't mention how desperately I'm longing to be back at our house in Exmouth; back with the sea views, the pristine herbaceous borders, and my little study at the end of the hallway where I do my private work. 'I'll need to see what they plan to do about Mum long term. And I've really got to do something about the cat.'

'Speaking of cats,' says Adam, scratching his nose. 'I can feel the effects of that thing already.'

'Maybe you shouldn't get so close,' I tease.

'I'll take my chances,' he replies, hugging me close.

Our visit to the stroke ward is excruciating. My mother's stats have improved slightly, but an unexpected spike in her temperature means they've decided to wait until tomorrow to remove her from ventilation. The back-and-forth treatment debate between Adam and Mr Emery, the consultant, is more like a medical conference between two old pals than a family-centred discussion. Eager to get it over with and leave, I find myself nodding without really listening. Maybe Adam is right. Maybe this place is so tied to tragedy and loss for me that I can't think clearly.

It's nearly three o'clock before we finally make our way back to the car park.

'Well, from what Mr Emery said it sounds like they'll be taking your mother off intubation tomorrow.'

'Provided her temperature is down,' I add.

'Of course,' says Adam as we walk to his car. He sounds almost pleased by the prospect of this potentially risky procedure, but I know him well enough to understand: diagnosis and treatment is his safe place. 'Are you sure you're all right?' he asks. 'You were very quiet in there.'

'It's just a lot to take in.'

'I'm worried about you being on your own tonight, in that house. You know how you get when you go back there.'

'I'll be fine, darling.' I try my hardest not to sound impatient. I realise that he's only looking out for me; I just wish he'd stop expecting the worst. It was over a year since my last episode, and that was only after I received that letter from our insurance company. *Have you considered coverage for the younger members of your family? It's really never too early to think about life insurance!*

'Really, Adam, I'm okay.' Why do I have to keep repeating that? 'We'll see how tomorrow goes and then we can look at getting an OH assessment for the house – handrails, stairlift, that sort of thing.' We both know I'm stating the obvious, but sometimes obvious is the safest place to be.

Adam takes my hands in his. 'I want you home by the end of the week.' It's a statement, not a request. 'Okay?'

'Of course.' I'm grateful, as always, for his directives.

He gives me a final kiss on the cheek before getting into his car.

'I'll see you tomorrow at eleven.' He taps a finger on his watch. 'Be on time.'

'Yes, darling.' I step back so a car can pass. 'I'll ring you later. Drive carefully.'

Giving him a final wave, I turn and head back towards the hospital. Behind me, I hear the Audi's engine rev and pull away. I stand alone in front of the main entrance, watching as the huge building ingests and repulses the steady stream of sick and injured. I should go back inside, sit by my mother's bedside, comfort her – but my head is thumping and my courage, always doubtful, has escaped me.

I decide to take the scenic route back to my mother's house, avoiding the bridge and following the lanes, where sun-streaked finches dart in and out of blossoming hedgerows. I drive past Yelverton and down through Gunnislake with its steep pines and dour granite churches. In the millisecond flash between trees and houses I catch the occasional glimpse of the moors, the landscape both breath-taking and bleak. I stop at a grocery store and buy eggs, cheese, biscuits, apples, coffee, milk, a loaf of bread, and cat food. I hesitate in the wine aisle, knowing that any more than a glass or two will mean I won't be able to drive back to the hospital tonight if needed; yet I settle, finally, on a couple of whites, two decent reds, and a small bottle of vodka for courage. If something comes up, I'll have to get a taxi.

When I finally arrive home, Tam is waiting for me. 'Don't worry, you old bugger. I didn't forget you.' I feed the cat, pour myself a large glass of red and head upstairs. If my mother is going to be in hospital for a while, she'll need some things.

I grab one of the suitcases from the Russian doll stack, and head into her bedroom. The room, like the rest of the house, is not so much dirty as *unkept*. Dust-covered knick-knacks cover almost every available surface, more romance novels are stacked high on her bedside table, and the wardrobe door is wide open, exposing a functional, yet drab catalogue of clothing.

I start in the chest of drawers: nightdresses, underpants, bras, and socks; then include a dressing gown hanging on the back of the bedroom door. I'm about to move to the bathroom for toiletries, when something strikes me. If my mother does successfully regain consciousness, there is one thing I know – no matter what its dubious history – may bring her comfort: her Bible.

I move to the wardrobe. Seeing my mother's old clothes is sobering. The long skirts and dresses she wore as Brethren are hanging as if ready to be put on once more. On the top shelf are a stack of carefully folded kerchiefs. Brethren beliefs dictate that a woman with an uncovered head causes herself and her community shame, and so she insisted we cover ourselves wherever we went. One more rule; one more humiliation. Nothing makes a teenage girl stand out more than having to wear a long skirt and a headscarf. I reach to the back of the shelf where I know my mother keeps a document box with all her papers.

The box is large, heavy; a ribbon is tied around the middle. My fingers struggle, but I finally pull apart the bow. Inside I find papers: life insurance; pension; mortgage. I find her Bible, and a letter from the Brethren headquarters in Plymouth, postmarked April 2000 – the month after Michael's birth, formally excommunicating us from the sect. Included, too, are childhood snaps; and surprisingly, a photograph from my university graduation. I push them aside to find a Nokia mobile phone, several years out of date. What was she doing with an old mobile? No matter how much Grace and I tried to encourage her to get one, she always refused.

Lying at the bottom of the box is something else; something black and shiny. It's an A4 plastic wallet: something you would find as part of any back-to-school kit, along with a pencil case and ruler. What is it doing in here?

The wallet has a slight bulge: there's something inside. I undo the snap and slide out the contents. It's a leather-bound notebook. A logbook? I open it, expecting to see a long list of Michael's training schedules and individual best swimming times. What I find, however, knocks me back so fiercely that my knees give, and I slump to the floor. This isn't a logbook at all. It's a diary. Michael's personal diary.

What was Michael doing with a diary? This can't be right. Michael was a fifteen-year-old boy; a normal teenager obsessed with technology – not just for social media and gaming, but also for its power to monitor, assess and improve his sporting performance. The idea that he would even think of keeping a hand-written personal diary is one that I find almost unfathomable.

For some reason I think of his MacBook, archived in the loft at home. Recovered from his dormitory at Edgecombe Hall, the police family liaison officer had explained, amongst other things, that the laptop would be forensically searched for any 'dangerous or suggestive websites'. What did she mean by that? When, a year after Michael's death, the coroner returned an open verdict, I had confronted that same officer, demanding to know why, if Michael's death was not deemed an *accident*, there was no further investigation taking place. She had spluttered and stumbled, clearly uncomfortable with how to respond. I think I had yelled, screamed at her for an answer. I recall people stepping away; gentle words of warning; then Adam beside me, leading, nearly dragging me away.

Keeping his voice to a low growl, he'd said to me, 'For Christ's sake, Kate – when they ruled an open verdict, they meant open to the possibility of suicide!'

I had felt my legs give, and, stumbling back against the courthouse wall, I'd screamed, 'He would never do that. Michael would never do that to me!'

Adam had taken me home and prescribed Valium and bedrest. I don't think I'd left the house for nearly a month.

I run my hand across the book's burgundy cover and gently strum the folds of crisp, cream paper. Opening the front cover, I run my fingertips across the fawn-coloured paper. Michael's handwriting – charming, childlike – fills almost every page. What on earth could a fifteen-year-old boy have to write about that would fill a notebook?

My heart is racing, my armpits damp. Resting my back against the side of the wardrobe, I lift the diary to my face and take in the rich smell of it; press my lips against the soft, cool leather.

'Now, my darling boy,' I whisper. 'Tell me what really happened that night.'

5

15 September 2014 – Exmouth to Edgecombe

*I stare out of the car window, letting Mum's voice
float around me. For some crazy reason she's telling
me about basking sharks, how even as late as
September they can be seen off the coast. She's talking
too much, worried about my going to some posh
prep school in deepest, darkest Cornwall, but there
you go. A so-so swimmer with an arsehole for a
stepfather – what better way to get rid of me than
to arrange a scholarship? I mean I'm good, but
Edgecombe good? I still wonder if my dear old stepfather pulled a few strings; made a few phone calls
to one of his old boys to get me out of the house;
out of his way. What an arsehole!*

*I let Mum's voice fade, and instead focus on the
hum of the motorway. It's only when we cross over
the bridge into Cornwall that I sort of come back to*

life. Mum opens the window a crack, letting the breeze drift in. Maybe it's the sea air, or crossing into Cornwall, but suddenly she looks happy.

I feel as if history is forcing its way back into me, as if Michael is beside me now, his shoulder against mine.

My mobile goes off; a deep, bass rhythm thumping its way through the silence.

'Hi, darling.' I force myself to sound chirpy. 'Yes, home safe and sound. Just sorting out a few things for Mum.' I press my blazing cheek against the cool leather of the diary. 'I stopped for a bit of shopping – you know, nothing in the house as usual.' The moment where I could and should tell Adam about the diary passes, and suddenly I am spiralling towards deceit. 'I'm just about to have something to eat. Can I ring you back a little later?'

It's surprising how easy it is to make something up. All I really want is to get back to the diary.

15 September 2014 – Cornwall

Mum glances over at me, knows I have a question. We've always been pretty close. Sometimes I think we can read each other's minds. Then Adam came along, fucking threats-behind-closed-doors Adam. Even though I'm a bit nervous about starting at a new school, leaving Adam behind will be one big plus! Only a mile to the turnoff so I'd better act quick, I take a breath and ask Mum if we can stop and see Gran on the way. The car jostles. I'm not sure if it's a gust of wind or my asking. She goes on about it being a bit late to stop and all, not wanting me to be late for the welcome barbecue at Edgecombe. It's a barbecue for fuck's sake! There's the silent tick of her deliberation; she's playing the game, but I know she'll give in. When I tell her I've already spoken to Gran about stopping, her head snaps to the left to look at me. I see her lips thin in that way that says she's really pissed. I don't want to upset her, but I don't feel bad either. Whatever issues Mum has with Gran, they're not mine.

The room feels hot, suffocating; I can't breathe. I stumble downstairs and somehow manage to pull on my shoes.

When the panic finally clears, I find myself standing by the river watching the sun being absorbed by the water like smoke into a vacuum. I walk for a long time, comforted by the steady huff of my breathing, the crunch of gravel beneath my feet. Time seems to still, my worries ebb. I return home, pour myself another glass of wine and go upstairs to telephone Adam. He answers after the first ring.

'Where the hell have you been?' He sounds furious. 'It's nearly eight o'clock. I've left about six voicemails.'

'I just went for a walk. I was—'

'A walk, at this time of night?'

'Honey, it's still light.'

'What if you fell over, hurt yourself?'

'It was the river path. There were loads of people.'

I hear his deep exhalation and his voice softens. 'Have you heard any more from Grace?'

'She's coming down on Tuesday.'

'Tuesday. Why not tomorrow?'

'Simon's away and there's school cover to think about.'

'How long is she staying for?'

'A couple of nights.'

'A couple of nights!'

A can feel my chest tightening. This is not how I want it. 'She needs to get back, Adam. Ellie's got GCSEs and she's struggling—'

'Can't Simon deal with it?'

'Grace seemed pretty stressed. I'm not sure how good things are at home.'

'Things are pretty bad here, too.'

'Adam, I can handle it – and Ellie needs her mother.'

'Will she be coming back,' Adam's voice is thick with censure, 'to take some of the weight off your shoulders?' His relentless line of questioning is making me anxious. I don't want to talk about Grace, Ellie or my mother. I want to talk about the colour of the evening sky as I wandered along the river path; the splash of trout; otter tracks in the mud.

There is a pause, and his voice deepens. 'Where are you sleeping?'

'In the spare room.'

'Michael's old bedroom?'

'It's a guest bedroom, Adam.' I take a large sip of wine, debating what to say next, and then, before I can stop myself – 'There's really nothing to worry about. It's just used for storage now.' I briefly consider confessing, telling him about the diary, but things have gone too far. I have descended into darkness.

'Well I'm glad you're handling everything so well.'

I give a rueful smile, slip the diary out from under my pillow where I hid it, and, without thinking, utter a phrase my mother was renowned for. 'Well, needs must.'

And I lift the wine glass to my lips.

6

15 September 2014 – Gran's House

Gran is waiting for us by the front door, a grey cardigan wrapped around her like a shroud. They face each other, my mother and grandmother, hostility lying between them. I slide past and into the house.

Later, I hear strained small talk from the kitchen. Not much has changed since I lived here with Mum after I was born. I hear Mum's voice rise and watch as she marches out of the kitchen. She mutters something about checking her tyres – lamest excuse ever. I go into the kitchen. Gran slides a cup of tea my way and asks me about Edgecombe; how I feel about going to a 'heathen school.' The criticism in her voice is clear. I tell her that I'm not Brethren and never have been. I can go to whatever school I want. I also tell her that she's not Brethren either and hasn't been for a long time. Her face closes, just like one of those

41

frilly plants that curl in on themselves when you touch them. I've seen her do this to Mum so many times, but never to me. I guess I deserve it. After all, it's my fault that Gran was rejected. It was the birth of me that caused all the problems. I've known it since I've been old enough to know anything. Sometimes I can ignore it – but sometimes it sits like a stone in my stomach.

I tell Gran that I'd better get going because I want to make it in to Edgecombe in time for the welcome barbecue and disco. Her eyes widen in horror and the words kinda fall away. It's like the oxygen is being sucked out of the room. My head starts to hurt. How did I get this so wrong? I lean over to give her a kiss and feel her arms fold around me. 'You be careful my boy,' she whispers. 'It's a grim world out there.'

I am halfway through the second bottle of red and am having trouble focusing. My cheeks are damp with tears and my head is pounding. I stumble to the bathroom, drink water from cupped hands and try to avoid my reflection in the mirror. Staggering back, I collapse onto the bed, the diary clutched against my chest.

I wake to the sound of seagulls: piercing squeals that slice their way into my brain. I turn over and rub my eyes. My mouth feels like flannel and tastes worse. I sit up, struggling with the nausea that partners my headache. I force myself to my feet and open the window for some fresh air, but I find myself assaulted by the bright morning light. I step back, my foot slips, and I hear the crack of leather. The diary is lying face down on the carpet, pages splayed, spine splintered. I take an involuntary breath – an inverse sigh – and, lifting it from the floor, cradle it against my chest as if it were an injured child.

As I go to set it down again, I notice that two of the end pages are stuck together.

I slip my thumbnail into the tiny gap and ease it open. Concealed between the thin sheets of pasted paper is a lock of short, brown hair. It's not Michael's. I stare at it in disbelief. With trembling fingers, I pick it up and lift it to my face. It smells of nothing. I hold it up to the window and sunlight glints on highlighted flecks of copper. *Who are you?*

After a moment I slip it back between the pages and close the book tightly. How long I sit on the bed with the diary on my lap I couldn't say, but when I finally look up, the sun has shifted and the sound of people going about their morning business drifts in through the open window: a car starting; a dog barking; the whirr of a lawnmower. I feel warm rays of sunlight stroke my face. I close my eyes to relax, but the diary calls to me, and I find myself returning to the pale pages.

15 September 2014 – Arriving at Edgecombe

It's nearly four by the time we get to Edgecombe. The light seems to bounce off every surface. We park up next to the 'elite swimmers' residence', a shitty looking prefab – but still mine, all mine. While Mum faffs about in the boot, I wander off. There's a small green at the back of the halls where two girls are playing Frisbee. A disc comes flying my way. One of the girls – blonde, fit, wearing cut-off shorts and a Radiohead t-shirt – looks at me and smiles. I am tempted to throw the Frisbee back, but instead I wait for her to come closer. Her skin is pale, and her cheeks are dotted with freckles. She smiles as I hand her the Frisbee, tells me her name – Shivie (what kind of name is that?) – and asks if I'm going to the barbecue. Her friend spots me and almost waves. She's taller, with mousey brown hair and a sulky expression that puts me right off.

When I make it back to the residence, Mum has already unloaded the car and stacked the suitcases and boxes in a pile next to the door. She raises an eyebrow and smiles. I like it when it's like this – easy, casual. We spend the next hour moving my stuff into the tiny closet that will be my room for the next few years, and then I make us a cup of tea in the shared kitchen.

We sit opposite each other. I try not to look too impatient. Mum sighs and says she'd better be heading back. We get up and she gives me a hug. When she steps back, I can see there are tears in her eyes. I don't think I've ever seen my mother look so sad or so pretty. I know it's not easy for her – I mean, I'm her only kid and all – but I really, really like that she gets me, and knows all I can think about right now is that girl in the Radiohead t-shirt.

We walk back to her car in silence. She gives me another hug. She looks like she's going to cry: properly, this time. She tells me she loves me. I tell her the same. She starts to give me another talk about drink, drugs, and safe sex, but I remind her we've had that discussion and that I'm not a kid any more – I'll be fifteen in March! She nods and gets into the car. My eyes shift in the direction of the green. I wonder if Radiohead girl is still there. I wonder if she has a boyfriend.

This is going to be the best year of my life.

I shower, have some breakfast, and then force myself outside to sit on the front step and get some fresh air.

It's as if I have discovered an entirely new Michael; one that fascinates and frightens me at the same time. Maybe I should have told Adam about the diary. He would know what to do. I grimace and shake my head.

Ever since I can remember, my way of dealing with problems has been either to avoid them or to let someone else handle it. At fifteen, I had told no one that my periods had stopped; I had hidden my swollen belly under an oversized school jumper. When the school nurse had finally confronted me, I hadn't even tried to deny it. That night, after the meeting in the nurse's office, my mother had beaten me with a wooden spoon.

The next night the church elders had been at our door, the three men lined up like crows. We were *shut out*, a temporary form of excommunication that involved being shunned by fellow Brethren, possibly permanently, unless we complied with doctrine. The only solution, the elders had said, was for me to marry a church member and raise the child as Brethren as a means of both penance and appeasement. The father, Ryan, was an outsider and *unclean* – a danger to our community – and must be treated as such. In an effort to appease the elders and prove her devotion, my mother had prayed, fasted, and relentlessly tried to coerce me into the arranged marriage; but I had refused, even threatening to go to social services.

Three months after that, it had been decided we were unredeemable, even in God's forgiving light, and we were cast out – excommunicated, rejected, scorned. All clearly outlined in that letter from Brethren headquarters my mother still kept. After that, if any fellow Brethren saw us in the street, they would completely ignore us or turn away in disgust. Our community, on which we relied so heavily, had abandoned us. My mother raged, but I had found it extraordinarily liberating. Being moved to the young mothers' unit at the local comprehensive school had also meant I was finally allowed to study GCSE Science. I uncovered a talent I never knew existed.

As for Ryan, he had left a few months before Michael was born to take up an apprenticeship in the West Midlands. I often wondered if the Brethren had anything to do with that, but never had the courage to ask. I saw him once or twice in the village when he was home for the holidays or attending a family do, but we lost touch. He married in his early twenties and had two daughters. Michael, it seemed, was easily forgotten.

I make myself another cup of coffee and go back upstairs to the bedroom. I pick up the diary and begin flicking through the pages, stopping only when I make the most astonishing discovery. It's a poem. Michael, my fourteen-year-old sporty, sweaty, socks-and-trainers son has written a poem. It was a struggle to get Michael to read a restaurant menu, let alone a collection of poetry. 'Books are boring, Mum,' he'd used to say when I'd suggest some new young adult title, 'and poetry is for girls!' Yet here he was writing – or at least trying to write – a poem. I suppose it could have been for his English coursework, and to be fair he did have a reasonable aptitude for language, but why the leather-bound diary? Knowing Michael, a Pukka pad would have been considered a luxury item for schoolwork.

Photo-frame (November 2014)

I keep a photo~~or photo-frame?~~ by the bed,
The frame is grey///gunmetal grey,
~~Holding in~~ and holds an image???
~~of~~ awkward affection,
Mother, daughter, and son,
Family but still strangers ~~still.~~
forever
Stand close ~~but~~ not touching.
Hurricane eyes and cyclone smiles

A storm ~~that~~ swirls beneath,
A/~~the?~~ riptide of rebellion
filling my lungs,
~~it~~ suffocates and stifles
~~the unending~~ the unending?? Overwhelming???
The love I harbour
~~Eternal, unending~~, sinking beneath
~~The water/the ocean~~ Murky seas

I stare at the page open-mouthed. This comes as a revelation like no other. When Michael was little, I used to love to read poetry to him at bedtime: Yeats; Blake; Wordsworth; A.A. Milne. I always thought he was indulging me – but could he have actually been paying attention? Maybe he'd somehow absorbed it all.

In places there are deep gashes where Michael has crossed a word out so fiercely that the page is torn: a ragged wound seeping fresh letters from underneath. I skip forward hoping for some sort of explanation. Instead I find this.

1 February 2015

You're waiting for me by the bike sheds (cliché eh) so gorgeous I can't take my eyes off you. I risk a smile and look around to make sure no one is watching. I'm not going to bite, you say, and kiss me. You taste like winter air and cigarettes. Diving Fish, I want you so much.

I feel my chest tighten. Had Michael been in love? He had never even told me he had a girlfriend. I feel the same wretched ache as on his first day of school when I had to leave him alone at the school gates, crying. I read on, my eyes scanning the pages. There are at least half a dozen other entries.

9 February

We meet by the lake. You're wearing my grey hoodie, your hair thrown wild by the wind.

3 March

No one about, we stay under cover all morning, our bodies entangled like seaweed on the shore

Beneath the entry is a rough sketch of a female figure lying naked on a bed, her face turned so that her profile is barely visible. The gentle swell of her hips, the roundness of her breast, points to an understanding and intimacy that makes me feel both shock and sadness. Michael was far too young for this kind of relationship, just a few months younger than me when I got pregnant. Yet part of me also feels an odd sense of relief. Michael had been in love, had experienced love.

Scribbled in small letters beneath the portrait is one final poem.

Carnation

Moonlight lingers on
the pale abandon
of
your
skin.

Sea-soaked tendrils,

Entwine
the smooth pillars of your thighs.

Encase
the cool whisper of your sighs
And

Await

My coming.

I am astounded. This is a poem of extraordinary skills and aptitude, a far cry from that first, clunky attempt. How could I not have known about this side of him? It's as if my son is suddenly revealing himself to be someone else – someone I would very much liked to have known.

I make sure I leave early for the hospital, recalling Adam tapping his finger on his watch yesterday: *don't be late*. I've put on makeup to cover my blotchy cheeks and wear glasses instead of my usual contact lenses to hide my bloodshot eyes. I'm just heading to the car when my mobile rings. It's Adam.

'We're short staffed in A&E and I'm not sure I'm going to be able to make it until after lunch.'

It takes a moment for me to formulate the correct response. 'That's all right, darling. I can manage until then.'

'They'll be trying to take her off ventilation if they haven't already. There may be complications and you don't know—'

'I'll be fine, Adam – really.' *How many times have I said this in the last few days?*

'You'll need to make sure that they—'

'Don't worry sweetheart; I know what to say.

I've got to go. I don't want to be late.' It's not often that I cut my husband off like this, but after last night's drinking session I just don't have the stamina to listen to his instructions. 'I'll call you when I get to the hospital.'

When I arrive, I'm surprised to see a trio of specialists surrounding my mother's bed.

'Mr Emery started the reduction in pressure support early this morning,' whispers the nurse, 'and your mother regained consciousness very quickly. She's been reasonably lucid, which is good news.'

Is it?

The nurse pauses and I realise she's doing the good news bad news thing.

'However, there appears to be some paralysis to the right side, which is why the specialists are with her now.'

'Ah.' I watch as the occupational therapist helps my mother to drink a glass of juice. Her gnarled, liver-spotted hand is holding the plastic beaker as if it were made of fine china. 'Is she able to speak?'

'Yes, but not very clearly,' the nurse replies. 'She asked after someone.' I can see her wracking her brain. 'Sam, is it?'

'Tam,' I reply. 'Her cat.'

'Oh.' The nurse giggles, a light, bell-like sound that seems oddly out of place in this room full of buzzes and bleeps.

'Can I see her?'

* * *

I wait until the physio, speech and occupational therapist have completed their assessments before approaching.

'Hi, Mum.' I place her Bible on the overbed table in front of her. 'I thought you might want this.' My mother's good eye flickers to it and then away. 'The nurse says you're doing really well.' She's finished her drink and I reach out to take it from her.

My mother pulls back, gives a low grunt, and then with agonising effort places the beaker on the table herself.

I feel tears prickling the back of my eyelids. 'Grace arrives tomorrow,' I say, with forced brightness. 'She should be here about one.'

My mother's face brightens, and I find myself flooded with resentment.

I clear my throat. 'So, I was tidying the spare room, and I found Michael's old rucksack. The one you hid in the suitcase.'

Those Gorgon eyes seem to be turning me to stone where I stand.

'And when I was looking for your Bible, something else.' My mother begins to shift uncomfortably. I lean forward to adjust her pillows. 'His diary.'

She gives a small groan.

'It's okay Mum – really. I just want to know how long you've known about it.' I can feel my nails digging into my palms. I glance down at the tiny half-moon indentations.

My mother's eyes narrow and her face begins to contort.

53

'You must have read it.'

Silence fills the space between us like a thick sludge.

'You must have known about his girlfriend too; the one he called Diving Fish?' I flex my fingers in an effort to regain some circulation.

There's a loud thud. My mother has knocked her Bible to the floor. Her mouth is twisted grotesquely in an effort to speak.

'What is it?' I say, leaning in so close that I can smell the orange juice on her breath. 'Do you know who Diving Fish is? Do you think she might know what happened that night?' I grip my mother's arm. 'Who is she?'

A primitive, almost animalistic howl comes from deep inside my mother's throat. I think I can hear words forming.

'Excuse me,' calls the ward sister, rushing towards us. 'What's going on here?'

'My mother's trying to tell me something.'

'This is really not—'

'It's about my son!'

'Mrs Hardy, that's enough!'

The nurse attempts to remove me from my mother's bedside; but the old woman, still surprisingly strong, grabs my wrist and pulls me in close. Her words are garbled, muted, as if speaking to me from under water.

'Michael's . . . moving . . . home.'

'Michael's moving home?' I repeat, bewildered. 'What do you mean?' My mother's lips move, but no sound emerges. 'What do you mean Michael's moving home?'

54

'I think that is quite enough!' The nurse unpeels my mother's claw-like fingers from my wrist and stands between us. 'You mustn't upset her.'

'I didn't. I'm not.'

'I realise how difficult this is for you.' The nurse's cheeks have gone bright pink. 'But you must remember that your mother is still in a serious condition.'

'She's trying to tell me something!'

The nurse's voice softens. 'Your mother has suffered a brain trauma. She might not fully understand what she's saying.'

'But—'

'Perhaps it might be best if you have a little break.' The nurse ushers me towards the exit. 'A cup of tea? A stroll around the grounds?' It's an order, not a request. I'm getting used to these now. 'I'm sure a bit of fresh air will do you the world of good.'

Outside, the sun shines, with the promise of a warm summer to come. I stumble my way to the car and sit with my head resting on the steering wheel. What was my mother trying to tell me? Was Michael really planning on leaving? Did she mean he was going to leave Edgecombe and return home to me, or had he decided to stay with my mother permanently because of his increasingly antagonistic relationship with Adam? I feel heartbroken and betrayed. Why hadn't he spoken to me about all this?

Adam arrives after lunch as promised and spends most of the afternoon speaking to specialists and reviewing my mother's treatment plans. It's too early for an occupational therapist's home visit – my mother can't even walk yet – but there's a physiotherapist's assessment planned for later in the week.

We eventually find ourselves sitting in the ground floor café sipping tea.

'Well, that was useful,' says Adam.

I put on my best, most cheerful smile, but I'm still haunted by my mother's words a few hours before. *Michael's moving home.* Maybe it wasn't Adam's fault at all – maybe it was me. Maybe I was overprotective; too fussy, domineering.

I am fragmented, conflicted; my mind keeps moving towards unbearable thoughts and places.

Adam checks his watch. 'I guess I'd better be heading back. Early start tomorrow.' I don't want him to leave. He looks up at me and smiles. 'Are you going to be all right?'

I do my usual. 'Of course.'

My throat is tight; my chest a deadweight. I speed out of the hospital desperate for home. Not the home I've lived in with my husband for the past twelve years – a place my son clearly felt out of place and unhappy – but back to the home I shared with Michael for the first few chaotic, yet happy years of his life: my mother's house in Cornwall.

I know I shouldn't – it's only half past one – but I down a coffee mug full of white wine in three large gulps and head upstairs. I go through the suitcases one by one, then the bags, and finally every drawer in my mother's bedroom, wondering if there is anything else of Michael's that she's hidden from me.

After nearly two hours of searching I find nothing. Tired and dejected, I refill my mug and tidy up. This is still my mother's house after all. I lift the lid on her document box and push aside the papers, files, and folders to try to find space for the Bible. My mother wouldn't even look at it in the hospital – so why did she still keep it carefully stored away? Maybe some things, no matter how painful, are connected to us in ways we really can't escape.

'What a load of crap,' I mutter. I'm drunk now, and having trouble fitting the Bible back in amongst all the other debris in the box. I come across the mobile phone and pick it up. It's smaller than a contemporary model and fits comfortably in the palm of my hand. What was she doing with a mobile phone? As I balance the solid black block in my hand, her words from a few hours before begin transmuting themselves into something new. *Michael's moving home*. My mother's words were garbled, unclear, affected by stroke, drugs, trauma. What she said wasn't what she meant. The realisation is a slow burn across my frontal lobe, bursting and fizzing like popping candy on the tongue. Not *Michael's moving home*, but *Michael's mobile phone*. I utter a small involuntary groan. This isn't my mother's mobile phone at all. It was Michael's.

I study the object in my hand more closely. It's a cheap pay-as-you-go model – Nokia 105. A phone that I'd never known had existed. I feel shaky; sick.

It's as if the past is being torn open and bleeding all over me. I press the power button idly – there won't be any charge left in the battery, surely?

Yet, after a pause, the screen flickers into life. The Nokia logo appears and swiftly shifts to the log on screen. Shocked that this is still possible after all this time, I take a deep breath and stare at the glowing screen.

Security code:

Without thinking I tap in 2 0 0 0; the year Michael was born.

Code error

I try again. 1 9 8 4, the year I was born.

Code error

I feel my heart pounding, a trickle of sweat rolling down my spine. One more wrong code and the SIM will be locked.

'Come on!' I shout, hammering my fist against my forehead. On my mother's bedside table sits a long-abandoned teacup; biscuit crumbs dust the saucer's faded cornflower patina. I am struck by an image of my mother sitting on her bed, sipping her tea, and sifting her way through Michael's things like a customer at a car boot sale.

Security code:

I enter the numbers 1 9 4 9, the year my mother was born. The home screen appears, and I find myself pressing the contacts icon. There is only one entry – 'D'. Without stopping to think, I hold it down and wait for the number to dial.

The screen splutters and goes black.

'What?' I tap the phone against my palm. 'No, no!' I fumble to try the power button again, my fingers like sticks. 'What's going on?'

Low battery – emergency calls only

'No,' I yell, 'please, no!' But the screen emits a final blush and then fades.

I ransack the wardrobe, tossing the document box and headscarves on the bed, the clothes on the floor, but there is no charger. I feel the panic rising in my chest like a fever. I race downstairs, grab my handbag, and almost tear the blue pills from their hiding place in the inside pocket. I pop one into my mouth and swallow it dry.

I wake up on the sofa covered in a musty old throw. I check my watch. It's nearly four o'clock – too late to make it into the mobile phone shop in Tavistock. Not like they'll have any chargers for a five-year-old Nokia anyway. I head back upstairs and begin tidying away my mother's things. Glad to be kept busy, I grab an old flannel and dust the figurines and knick-knacks that dot the shelves, windowsill and just about every other available surface.

'Where did you get all this rubbish?' I exhale deeply. Then something strikes me. I check my watch, grab my trainers, and try to put them on while combing my hair at the same time. My reflection in the entrance hall mirror is grim, but I'm not interested in how I look.

I race down the narrow road that leads from my mother's house to the tiny high street. Pub, hairdressers, convenience store, and to my left, a smart gallery that garners most of its income from well-off tourists buying overpriced art. I stop in front of a small shopfront with a large hand-painted sign that reads *Bling and Things*, and, in smaller letters, *all proceeds to Children's Hospice Southwest*.

This charity shop has been around for as long as I can remember and has had more incarnations than Dr Who. Cats Protection League, RNLI, Macmillan Nurses – they all start off well, but it's not long before business drops off and eventually the shop window is soaped up and a *To Let* sign stuck on the front door. A bell attached to the door chimes as I enter, and somewhere in the background I can hear classical music playing. The old, mottled carpet I remember from my childhood has been removed to expose freshly polished oak floorboards. There are boxes of china, still wrapped in packing paper, and to my right a small mountain of Ikea shelving units waiting to be installed. Racks of old clothing have been pushed to a far wall and someone has started to put together a modern-looking corrugated iron hanging unit. As I move further to the back of the shop, however, it becomes more and more like the charity shop of old. Shoes that have seen better days are stacked in piles next to cuddly toys, and a nearby table is overloaded with lamps, kettles and even a sandwich toaster.

'They've all been PAT tested,' comes a voice from behind me.

I turn. 'Pardon me?'

'Electrical safety test.' It's an older woman, around

my mother's age. 'That's what that little sticker indicates.'

I nod. 'I'm not really after a sandwich toaster.'

The woman tilts her head. 'Katie, is that you?'

I feel my heart sink. I was hoping to avoid old acquaintances as much as possible while I'm in Cornwall – not that I had very many when I lived here in the first place.

'Katie, it's me. Helen.'

'Helen?' I feel my face flush in embarrassment. How could I forget the teaching assistant who singly helped me get through A Level Biology? 'Helen! I'm so sorry I didn't recognise you.'

She emerges from behind the counter and engulfs me in an enormous hug. I stiffen, but the warmth of her body reminds me of all those hours in the Sixth Form Centre, just the two of us, side by side, trying to learn about microbiology and pathogens. I find myself relaxing into her embrace. After a moment she steps back.

'I heard about your mum. How is she?'

'Not bad. Still in ICU but conscious.'

'Well that's good news.'

'It is.'

'And how are you finding it?' she asks gently, knowingly. 'Being back here I mean?'

'Harder than I thought.' She nods but says nothing. I don't want to be having this conversation, but this woman was instrumental in helping me get away from here, from my mother. 'I'm sorry I haven't kept in touch.'

'It's fine, love. I understand.'

'It's been a while, hasn't it?'

'Six years now.'

Now I remember. The last time I saw Helen was at Michael's funeral.

'I'm sorry I haven't . . .' I realise I'm repeating myself and decide to change the subject. 'What are you doing here?'

'Well, I'd been helping out now and again in the shop, whatever form it took, for years,' she says, smiling. 'So when I retired last year, I decided to take it on full time.'

'I can't imagine you retiring.'

'Nor could my husband. Said I was driving him crazy.' She spreads her arms wide. 'So here I am.' I forget the diary; the mobile; my mother; I just feel calm. 'I'm trying to posh it up a bit,' she continues. 'I want to increase footfall and revenue. There's still loads of work to do but I'm getting there.'

I find myself smiling. Just like Helen to take on a project with absolute determination. Just the kind of person I need on my side.

'Helen,' I say with unexpected shyness. 'I wonder if you might be able to help me?'

We spend the next half hour looking through shelves, boxes, and the storage cupboard. With her eye for detail, Helen is able to go through a snakes' nest of old electrical cords and phone chargers, handing me one possibility after another: *try this one, love*. When we exhaust that search, she moves on to the crawl space behind the boiler, emerging with a large shoe box.

'There's always more junk to be found,' she says, pulling cobwebs from her hair. 'I could do with a cup of tea. You?'

I nod and follow her to the tiny kitchen at the back of the shop. I'm burning with impatience, but I can't be rude – not to Helen. She flips on the kettle, tosses teabags into mugs, then begins trawling through the shoe box. I can't seem to keep myself still, even though I have a thumping headache. I just want to find the right charger and get out of here, but Helen seems eager to alleviate my obvious unease.

'Did you know that Michael used to come to the shop sometimes when he was staying at his nan's?'

This is surprising news. 'Did he?' I ask. 'To say hello?'

'Well, yes and no.'

'Yes and no?'

'He was so sweet,' she smiles with such tenderness it makes my heart ache. 'He'd come in on the premise of a visit, you know. But really he was looking.'

'Looking?'

'For jewellery mostly; necklaces, bracelets, that sort of thing. It all had to be gold though – none of that cheap stuff – which is a bit of a challenge in a charity shop to say the least.'

I am now on automatic. 'I can imagine.'

She sighs heavily. 'I used to try and put the good stuff aside, but he was always so particular.'

'Particular?'

She shakes her head and stares out of the window. 'Fish.'

'What?'

'It always had to be fish. The jewellery, I mean. It had to be a fish. I remember I found this one piece – sterling silver, not gold, mind – with this lovely little fish charm made of sea glass.'

I need to take a moment before speaking. Don't go in too eager, Kate. 'Did he, um, ever say why? Who the jewellery was for, I mean?'

Maybe it's something in my voice, but Helen looks uneasy.

'No. I mean, I thought it was maybe for a . . . for a . . .'

'Girlfriend?'

'Yes, a girlfriend.'

I force a smile and decide to offer up the happy narrative she so clearly desires. 'I wondered that myself.'

'It's a nice thought, though, isn't it?'

I nod in agreement, but in truth I'm not really sure.

'Is this it?' An excited Helen pulls a bit of black wire from the box. 'I think it is!' She reaches for Michael's phone.

Before she can reach it, I grab the phone from the counter then carefully slide the plug into the connector. It fits perfectly.

I stumble my way home and, handling the mobile as if it were a priceless object, I plug it into the mains. At first there is nothing, but after a few seconds an icon of a battery appears on the screen. I'm about to pour myself a glass of wine when a reminder goes off. It's *my* mobile. *Ring Adam.*

'Were you at the hospital all day?' he asks.

'Yes, darling,' I lie.

'And?'

'She slept most of the afternoon, so I just sat by her bedside.'

'You sound odd.'

'I'm just tired.'

'Would you like me to drive back down?'

'You've had a long day.' As much as I'd like Adam here to support me, I also want to keep him away from my recent findings – at least until I can find out more. 'I'm going to have an early night anyway.'

'What about tomorrow?'

'Grace is here tomorrow.' Adam and Grace don't get along. She feels that I married him as an escape. He says she's a bad influence. Neither seems to care much about what I think. 'Maybe not such a good idea.'

'Maybe not. But you'll be home on Thursday, right?'

'Yes, darling, for tea, just like I promised. Maybe we can order a Chinese and finish it this time.' In the corner of my eye, a light catches my attention and, turning, I see the mobile is charged up enough to display the passcode screen. 'I've got to go.'

'Are you all right?'

'Yes. The cat's just been sick.'

'That bloody cat.'

'I'll call you tomorrow, sweetheart. I love you.'

'I love you too.' He puts on his consultant's voice: deep, serious, undisputable. 'Now you're not to over-burden yourself, and don't forget to take your medication. It's important. And, for God's sake, don't mix it with alcohol.'

I glance at the near-empty glass of red on the bedside table. 'Of course not. I'd never be that foolish.' When did I start lying so proficiently? Is it a newly acquired trait, or one that has been lying dormant for all these years? 'Sleep well, darling. I'll call you in the morning.' I hang up, toss my mobile on the bed and take another sip of wine.

Unplugging Michael's phone from the charger lead, I enter the digits of my mother's birthdate, then pull up the contacts list. Only that one contact. Why a burner phone and why only one contact? What was he trying to keep a secret? I press that mysterious 'D' and wait. Hope. There is no dial tone: just a long, slow hum. The number is dead.

I check incoming and outgoing messages. There is only one, sent by Michael on the day he died.

My silent Diving Fish, please no more waiting. It's time for us to speak. Meet me by the water's edge tonight.

I place the phone on the bed and begin to cry.

8

I have a restless night, finally resorting to medication at three a.m. in a desperate attempt to gain a few hours' sleep. I'm meeting my sister at eleven and I have to be at my best – top form and inscrutable. I really can't handle any more of these 'are you sure you're all right, Kate' conversations.

I get up early and make a special effort, washing, blow drying and straightening my hair. I also spend an inordinate amount of time on my makeup, concealing, contouring, and powdering away any indication of my true state. When I meet Grace I want her to be presented with a composed and capable individual, not the woman on a verge of a nervous breakdown everyone seems to expect.

I complete the now-familiar journey to the hospital and find myself at the same table in the canteen that Adam and I had sat at only a few days before. I push aside my pale cup of tea and retreat to the hospital's sensory garden, where I soak up the morning sun and the scent of lavender and camomile. I feel myself nodding off when I hear the ping of an incoming text.

Just checked in at hotel. Will meet you at the café inside main entrance in ten. Gx

I return to that same table, check my mobile, fiddle with the clasp on my bag, reapply my lipstick; but most of all I try to keep my breathing deep and steady. I imagine every possible scenario in the few minutes before my sister's arrival. Hearing the click of high heels, I look up and see Grace. Her hair is longer than I remember, falling in soft curls around her shoulders. We have the same strong bone structure – high cheekbones inherited from Celtic ancestors – and blue-green eyes the colour of a glacial lake. Unlike Grace, however, I'm a Nordic-looking blonde. Both of us are tall and long-limbed, with narrow hips and small breasts. Adam used to comment that we were built for sport; too tall for gymnastics but perfect for athletics.

I watch my sister as a stranger might – interested but removed, as if she were a model on the catwalk. Grace wears designer jeans and a cream-coloured jumper that slips down from one shoulder, exposing a long, pale neck.

'Don't you dare turn and look back at that boy, you Jezebel!'

Grace is thirteen and I am ten. We've travelled with our mother to Plymouth for the day to buy school

68

shoes. Both of us, forced to wear the drab headscarves and long skirts of our sect, attract attention.

'I didn't,' replies an indignant Grace.

Both intrigued and confused by the argument, I look back to see what my mother is referring to.

'And you as well!'

I feel a sharp pain as she pinches my arm.

'You can't stop people from looking at us,' says Grace in a tone I recognise as dangerous. 'It's because they think we're a bunch of freaks. They're not leching!'

It is the first time Grace has ever raised her voice to our mother, and although I don't know why, I'm certain that things will never be the same. In a fury, Grace tears the headscarf from her hair and throws it to the ground.

'I hate these things!' she screams. 'I hate not having any friends, and I hate not being allowed to watch telly!'

My mother moves forward to silence her, but Grace is too agile and too quick. 'And I hate you!' Turning, she runs and disappears into the Saturday morning crowds.

Shaking the memory away, I get up and walk towards my sister. At first Grace doesn't recognise me, but then her eyes widen, her face changes, and she smiles.

'Kat!' she cries, and, pulling me into her arms, she kisses me fiercely on both cheeks. 'How are you? She steps back and scrutinises me closely. 'You look tired, and thin. Are you eating?'

'I'm fine.' I respond, and Grace raises an eyebrow. 'Well there's been so much to think about, and I haven't really had the time to . . .' I begin to feel unsteady, as if I'm standing on the juddering floor of a funhouse. Grace takes my arm and leads me to a bench opposite the lifts.

'Are you *really* okay?'

'I'm managing.' I dab at the thin film of perspiration that has appeared above my upper lip. 'It all just gets a bit much sometimes.'

'I'm not surprised,' says Grace. 'I just wish I lived a bit closer.' I'm not quite sure what response she expects, so I remain silent. She reaches over and grips my hand. 'I'm sorry I didn't ring on Michael's anniversary.'

'It's okay.' I know what to say. 'I got your card.'

'No, it's not okay. I should have called.' Grace closes her eyes, revealing dark circles hidden beneath expensive concealer. 'I was thinking about you,' she says, and she looks as if she's going to cry. 'And about Michael, of course. God knows I was.'

'Grace, it's all right.'

'It's just that,' she pauses as if struggling with what to say next, 'we've been having a terrible time with Ellie.' She bites her lower lip. 'Simon thinks we should get her to see someone.'

'Someone?'

'A therapist, counsellor, whatever.' She pushes the sleeve of her jumper up to expose a large, fist-shaped bruise on her arm.

'Jesus!'

'All the crap we've had to put up with. Swearing, throwing things, cutting herself. She even . . .' Grace shakes her head, unable to continue.

'I'm sorry.' I try hard to sound sympathetic, but I wish more than anything that I was in her place.

'But this isn't the time, is it?' says Grace, aware of my discomfort. Taking a deep breath, she seems to gather herself in, as if buttoning a coat up tight. 'So, aren't you going to ask me how the drive was?'

'How was the drive?'

'Roadworks and an overturned caravan on the M25; the usual.' She grimaces and tucks a long strand of chestnut-coloured hair behind one ear. 'So, you'd better give it to me straight, Kat. How's Mum?'

At first, Grace is calm, almost stoical; but when our mother starts to cough and the saliva trickles down her chin, her composure crumbles.

'What's going on?'

'The stroke and associated dysphasia can sometimes make swallowing difficult,' I say, adjusting Mum's pillows. 'All pretty standard stuff.' After a moment Grace sits down, rests her arm on the edge of the bed, but refrains from taking our mother's hand. She talks about the weather, her teaching job, Simon's new car; a fixed smile masks the emotion that I know is bubbling just underneath. Once or twice I catch her desperate expression: *get me out of here*, she seems to be pleading, but I don't know how. My mother is so pleased to see her.

Finally, a nurse arrives with medication, giving us

both an excuse to leave. We take the stairs to the back entrance, follow a woodchip-covered path to the nature reserve that borders the hospital, and sit on a bench carved out of an old tree trunk. I hear birdsong, the gentle warbling reminding me of Michael's fascination with a family of house martins that had nested in the eaves outside his bedroom window every year. Adam had grown impatient with not being able to clean out the guttering, but I still have the series of black-and-white photos Michael had taken of each generation as they hatched and flew to freedom. I can hear Grace breathing and feel the steady rise and fall of her shoulders next to mine.

'Are you all right, Grace?'

Reaching into her handbag, Grace retrieves a small packet of menthol cigarettes. 'I know I said I was going to quit.' She looks as if she is sitting in shadow, even though the sun is bright. Something in her tone makes me look closer. Her expression – eyes narrowed, mouth in a firm, hard line – is one that I recall from years ago when we were both children and she was hankering after a fight.

'Better give me one,' I say, reaching for the packet. 'I'm not going to let you go astray on your own.' I feel her relax; her deep exhalation seems to swirl the leaves at our feet. She lights our cigarettes, the stone in her engagement ring catching the afternoon sun and splitting it into infinite splinters of light.

'Be honest with me, Kat,' she says, taking a long drag. 'Will she be able to return home? Live on her own, I mean?'

I shrug, relishing the sensation of nicotine seeping through my lungs. 'Depends,' I reply. 'Mobility will be a problem of course. I'm not sure how she'll get up those narrow stairs.'

'Should we be having *the* conversation?' I feel my throat tighten. Over the years, as our mother has grown older and increasingly frail, we have both skirted around the question of residential care. The fact that I haven't seen my mother in nearly six months has made it seem all the worse. Grace has kept in touch, even if it has only been by phone and the occasional visit. I've only been sporadically engaged.

'When it comes time,' Grace lays her hand on mine, 'I'll make the decision. You've had enough crap from the old bat to last you a lifetime.'

'Maybe I should have visited more often.'

'Are you kidding?' Grace flicks her cigarette into the distance, the glowing end creating a crimson arc through the air. 'After her little *pièce de résistance* at Michael's funeral?'

'But—'

'I know she must have loved us once,' says Grace, her voice flat. 'Maybe when we were very little. Whether she blamed us for Dad leaving, or for her being cast out . . .'

'That was my fault not yours.'

'I did plenty.' Grace gives a little chuckle and I wonder if she's remembering the time when she was collected, drunk and bedraggled, from the quayside, or the Sunday when she refused to attend a Brethren

73

assembly and locked herself in the bathroom. We finally arrived nearly half an hour late to the soft tutting of the elders, with Grace, chin held high, sporting a vibrant purple bruise on her cheek.

'But *you* didn't have a baby out of wedlock.'

'That was next on my list,' says Grace, squeezing my hand tightly.

9

I follow Grace back to her hotel, and I'm surprised to see her heading straight for the bar.

'I need a drink,' she says, ordering a Jack Daniels for herself and wine for me. She downs hers in one and orders another. 'It's going to take a lot more than one drink to deaden what I've just seen. You?'

'Just the one,' I say. 'I need to ring Adam and then I'll be driving back to Calstock.'

'You're not still at Mum's, are you?'

'Yes, why not?'

'It's just that . . .'

'Well, someone needs to watch the house.' I'm coming across as a little belligerent; not a good thing. I need Grace on my side. I smile and reset. 'It's easier on my own. And there's the cat to think about.'

'Ah yes, the cat.' Grace is clearly not convinced. She swirls a piece of ice around her glass.

'Why don't we have something to eat?' I suggest,

hoping to change the subject. I slide a menu her way. We order game pie and mash, which neither of us finish, and a bottle of wine, before finally winding our way back to Grace's room.

'There's no way you'll be able to drive home now,' she says, collapsing onto the double bed and kicking off her heels.

'Maybe I should book a room.'

'Don't be ridiculous.' Grace glances through the room service wine list. 'Stay here with me. I've even got a spare t-shirt you can wear.' She grins mischievously. I shake my head and smile, reminded of the transgressions Grace had enticed me into as a child.

'Ah well,' I say, forcing myself to join in on the fun. 'You know me . . .' Reaching into my shoulder bag, I remove a travel toothbrush and spare pair of pants. 'Always prepared.'

Holding up the white cotton briefs for my sister to see, I watch as something drops from amongst the delicate folds of lace and spirals its way to the carpet. Bending down, I find it's the last remnants of the lilies I'd taken to the lake only a few days before. The pale gossamer petals are browning around the edges and the membrane is almost translucent in its decay. The faint scent of rot lifts to my nostrils and in an instant, I am transported back to the day Michael's remains were lowered into the ground; the release of handfuls of earth into the gaping black hole, and the agonising desire to throw myself in after it; a demented Alice tumbling into darkness.

'And a bottle of the Sauvignon Blanc please.' I look

over to the bed where Grace, legs dangling in the air, has the telephone pressed to her ear. On seeing my expression, she adds: 'Actually, you'd better make it two.'

I'm having trouble focusing on the numbers on my mobile phone. I've forgotten to ring Adam again and I'm now desperately trying to make up for it by sending him a grovelling text. The letters on the keypad are quivering as if I've just stepped off a funfair ride. I'm certain I've written the words *sorry* or *I am very sorry* at least five times.

'Give it here,' says Grace, prying the phone from my hand and replacing it with a glass of wine. 'You rang him before tea anyway. Is he keeping tabs on you or something?' She sits down on the bed. 'The trick is to keep it simple. The more you say, the more you give away.' I watch my sister tap away. 'How's this? "Hi darling, sorry for not ringing. Grace was upset and wanted to stay at hospital until as late as possible. Had to get her settled in hotel first (she had a few drinks!) and just got back to Mum's. Shattered and know you have a long shift tomorrow so will ring you first thing. Love you. K." And . . . send.'

I regard my sister with appreciation.

'Why did you say I was at Mum's?'

'Why not?' Grace takes a sip of wine. 'I mean we both know what Adam's reaction would be if you told him where you really are tonight; pissed as shit in some sixty-quid-a-night Travelodge with your older sister, who is a notoriously bad influence.'

'Oh, stop it,' I say, taking the phone and re-reading the message. Even though I know she is right, I still resent her saying it. The truth is that if Adam decided to call me at this very moment, there is absolutely no way I would be able to answer; not just because I can barely string two words together, but more importantly because I would be caught in a lie. Adam doesn't like lies. I need to clear my head, and right now Adam isn't my main priority. I have something more important to deal with.

'Grace,' I say, draining my glass. 'There's something I need to tell you.'

At first Grace says nothing, just listens, as I drunkenly spill out my story, illustrating my suspicions with photographs from the pages of Michael's diary taken on my mobile.

'There's even one entry, look!'– I point to a highlighted entry – 'Where Michael says that this Diving Fish girl got nasty when he wanted to make their relationship public.'

'He was fifteen,' says Grace calmly. 'How much trouble could two fifteen-year-olds get into for dating?'

'It was a little more than dating.'

'You were pregnant at fifteen!'

Seeing my hurt expression Grace takes my hands in hers. 'I'm sorry, Kat. It's, well, just – how dangerous can a fifteen-year-old girl really be?'

'Maybe she wasn't fifteen,' I say. 'Maybe she was older?'

'Even so.'

'And what about the mobile?' I will not let her dismiss my suspicions. 'Why would he need a pay-as-you-go burner?'

'The phone thing is a bit weird,' concedes Grace, 'but if she was older and they were sleeping together,' she takes a sip of wine, 'I mean Michael was underage and legally she could have been done for it. We had a similar case in school a few years ago, but it was a sixth former sleeping with a year ten girl—'

'It's not about the sleeping together, Grace!' I'm struggling with my growing impatience. 'He arranged to meet with this Diving Fish person that night.' I flip through the diary images on my phone until I find the one I'm looking for. 'She was there, Grace, at the lake. Diving Fish was with Michael the night he drowned.'

My sister stares at me, her expression unreadable. 'Don't you think that's a bit of a leap? And don't you think the diary entries, even the text,' she speaks slowly, as if measuring every word, 'are all a little . . . *fanciful*?'

'Fanciful?' Even drunk, I can't believe what I'm hearing. 'Are you suggesting he made it all up?'

'Of course not.' She pauses, as if carefully considering what to say next. 'It's just that he did tend to . . .' I watch as she struggles for the appropriate word, 'embellish things a bit.'

'Embellish things!'

'Oh, come on, Kat.' We're sitting only inches apart, but it feels like miles. 'Let's be honest. Michael could be slightly over-dramatic. Remember that thing with

79

his Art teacher? You went storming into school only to find out that he'd copied the image from the internet.'

'That was different.'

'Was it?' Grace looks troubled, then sad. 'Michael drowned, Kat. He had a few too many beers, accidentally mixed it with some medication, went swimming and then drowned.'

'Michael wasn't on any medication.'

I can feel her tense. 'We've talked about this before. The pathology report said there were traces of cyclizine in his blood.'

'Not enough to indicate abuse!'

Grace drops the phone on the bed next to me. 'You're the nurse,' she says, now clearly annoyed. 'You're the one who told me that cyclizine causes drowsiness. What the hell else am I supposed to think?'

I close my eyes, praying for calm. 'Michael didn't suffer from travel sickness,' I whisper. 'There's absolutely no reason he should have been taking that sort of medication.'

'For fuck's sake, Kat. Are you seriously telling me that there's no buzz when it's mixed with alcohol?'

I stand up quickly, the contents of my wine glass sloshing over my hand. 'Michael may have liked a beer or two,' I say, through gritted teeth. 'What teenager doesn't? But he wasn't into drugs.' Before my sister can reply, I add, 'And even if he was, why would he take travel sickness medication?'

Grace shakes her head. 'He was an athlete, Kate,

80

competing against a lot of other top-notch athletes. Maybe it wasn't for the buzz, maybe it was—'

'Don't you dare!' I cry. 'Michael was not doping. How can you possibly even say that?

Grace's blue eyes flash. 'There was that GHB scandal at the nationals.'

'Michael tested negative, as did all his classmates.' I stare at my sister, bewildered. 'Why would you bring this up?'

'It's no more bizarre than suggesting he was drugged by some psycho classmate.'

'What exactly are you saying?'

Grace sits back down on the bed and after a moment motions for me to join her. 'Honey,' she says, her voice thick with Sauvignon Blanc. 'Do you know how ridiculous this all sounds?'

I am taken aback. 'You *do* think he made it up.'

'I'm not sure what to think.' Grace reaches for her glass. 'All I know is that before you found this stuff at Mum's you were starting to get your life back together.'

'My life will never get back together.'

Grace stares at me, her lips parted slightly as if in surprise, her slim fingers clutching the wine glass. It's a moment before she speaks again. 'I'm sorry,' she says. 'I suppose six years isn't really that long, is it?' She takes a tissue from the bedside table and hands it to me. I haven't realised I've been crying. 'I'm worried about you though. Fixating on Michael's death like this – it just isn't healthy.'

'I just want to know the truth.'

'What difference will it make? Will it bring him back?'

'Of course not, but at least I can be sure justice is done.'

Grace frowns. 'What do you mean by *justice*?'

'For whoever was responsible.'

Grace replies so softly that I have to lean in closer to hear. 'No one was responsible. It was an accident.'

'It wasn't,' I say, finally able to voice the suspicions that have haunted me since the night my son died. 'Michael may have been a bit dramatic, but he wasn't a lunatic.' I can feel my heart pounding and long to reach into my bag for a tiny blue piece of calm. 'And I'm his mother. If it was an accident, why does every bone in my body shout out that it wasn't?'

'What else could it be?'

'Someone did this to him, Grace. Someone killed Michael.'

Grace turns very pale. 'You can't really believe—'

'Why not? The police report was inconclusive. The coroner's verdict was open.'

Grace puts her wine glass on the bedside table, turns to me and grabs me fiercely by both shoulders. 'I will not let you do this to yourself again.'

'What do you mean *do this to myself*?'

'Create some ridiculous scenario in your mind.' Her eyes have gone very blue. 'Do I have to remind you about last time?'

'Oh, for Christ's sake!'

'Your trips to the school? The police station? Harassing that family liaison officer?'

'I didn't harass her!'

'Kate, you were charged. If Adam hadn't got that psych report—'

'So, you're on his side now are you?'

'Of course not,' says Grace. 'I'm on yours. I'm always on yours.'

I don't believe her. No one is on my side. This has become more and more obvious in the six years since Michael's death. The police, the coroner, the school, social services; everyone including my husband and now my sister would rather let the truth lie than face the facts. My questions and subsequent confrontations with the so-called *experts* were in no way hysterical or unfounded – not like Grace is suggesting. It was all evidence-based enquiry. I have collected a lot of facts in the last six years. I know what I'm talking about. The realisation that my sister is one more doubter is more painful than I could have ever imagined. It's time for me to shut down this conversation.

'If this were Ellie—'

'Don't!' Grace jumps up as if stung. She fumbles through her bag for the packet of cigarettes, swearing as the contents scatter across the floor. Pulling on her jacket, she heads for the door. I sit on the bed unmoving, resolute. I hear the metallic click of the handle and the sound of the door being thrown wide open. There is a pause and then Grace speaks.

'Are you coming outside for a smoke or not?'

We stand by the back door of the hotel, smoking in silence, not even daring to look at each other. Even though I love her with all my heart, I know now that my sister is just one more obstacle keeping me from the truth. I also know from experience that it is best not to push her: she will talk when she's ready. What I won't do, however, is give in. If anything, our argument has only strengthened my resolve.

'Does Adam know?' Grace exhales loudly, the cigarette smoke curling around her ears like horns. 'About the diary and mobile?' I shake my head. 'What do you think he would say if he did?' I know where she is going with this, but I choose not to reply. Instead I think of the diary; of the gently sloping letters of Michael's handwriting; of the heartfelt poems. 'Don't you think telling him might help?'

'Help?' I stub the cigarette out fiercely beneath my shoe. Leaning back against the metal railings I stare up at the night sky. 'Do you know that after Michael died I wanted to hire a private detective?' I wait for Grace's response but there is none. 'There were so many mistakes with the police investigation; so many inconsistencies. Do you remember when they lost some of his blood samples? I knew something wasn't right. But Adam wouldn't let me hire somebody to look into it, and the only way I could have afforded it was to use money from the joint account.'

'And then he would have known,' says Grace.

'He said he'd put a block on the account if I did.'

'Could he do that?'

'I don't know . . .' I shrug. 'But by then I'd sort of lost the confidence.'

'I'm sorry,' says Grace, putting an arm around my shoulders. 'Your husband can be an arse sometimes.'

'I left it because I had no choice.' I take a deep breath, drawing in the scent of bergamot and sandalwood from her perfume. 'But now – finding the rucksack, the diary, and that strange text – well I just can't let it rest. Even if I'm completely wrong, at least I'll know I did everything in my power to find out what happened.' I rest my head on Grace's shoulder. 'Everyone is always going on about the need to move on. Why don't they understand that solving the mystery of how Michael died that night is the only way I *can* move on? If this Diving Fish person can help, whoever they are, isn't that a good thing?'

'I understand,' Grace whispers, and, kissing me softly on the forehead, she adds, 'I'll always understand. I just worry you'll get carried away, make yourself ill again.'

'I appreciate your concern, really, but I'm fine.'

I fact, I have never felt so sane in my entire life.

We wake at eight – groggy, hung over and with tongues like sandpaper. I make tea and sit on the bed next to Grace. She's reading her text messages, the bruise on her arm a kaleidoscope of purples, greens and yellows.

'Everything okay?'

Grace sighs. 'Ellie and Simon have had a row and she's buggered off.'

'Is she at a friend's?'

Grace rubs her eyes. 'Who knows. I was hoping to stay a bit longer, but with this—'

The words come out before I can stop them. 'She can always come and stay with us for a while if that would help?'

'What?'

'You know, maybe over the summer? She likes the seaside, and I could take some time off from work, take her to Cornwall?' It's nice to be the one offering advice and support for once. 'It could give you all a little space.'

There's a telling pause before Grace replies. 'I'm not sure that would be such a good idea.'

'Why not?'

Grace avoids my gaze. The first time she has done so all evening. 'Just leave it, Kate. Okay?'

'*Why not?*'

Grace sighs, long and slow. 'First of all, my darling, this isn't about me and my family problems. This is about us, our mother and what we're going to do. Secondly,' she has her teacher's voice on now, 'to be perfectly honest Kat, I'm not sure I want my daughter staying in the same house as your husband.'

'*Oh.*'

'I'm sorry.'

'Don't be.' I get off the bed and make a show of filling up the tiny kettle. Even though I understand why Grace said what she did, it still hurts.

'Anyway,' she says, changing the subject. 'You've got enough on your plate with Mum, and now this diary thing.' I've moved to the window and I'm staring out at the car park. Grace gets up and stands beside me. 'After everything you've been through,' it sounds

86

as if she's fighting back tears, 'I just don't know how you do it.'

I give a little shrug. It's a question I have heard time and time again since Michael's death. Over time, I have come up with a few faultless responses to make everyone else feel better.

Michael would have wanted me to carry on.

Michael would have wanted me to remain positive.

Adam and I made the decision to celebrate Michael's life rather than his loss.

This morning though, I am too tired to reach for that sort of default reply. This morning I speak the truth. I turn to my sister.

'I fake it.'

10

'Why don't you have the day off?' says Grace after breakfast. 'Go back to the house, see to the cat, get some rest. I'll spend the day with Mum.'

I don't argue. The thought of having to spend another day with my mother had woken me before dawn. I had lain next to Grace watching the early morning sun steal its way in through the half-opened curtains to settle on her face. The large wide-set eyes, so much like our mother's, had flickered as she slept. High on her forehead, just below the hairline, is a thin white scar, a relic from when we were children and I had thrown my Bible at her. I still remember the terror I had felt when our parents returned from their church meeting – I had expected Grace to pronounce my sin. Instead, I watched in amazement as my sister emerged from the bathroom with her hair newly parted to the left, her fringe hiding the injury.

As I had lain there gazing at my sister's beautiful,

sleeping face, I had felt overwhelmed by love, loyalty, and a profound sense of gratitude. I had also realised, after our discussion the night before, that there is only so much I can tell her. If I am going to find the truth about the diary, Diving Fish, and what happened to Michael that night, I'll have to keep my investigation to myself.

'I can come back for visiting hours this evening if you'd like,' I tell her, grateful for the hit of caffeine to clear my foggy brain.

'Tomorrow,' Grace insists. 'Come back tomorrow. We can visit Mum, have lunch together and then I'll head back about three.'

'I must admit I could do with a bit of a break.'

'Are you going back to Mum's?'

'Tonight, yes, but I promised Adam I'd go home tomorrow. I could do with a change of clothes and to sleep in a decent bed for a couple of nights. That old one of Michael's is a killer.'

'Why can't he come here?' There's a hint of criticism on Grace's voice that I choose to ignore. 'After all, you're the one coping with a critically ill mother and driving back and forth to the hospital. And what about the cat?'

My sister always won the arguments when we were little.

'Adam's work schedule is crazy right now, and Doris doesn't mind looking after the cat for a day or two.' I give her a hopeful look. 'You could always come back for tea tonight. Stay over? See the old place again?'

Grace shakes her head. 'Too many shitty memories.'

I nod in grim understanding. Part of me wants to say *I have them too, you know.*

I wave as Grace drives off towards the hospital, and then give a great sigh of relief. I could do with a day off and the opportunity to investigate the diary and mobile phone more deeply. Six years or yesterday – it doesn't matter. My burden will not be lifted until I find the absolute truth. I desperately need to find a new inroad; a new source of information. Something has been playing at the back of my mind; a half-formed idea trying to work its way forward. With all the craziness of the last few days, however, I just can't grasp it. Maybe some time away from the stress of the hospital will help. Climbing into my Mini, I feel the morning sunlight swaddle my skin. I give in to the dreamy sensation and close my eyes. My eyelids flicker, head nods and I find myself falling somewhere between consciousness and sleep.

I am descending a narrow spiral staircase with no handrails. It shifts to a multicoloured vista of eye-watering green sprinkled with daisies. In the distance something draws my eye: a disc spinning its way towards me. A flash; and then a smiling freckle-faced girl follows. Even though her words are hushed I can still make out what she is saying. 'I'm Shivie,' she mouths, before dissolving into dust.

I jolt awake with a new understanding. I know what I need to do.

I head out of the hospital car park and instead of turning left towards the bridge for Cornwall, I head

90

inland instead, towards the moors. Beyond the A386, past Princetown, the towering stone walls of Dartmoor Prison rising above the landscape like a granite giant. Stopping at a vantage point near Widecombe-in-the-Moor I gaze up to where the remains of twenty-four roundhouses, remnants of a medieval settlement are laid out across the hillside like draughts on a board. Michael and I used to make this journey every summer. We would hike to the top of Hound Tor and sit on the rock drinking hot chocolate from a flask, our legs dangling precariously over the edge.

It's sudden snapshots like these which still make my loss so unbearable. I give myself a little push and tighten my jaw in determination. It's clear that Michael's connection to this mysterious Diving Fish may finally provide the answers I so desperately need. If I can find out more about her, about their relationship, then maybe I can find out what really happened that night. The police report mentioned the presence of two sets of footprints in the sand by the lake, but concluded that they may have been made earlier in the day by someone unconnected with Michael's drowning. Couldn't they have been made by Diving Fish? Could she have been there that night? Maybe she was too afraid to come forward? Maybe she has something she can tell me that will finally allow it all to make sense. The diary and mobile phone are just the beginning. I must know more. This is the only way my life can ever return to even some semblance of normal. I have no choice.

I drive on, stopping for some petrol and a takeaway

coffee. Conscious Adam's shift doesn't start for another two hours, I take my time. I need to make sure the house is empty when I get there.

I slow the car before reaching the house, all the time scanning the front drive for any sign of Adam's car. I hate keeping the truth from him, but he wasn't as supportive as he could have been when I first started looking into Michael's death. Like the police and the coroner, he only seemed to want an easy solution. Open and shut. I've always sensed there was much more to it than that. Now I need to prove it.

I know that he's on a twelve to twelve shift today, but I still feel a wave of relief when I see the empty drive. I pull up and check the neighbour's bay window. The curtains are closed. I creep out of the car and around to the side entrance, feeling like a criminal trying to break into my own house.

Once inside, I head upstairs to the spare bedroom. I take a wooden pole from behind the wardrobe door. Giving the loft hatch a gentle tap, I wait for it to pop open and then, using the hook attached to the end of the pole, I pull the ladder down and climb into the loft.

The dry heat descends like a shroud. I switch the light on and wait for my eyes to adjust. Set out before me are the remnants of my life. Boxes of books from my student days, Michael's Moses basket – a little saggy after all these years – and suitcases filled with baby clothes that I had been saving for the children Michael might have had one day. There are a few clearly labelled boxes of Adam's things, and towards the back, just under the eaves, is another box, wide and flat, the tan packaging tape glimmering in the light.

I make one final check of the house, making sure the loft hatch is closed properly and the pole put back in its exact position. Making my way to the bedroom, I open the closet door and rummage through boxes on the top shelf to find it. The book of condolence. Every friend and classmate who had attended his funeral, and who may have known anything about Michael's life at Edgecombe Hall, would have signed it. *It's a long shot*, I think, as I trace the gold embossed lettering on the cover, *but at least it's a start.*

The drive back to Cornwall seems blighted by road works and slow-moving traffic. Stealing into the house to avoid having to chat with any neighbours doing some afternoon gardening, I grab a packet of crisps and take the box from the loft straight up to Michael's room. Once on the bed, I carefully remove the packaging tape, slide out the laptop and charger, and plug it in. I run my hand lightly across the brushed silver lid, tracing the outline of the apple. I wonder if the latex-gloved hands of the police officer who recovered it from Michael's room at Edgecombe Hall had done the same. I turn it on and type in the password *Bobby 123* – based on the name of one of Michael's childhood teddies. It takes a few seconds for the screen to come to life, and then the flat nothingness is slowly consumed by a catalogue of small icons and images.

Folders entitled *Coursework, Music, CCleaner* and *File Manager* emerge from the smoky blankness. There is a shortcut to Facebook, and at some point, Michael must have downloaded the Jack Wills summer catalogue. I move the cursor to the left side of the screen, to a small icon of an eagle in flight.

There are a few emails dated just before Michael's death. One is from his best friend Joe, telling Michael about his upcoming holiday to Ibiza, and another is from someone I don't recognise with the subject heading 'Mental Strength in Sports'. I scroll down further, finding nothing of interest. I check his deleted items and then methodically begin going through his archive folder, which contains dozens of emails, including notices about training days, swimming competitions and tips from fellow swimmers including *how to jack up those lame timings bro!* I'm about to give up when I spot an email from someone called Lisachick. Who the hell is Lisachick?

Re: last night

Lisachick@gmail.com
Sent: Wed 27/05/2015
To: Michael Penrose

I SAW YOU AGAIN LAST NIGHT!
WHY ARE YOU DOING THIS TO ME!
I WISH YOU WERE DEAD!!

The email was sent just before Michael's death. I feel my head spinning. Was Lisachick Diving Fish? Had Michael been cheating on her? It seems to me that the more I discover, the less I know. What about the police? They had examined the laptop. Didn't they find a hysterical email from someone wishing my son dead days before his *actual* death suspicious? Had they even bothered to question this Lisachick person? Why haven't I heard about this before?

An entirely new line of investigation has opened up. For the first time in days I feel strong, determined, clear-headed. Something about having a focus – a mission – seems to have settled my nerves. I search through the Facebook alumni page from Michael's year to see if I can find any record of a Lisachick.

After a frustrating hour, I concede defeat. Who is this woman? And what is her connection to Michael? There's no doubt in my mind now that what happened to Michael at the lake that night wasn't an accident – it wasn't suicide, but something else; something I'm not ready to name yet. All I have to do now is prove it.

After a glass of Merlot, I feel able to tackle the book of condolence. The black leather smells nothing like the warm, buttery scent of Michael's diary. Maybe it's the silica gel pack, but it has an oddly toxic quality; like burning rubber. I race through the list of names, read them out loud, hoping for some definitive recognition: *Thomas Davies. Astrid Strom. Sarah Thomas. Daniel Stacy.* There is no record of anyone named Lisa, but on the final page, three quarters of the way down, I spot something just as important. Written in elegant looping handwriting is the name Siobhan Norris. Shivie, the Frisbee-playing student who Michael met on his first day at Edgecombe Hall. I can still recall the girl's soft cheek against mine as she offered me her condolences at the funeral. Now that I know her surname, I'll be able to find her.

I'm amazed by how much I can find out about Siobhan Norris on Instagram. I learn that the twenty-one-year-old has recently secured a job in the Human Resources department at Edgecombe Hall (she posted a photo of her contract!), bought her first car (a white Fiat 500), and is saving up for a trip to Australia (lots of images of beaches). I contemplate messaging her, but suspect that like a lot of Michael's old classmates, she has moved on. The intrusion of an obsessed, grief-stricken, mentally unstable mother – because that is how I'm beginning to think people see me – won't be the best approach. It could take days, even weeks, before Siobhan replies; if ever.

I check my watch. It's too late to travel. Tomorrow is going to be a long day.

I meet Grace the following morning, as promised, for another depressing visit to the hospital. Our silent mother mostly sleeps.

'Is it just me,' says Grace during lunch, 'or does she seem to be getting worse?'

'I had a word with the ward sister,' I reply, picking at my baguette. The pale, plastic-looking chicken and

96

wilted rocket is made even more unappealing by the café's bright lighting. 'It's not so much that she's getting worse, as that she's not getting better.' I push the sandwich aside. 'With these kinds of strokes, any improvement will generally be seen within the first few weeks; the return of motor functions, speech.' Grace nods in understanding. 'After that, well . . .'

'It's off to the care home?'

'It looks that way, but you never know.'

'I wish she'd died.'

'Grace!'

'Tell me you don't wish it too.'

I look up at my sister and just as quickly look away. 'I just wish sometimes that things had been different.'

Grace reaches across the table and takes my hand. 'I love you, Kat.' And, then glancing at her phone, she exclaims, 'Bloody hell, look at the time!'

'I'd better go too,' I say, and without thinking, I add, 'I need to get to Falmouth before five.'

'Falmouth?' Grace's eyes narrow. 'Why Falmouth?'

My mind whizzes, but I have grown so accustomed to lying that I don't even blink.

'Just some fundraising stuff for Michael's scholarship,' I say, dismissively. 'I'm not sure if it will amount to anything, but it's worth checking out.'

'As long as it's not too much for you,' Grace says in a motherly tone. 'I mean with Mum, Adam, the house and that bloody cat.'

'Of course not,' I reply brightly. 'I'm absolutely fine.'

*　　*　　*

I time it carefully, checking the estimated travel time to ensure I arrive just before office closing time. I drive on automatic, the countryside flashing past me like a fast-forwarded film. I stare straight ahead and focus on one place, one outcome.

The Edgecombe Hall estate just outside Falmouth isn't much different to how I remember it; still a mixture of crumbling Georgian architecture and modern dormitories, with their prerequisite solar panels and living grass roofs. I find myself fumbling for a tissue from the glove compartment, recalling my last visit.

I had come to collect Michael's things, insisting Adam wait for me in the car park. This had seemed like my final duty, and mine alone. I passed a sea of solemn faces as I made my way to the headmaster's office, where the cardboard boxes were stacked impatiently by the door. *Rice pudding.* One of the boxes holding my dead son's precious belongings had once contained tins of rice pudding. If Michael were still around, he would have found it hilarious.

I take a deep breath and blow my nose. My loss feels as intense today as it did six years ago, but there's work to be done. I set my shoulders and carry on. It won't take me long to find a brand-new Fiat 500 in the staff car park.

I hear the jingle of car keys before I see her. Turning, I'm surprised by how different Siobhan looks. Gone is the perpetual ponytail, t-shirt and jogging bottoms, replaced now by a tidy bob and standard office uniform of black pencil skirt and white blouse.

'Shiv . . . Siobhan?' My voice is shaky, weak.

'Yes?' I can see uncertainty in the girl's eyes, and then suddenly, the clarity of recognition. 'You're Michael's mum aren't you?'

I smile and hold out my hand. 'Kate,' I say softly, 'Kate Hardy.' Then conscious of the uneasy look on her face add, 'I hope I didn't frighten you.' I can sense her unease. 'I was in the area, visiting friends.' The words feel as false as they sound. 'And, well, I was wondering if I could ask you a few questions.'

'Questions?'

Siobhan watches as I remove Michael's diary from my shoulder bag. 'Yes,' I continue. 'Questions about Michael.'

'I'm not sure—'

'Please,' I say, near tears. 'You're the only one who can help me.'

Siobhan gives a reluctant nod and leads me to a nearby bench. We sit in silence.

'I still think of him, you know,' she whispers.

I smile gratefully. 'I've been staying at Michael's grandmother's house. She's recently had a stroke.'

'I'm sorry to hear that, Mrs Hardy.'

I turn to Siobhan. I can see that her earlier look of uncertainty is now replaced by one of sympathy.

'While I was at Mum's I found a few of his things.' I swallow hard. 'Things I never knew existed.' I hold out the diary, the page opened to 'Jawbone Ridge', one of his poems in progress.

'I know this,' Siobhan whispers, her eyes scanning the page. 'I told him it was amazing.' She shakes her head and grins. 'Whoever thought a macho swimming star could write poetry?'

I turn the pages to his entries about Diving Fish. I watch as Siobhan's cheeks redden.

'I don't think,' she says, 'I can do this.'

I feel hope drain away like water into sand. 'Please,' I beg. 'That's not all I found.' I get out my mobile and show her the photos I've taken of Lisachick's email, and of Michael's text to Diving Fish. 'Can you see why I'm so confused? I need to know who these people are, and what connection they had to Michael.'

Siobhan sighs and hands the diary back to me. 'There's a pub just down the road,' she says. 'I think you're going to need a drink.'

11

The Old Wheel is as drab and run down as its name suggests; worn carpets, sticky tabletops and a constant jangle and flashing of lights from a fruit machine. I get us a couple of white wine spritzers and find a secluded table in a tiny alcove. We sit sipping our drinks and gazing at the faded photographs of local football teams, before finally daring to make eye contact.

'What exactly is it that you want to know, Mrs Hardy?'

'Everything.'

Siobhan takes a sip of her drink and clears her throat. 'I don't know a lot really. Only that after October half term things really started to change with Michael.'

'What do you mean by change?'

'He just seemed different. You know, got very secretive about everything. He stopped hanging out in the common room, didn't spend his free time with us.' Siobhan takes another sip. 'He always seemed to be sneaking off somewhere. It was pretty clear he was up to something.'

It takes a moment for me to remember to breathe. 'And this Diving Fish person. Do you know who she is?'

Siobhan shakes her head. 'Not a clue.'

'Why do you think he called her Diving Fish?'

Siobhan smiles sadly. 'I think it might have been something to do with a story our Swimming Coach told us. She was always throwing motivational quotes and stories our way, most of them rubbish. There was this one she told us whenever we were messing around or getting distracted from our swimming,' her brow furrows as she tries to remember. 'A Chinese proverb or something about someone so beautiful that when the fish saw them, they forgot to swim, dived to the bottom of the sea and drowned.'

The word *drowned* sends a sliver of ice through my heart.

'I'm sorry Mrs Hardy – I didn't mean to—'

'It's all right.' People say things like that to me all the time. They don't realise that six years, six days, six minutes is irrelevant. Time has no meaning, no perspective, when you've lost someone you love. But I don't have time for sentimentality. 'If it was an actual relationship, why would he keep it a secret?' I take a sip of wine to steady myself. 'I get that he may not have wanted me to know – his mother, I mean – but wouldn't he have told his friends?'

Siobhan seems reluctant; coy. Running her finger-tips along the side of the wine glass, she makes tiny circles in the condensation. 'I'd heard things, rumours; but he never told me anything. And if they were both under sixteen—'

'And in an intimate relationship, you mean?'

She nods and then continues, 'If things got messy, not only could he have been kicked out of school—'

'But he could have also been charged with statutory rape.' Now it's starting to make sense. 'Do you think that's why he kept it a secret?'

'Maybe.' She takes a sip of her drink and seems to be thinking over my question. 'Or maybe he just wanted to keep it private.'

'But you knew.'

Siobhan shifts in her seat. 'He was on a mobile one night. Not his normal one, but some cheap piece of rubbish.'

The burner phone.

I'm trying desperately not to push too hard, but I need answers. 'And you thought?'

Siobhan's eyes meet mine then almost as quickly look away. 'I didn't think anything. He said the battery on his iPhone was going and that he kept his old one for emergencies.'

'But you didn't believe him.'

'We slept, ate, trained and studied next to each other. It was virtually impossible to keep a secret in that house.'

'So what happened?'

Siobhan sighs heavily. It's almost as if a weight is

being lifted. 'I could see he was texting, and, well, I was curious. So when he went to make himself a smoothie, I took the phone.'

'You what?'

'Well he left it sitting on the arm of the chair.'

'And you were, as you said, curious.'

'I thought he had a secret girlfriend and was going to tease him about it.' She gives an embarrassed, cheeky grin. 'And maybe text something back.'

'But Michael found out.'

'It was stupid really. I mean the house was all open plan. He just had to look up from where he was making his drink.'

'And when he did? When he saw you on his mobile?'

'He went absolutely ballistic.'

I put my glass down and lean forward. 'What *did* you find?'

Even in the dim light of the pub I can see her blush. 'The texts,' her voice is deep, hoarse. 'They were, um, pretty explicit.'

I put my hands to my face as if trying to blank out the world. It takes a moment before I can speak again.

'Do you think it was someone from Edgecombe? Someone in your year?'

'I couldn't say.'

'Oh come on!' This faux bashfulness is getting on my nerves. 'You've told me this much, why not the rest?'

Siobhan appears to be looking to the ceiling for

an answer. 'I thought maybe he was seeing a sixth former,' she says, finally. 'I mean why else would they be keeping it a secret?'

I exhale softly. *At last*. There is one more thing, however, I do want to ask.

'Do you think they might have been together at the lake that night? The night he died?'

'What?' The girl's expression changes from one of caution to one of fear. 'Look, Mrs Hardy – I'm not really sure there's any more I can tell you.'

I feel my heart sink, but I won't give up. 'Do you think Diving Fish was there?'

Siobhan looks as if she is about to burst into tears. 'I . . . I don't know!' A few of the other customers have turned to look at us.

'Why don't I get us a couple of coffees?' I say, forcing a bright tone. The last thing I want is a bunch of do-gooders sticking their noses in and stopping me from getting the information I so desperately need. I must keep everything under control.

I'm back a few minutes later, and, placing the coffees on the table, say, 'Why don't you tell me a little bit about yourself? What have you been up to since leaving Edgecombe Hall?' A look of doubt crosses Siobhan's face and I know I'd better think fast if I'm going to keep her on side. 'I always imagined that you and Michael would have stayed friends after graduating.' I pause. 'Had he lived.'

She smiles as if she had imagined the very same thing. 'Popped my knee playing five-a-side football during my final A Level year, which pretty much put an end to my swimming career. Started a Sports Science degree but screwed that up too.' She gives a bitter laugh. 'So here I am, in some lousy admin job at a posh prep school with all the swimming super-stars of the future just rubbing my nose in it.'

'I thought you liked Edgecombe?'

'It's a great place when you're a winner. Crap when you're not.'

'What about the lovely car I saw in the car park? It looks quite new?'

'My parents lent me the money, but now that I've decided to go travelling, they're hassling me to make sure I've got at least a year's car payments in the bank. I've been saving like crazy, but that and travel expenses mean I'll need at least another grand.'

'I'm sure something'll come up.'

Siobhan checks her phone. 'I've got to go,' she says, clearly desperate to leave the bleak hollow of the Old Wheel.

'But I still have so much to ask you.'

'Look, Mrs Hardy, I've pretty much told you every-thing I know.' She takes a deep breath and I know at once there is something else. 'There is one thing. Lisachick is Lisa Edwards. She was in her first year of A Levels when Michael arrived. Weekly boarder, went home for weekends. A real pain in the . . .' Siobhan stops herself. 'I'm pretty sure nothing was going on between them – as far as I knew, Lisa was only interested in girls. Things may have changed of course.' Siobhan gives a wry smile. 'Some kids were

106

always experimenting. The only thing I can tell you for sure is that she did not like Michael.'

I feel as if I am travelling deeper and deeper into darkness. 'What do you mean, did not like Michael?'

'She was always slagging him off, saying he was undisciplined. *Using.*'

'Using?'

'You know.' Siobhan looks uncomfortable, as if realising she has said too much. 'Performance-enhancing drugs.'

'What?'

'Nobody believed her.'

'Why would someone who barely knew Michael say that about him?' My maternal instincts kick in, even though I no longer have someone to mother. 'Why did she dislike him so much?'

'I really don't know.' The girl's voice drops, and I find myself leaning forward to hear. 'There was one time, a few weeks before he d—' Siobhan pulls herself back from saying the dreaded word, 'before it happened, when they were arguing in the kitchen and she actually pulled a knife on him.'

'Why didn't you tell me this before? Or tell the police?'

Siobhan cowers slightly. 'Things like that happened sometimes. I'm sure she didn't mean it. We were all pretty highly strung. Regionals were coming up.'

'So, you just let it go?'

'I really don't think she would have done anything, Mrs Hardy. She put the knife away just as quickly. And anyway Michael was winding her up something awful.'

'Winding her up?'

'He kept on singing "Creep" to her.'

'"Creep"?'

'You know – the Radiohead song. "I'm a creep, I'm a weirdo" – but Michael just kept on singing "you're a creep, you're a weirdo" to Lisa. It was really pissing her off.'

I force myself to remain calm and not get carried away with this new information.

'And she threatened him?'

Siobhan's expression returns to one of guarded alarm. 'I wouldn't go that far.' She whispers. 'I mean I'm sure Lisa wouldn't have actually done anything.'

'But she *did* threaten him.'

Siobhan stares at me, unwilling to reply. Standing up, she wipes imaginary crumbs from her skirt and glances towards the exit. 'I've really got to go.' She gives me an awkward smile and, picking up her handbag from the chair, adds, 'I hope you find what you're looking for, Mrs Hardy. I really do.'

'Lisa Edwards. Lisa Edwards,' I mumble, as I walk back to my car. Frustrated and tired, I ease myself into the driver's seat, but there's no time to waste, and taking my mobile out of my bag I begin searching the internet for any information on '*Lisa Edwards, Cornwall.*' My mobile gives a desperate buzz and then suddenly goes blank.

'Dammit!' I begin searching through my glove compartment for my car phone charger but only come across some tissues, a torch, old sweet wrappers, and, in the far corner, a leather bracelet I bought Michael for his fourteenth birthday. Worn once too often when training, the chlorine had started to erode the leather and the clasp had rusted. I clutch it in my fist like a talisman, then forcing myself to remain calm, I slip it into my handbag, start the car and begin my journey back to Calstock. I'll have to wait until I get home before I can do any searches on Lisa Edwards.

When I reach the cottage, Tam, as usual, is sitting by the front door meowing loudly. Inside, I can hear the muted ringing of the telephone.

'Out of the way,' I say, gently pushing the cat aside with my foot and opening the door. The cat races past me and into the kitchen. 'There's a cat flap in the back door you idiot!' By now the ringing has stopped. 'They'll phone back,' I mutter, and head towards the kitchen to make myself a drink. I take it upstairs, settle back on Michael's bed, and scroll through my laptop looking for any information on Lisa Edwards. It's been a long week and my brain feels as heavy as wet cotton wool. I lean back and rest my head on the pillow.

In my dream, Michael is swimming towards me, his muscular body powering through the water. He lifts his head, and I can see the delicate filaments of gill tissue on his neck gently pulsating. His eyes are shiny, glutinous orbs. He glances at me, then away, his attention fixed on some distant point.

I jolt awake. I reach for the blister pack of blue

pills on the bedside table, then stop. My stash, which I deliberately started hoarding during that unbearable period after Michael's inquest, is running low. I'm going to have to find some other way to cope. I hear the soft hum of Michael's laptop. It's open on the bed next to me, and, with little airflow, the fan has started running to cool down the machine. I glance at the screen. My Google searches for Lisa Edwards threw up dozens of hits, including a hairdresser, a quantity surveyor and a chiropodist, none of which fit the profile of a twenty-three-year-old ex-competitive swimmer. It seems like the closer I get, the further away it all becomes.

I run a steaming bath and sip from a tall glass of vodka and tonic. I wash my hair, shave my legs, and apply body lotion from a gift set I bought for my mother years ago which has never been used.

I'm just nibbling on a cracker and pouring myself another drink when I hear a knock at the door. Tightening the belt on my bathrobe, I glance at the clock on the cooker. Nine thirty. Who would be coming by this late?

There is another knock, this time louder. I hide my glass behind the toaster and make my way to the front door. Through the frosted glass window, I can make out a familiar shape. My stomach tightens and apprehension floods through me. Holding my breath, I open the door.

'Adam.' I try to look pleased, but a multitude of questions are firing through my brain. *Why is he here? Does he know something?*

'Are you going to let me in or not?' Adam's face is cold, pinched, his pupils two angry pinpricks. He doesn't wait for an answer but strides past me and into the lounge. 'Close the door, Kate,' he calls to me. 'Then come and sit down. We need to talk.'

I think about fleeing. Flinging open the door and racing towards the river, diving, and swimming until I am nothing but a tiny speck on the horizon. When Michael was thirteen, I helped him train for the under-sixteens triathlon. I would get up with him at dawn, and, wetsuit clad, I would swim with him in the early morning sea, our lips blue, eyelashes encrusted with salt. Some days I would leave him alone in the water and sit sipping hot chocolate on the shore. I would watch him swim on and on, never seeming to tire. My beloved dolphin boy.

I make my way into the living room. Adam is standing by the mantelpiece, his back towards me. I perch myself on the edge of the settee and wait.

'What day is it?' he asks, not turning.

'Pardon?'

'What day is it?'

I hesitate, conscious that any response that I give might not be the right one. 'Thursday?'

I'm flooded with a sudden, terrible realisation. 'Oh God. I was supposed to be home for tea tonight, wasn't I?'

Adam turns. 'Yes. You were.'

'I'm sorry, honey – with Grace here and all the running back and forth, I just lost track of the time.'

'I called your mobile; the house.' He points towards

the telephone with its blinking answerphone light. 'Why didn't you answer?'

There's no point in trying to lie my way out of this. I think of Grace's advice last night when she was texting Adam on my behalf. *The trick is to keep it simple. The more you say, the more you give away.*

I try to keep my voice light. 'It's been a bit of a day.'

'So I've heard.'

'I'm sorry?'

'When I couldn't reach you, I got worried.'

'I was—'

'*Fine,* I know.'

'I just needed a little space.'

'Well, I called Grace.'

'You what?'

'I called your sister.'

My mind races as I try to imagine what Grace may have told him, but I stop myself from asking. 'Look, I'm sorry I worried you. It just slipped my mind that I was supposed to be home tonight. I really am sorry.'

'Grace said you drove to Falmouth?'

There's a sudden sick feeling in my stomach.

'It was just to sort out a bit of admin about Michael's memorial scholarship. Nothing serious.'

'But driving all that way with everything that's going on?'

Adam has always been good at getting to the heart of the matter.

'I just needed a change of scenery.'

'You were supposed to come home.'

112

A look of worry is etched into his handsome features and I feel overwhelmed by remorse.

'I'm so sorry. I really should have come. It's just that I never know quite what to expect when I get to the hospital, and with Grace here, well . . . to be perfectly honest this week has just flown by.' I give a hopeful smile. 'But you're here now. Why don't I make us a cup of tea and you can tell me about your week?'

Adam is silent for a long while, his eyes searching mine. 'You look tired.'

I nod, and then the tears come. I feel a sob rising in my chest, the desire to scream and thrash about like some tragic heroine, a Dido at the pyre, but that would only worry him more.

'I said this would be too much for you.'

I really must close down this conversation. The last thing I want is for Adam to try and force me to come home. 'It's hard, Adam, I won't deny that; but it's also my duty.'

'To her?'

He's fallen very nicely into my line of thinking. I keep my voice soft so that he doesn't think this is a confrontation. 'It's not really that different to when your father was ill.'

I've hit home with that one, but I don't feel pleasure, only relief. Adam sighs deeply and his expression softens.

'I suppose you're right.'

He moves closer and then his arms are around me. I can feel the warmth of him; I can smell the woody scent of his aftershave. His arms tighten. I feel his hands loosen the belt on my robe, slip around my waist and then down to cup my buttocks. He pulls me towards him and slips his fingers between my thighs. Grabbing my wet hair, he pulls my head back and begins kissing my neck, working his way down to my breasts. I feel odd, distant, as if this scene is being reflected through a broken mirror, fractured and distorted. My robe is thrown off and I find myself being pushed back onto the settee. I hear a zip and the thump of his jeans hitting the floor. Suddenly Adam is inside me. Forcing his way inside me. I run my fingers across his back, gripping the taut muscles above his shoulder blades. I feel him buck and thrust harder. I close my eyes, willing it to be over. The warmth of his body, the salty taste of his skin should be comforting, pleasurable. Could this at last be a way to free my restless mind? Instead I feel soiled; polluted.

Adam grunts, rolls off me, and lays on the settee panting. He wipes the sweat from his forehead and slips his jeans back on. I pull my robe tightly around me and double knot the belt. He clears his throat.

'How about that cup of tea?'

12

We sit on the Queen Anne chairs sipping our tea and not speaking. Adam, still with a post-coital flush, looks troubled. I wait.

'When I spoke to Grace earlier . . .' he says, finally, 'along with telling me about Falmouth, she said you found something?'

'Something?'

'Of Michael's – she said you found something of Michael's. A notebook?' My eyelids flicker. My heart pumps fiercely in my chest. Has Grace betrayed me? How could she betray me? I struggle to contain my feelings. How could my sister give up my secret? A secret that was mine alone to tell?

'What notebook?'

'Oh, come on, Kate. Stop playing it so coy.'

'I don't know what you mean.'

'Grace said you had found a notebook of some sort . . . no, not a notebook. A diary. Michael's diary.'

He sounds dismissive, patronising. I know what he's thinking. *What kind of teenage boy keeps a diary?* I feel as if I'm balancing on a tightrope and any wrong move could send me hurtling into the pitch-black depths below. As a child I had been afraid of the dark – that unseen space beyond my bed. I had so desperately wanted to be like Grace, striding head-strong and fearless into the unknown. I did try, once.

I was fifteen and Michael's father, Ryan, had offered to take me upriver from Cotehele to Calstock on his homemade dinghy. We had sat next to each other in Geography for the entire year, me discreetly holding my notebook open to share my answers, while he kept the bullies at bay. He was kind. Not like the other boys, who called me *loser* and *freak* because of my hand-me-downs and headscarves. We would walk together from the bus stop until we were forced to go our separate ways to avoid being spotted. In those magical ten minutes he would fill me in about the latest episodes of *The Simpsons* and *Stargate* and let me listen to The Verve on his iPod. The afternoon of the boat trip, my mother was working late then going on to a Bible reading. It was a sunny Friday, only weeks before school breaking up, and I was haunted by the knowledge that I would be spending the entire summer either babysitting for one of the Brethren families, or, even worse, having to sit through endless prayer meetings and Bible classes in the hot, stuffy church hall. It was windy and for some reason the breeze made me feel rebellious. When Ryan asked if I would like to go for a sail in his dinghy, I thought of Grace's daring: *Donna-Marie and me have got ourselves jobs at a hotel in St Ives.* I raced home, changed into one of Grace's abandoned t-shirts and a pair of cut-off jeans she had kept hidden under the floorboards in our bedroom, and went to the river.

Then I waited. It seemed like ages. Just as I was convinced he had abandoned me I saw a small flash of white as the sail floated downriver towards me. After tacking, Ryan eased the boat towards the jetty.

'I'm going to pull up as close as possible and then I want you to jump.'

'Jump?'

'Don't be scared, Kit Kat. Just one big jump and you're on!'

I watched him approach with a mixture of excitement and terror, holding my breath as I launched myself from the jetty, across the swirling water, and into the tiny boat. That airborne second had seemed like an eternity – an infinitesimal moment of possibility. When I landed safely in the boat next to Ryan, he smiled proudly and kissed me.

That evening, as the sun dipped behind the Tamar Valley, we made love in the boat shed. My first time. Nine months later, Michael was born.

No matter how fierce the intimidation, how frightening the threats, I never told the elders who the father was. Even then, I knew the value of keeping secrets. We spoke once or twice afterwards, but a few months after that dinghy trip, Ryan left Cornwall for good. Maybe being fearless and headstrong wasn't such a good thing after all.

When Michael was three and I was just about to start university, I contacted Ryan. He didn't seem surprised to discover Michael was his son – how could he be? – but he didn't seem bothered either. That's when I understood it would always just be Michael and me. Everyone else existed on the periphery.

Ryan's divorced now, with two teenage daughters and an ex-wife called Jackie, and living in Bromsgrove. Not quite the father I'd hoped he would be.

'*Kate!*'

Adam is standing in front of me, hands on hips.

'It's just a notebook,' I say, hoping with all my might that's all Grace has told him. 'Nothing special, just a few scribbles.'

'Where is it?'

'What?'

'The notebook, where is it?'

'Why?'

Adam gives a little cough. 'Well, the thing is, I can understand how finding a notebook, or diary, whatever, must have been upsetting for you. No wonder you're all over the place. After all, we've really been moving on, haven't we?'

I open my mouth to protest. I'm not about to let him think that finding Michael's diary has made me unstable or unwell. That would just be too easy. It did, of course, but only for a little while. I'm now feeling the most focused and clear-headed I have been in months.

Adam speaks first. 'I thought we agreed that we'd

work hard to try to put some of those painful memories behind us.' Why does he keep saying *we*?

'Michael is not a painful memory.' *How many* times do I have to repeat this? Adam and Michael had never been particularly close, but after he left for Edgecombe their relationship deteriorated to the point where any communication between the two of them, on the few occasions Michael did come home, either consisted of yelling or sullen silence. They had clashed over everything: schoolwork, Michael's social life, and especially his training routines. Adam, a former university rugby fly half, favoured a regime based around weight training, while the more adventurous Michael was exploring innovations such as plasma volume and decreased body temperature as a means of enhancing athletic performance. I smile as I recall producing endless jugs of homemade beetroot juice to help him reduce his oxygen uptake. My hands seemed to be constantly stained red.

'This is not something to smile about, Kate.'

'Will you just leave it, Adam? Please?'

'But we agreed.'

We didn't agree.

'It's nothing.' I sound guilty, defensive, as if I am a naughty pupil being chastised. 'A bit of life history, a few poems; that's all.' I think of the diary, nestled under my pillow where I sleep with it each night. 'It's just a sweet reminder – something that gives me a little bit of my son back.'

'So, where is it?' Adam stands up and scans the room. 'Is it upstairs?'

Now I'm terrified. I'm certain Michael's laptop is still on the bed. If Adam knew that I snuck into the house to get it without telling him he would be furious.

'I'd like to see it,' he adds.

The tension in the room becomes solid. A wall of ice. Normally in these situations I acquiesce, roll over like an obedient dog to keep the peace and avoid confrontation. For weeks afterwards, I berate myself for being weak, giving in. Today, however, it's as if some unseen force is guiding me to stand my ground.

'Why do you want to see it?' Sitting up straight, I add, 'It's private. It's Michael's.'

Adam has gone very still. 'I just want to help you, Kate,' he says. 'Help you to move on.' He's always talking about *moving on* when I know all he really wants is for me to forget – toss Michael aside like some old photograph, like the laptop hidden away in the loft and the clothes he made me pass on to the charity shop. 'Just give me the diary. I'll put it somewhere safe.'

From deep inside I feel the rumblings of rebellion. 'No.'

For a few seconds there is silence: only the tick of the mantel clock and the beating of my heart. I see Adam's left eye twitch.

'What do you mean *no*?' His voice sounds as if it's coming from deep underground, slowly thundering its way through the dirt.

'I mean no.' I can see his chest rising and falling; hear anger in his every breath. For some reason it only makes me more determined. 'You cannot see it; you cannot have it; you cannot take it.' I think that I've gone completely mad. The events of the last week, including finding the rucksack and the information from Siobhan, have driven me over the edge, and my defiance reflects it. I can't imagine what Adam is making of it all, but I have never felt so exhilarated in all my life.

'Kate.'

'You can't have it.' I'm standing now, slowly trying to edge my way towards the stairs. If necessary, I will run up and barricade myself in the bedroom. 'It's *my son's* diary. Probably one of the last things he ever touched. I'm keeping it.'

'Jesus Christ, Kate!' Adam's outburst, the ferocity of it, sends me stumbling backwards onto the chair. He's on top of me now, his hands gripping my shoulders, shaking me. 'Give me the diary!' I see his eyes shift to the upstairs landing.

'No!' I scream and breaking free of his grip run towards the stairs. Positioning myself on the bottom step, I block his way. 'Get out!'

'For God's sake, Kate,' he yells, his face an unappealing shade of red. 'Don't you know that I'm only trying to help you? Trying to save you from yourself?' I have never seen him like this before.

There is a knock at the door and a soft voice follows.

'Katie, are you all right?'

It's Doris. Thank God. I feel relief flood through me. I turn to Adam.

'Get out,' I repeat, and with every ounce of strength I possess, take a step towards him. 'Get out and don't come back.'

I sit at the kitchen table clutching the balled-up tissues in my tightly clenched fists. Occasionally, I release my grip to dab at my eyes or runny nose. Doris hands me a cup of tea and, finding a spare foldaway chair, sits down next to me.

'I was just putting my recycling in the green bin when I heard yelling.' She takes a sip of tea and I can see that her hands are shaking.

'I'm sorry, Doris.' I desperately want to join her in a sip of tea, but don't think I will be able to swallow. 'Things got a bit out of hand, that's all.'

Doris nods and reaching across the table takes my hand. 'Did he hurt you?'

I shake my head. In the past there have been occasional bruises where he has grabbed my wrists in frustration, but there's no way I can tell Doris any of this – I'm embarrassed enough.

'Oh, my love,' she says, and as if reading my mind, adds, 'You've not had an easy time of it, have you?' We sit for a while in the kitchen's soft neon glow, not speaking. Finally, she says, 'What are you going to do now?'

I shrug. 'I'm really not sure.' I don't realise I've started crying again until I see my tears softly plopping into my teacup. 'It's not been the same, you know . . . since Michael.' Doris nods in understanding. 'Maybe it never really was that good.' I could confide in Doris about Michael's diary entry describing his stepfather as *threats-behind-closed-doors Adam*, but that would be unfair. It's a burden no one else should have to shoulder.

Doris pats my hand. 'You know you always have my support, no matter what.' I lean across and give her a hug, wishing, as I so often had done when I was younger, that she were my real mother.

13

I spend most of Friday morning in bed ignoring the
barrage of phone calls and texts from Adam:

*Kate, I'm sorry about last night. I got carried away.
I was just so worried.*

*Kate, we need to talk. Last night was a mistake, I
overreacted.*

Kate, please come home. Let me make it up to you.

*Kate, I'm concerned you'll become unwell again.
Let me help you.*

There's a long voicemail pleading for forgiveness,
justifying his behaviour, saying it was just the worry
of it all. Hadn't he looked after me all these years?
Didn't I believe he had my best interests at heart? By
midday, my head is spinning, my resolve weakening.
With everything that's going on, I'm not sure if I have
the resilience to deal with a marriage break-up as
well. It's not just the emotional impact of separating,
but the financial implications. The house, the cars,

the credit cards – most are in Adam's name. My bank account contains less than a thousand pounds; certainly not enough to start afresh. I've also had to take unpaid leave while Mum is in hospital – it's not like my salary was enough to live on anyway – and I will need his financial support if I'm to continue my investigation.

The thought of being financially vulnerable strikes a deep chord. After my father left us there was little money. Though not common for Brethren women, my mother took a job as a secretary for another member – a farmer. She did accounts, admin and arranged deliveries. But even then, the money was basic, and certainly not enough to keep a house and two children. Food parcels were regularly left at our back door: homemade bread, casseroles, the occasional cake. Also left were bags of hand-me-down clothing: skirts, blouses, cardigans, shoes. I don't think I had a pair of shoes that fit properly until I was sixteen.

My mother accepted their charity with reluctant grace, but underneath she seethed at the unbearable humiliation, growing angrier and more bitter every day. She became like one of those homemade apple dolls: faces carved out of fruit and left to wither and dry until they take on the appearance of a wizened old woman. After we were cast out, her drinking got worse, and that, along with our lack of connections outside the Brethren, made it even harder for her to find work. Eventually we were forced to live on benefits, a further humiliation.

The additional benefits I brought in as a single mother in education were also crucial, and even though I desperately wanted to find a little flat of my own, just me and Michael, I knew I couldn't leave her. Grace, just a silhouette on the horizon – a voice on the phone espousing the virtues of freedom and a fun time – had absolutely no relevance to my life. My plan was clear: finish my A Levels, get a place on a nursing course, get a job, and get out. I was perfectly happy to play the long game; I always have been.

My brain feels heavy, overburdened. I know I will have to deal with it all, but maybe a little later. I wonder if it's too early to have a drink. My mobile goes off; the ringtone tells me that it's Grace calling. I could ignore it – that would be so much easier – but instead I push the little green circle with the phone icon on it. I have a few things I want to say to her.

'Kat, it's Grace. I've been trying to reach you for ages.'

'I've been busy.'

There's a long pause. 'I guess you know about Adam.' Grace sounds uncomfortable. 'And the diary thing.'

'Yes.'

'I didn't mean to tell him, Kat. I really didn't.'

I smile grimly to myself. 'Adam has a way of getting things out of people.'

'When he called me last night to say that you hadn't come home, I was really worried.' She rattles out the

126

words, *rat-a-tat-tat*. 'You said you were driving to Falmouth and I thought you might have had an accident or something.'

'I got home late and forgot to call.' I feel as if I'm reading the lines from a script.

'He was in a real shitty mood when I spoke to him.' I rub my aching shoulders. 'I know.'

'Did he give you a load of aggro over the phone?'

'It was in person actually.'

'What?'

'Adam drove down, late last night.' I long to add *Giving me hell over the phone just wasn't enough for him*, but I stop myself. *The more you say . . .*

'Oh God,' Grace sounds remorseful. 'I never thought he'd do that. Are you all right?' I don't answer. 'I'm so sorry Kat. I should have never left you on your own. I told Adam that it was probably all a bit too much for you. I mean the last thing we want is for you to get ill again.'

Here we go. Let's all just revert to the familiar scenario of Kate as the helpless lunatic: weak, unbalanced and unreliable. I feel so, so tired. I search through my bag for the blister pack.

'Only three left.'

'What?'

I hadn't realised I had spoken aloud. 'Nothing.'

'I just feel so bad for leaving you to handle it all,' continues Grace.

I love my sister, and respect her enormously, but at this very moment I couldn't give a toss how she's feeling.

'Kat? Are you there?'

'Why did you tell him?' I ask. 'About the diary?'

There is another long pause and I hear my sister sigh. 'I'm worried about you, Kat – about the effect all this might have on you. All that stuff you told me about Michael, about this Diving Fish girl. It just sounded—'

'Crazy?'

'No, not crazy,' says Grace, almost too quickly. 'Just . . . not healthy.'

'And did you really think telling Adam would help?'

'Well, I just—'

'After everything I told you at the hotel about him refusing to let me hire a private detective, and not supporting me?'

'Kat, listen to me.' Grace's voice has grown stern. 'I simply said I was worried about you and when he asked me why, I mentioned the diary.'

I can feel the heat rushing to my cheeks. 'Why does everyone want to stop me *feeling* anything? Michael was my son – my boy – and I lost him. I will be experiencing this for the rest of my life. I'd rather have painful memories than nothing.'

'I thought it would be too much for you.'

'Why couldn't you just give me the benefit of the doubt?'

'It's just so—'

'Mad?'

'Oh, come on, Kat!'

It's as if I'm leaning against a brick wall in winter – I can feel the heat seeping from my bones. 'I'm the

128

one dealing with this, Grace, and as far as I can tell I've been doing okay. I wish, instead of expecting the worst, everyone would just cut me a bit of slack. Maybe then I wouldn't forget to go home for tea, or forget to call Adam!'

'Kat, I'm sorry.' Grace's tone has changed from stern to desperate.

'It doesn't matter.'

'Why don't Adam and I draw up some sort of rota to make sure you're not on your own?'

'I'm perfectly capable of looking after myself, Grace, and considering the circumstances I think I'm allowed at least one lapse of judgement without people turning it into a complete drama.'

'We overreacted, Kat – clearly we did.'

'I've got to go.' Something about the way I say the words seems final. Grace senses it too.

'I'll see you soon, Kat. Ellie's staying at her friends for a couple of days next week, so I'm hoping to get some time off work and come up then. I thought maybe I'd stay with you at Mum's?'

I feel like ending the call – just slamming down the phone. As angry as I am right now, I still love my sister. That doesn't mean I want her staying with me, getting in the way, dismissing my suspicions and offering the usual safe, generic explanations. *None of this is concrete, Kat. Are you sure you're not just imagining it?* What I want now is to find Lisa Edwards, find out what she knows about Diving Fish, and make her tell me what happened to Michael.

'Of course,' I reply, trying hard not to let irritation

creep into my voice. I hope, however, without wishing any hardship on my sister, that something comes up to keep her away.

'Are you sure you're okay? What about Adam?'

'What about him?' This time I can't contain the vitriol in my voice.

'Have you two had a row? Did he do anything to you?'

A bit late for you to ask that now, don't you think?

'Everything's fine, Grace. I'll call you later, okay?' And in a herculean effort to sound bright, normal, I add: 'Give my best to Simon and Ellie.'

I've just ended the call when my mobile rings again. It's Adam.

'In for a penny, in for a pound,' I mutter, and take the call.

14

I make a quick stop at the hospital – no change with my mother – then head up the A38 to Exmouth. The phone call from Adam was civil, apologetic. *Kate, please try and understand, I'm just concerned. I care about you. I love you. I can't live without you.*

I feel angry, guilty, and terribly uncertain. Adam has always been my lifeline, my strength, someone who was always able to make things right again. If I'm ever going to get through this, I need him on my side, at least for the moment. *Choose your battles, Katie*, my father used to say. As focused as I am on finding Diving Fish, I need to maintain my perspective and make sure everyone else knows I've maintained it as well.

I text Adam to let him know I'll be coming home for the weekend. I add a few banalities about starting afresh. I checked my bank balance online this morning and realised I'm going to need some financial support if I want to get the answers I need. When did I become so mercenary?

The house is warm and welcoming. Vibrant purple irises line the drive, and the Bride and Groom rosebush – a wedding present from Adam's mother – is just beginning to bud. Everything feels so normal. A reminder of what was . . . and what could still be?

He's waiting for me at the door, his expression warm and welcoming. He hesitates before enveloping me in a hug. 'I'm so glad you're home.'

'Me too.'

'Come inside.'

The house is pristine and orderly. A large vase of flowers is prominently displayed on the dining room table.

'An apology,' he whispers.

'No need,' I reply.

Our lovemaking is passionate, frenetic; a place of forgetfulness. Later, when we're lying in bed sipping ice-cold beer, Adam reaches over and touches my arm.

'I spoke to Claire today.'

'Claire?' I know several Claires.

'Your therapist. She's got a cancellation tomorrow morning.' He takes a sip of Peroni. 'I've booked you in for eleven.'

The next morning, I make the half-hour drive to Exeter and pay for overpriced parking in the city centre. It's just after ten and the streets are already crowded with Saturday shoppers. I turn left just past the Royal Albert Memorial Museum and enter Gandy Street, a pretty cobbled lane with hanging baskets and endless bunting. I'm not interested in the sights, however, and I keep my eyes low. A little more than halfway down the alley is the jeweller's where Adam and I bought our wedding rings. Next to it is a door, and to the left a sign that reads *Claire Hodgeson: Integrated Therapeutic Counsellor. Please ring buzzer to enter.* I push the buzzer; the door clicks open and I climb the narrow stairs to the second floor.

'How lovely to see you,' says Claire, welcoming me into her office. To the right is a two-seater settee with a colourful throw strewn across it; next to that a comfortable chair, and, opposite, a small desk and chair where Claire usually positions herself. 'Come in. Sit down.' I do as instructed. 'Coffee? Tea?'

'Water, please.'

She pours me a glass of water then sits, hands folded on her lap, watching me. 'So,' she says, finally.

I take a sip of water. 'So.'

'It's been a few months, hasn't it?'

'Three, I think.'

She nods. After Michael's death, my sessions were as regular as clockwork. Once a week you would find me sitting on her settee, wrapped in a throw, bawling my eyes out. God, I was a mess. 'It's lovely as always to see you again, Kate. Is there a particular reason you felt you needed to meet today?'

'I didn't make the appointment. Adam did.'

Claire nods again. 'That's why I asked the question.'

We talk about my mother, the hospital, Adam, the weather; but I keep clear of the diary, the mobile phone, and the scene with Adam the other night.

I like Claire, she's understanding and accepting no matter what I say. In the early days after Michael's death when I was challenging the authorities and scrutinising the evidence, she didn't try and stop me, didn't say I was paranoid or mad with grief; she simply listened. She also provided the psych report, which helped to get the harassment charge against me dropped – although I fail to see how asking a few questions, demanding a few answers, constitutes harassment.

'So how *do* you feel about Adam making this appointment for you?'

I shrug. 'He's only trying to help.'

'You don't sound like you believe that.'

'It's been difficult.'

'For him or for you?'

Something about the way she says that last sentence makes me decide that, of course, I can trust her. 'I found some things of Michael's.' I tell her about the diary, the mobile phone. We talk about Michael's poetry, the beauty of it. We talk about Diving Fish, about his experience of love. It feels good, healthy. Claire, as always, senses something deeper.

'And Adam,' she asks. 'What does he think about it?'

'He wants to put it somewhere safe.'

'He wants to take it from you?'

134

'Yes, but I won't let him.' I pause to let that last statement lie. 'Michael wrote something about him in his diary.'

'About Adam?'

'Referred to him as *threats-behind-closed-doors Adam.*' Claire raises an eyebrow, but remains silent. 'If he did something to hurt him . . .'

'Do you think he did?'

'He was strict with Michael; controlling. But I never witnessed any actual physical violence.'

'But?'

I reach over for my water, take a sip. 'I never told you this before.'

Claire responds with her usual kindness and composure. 'You know you're safe with me.'

I take a deep breath. 'When Michael was thirteen, Adam prescribed Ritalin for him.'

My therapist suddenly looks interested. 'Ritalin? Was Michael having difficulties?'

I think back to his mood swings and manic behaviour. 'Not more than any teenager. In my opinion, at least.'

'Can he do that?' Claire asks. 'Prescribe for a family member?'

'Whether he could or not, he did.'

'And how did Michael respond?'

'How do you think?'

'And you? How did you feel about it?'

Claire is one of the few people in my life who still asks how I feel about things. 'I was furious. Even threatened to leave him. Well I did leave, actually.'

Claire nods. 'We spoke about that period, didn't we? You went to stay with your mother for a bit.'

'It didn't work out.'

'So you went back home.'

'Adam apologised, claimed it was a misjudgement, said he was only trying to help, couldn't live without us.' I'm shivering and pull the throw over my shoulders. 'The following year, Michael started his GCSEs at Edgecombe.'

'And how was that for you?'

'Unbearable.'

'But Michael was happy?'

'Yes, so I coped.'

'And now? How do you feel now, particularly with this new information?'

I take a moment to frame my response. 'What I'd like to do is find out who this Diving Fish is. If she knows anything about the night Michael drowned.'

'Would that be helpful to you?'

'Very helpful.' Now we're getting to the heart of the matter. 'I understand that Adam is concerned for my well-being, but finding this diary has finally offered me an opportunity to get answers to the questions I've been asking for six years. I can't understand why he thinks this is unhealthy.'

Claire does the usual therapist thing. 'Why do you think that is?'

I remember him on Thursday night, towering over me, shaking me by the shoulders, but I don't tell her that. 'I'm not sure.'

Claire's expression is neutral, but there's something

in the tone of her voice that catches my attention. 'Putting your mental health aside – and let's be clear, this is an important issue and must be addressed if you intend to pursue this course of action, but putting it aside for the moment – have you really considered why Adam is so adamant about the diary?'

'He just goes on and on about our need to move forward.'

'Yet from what you've told me there are still plenty of questions – about the investigation into Michael's death, the ambiguity about the inquest findings.' I get the feeling Claire is moving beyond professional boundaries. 'Why would someone want to stop you from finding the answers to questions that are so essential to your being able to move on?'

I leave Claire's office invigorated. After the scene with Adam and my conversation with Grace I had, briefly, considered putting the diary aside for a bit – maybe just to get my grounding back – but my conversation with Claire has made me realise my need for answers, for closure, is not mad, unreasonable, or unhealthy. It's perfectly normal. I am perfectly normal. It's just everyone else around me that's not on point.

The main thing now is to keep up my relationship with Adam. What to do about the diary is another matter. I'm going to have to try and find some way to keep the diary and keep Adam satisfied at the same time. I text Adam saying I'm going to spend a few hours doing a bit of shopping, but instead I sit by the cathedral green with a latte and a notebook, planning my strategy.

I arrive home to the smell of lamb roasting and a cold glass of Chablis. I help Adam in the garden; the gladioli bulbs I planted after Easter are starting to sprout, and, with each gust of wind, freshly washed sheets flap and flutter on the line. As conflicted as I am it's nice to be home, in my own space, with all my things around me. Later, when Adam is watching the telly, I'll sneak into my office to continue my research.

We eat outside, a delicious meal of lamb tagine and couscous. It's been a good day. My conversation with Claire, the pleasant atmosphere at home. Maybe things will be all right after all. I'm just finishing my last morsel when Adam pushes back his plate and clears his throat.

'So,' he says. 'Did you bring the diary with you?'

I've been expecting this, but not quite so soon. 'No.' My heart is thumping but I hold my nerve. 'The diary is safely locked away at my mother's house.' In fact I have given it to Doris for safekeeping. 'It won't be a problem; I promise you that.' *Well not for you, anyway*. He looks at me with a mixture of frustration and what might just be admiration. Hopefully this will be the end of it.

Sunday afternoon, just before leaving to head back to Cornwall, I sneak into my tiny office – just a box room really – with a desk, filing cabinet and a few diplomas on the wall. I reach into the very back of the filing cabinet, where hidden behind some old warranties and instruction manuals is a green file folder. I wait until Adam is outside checking the tyre pressure on my car, before slipping it into my overnight bag.

15

I arrive back in Calstock just after five. I'm feeding the cat when I hear a soft tapping at the front door. I smile and pop on the kettle.

Doris and I sit shoulder to shoulder on the settee looking through Michael's diary. I've been careful not to share some of the more explicit entries.

'So many hidden talents,' she whispers, gently running her fingertips across one of the pages.

'Do you see why it's so important to me? Why I couldn't let Adam have it?'

'Of course.' She straightens her shoulders as if about to say something difficult. 'Do you really think this person will be able to provide you with some answers?'

'I don't know,' I reply. I decide to admit my greatest fear. 'The idea that Michael's death may have been a stupid, pointless accident is something I just can't accept; something that has haunted me for all these years. I'm scared someone did something terrible to him.' I tell her more about Diving Fish, the threatening email from Lisa, and the information I have acquired from Siobhan.

Doris's deep brown eyes seek out mine. 'Hardly enough there to prove any actual wrongdoing,' she says, referring to Lisa's message. 'But all this talk about secret relationships, fights in their lodgings . . .' She shakes her head. 'What kind of person brandishes a knife?'

I stare at her in disbelief. Does someone actually believe me? I'm so used to being doubted, first by the police and coroner, then by Adam, and even Grace.

Doris pours herself another cup of tea from the teapot and I can see that she is deep in thought. 'The danger, of course,' she says, adding a teaspoon of sugar and stirring it fiercely, 'is that this is all very much second-hand information. A few notes in a diary, a text to an unconfirmed number, an email that could be threatening, depending on the context.' Doris takes a sip and puts her cup down with a clatter. 'What you're going to need, Katie, is good, solid evidence.'

It's Monday morning; nine-thirty a.m. I'm sitting anxiously pulling the threads from the old throw on my mother's settee, listening as the telephone, clasped to my ear, rings for a fourth time. Doris's idea has been bubbling around in my head since yesterday; I've had a restless night waiting for the working week to begin. I'm just about to hang up when I hear a voice at the other end of the line.

141

'Human Resources, Siobhan Norris speaking.'

'Siobhan.' I know it's risky ringing her at work, but I have no choice. I need information. 'It's Kate Hardy.' There's a pause and I can imagine her glancing around the office, hoping no one will hear.

'I can't really talk,' she whispers, sounding nervous. 'I—'

'You don't have to,' I interrupt. 'Can you look through the student records for me to see if you can find a contact number for Lisa Edwards?'

'What? I don't really think—'

'I just want to talk to her, Siobhan.'

'It's against GDPR. I've just had my training. I could lose my job.'

'I need to find out more about what happened to Michael, and you're the only one who can help me.'

I hear voices in the background.

'My manager is coming; I've got to go.'

'Siobhan, *please*, I only want—'

'I'm sorry, Mrs Hardy, I really am.'

There is a loud click as the line goes dead. I throw my mobile down in frustration. For the first time in years, I seem to be getting somewhere; but every tiny step forward seems impeded by obstacles and setbacks. I'm just about to try another online search when the phone rings.

'Mrs Hardy?'

'Siobhan, is that you?'

'I've got something for you. It's not a lot, but it may help.'

'Did you find Lisa's phone number?'

'Even if I had it, I couldn't give it to you, Mrs Hardy, but there is something I can send to you. I just need your email address.'

I run upstairs, take the laptop from where I've hidden it under the bed, just in case Adam drops by again, and turn it on. Wildly impatient, I have to hit the refresh button several times before the email finally arrives.

Re: photograph of student fundraising event

admin@Edgecombehall.co.uk
To: Kate Hardy

Dear Mrs Hardy,
Thank you for your enquiry regarding Edgecombe Hall's photographs of your son Michael during his time as a student with us. I have searched through our newsletters archive and came across one of him at a school fund-raising event in 2015. As a Scholarship Committee member, Michael was highly active in raising funds for the school.
In the attached photograph you will see Michael seated with Junior Swimming Coach and Scholarship Committee staff member Susan O'Neill, and Sixth Form Student Committee member and scholarship recipient Lisa Edwards.

> *I hope this photograph will be a useful addition to your memory book.*
> *Kind wishes*
> *Siobhan Norris*
> *Administrative Assistant*

'Clever old Siobhan,' I whisper, clicking on the attachment. In the photograph, three people are sitting at a table in the student common room at Edgecombe Hall. In the centre sits Michael. He's smiling at the camera, his brown eyes sparkling. On his right sits a girl about his age. She is pale skinned with narrow eyes that give her a guarded look. Her mousy hair is pulled back in a tight ponytail and she isn't smiling. 'Lisa Edwards,' I mutter. Was my son really in love with this apparently unremarkable young woman? My attention shifts to the woman on Michael's left, the swimming coach and the scholarship committee's staff supervisor Susan O'Neill. Small and fine boned, her hair is styled in a fashionable asymmetrical cut. It is clear she hasn't wanted to be photographed and has turned away so that her face is in profile. She should be pretty, but something about the set of her jaw and her fierce expression makes her look more like a sulky teenager than an academic.

My mobile suddenly goes off and I jump. I glance down to see that it's Adam. Checking up on me no doubt. I force myself to sound calm, normal.

'Morning, darling.'

'Hi, sweetheart. Any plans for today?'

'Hospital at eleven. I'm going to try and see if

144

there's any progress on the right side, and then,' – I glance around the bedroom hoping for some inspiration – 'a bit of housework, I think. The place needs a good dusting, and it looks like my mother has become a bit of a hoarder in her old age.'

I consider mentioning I'm planning a long walk along the river path later, but knowing Adam he'll warn me against it. *I don't like you walking on your own. What if you fall over and hurt yourself?*

'They should be looking at another ECG and Doppler.'

'I'm sure they are, but I'll ask.'

'What about follow-on?' He's referring, of course, to aftercare – most likely a rehabilitation unit a few miles from the hospital. The way it's looking now, it's very unlikely my mother will be returning home anytime soon.

'It's a bit early to discuss this now, isn't it?'

Adam gives a little tut of irritation. 'You know as soon as she's stabilised, they'll need to move her on, for the bed.' Spoken like a true doctor. 'Have you thought about long term?'

I really don't want to be having this conversation right now. 'Grace and I have already spoken about it.'

'And?'

'When the time comes, Grace said she'd handle it.'

'Thank God for that.'

I'm feeling impatient to get back to my work. 'Aren't you on at eleven?'

'You're right, I'd better go.' He takes what sounds

like a large slurp of coffee. 'I'm on a twelve hour, so may not have a chance to speak to you later.'

'I'll text you.'

'Promise?'

'I promise.'

'Love you.'

'Love you too.'

I end the call with relief and guilt, and I'm about to put my mobile on silent when I receive a text from Grace.

Hope you had a good weekend and you and Adam worked everything out. Call me Gx.

I sigh and return my attention to the laptop; to the photograph of Lisa Edwards. I wish everyone would just mind their own business and leave me alone. I still have a lot to do.

16

I am now beginning to actively dread the hospital visits. Every day I greet my silent, angry mother with a fixed smile and one eye on the clock. Visiting hours are from eleven a.m., and I try to get there as early as possible to avoid lunchtime when families are encouraged to help their loved ones with eating and drinking. This afternoon when I arrive at the ward, I'm shocked to learn that my mother's bed is empty.

'No need to worry,' says the nurse, seeing the look of panic on my face. 'After last week's assessment it was decided she could have a bit of physio.'

'Physio?' I hadn't realised my mother had made such progress. 'Does that mean she'll be coming home soon?'

'It might be a little while yet,' says the nurse. 'But we will need to discuss next steps, and probably a visit home by an occupational therapist to determine any access difficulties.'

How long is a little while? I think, and then imme-diately feel guilty. It's been nearly a week since my mother's stroke, but in that time my life has changed so drastically that I'm beginning to not recognise myself. With that shift comes a tentative yet terrifying sense of freedom and fear. Last night I had dreamt I was walking through a pine forest, the sticky trees towering high above me, blocking out the sun. I was barefoot and could feel the sting of needles between my toes and the dusky smell of damp earth. As I walked, I felt myself sinking deeper and deeper into the ground. Then it changed, and I found myself wading through murky water, seaweed tugging at my toes. In the distance I could see a log floating towards me. As it drew closer, I could see that it wasn't a log at all, but a body, blue-hued, the lips and eyelids eaten away by fish. I had awoken with a start before sunrise, and, afraid of sleep, had stood at the bedroom window watching the pumpkin glow of bedroom lights being switched on across the river.

'Mrs Hardy?' I realise with a start that the nurse has been speaking to me.

'Sorry?'

'I asked if you would like a cup of tea while you're waiting.'

'No, thank you.' I check my watch. 'Maybe I'll just nip out for a bit of fresh air.'

I sit in the shade of a weeping willow and continue my search through the internet for any record of Lisa Edwards. As far as I can tell there is no active Facebook page or Twitter feed, and surprisingly no Instagram.

What twenty-something doesn't use Instagram? I am beginning to lose hope. How will I ever find her? How will I ever find the truth?

The afternoon brings a deep, driving rain that rattles the window frames of my mother's house and makes me fretful and uncertain. I toy with calling Siobhan again, asking for more information, but the girl has already put her job on the line by sending the email. Opening the laptop, I study the photograph once more: Michael is happy and open, smiling at the camera as if he hadn't a care in the world. On one side the unremarkable O'Neill, a dark blot of a thing who seems to disappear into the leather chair, and on the other the scowling Lisa. Anger spills out from her image and into the room. I study the girl's face; the narrow, resentful eyes.

As I look closer, I realise that there's a logo of some sort on her t-shirt. It's circular with lettering around the edges that I can't quite make out. In the centre is a drawing of a mermaid. Enlarging the picture doesn't help, as it only makes it even more blurry.

'Does that say *club*?' I mutter, squinting to read the tiny writing. I stare at it for what seems like hours before finally closing the attachment and turning off the laptop. I seem to be hitting dead end after dead end, and it's tiring me out.

I need some space to figure out what to do next. Maybe I would like a visit from Grace after all; maybe then I wouldn't feel so lonely. Relief and regret seem to mingle together like colours on a paint wheel. I'm not sure what to feel any more; or even *if* I feel any more. Visits with my mother are anything but uplifting; just my stilted monologues about village life and how the cat is coping. I never speak of the future. The few friends I do have are so connected with Adam; either fellow doctors, or wives of his friends, that I know speaking to them will be impossible.

Where are all my friends? When and how did they drift away? I stumble upstairs to the bedroom, find what's left of my blue pills and swallow one with a gulp of water from a half-empty glass that has been sitting on the bedside table for days. Collapsing onto the bed, I slip Michael's hoodie from beneath my pillow and lie with it nestled against my chest. I have never felt so alone in all my life.

I wake an hour later. The rain has cleared, leaving glistening streets and muddy puddles that will be the downfall of any mother trying to get their child home from after-school club without wet socks. I feel my stomach grumble and make my way to the kitchen. I've been so preoccupied with pacifying Adam and looking after Mum that I haven't done a proper shop in days. As expected, the fridge is empty – only milk, bottled water and a piece of ham hardening around the edges. I check the time and give a little huff. The corner shop is long closed. I open the pantry and scan the contents for possibilities. Hearing the door creak, Tam races in from the lounge and begins circling my ankles. Did my mother really say a few months ago that his hearing was going?

'The one thing I *do* have is cat food,' I say, emptying a pouch of something foul smelling into a bowl. 'Looks like it's the pub for me.'

Once upon a time The Bell and Anchor had been a prosperous watering hole for the small narrow-hulled sailboats that transported goods up and down the River Tamar during the late 1800s. As a child I was fascinated by the pub; the sounds and smells, and the conspicuous sense of danger that hung like pipe smoke in the air. There had been a stabbing one Friday evening when I was eight, and my father, a trained first aider, had been summoned to help. He returned a few hours later with blood on his shirt and a pale look of disbelief on his face. The next morning, when Grace and I tried to ask him about it, my mother silenced us with a glare. Later, when we were sent to the shop to buy milk, we wandered on, desperate to see the bright splash of blood that would stain the pavement for months to come.

This evening, however, the newly replaced pub windows glow with light, and smoke curls its way upwards from the repointed chimney. I've been told that a Londoner has recently arrived in the village and bought up the site with the view to converting it into a gastropub and B&B, catering mostly to well-off holiday makers. I duck through the squat front entrance and head for the bar. The place is buzzing. I feel a flutter of panic as I make my way through the crowd but force myself to carry on. I find a seat at the bar and order a glass of wine and an omelette and chips. I take a sip and look around. The scarred wooden panelling has been removed, exposing beautiful red brickwork. Bleached pine tables with chunky leather-backed chairs take the place of standard pub furniture. Near the front, the landlord has placed a couple of settees for a more intimate seating area. A young couple, clearly hikers, are sitting opposite each other sipping from pints of Guinness and leaning over after every second sip for a kiss. The clientele seems to have moved upmarket as well; moneyed tourists, well-off landowners, and the occasional local to keep the place going in off season. *Still smells the same though.*

While I wait for my food, I find myself doodling on a serviette; anything to avoid having to make eye contact with the heavily fragranced man sitting next to me. I find myself drawing a circle and, within that, a very rough depiction of a mermaid, just as I had seen on Lisa's shirt in the photograph. The barman arrives with my meal and clears a place for the sauces.

'You a rower?'

I reluctantly look over at the man sitting next to me.

'Pardon?'

'A rower.' He points to the doodle of the mermaid I have drawn on the serviette.

'I don't know what you mean.'

He frowns at me. 'This here is the symbol of the Cadgwith Cove Gig Club,' he says, tapping loudly on the bar. 'My brother-in-law rows for them.'

'Gig club?'

He shakes his head at my ignorance. 'The Cadgwith Cove gig rowing club, 'bout ten miles from Helston.'

I can feel my heart pumping. 'Are you sure?'

'Of course I'm sure.' He gets his phone out and Googles the club. Within seconds the screen is filled with an image of a mermaid enclosed within a circle of words. It's exactly like the one on Lisa Edwards's shirt.

The next morning, I don't have much of a plan except to get to Cadgwith Cove and find out as much as I can about the gig club and Lisa. I could ring the club secretary, but I wonder what on earth I would say when he or she asks why I'm looking for her: *Well it's like this, Bob. I think that Lisa may have been responsible in some way for my son's death. So, can you give me her home address?*

I am now experienced enough to know that even the tiniest sniff of weirdness or desperation is sufficient for people to shut down. Nobody wants the truth. They just want tidy stories that maintain the status quo.

'Just find Lisa,' I whisper as I pull out of Calstock. The morning sun is a blood-orange glow.

17

The sky above Helston is angry indigo, and in the distance, there is thunder. As I drive along the narrow lanes towards Cadgwith, I pray for no approaching cars. The thought of having to back up to a passing point makes me feel queasy. I spot the sign indicating parking and pull into a small, gravelled area. As I get out of the car, the first drops of rain begin pelting my skin. I don't have a clue where I am or where I should be going. A fierce south-westerly wind nearly knocks me off my feet and I wish I could race home to the relative safety of my mother's front room. For some reason, Michael's words in his diary from nearly seven years before pop into my mind: *This is going to be the best year of my life.* I carry on.

After a bit of wandering, I find a sign for the coastal path to Cagdwith Cove. The rain is lashing down, but I grit my teeth and push on. I make my way along a wooded path that shelters me from the worst of the rain and find myself going steadily downhill. To my left I can see a small cluster of stone and slate roof buildings. The narrow streets are empty: the tourists have escaped to a warm pub for lunch and the locals are far too sensible to be wandering about in this weather. By the time I make it to the village, the wind has eased, and the sun has managed to battle its way through the clouds. It doesn't take long for me to find the gig club, a small, squat building that faces the bay. The wide doors have been thrown open to welcome the emerging sun, and from inside I can hear hammering. I move forward. I can see a man, tall and lanky, bending over what looks like an oversized rowboat.

'Can I help you, Missus?' comes a muted voice.

The man has extracted himself from the boat and is wiping his hands on a faded handkerchief. He must be in his late fifties with a lean body and heavily lined face that speaks of hard work and long hours in the open air. He has a shock of white hair and the most piercing green eyes I have ever seen.

'I, ah . . .' I'm having difficulty finding words. 'Is this the Cadgwith Cove Gig Club?'

The man doesn't reply, only points to the sign above the door. I stand silent and still, uncertain of what to say.

'Is there anything I can do for you then?' asks the man, studying me with a mixture of curiosity and impatience.

'Ah, yes, well, the thing is . . . I'm looking for someone.'

'Aye,' he says. 'And who might that be?'

'It's a girl, a woman I mean. Her name is Lisa, Lisa Edwards.'

Try as he might, the man can't conceal the look of recognition on his face. Instead of answering, however, he turns and resumes working on the boat.

'Can't say that I knows her,' comes his reply.

'I have a photograph.' I take a printout from my bag and walk over to stand next to him. The gig boat is in the process of being sanded down before painting. I am mesmerised by the pale beauty of the wood, and the streamlined perfection of the structure. At least eight metres long, it's large enough to hold six rowers, a cox and pilot.

The man turns to me, his striking green eyes seeking mine.

'Why do you want to know about her?'

I take a breath. I have been working out my story for the whole two-hour journey from Calstock.

'Well . . . this is my son Michael; well, was my son Michael.' I point to the photograph, and I must swallow hard before I can continue. 'He passed away six years ago.'

'Sorry to hear that,' says the man, studying the photograph.

'Michael and Lisa were at Edgecombe Hall together, you know, the school near Falmouth? They were swimmers. She was a couple of years above him.' Even though I have practised the speech in my head numerous times, I still feel as if it sounds stilted and unconvincing. 'Now that a little time has passed, I've decided to put together a sort of memory book of his life.' I hadn't realised how hard it would be, saying it aloud. 'I've got plenty of things from his childhood, but not so much from later years. I thought if I could speak to a few of his classmates . . .' My voice cracks. I'm furious at myself for getting so emotional. This will require careful planning and clear thinking I had told myself only a few hours before. When I look back at the man, however, his wary expression has been replaced by one of kindness.

'She's Lisa Gannon now,' he says. 'Married a few years ago. Not long started as a Teaching Assistant at St Michael's C of E Primary in St Keverne.' He indicates back towards the car park. 'Eight mile or so inland.' I give him a grateful smile but cannot speak. He nods and returns to his work. 'Not easy losing a child,' he says softly. 'You never get over it.'

18

The school is a solidly built stone and slate building, which sits on a busy street corner. Against all odds, I find a spot directly across from the school, and watch as a seemingly endless parade of cars park on the pavement and double yellow lines as parents arrive to collect their children. I wait until the playground is completely empty before approaching, and catch the main entrance door just before it shuts. The earlier rain showers have died away leaving the air thick and humid, but inside the school feels fresh and cool. A large display about the Lizard lifeboat crew adorns a wall near the entrance, and next to that are rows of class pictures framed in colourful displays. I look around nervously. I'd considered telling a story about being a concerned relative, or saying I'm from the scholarship committee at Edgecombe, but it seems it won't be necessary. The receptionist's office, secured behind glass, is empty. The computer is still on and there are papers on her desk suggesting she's just stepped away for a moment. The double safety doors leading to the staff offices and classrooms are blocked open. Somewhere in the distance I can hear an electric floor polisher. I don't have much time – the longer I loiter, the more suspicious I'll look. I just need to find Lisa.

I turn towards the wall of class photos and study the faces of the teachers and teaching assistants before finally spotting her. Lisa Gannon isn't much different to the girl in the photo Siobhan sent me. There is still the guarded look, softened slightly now with a tentative smile and a good haircut, but the eyes are still wary, and the sense of overwhelming vulnerability almost too much to bear. I feel that ever-present tug of regret as I contemplate what Michael would have looked like, what he would be doing right now.

A sign next to the office points to the first year and reception classrooms. I slip through the open doors and make my way down the empty hallway.

Lisa is wiping down the whiteboard when I finally find her classroom. Hearing me enter, she turns and smiles, clearly thinking I am a parent of one of her pupils.

'Can I help you?'

'Lisa Ed . . . ah, Gannon?'

Her smile falters slightly. 'Yes,' she replies, caution creeping into her voice.

'My name is Kate Hardy.' I close the door behind me. 'My son was Michael Penrose.' There is a moment of absolute stillness and then Lisa's face starts to change. First there's a noticeable widening of the eyes and lowering of the jaw, and then the slow depletion of colour from her skin, as if a sheet is being pulled across her face.

'I wondered how long it would take for you to find me,' she whispers, and then bursts into tears.

'I don't understand why you're so upset,' I say, handing Lisa a tissue. It's unlikely I'll get anything out of the blubbering young woman until I can calm her down. I wait until she's seated before I continue. 'I got the distinct impression that you and Michael weren't particularly close.'

'We weren't,' says Lisa through a gulp of tears. 'I hated him.' She wipes her eyes, and seeing my shocked expression attempts to explain herself. 'Well, I suppose I didn't really hate him, Mrs Hardy. It was just teenage stuff. He was okay.' She lowers her head in humiliation. 'I was just jealous.'

'Jealous?'

'He was so talented and good-looking. Everybody loved Michael. He had everything.'

'Is that why you threatened him? Because you were jealous?'

The girl's mouth forms itself into a silent 'o'.

'Who told you that?'

'It doesn't matter who told me anything.' I slide my mobile phone across the desk. 'Read it.'

I can see Lisa's hand beginning to shake as she reads a copy of the threatening email that she sent to Michael six years before.

'It's not what it looks like, Mrs Hardy. I didn't mean anything by it. I was just angry.'

I take a chair from the corner and bring it to where Lisa is sitting. Placing it directly opposite, I sit down. 'How angry?'

'What do you mean?'

I reach into my shoulder bag. Along with a copy of the photograph Siobhan has sent me, I also have the file folder with copies of the police and coroner's reports. I make a point of ensuring that Lisa can see all the documents, photos, and official logos before I begin sorting through the paperwork.

'The police report says there were a few anomalies.'

'Anomalies? What anomalies?'

I pretend to read from the file in front of me. 'It says here there was some suggestion that Michael may not have been alone at the lake that night.'

Lisa's already pale complexion turns ghostly. 'Oh my God, oh my God.'

I have one more trump card to play to break down her flimsy facade.

'And who is Diving Fish?'

Lisa makes a retching sound. 'I can't,' she wails. 'I can't!'

I grab my phone and begin scrolling through my contacts. 'I've still got Devon and Cornwall Police on speed dial.'

'Don't,' she whimpers. 'Please don't.'

The young woman is a wreck. Her nose is bright pink. There's a damp patch on the front of her blouse, and mascara has streaked its way down her cheeks.

161

'Well, then, you'd better tell me everything.'

It takes a few minutes before Lisa can collect herself and continue.

'First of all,' she says, dabbing at her streaming nose with a tissue, 'I don't know anything about that night.'

I find my voice rising. 'Then why did you get so upset when I introduced myself?'

'Please be quiet,' Lisa begs. 'The head teacher is in her office. I'm still in my probationary period. I don't want any trouble.'

I take a breath and steady myself. 'Just tell me what you know.'

'That day, before Michael, well, you know . . . he was really on edge.'

I try not to think of that period in his early teens when Adam thought Michael's behaviour was so extreme that he had tried to medicate him.

'He was a wonderful guy – really he was – but he knew exactly how to get under your skin – especially when he wasn't feeling right in himself.'

I'm not interested in her feeble attempt at shifting the blame. 'Is that why you went for him with a kitchen knife?'

'Who told you that?' Lisa makes a small hiccupping sound as if unable to breathe, and I realise I'm going to have to take it slowly if I want to get any useful information out of her. 'It was a bread-and-butter knife, Mrs Hardy, and I put it away almost as soon as I'd taken it out.'

Looking at the whimpering young woman in front

of me now, I'm finding it hard to believe that she could be capable of any actual violence.

'But what made you angry enough that day to get the knife out in the first place?'

Lisa's bottom lip trembles. 'Michael was winding me up, making fun of me, making fun of the fact that I . . .' she places a hand over her mouth to try to stifle her sobs.

'What?' I demand. 'That you what?'

'That I was in love,' she blurts out finally. 'Desperately in love.'

'With . . . Michael?'

She shakes her head vehemently and I make the connection. In those eight simple words the truth begins unfolding itself to me like an origami swan. Lisa wasn't jealous of Michael; she was jealous of his relationship.

'Diving Fish,' I whisper. 'You were in love with Diving Fish.'

Lisa rests her head in her hands and wails. *'Diving Fish'* – she spits the name – 'took everything, absolutely everything – and then threw me away like a piece of rubbish!'

'Because of Michael?'

'Michael!' She snorts. 'He was just one more toy!'

Suddenly I feel very cold. I lean in closer. 'Who *was* Diving Fish?'

She looks up at me with wide, wild eyes and chews on her fingernail so fiercely that it tears away, then whispers, 'I promised I'd never tell.'

Her voice has that faraway tone that reminds me

of a time when as a trainee nurse I had been working an overnight shift in A&E. A woman in her early twenties had been brought in accompanied by two policewomen. One eye was bruised, her nose bloodied. As I helped her out of her clothes and into a hospital gown, I noticed clearly delineated finger marks around her neck. 'Fell over,' she had muttered numbly as I applied a butterfly closure across a gash on her forehead. That was all she would say until the police had no other choice but to let her go home.

'Lisa, were you hurt?' I ask, gently.

She leans her head back on her chair and stares up at the ceiling. I can hear her laboured breathing, see her chest rising in tiny intermittent jumps. 'More than that,' she says. 'I was destroyed.'

It takes a few minutes before Lisa can compose herself so that we can continue our conversation.

'I was going through some pretty awful stuff at the time.' Now that she's calmed down a bit, she can't seem to stop talking. 'My parents were divorcing. I got into a bit of trouble.' She tilts her chin forward so that her hair forms a soft curtain in front of her face. 'Michael wasn't the one using performance-enhancing drugs; *I* was.'

Conscious of her reluctance to divulge any details I decide to tread carefully. 'And this Diving Fish person found out? Used it against you?'

There is a slow, steady nod. I think of my fourteen-year-old son vulnerable, needy, away from home for the first time, trying to integrate into a new routine, make new friends; estranged from his natural father, furious with his stepfather, and unwilling or unable to seek support and solace from the most important person in his life: me.

'I tried to speak to someone about it,' she continues, 'but . . .'

'They didn't believe you?'

'I wished I'd never opened my mouth.'

'How could they not believe you?' I'm still desperately struggling to take it all in.

'They said I was treading on very dangerous ground.'

'What?'

'Said making false accusations could get me in big trouble.'

I feel that familiar, painful sting of injustice. Even though I'd been determined to break the girl, I'm becoming aware that the truth surrounding Michael's death is much more sinister than I could ever have imagined. Attacking her won't help. 'I want to help you, Lisa.' I reach out for her hand, but she pulls away.

'It's too late.' Her voice is lifeless, flat.

'It's never too late,' I reply, and believe it.

She looks up at me and gives a slow, sad smile.

'He was a lot like you, you know.'

'Pardon?'

'Michael. Willing to put himself out to help others.' She stares into the distance. 'Do you know he used to stay after evening training sessions to help the junior swimmers?' She shakes her head in a mixture of exasperation and wonder. 'He could have been back in the house watching telly, or at the gym doing strength training, but instead he would stay late to help the year seven scrotes perfect their front crawl.'

I find myself smiling. 'He was always doing things like that.'

'Do you know, Mrs Hardy, even though we didn't always get along – well, I really admired him.'

Something about the way she says the words suggests deeper feelings. For someone who supposedly *hated* Michael, she certainly had a lot to say about him.

I force my thoughts away from my dead son. For the moment there's something more important that needs my attention. 'Why don't you come with me to the police station right now?'

Lisa stares at me, incredulous. 'You think I haven't tried that? The first time I tried to get help it was just after I got married.' She absent-mindedly twirls her wedding ring around her finger. 'Joe and I were already thinking about having kids . . . and I wanted to make sure I'd be a good mum. To be free of the past.'

'Is Joe your husband?'

'*Was.*'

'Oh, I'm sorry.'

'Don't be.' Again, that sad, resigned voice. 'The truth is we got married way too fast and way too young. I'd just turned nineteen, not long left school. I guess it was a bit of an escape route for me, after everything that happened.' I'm not sure if she's referring to Diving Fish abandoning her or Michael's death. 'And anyway,' she gives a little shrug, 'he'd

166

been messing around the entire time. While we were dating, afterwards. I wouldn't have been surprised if he had screwed the maid of honour on our wedding night, except of course that she was my sister.'

'I'm so—'

'Please don't say you're sorry.'

'No, of course.' I can feel the words slipping away. 'I just want to help you,' struggling to offer some form of reassurance, I find myself repeating my most hated phrase, 'to move on in some way.'

'I don't have the luxury of moving on, Mrs Hardy. I'm living in a house I can't afford – which is just about to be repossessed, by the way. I'm doing a shitty part-time teaching assistant's job, and I'm surviving on a diet of anti-depressants and alcohol just to get to sleep every night.'

Ah, something in common.

'Well, if not me, then what about friends? Are there others – people that were there – that you could talk to?'

'There were a couple of friends in the house, but I don't think they'd want anything to do with someone who was considered *mentally unstable*.' She gives a long, jittery sigh. 'Ever since I tried to come out about it, everything has gone wrong.'

I fight back the fury that threatens to overwhelm me, and instead I think of the eager and hopeful teenage Lisa opening herself up to such cruelty and exploitation.

'So, you see,' she says, 'there's nothing I can do. Nowhere I can go.'

I look at the Lisa in front of me now: broken, traumatised, with a failed marriage behind her, a life in ruins, and nowhere left to go.

The words come out before I can stop them. 'You could come and stay with me for a while.'

'What?'

'At my mother's house in Calstock. Until you get things sorted. The last thing I want is for you to be out on the street. I'll even try to help you find a better paying job.'

'Stop, Mrs Hardy – please stop!' Lisa buries her face in her hands. 'I can't accept your help.'

'Why not?'

'I don't deserve your help, or anyone else's for that matter.' Lisa picks at an imaginary scab on her elbow. 'I saw them. Together. That afternoon. The day he died.' Her long-held confession emerges in a series of short sharp sentences. A Morse code of admission. I am too stunned to reply. 'They were on the green in front of the swimming centre,' she continues. 'Smiling, laughing. I was so angry I just ran away.'

'And the police?' I ask. 'Afterwards did you tell the police?'

The look of shame on her face is so manifest that I find myself turning away.

'Just because they were together that day, doesn't mean she was with him the night he . . .'

'The night he drowned.'

'Yes.'

'But you suspected?'

'I saw her later.'

'And?'

'She looked like she was on her way to meet someone.' Lisa lets out a tiny sob. 'She was wearing lipstick. She always wore lipstick when we met.'

I scramble for my phone and show her the screenshot I took of Michael's text to Diving Fish. *Meet me by the water's edge tonight.* 'They did meet that night, Lisa. The night Michael died, and yet you did nothing about it.'

Lisa's expression deepens. 'I did try to speak to the head teacher.'

This is becoming more and more unbearable. 'And what did he say?'

Lisa's voice has gone very low and there's bitterness in every syllable. 'He told me I was being ridiculous and to mind my own business.'

That's it. I've had enough. 'We need to go to the police, Lisa. Right now.'

'I won't go back there.' The skin on Lisa's elbow is now raw and bleeding. 'Not after the way they treated me.'

'But I'll be there with you this time.' I could report this to the police myself hoping that Lisa would be questioned, forced to cooperate. 'I'll make sure you get all the support you need. I'll make sure they listen.'

Lisa's eyes look hopeful before quickly fading back into despair. I'm losing her. I must think fast. 'I know a lawyer in Truro – a friend of my sister's. I could ring her and arrange for her to come with us.'

'I don't want anyone else involved,' says Lisa. 'And anyway, what good would that do?'

169

I take an antiseptic wipe from my bag and pass it to her, watching her gently dab it on her elbow. 'She'll make sure you're taken seriously.'

Lisa's face is a fortress. 'I'm tired. I want to go home.'

'I'll drop you off if you like.'

'No, Mrs Hardy. I have a car.'

'But what about the police? The sooner we tell them everything, the sooner they can start to investigate?'

Lisa looks as if she's about to burst into tears again, but instead takes a gulp of air and steadies herself. 'You shouldn't get involved in this, Mrs Hardy. You've suffered enough.'

Somewhere in the distance I hear a door slam and the sound of approaching footsteps.

'That's the head,' says Lisa, clearly terrified. 'You shouldn't be here – she'll hit the roof. I've already been late twice this month. I can't get in trouble again.'

Using the bloody antiseptic wipe, she rubs the mascara from her cheeks, then, jumping up, returns to wiping down the whiteboard. I'm about to suggest going to the police again when we hear the door open.

'Mrs Gannon?'

The head teacher, a tall willowy blonde in her late forties, is standing in the doorway eyeing both Lisa and me with suspicion.

'Yes, Mrs Drake?'

'You're aware we don't encourage parents in the

170

school after four p.m. unless under special circumstances.' She gives me a polite once-over. 'And you are?'

'Kate Hardy.'

She looks momentarily perplexed but, used to the ever-changing nature of the modern nuclear family, she smiles. 'And your child is?'

'Mrs Hardy isn't a parent.' Lisa puts down the whiteboard eraser and I can see that her fingertips are stained with red marker. 'She's the mother of one of my former classmates.'

Mrs Drake arches a perfectly threaded eyebrow.

'My son, Michael, attended Edgecombe Hall School with Lisa.' I'm eager to keep her from getting into any further trouble, at least until I can get some answers out of her. 'He passed away a few years ago. The anniversary was only last week. I just came to see Lisa to ask her a few questions about Michael's time at Edgecombe.'

'I'm sorry to hear that, Mrs Hardy, I truly am, but we have a strict safeguarding policy here at St Michael's.' She frowns slightly, clearly irritated at a possible transgression. 'Rule number one is that no unauthorised persons are allowed into the school without prior permission. Mrs Gannon is aware of that, aren't you?'

'Yes, of course, Mrs Drake.'

'Please don't blame Lisa,' I say, feeling that automatic response to fight for the underdog. 'I did try to find someone at the front desk but there was no one.'

'That should not have happened,' the head teacher says with barely contained fury, 'but that still doesn't excuse—'

'She was only trying to help,' I interrupt, 'and she did ask me to leave, but I'm afraid I just needed to talk.'

The head teacher's stern composure softens. 'Of course, and I *am* sorry. It would be more appropriate, however, if you met outside school.'

'I understand. It won't happen again.' I get up and turn to Lisa, who is standing by the whiteboard, wide-eyed and mute. 'Lisa and I were just going anyway, weren't we?'

'I'm afraid I'll need a word with Mrs Gannon first,' says the head teacher, now restored to stern mode. 'We may be a little while.'

'I'll wait.'

Her nostrils flare. 'Unfortunately, that won't be possible. I'm going to have to ask you to leave.'

'But I—'

'Why don't you leave me your mobile number?' says Lisa, attempting to sound calm, but clearly in a state of panic. 'I'll give you a ring when I'm done.'

I am reluctant to leave now that I have found her. It's clear, however, that I have no choice.

'Of course.' I rummage through my bag for a pen and paper, write down my details on a Post-it note and hand it to Lisa.

'My office, Mrs Gannon,' says the head teacher, and, leaving the classroom, adds sharply: 'Straight away please.'

Lisa's complexion turns ashen, and when she speaks her voice sounds childlike. 'I've got to go.'

'What about the police?' I try not to sound too demanding, threatening. 'Shall I wait for you somewhere?'

'Tomorrow,' says Lisa impatiently. 'Meet me at four at the QE Cafe on Godolphin Street. We'll talk then.'

'And you'll come to the station with me? Tell them everything?'

'Yes,' Lisa snaps, 'I'll come to the police station with you!'

As she turns to leave, I step in front of her, blocking her way. There is still one more thing I need to know. 'You never told me about Diving Fish.'

'I've got to go.'

I don't move. 'Who is she?'

From the hallway comes the muted voice of Mrs Drake. 'Mrs Gannon – now, please?'

Lisa, pale-faced and humming with anxiety, turns back to the desk. I watch as she searches through my papers, pushing aside the police and coroner's report until she finally finds what she's looking for. She picks up the photograph of her, Michael, and their swimming coach sitting together at the Edgecombe Hall fundraising event and thrusts it at me. 'You already have your answer,' she says. Gone is the frightened, panicked expression, replaced momentarily by one of power and control. Grabbing her planner, she speeds from the classroom towards the head teacher's office, calling back to me, 'I'm sure you can see yourself out.'

19

My meeting with Lisa has been both astounding and perplexing, providing me with far more questions than answers. I should go straight to the police, but I'm not sure how to explain what she told me, or even what it means. Was Diving Fish someone in Michael's year? Or a sixth former? Or someone else, someone older? I find myself struggling with Michael's version compared with Lisa's. In his diary he describes his lover as beautiful, loving, sensual; there's no indication of manipulation or abuse. Yes, there were comments about things getting nasty when he wanted to go public with their relationship, but that's hardly on the scale of what Lisa described. What exactly is the truth, and who's telling it? A vulnerable young woman, or my dead son?

I give myself a shake for letting my imagination run away with me. Conscious of the long drive home, I stop for a coffee and something to eat. I can't stop myself from returning to the photograph. What did Lisa mean when she pointed to the image? *You already have your answer.* Was it someone on the scholarship committee, or at the meeting where they were photographed together? What about Susan O'Neill, the sullen-looking swimming coach sitting on Michael's left? Could she have been Michael's lover?

The more I find out, the less it makes sense. Unable to contain my curiosity or impatience any longer, I decide that there is still one more thing I can try and do before my meeting with Lisa tomorrow. Something that might just help us when we go to the police.

I make a quick phone call, and then drive the twenty-three miles to Falmouth, making it to the bank just before closing time. It's half past five when I arrive at the Old Wheel. Siobhan is already waiting.

'Mrs Hardy.'

'Why don't we go outside?' I lead Siobhan around the back to the beer garden. She looks nervous – but even more than that, she looks hugely curious.

'Thank you for coming,' I say, finding a table under a large chestnut tree.

'I can't stay long.'

'You won't need to.' I reach into my bag, remove a white envelope, and slide it across the table.

'What's this?'

'I told you I'd make it worth your while to meet with me. Open it.'

Siobhan glances around and then, slipping a manicured fingernail between the seal, gently rips open the envelope. My eyes never leave her face. At first, she seems confused, uncertain; but slowly understanding dawns. I watch in satisfaction as she counts the notes.

'There must be at least five hundred quid here,' she whispers, finally daring to make eye contact.

I smile, confident she is mine. 'Five hundred pounds now,' I say, 'and another five hundred when you deliver to me a copy of Susan O'Neill's HR file.'

'The old swimming coach?' Siobhan gives a chortle of disbelief. 'You're kidding me, right?'

'Just a photocopy. Or screenshots,' I confirm. 'Whatever's easier.'

'But it's against the law.'

I can see her struggling with her conscience; but not too hard.

'It'll just be between you and me. No one else needs to know.'

We leave the pub without speaking. I watch as Siobhan slips the envelope into her handbag and clips it shut with a heartening determination.

'I'll just pop back and say I left my mobile in the office,' she says, sliding elegantly into the front seat of her Fiat. 'The hall porter won't care. He'll be too busy watching online porn. I'll be back here in an hour. Wait for me in the car park.'

I drive a few miles west and, spotting a lay-by with a scenic view, spend the next hour gazing out at the sea. For so long, I've doubted myself: first as a daughter, then as a mother, and most recently during my marriage to Adam. Now, however, I feel a new and fresh power in my bones; a vitality and assurance that I have never experienced before. I check my mobile. Siobhan was supposed to text me when she was ready to meet. It's nearly seven and I still haven't heard anything. Has she lost her nerve?

I hear a ping and, checking my messages, smile and start the engine. I might just make a decent private detective after all.

Pulling into the pub car park, I quickly spot the Fiat. Siobhan steps out of the car, an A4-sized envelope in her hand. I feel my heart soar. I'm getting closer.

'It was as easy as could be,' she says, handing me the envelope. 'The porter couldn't have cared less, and I know most of the CCTV cameras don't work because of the shit electrics in the older buildings.' She tuts self-righteously. 'If only the parents who fork out thirty-five grand a year knew what really went on.' I hand Siobhan a second white envelope. She slips it into her handbag without bothering to examine the contents. 'I think it might be best, Mrs Hardy, if you don't contact me again.'

'Of course,' I reply, surprised but impressed.

Without another word Siobhan gets into her car and drives off, the glint of excitement at the prospect of six months in Australia still in her eyes.

177

20

I sit in my car, the white A4 envelope on my lap. Inside are photocopied pages of Susan O'Neill's job description, health questionnaire and permanent contract with Edgecombe Hall School and Sixth Form College. I scan the pages. She had been twenty-six and at Edgecombe for nearly three years when Michael started. She had had an exemplary record. Few absences; comments on her great rapport with her students; accolades from her peers. The woman was a saint. I continue searching through her peer reviews and teaching observations, and I am just about to give up when I spot it.

A document, dated just a week after Michael's death, signed by the Head of HR agreeing to Susan O'Neill ending her contract early without giving the standard term's notice. Her last day of employment was less than a month after Michael died.

I examine the documents for any indication of

where she might be living now. The address listed is a staff flat on the school grounds. Clearly, she would have had to give that up when she left. The mobile number given is different to the one on Michael's pay-as-you-go phone. I won't be surprised if that one is dead too. There is no forwarding address, no next of kin. It appears that Susan O'Neill has disappeared without a trace.

Sleep that night is elusive: a wave that drifts in, hovers, then just as quickly withdraws. Tired of watching the shifting shadows, I get up and make myself a cup of tea and then spread all the documents out on the bedroom floor in front of me. The HR files; the photograph; my research documents from home. I turn on the laptop and log into my emails, scrolling through the messages I received from Michael before his death. There are a few initial ones reporting on the school's poor catering and lack of central heating, but after that he seems to have settled in well. He wrote of his housemates in their special boarding house for elite swimmers; their quirks and eccentricities: *My roommate likes peanut butter and ketchup sandwiches!* and of the rigorous training regime: *ball busting!* There are two mentions of his introduction to writing poetry as part of his English GCSE: *I always thought I hated poetry, but I guess it's sort of okay after all,* and then a little later, something more subtle, more private. *I actually kind of like writing poetry.*

'He seemed happy,' I mutter. I scroll through the

pictures saved on his laptop, but there's nothing to connect him to Lisa or Diving Fish, not even the photo from the scholarship meeting. In an age where young people keep a digital record of almost every aspect of their lives – Michael had countless photographs of him and his mates doing nothing – I am surprised that there is so little evidence.

I do yet another Google search on Susan O'Neill. Aside from a few postings from Edgecombe Hall about her coaching successes and something about a creative arts club, there's nothing. I check the time and wish away the hours until I can take Lisa to the police station and expose the truth about Michael's death once and for all. I am tempted to call Grace and tell her about my meeting with Lisa: tell her that I, the hysterical, grief-stricken fantasist, have been right all along. I make my way to Michael's bedroom, eager for tomorrow to begin.

I wake to a chaos of paperwork all around me. It's another stormy day, but nothing can deaden the feeling of triumph I hold in my heart. I shower, eat a proper breakfast, and spend the rest of the morning tidying the house. I dust, hoover, and after cleaning the fridge and wiping down the kitchen surfaces, pour the last of the vodka and red wine down the sink. Finally, I collect my papers, reports, photos, the diary and the burner phone, and leave.

The drive to Helston seems interminable; every red light and section of roadworks is a personal affront. Eventually I make it to Godolphin Street and the café where Lisa and I have agreed to meet at four. I check my phone. It is ten past three. I order a coffee and find a table near the window: I want Lisa to be able to see me when she arrives. The street life outside the café ebbs and flows; a dribble of construction workers popping in for takeaway coffees and cakes, a stream of young mums passing on their way to the school pick up, and again on their way home. I order another coffee, and then a sparkling water, before finally checking the time. It is nearly twenty past four. *Probably just tidying up or waiting for a late parent.*

'Excuse me,' calls the sullen-faced waitress. 'We close at half-past.'

I leave the café and walk straight to the school. I'm just turning the corner when I spot the first police car. It's parked near the front entrance. A second is parked in a lay-by opposite. I slowly make my way through the school gates and into a nightmare.

The tiny entrance is crowded with people. By the plastic ID badges dangling from their necks, I can see that they're all school staff or police officers. A middle-aged woman, clearly the school receptionist, is sitting at her desk weeping. Next to her a female officer makes a feeble attempt to try and comfort her. Other staff members appear shocked and uncertain, and I hear someone whisper, 'I just can't believe it.' I'm about to step forward and ask for Lisa when I see the head teacher, clearly distraught, emerging from her office, and being escorted by an overweight man in a poorly fitting suit. Spotting me, she grabs the man's arm and points animatedly in my direction. For some reason I have an overpowering urge to run, but I resist the impulse and wait for them to approach.

'Mrs Hardy,' says Mrs Drake. 'Could you come with us, please?'

I find myself on a stiff wooden chair in the head's office sitting under a poster that reads *Stand up for what is right, even if you stand alone.* Next to me, DC Ron Verby sits with a small leather-bound notebook balanced on one knee.

'Can I ask what this is all about?'

The detective and head teacher exchange a glance.

'Mrs Drake informs me that you were talking to Mrs Gannon yesterday afternoon. Mrs Lisa Gannon?'

'Yes, I was.' My unease grows with every syllable. 'Why, what's the matter?'

DC Verby clears his throat. 'I'm sorry to have to inform you that Mrs Gannon is dead.'

I wasn't sure if his habitual approach is always so blunt, or if he is simply testing me, but it is a good ten seconds before I can reply.

'Dead?'

'I'm afraid so.'

'When? What? How?'

'Mrs Gannon was found this afternoon in her home. We believe she may have taken her own life.'

I feel a clenching in my gut as the blood runs from my cheeks. My brain seems to have shut down.

As the reality of what I have just been told strikes, words form.

'But . . .' My throat closes. I am unable to continue.

182

'It would be helpful if you could tell me about what you and Mrs Gannon discussed yesterday.'

'Discussed?'

'Mrs Drake seems to think that Mrs Gannon was quite upset.'

I'm finding it hard to think. Lisa is dead. How is this possible? I have planned everything so carefully: the visit, the paperwork, the call to the solicitor in Truro. I've even dusted my mother's bedroom and changed the sheets in anticipation of her coming to stay. 'Mrs Hardy?'

'I'm sorry.' I feel hazy, sick. 'Could I have a glass of water please?'

Mrs Drake disappears, returning shortly afterwards with a glass of water. I sip it gratefully. 'I was supposed to meet her today at a café on Godolphin Street.'

'What time was that?'

'Four.'

The DC gives an almost imperceptible shake of his head, which I take to mean that Lisa had been long dead by that time.

'And your discussion yesterday?'

I take another sip. 'We were discussing the death of my son Michael at Edgecombe Hall six years ago.'

'The public school near Falmouth?' enquires Verby. 'Where that gold medallist went?' I think of the pretty, blonde teenager waving her arms high above her head as she stands front and centre on the Olympic podium.

I take a breath. 'For some time now, I've been convinced that my fifteen-year-old son Michael wasn't alone the night he drowned.' Verby looks confused.

'My son drowned in 2015 at Argal Lake, Detective. Your own division investigated.' He gives me an *ah yes* look and I carry on. 'Recently I found a diary he wrote suggesting that he was in a sexual relationship with someone while at the school. He referred to this person as "Diving Fish".'

'Diving Fish?' says Verby, clearly confused.

'Chinese proverb,' pipes up Mrs Drake, as she hovers near us both. 'About a woman so beautiful that the fish forgot how to swim when they saw her and drowned. There's also another version where the geese forget how to fly and fall to the ground.' I look at her in surprise. 'I did one of my undergraduate modules in Chinese studies.'

'And did you get a proper name?' asks Verby.

'No,' I reply, 'but yesterday Lisa confirmed to me that she had also been in love with this Diving Fish person.' By this point the DC has stopped writing.

The head teacher steps forward. 'Lisa told you this?'

'Yes. And though she didn't say it in so many words it was clear that she was also sexually exploited by this person.' I begin to cry. 'That's why she was so upset.'

'Jesus,' mutters Mrs Drake. 'As if that girl hasn't hurt enough people already.'

I look up at her in astonishment. 'How can you possibly be so cruel? Lisa was a victim.' Turning to DC Verby I say. 'Why aren't you writing this all down?'

'Mrs Hardy,' says the head teacher. She sounds kind, sympathetic. 'Lisa was—'

'You'd better let me,' interrupts Verby. He pulls the

chair a little closer. 'I have to inform you, Mrs Hardy, that Lisa Gannon was known to the police in Helston.'

'Of course she was. That's where she reported the abuse.'

'I'm afraid that's not the case,' says Verby. 'As far as I'm aware there is no record of Lisa Gannon née Edwards reporting any abuse, or in fact anything else to do with any incident at Edgecombe Hall.'

'But she said—'

'The only police record we have for Mrs Gannon is for drink-related public disorder offences.'

I am dizzy with confusion. 'But she said she reported it.'

'You weren't the only one caught out,' says Mrs Drake. 'We took her on with an excellent reference from a school in St Ives and having seen the DBS check they'd run.' The head teacher gives a loud sniff. 'I had a call yesterday afternoon from the HR department at our lead school. Lisa's new DBS came back with community orders listed. I just thank God she was never left alone with the children.'

'Was she dangerous?'

'Not as far as I could tell,' says the head teacher, 'but she clearly had some issues with substance misuse. She also failed to disclose her public order offences on her application form. Not only is that illegal, but it's also cause for immediate dismissal.' Mrs Drake reaches for a tissue from the box on her desk and I realise what their meeting had been about yesterday afternoon. Lisa was being sacked. 'It could have put the school in an exceedingly difficult position.'

All I can think about is the blood dripping down Lisa's arm as she picked at her imaginary scab.

'I just can't believe it.'

'There is something else,' says Mrs Drake, her tone a warning.

I can't imagine it getting much worse.

'During our meeting yesterday afternoon, Lisa confided in me that she had been detained at the West Cornwall Hospital earlier this year.'

'I'm not sure—' says Verby, clearly irritated at this disclosure of confidential information.

'The poor woman has a right to know,' says Mrs Drake.

'When you say detained, you mean sectioned, don't you?' I ask, and Mrs Drake gives a tiny nod of confirmation. 'And the diagnosis?' She looks at me in surprise. 'I'm a nurse. I did a couple of rotations in the mental health ward at Royal Exeter.'

'She wasn't specific,' she replies, 'but from what she told me I gather it was rather serious; some form of psychosis. She had not disclosed this on her application form either.'

I can't believe this is happening. I am completely overcome. 'After everything she told me yesterday.'

'She was a very unwell young woman,' says Verby, opening a fresh page of his notebook. 'I would appreciate it if we could start from the beginning and you tell me everything you and Lisa talked about yesterday.'

21

It is nearly seven by the time I leave Helston. Following my interrogation by DC Verby and Mrs Drake, I also had to make a formal statement at the police station – the very same one that I had been expecting to attend with Lisa before this day was turned upside down.

I'm exhausted, confused, and utterly, utterly dejected. It's only after going through a red light and hearing the honks of furious drivers that I finally decide to stop to try and collect myself. Pulling into a lay-by, I remove the photograph from the folder and trace a fingertip around Lisa's image, her sullen, frightened expression.

'Oh you poor, poor girl,' I whisper, and then, unable to hold back any longer, I break down and cry for a solid twenty minutes.

Once the tears have dried and my emotion is spent, I am able to re-examine my notes from yesterday's meeting. Less than half an hour ago I had been sent away by DC Verby with a patronising pat on the arm and a list of bereavement services in the southwest.

'She was a disturbed young woman, Mrs Hardy,' he had said, barely glancing up from the computer screen where he was completing his report. 'I have no doubt it wasn't her intention to deliberately mislead you, but unfortunately it seems to be the case.'

I hear the buzz of my muted mobile and notice that it's a missed call from a Plymouth number. My pulse quickens as I press the recall button.

'Acute stroke unit.'

'This is Kate Hardy.'

'Mrs Hardy, we've been trying to reach you.'

'I'm sorry, I'm in Helston and couldn't get a signal. Is everything all right?'

'I'm very sorry, Mrs Hardy. Your mother has had another stroke. You need to get to the hospital as soon as possible.'

The drive back to Plymouth is a blur of road signs and traffic lights. As I push through the swinging doors and into the ward, two nurses spot me and quickly approach. My mother's bed is empty.

'Mrs Hardy,' says one nurse, softly. 'Would you like to come and sit down?'

They've laid my mother out in a private viewing room so that I can sit with her for a while before they take her to the hospital mortuary.

'We thought it would be easier for you here,' whispers the nurse I met on my very first visit. She places a cup of tea on the table next to me. 'Take as long as you need.' I'm overcome with gratitude and heartbreak. 'It was very quick,' she adds. 'She didn't suffer.' I wait for her to leave before telephoning Grace.

The call is as difficult as I had expected. Grace, never one for emotional restraint, howls like a wounded animal. I envy my sister's ability to express her pain so openly. I, unfortunately, have held back my heartbreak for much too long. I'm not certain I can ever access those feelings again.

I reach out and touch my mother's face, something I would never have been allowed to do when she was alive. Her expression is serene, as if death has finally granted her some peace. I wish for tears – would welcome them – but all that comes is a numbness so profound I could push a sewing needle through my finger and not feel a thing.

What else is there to do? Talk to her, kiss her icy cheek? Instead I sit upright staring at the wall until my eyes ache. I think of my blue pills; sadly only two left, certainly not enough to make a dent. If there had been more, a multitude of blue babies, I would have taken them all without hesitation, all with a gulp of cold tea and a smile.

At some point a nurse comes in and tells me that they need to move her body to the hospital mortuary. When all is done, and the body is removed to that little white room on the lower ground floor, I find

189

myself on the pavement outside the hospital, watching as the hopeful and desperate are ejected and engulfed.

On the way home, I stop for a large bottle of vodka and some painkillers. My head throbs and my shoulders ache from sitting for so long. It is after midnight by the time I make it to the house. I don't bother with proper food, just a tall shot and a packet of crisps. I run a scalding bath and lie amongst the lavender-scented bubbles trying not to think. There will be funeral arrangements of course, and the house to sort out and sell. The thought of it all makes me feel dizzy. Not for the first time, I wish I could sink into the water and never re-emerge. Next to me on the bath is a disposable razor. I run my fingertip across the blade, wondering briefly if it is strong enough to sever a vein. A drop of blood trickles into the bathwater and I watch it swirl amongst the bubbles.

Once downstairs, I continue working my way through the vodka, hoping instead of numbing any feeling, it will evoke some.

By two in the morning I am near oblivion. Staggering my way to the stairs, I bump against my mother's display cabinet. A glass giraffe quivers and then topples, shattering into sparkling pieces that scatter across the cabinet top. With a shaking hand I reach for a white glass swan.

After being cast out, my mother had seemingly replaced religion not with helping her youngest daughter negotiate the ins and outs of teenage motherhood – *you got yourself into this mess after*

190

all – but with an obsessive desire to collect tatty glass animals. God forbid anyone even dream of touching her menagerie. When Michael was three he had toddled over to examine a newly acquired penguin family. She had pulled him away so fiercely that he had gone hurtling to the floor. I vowed then to get us out of that house.

Cold, hard, unmoving, the swan glitters in the overhead light. I close my hand around it and squeeze. Squeeze until the glass wings shatter; squeeze until the long white neck breaks in two; squeeze until the blood runs down my arm.

As I drift in and out of sleep I think I can hear knocking. My eyelids flicker but the front door is just too far away. There is a sound of a door opening, and then someone is screaming.

'Kat!' I recognise Grace's voice through my alcohol fog. 'What the hell have you done to yourself?'

My sister reaches for the phone. I put a blood-stained hand on hers.

'What are you doing?'

'I'm calling an ambulance, what do you think?'

'No.' I sit up quickly, causing my head to spin and the wound in my hand to reopen. 'No ambulance! I don't want an ambulance.'

'But Kate, you're bleeding.'

'It's just a few cuts.'

I grab the towel I had been using to staunch the bleeding and wrap it around my hand. Grace's attention shifts to the display cabinet.

191

'Sit back,' she says. 'Don't move!' She returns a few minutes later with a bowl of warm water, disinfectant, and plasters. Pulling up a chair next to me, she carefully unwraps the tea towel. My left hand is a crisscross of cuts and puncture wounds. '*Jesus*,' she mutters. 'At least there doesn't seem to be any glass in there.' She gently dips my hand into the warm water. 'What the hell were you thinking?'

'I don't suppose there was any thinking involved.'

Grace gives a shaky sigh and after drying my hand with a clean towel begins bandaging it. 'Kat,' she says after the last plaster has been applied. 'This isn't like before, is it?'

I know exactly what she means. Grace is asking me if I'm having another breakdown.

'I'm okay,' I say. 'Really.' She looks at the small pile of broken glass on the cabinet top.

'Did it make you feel any better?'

'At the time, yes,' I reply sadly. 'Now, maybe not so much.'

The unforgiving darkness brightens into morning. Sunlight streams in through half-opened curtains and my eyes wander to the mantel clock, then I drift back to sleep. When I open my eyes a few hours later, I momentarily forget the night before, yawn and stretch, then wince in pain as my injured hand protests. On the settee next to me, my sister stirs.

'What time is it?' says Grace, rubbing the sleep from her eyes.

'Nearly eleven.'

I feel the settee give as she moves closer. 'Fancy a cup of tea?' she asks, and then unexpectedly kisses me on the cheek.

'Yes please.' I smile, realising I have never felt so grateful for my sister's presence in all my life.

We sit on the sofa, cover ourselves with a throw, and eat hot buttered toast washed down with sweet, milky tea.

'What are you doing here anyway?' I say, just beginning to feel like myself again.

'I'm not really sure,' Grace replies. 'The only thing I know is that the minute I put down the phone after speaking to you last night, I knew I had to get here.'

'Just like that?'

'Well I couldn't let you deal with this all alone, could I? So I just threw a few things in the car, told Simon and Ellie if they fell out with each other while I was away, I would never forgive them, and here I am.'

I rest my head on my sister's shoulder. 'I'm really glad you came.'

'Me too.' Grace reaches her arm around my shoulders and gives me a hug. 'But you can't keep going on like this Kat.'

'I know.'

'I want you to promise me you'll see a doctor, make sure you're okay, and if necessary, get some medication.'

More pills are the last thing I need, but I don't want Grace to worry. 'I promise.'

'Good,' says Grace, shaking out the throw. 'Why

don't you go back to sleep for a few hours? I can sleep in Mum's room tonight.'

'I've cleaned and dusted it,' I say. 'Changed the sheets too.'

Grace smiles. 'It's almost as if you were expecting me.'

I wake two hours later to the smell of bacon frying and freshly brewed coffee.

'Hi, sleepyhead,' says Grace, as I wander into the kitchen. 'Have a seat.' She pours me a steaming mug of coffee from a cafetière.

'Where did you get that?'

'Don't you remember? I bought it for Mum ages ago.' She points to a box on the counter. 'It's never been taken out of the packaging.'

'And the bacon?'

'I can still remember how to get to the Spar.' Grace places a plate of bacon and scrambled eggs in front of me. 'How's the hand?'

'Sore.' I can see my sister's eyes are red and puffy from crying. 'How are you?'

Grace gives a resigned sigh. 'A little sad,' she says. 'But even more sad that I feel so little.' She discreetly wipes a tear away from her cheek. 'I've arranged for a funeral director to collect Mum from the hospital. We'll be able to see her tomorrow morning.'

'Thanks Grace.'

'The sooner we get this settled and over with, the sooner we'll be able to get on with our lives.'

I nod in agreement, but I don't know exactly what

194

I have to get on with. Grace has Simon, Ellie, her students, and a wide circle of friends. All I have is an uncertain marriage, a dead child, and a ridiculous obsession with finding out what happened to him.

The funeral is held on a sunny Thursday afternoon in a small Methodist church in nearby St Dominick. Only a handful of people attend, including Doris, Simon, Ellie, and Adam. There are the obligatory hymns and readings, but Grace and I find we are unable to manage a eulogy, so instead the minister says a few words about Christ's undying love, and then it's over. She's buried in a small plot near the car park: the note in her will said *as far away from any Brethren as possible*. The wake is held in The Bell; just some pale sandwiches and teas and coffees in a back room. By four o'clock it's all over. As we wish the last of the mourners goodbye, I spot a vehicle in the pub car park. It's only when I see the driver's face that I'm certain.

'Ryan,' I whisper, but stay frozen to the spot. I feel Grace's hand on my arm.

'Do you want me to speak to him?'

'No. I can manage.'

'What the hell is he doing here?' Adam has noticed him too. 'I'm going to go over there and tell him to bugger off.'

I hear the hiss of a muted argument as Grace tries to rein Adam in. 'Let her handle it, for God's sake. She's perfectly capable.'

I take a breath and walk towards the car. Even

from a distance, Ryan looks old. His brown hair is flecked with grey and thinning at the temples. His face is lined and there is the beginning of a paunch. Where is that beautiful boy who took me upriver in his dinghy? As I approach, he appears to relax.

'Hello, Ryan.'

Behind me, I hear Grace's voice. 'Leave her be, Adam. Simon, take him inside and get him a drink. I'll stay out here.'

Ryan steps closer. 'Katie.' His voice is soft, tentative. The last time I saw this man was at our son's funeral.

'What are you doing here?'

'Me and the girls are visiting Mum and Dad.'

'Oh.'

'I heard about your mum.' His eyes shift to where Grace is standing. 'I'm sorry.' Then, with a regretful smile, adds, 'I just wanted to pay my respects.'

'Pay your respects?' I'm finding it hard to believe that Ryan, who, as far as I'm aware, has never even met my mother, would feel this way.

'I was a coward,' he says. 'I should have stayed and fought for you.' This admission is so unexpected I don't know what to say. 'I abandoned you, Katie, just because it was easier.'

'You were only sixteen.'

He steps a little bit closer. 'The apprenticeship in the West Midlands,' he says, his tone cautious, 'it was set up by them – the Brethren.' I stare at him open mouthed. 'I only found out later; and by then, well, it was too late. I was working, had a . . .' He stops himself.

'Girlfriend?'

He nods.

It was never too late for me, I feel like saying, but I keep it to myself. I stare at him, angry and perplexed. 'Why are you telling me all this now?'

He swallows hard and I see his Adam's apple bob up and down.

'Maisie is pregnant.' Maisie is Ryan's oldest daughter, born six years after Michael. 'Same age as you were when you fell pregnant with Michael.'

'I don't understand.'

'Seeing what she's going through has made me realise just how difficult it must have been for you. On your own, in that house with *that woman*.' The mask is off, and Ryan's resentment flashes like a beacon. 'I should never have abandoned you. I was a coward and I'm ashamed of myself. Forgive me Katie,' he begs. 'Please say you'll forgive me?'

My brain, already struggling to process everything that has happened in the last few weeks, falters, like a computer program with a sudden blip. I try to speak but I can't form words. I close my eyes to try and steady myself, but the opaque veil has already descended.

A paramedic is leaning over me, calling my name.

'Kate? Can you hear me, Kate?'

I lift my hand to my throbbing temple. 'It hurts.'

'You had a bit of a knock,' says the paramedic, 'and a bit of a gash.' There is some sort of dressing against my temple. 'You were out for a little bit, so we'd like to take you to hospital to have you checked out.'

'No hospital,' I whimper, and pushing the paramedic's hand away, I try to sit up. The pain in my head is so excruciating that I collapse back onto the stretcher.

'It's all right, honey.' Adam is beside me now. I can smell his cologne. 'They just want to check that your head is all right. That's all, nothing else.' He mutters something to the paramedic about checking my GCS.

'Okay,' I mumble, wishing only for the pain to go away and that I can sleep forever.

A foam support is slipped around my neck, and I feel the stretcher being lifted into the ambulance. I hear another voice. Grace. She's speaking to Adam.

'I want to ride with her in the ambulance.'

'Only one person is allowed,' Adam replies, sounding testy. 'You can meet us at the hospital.'

I want Grace there, I think; and Simon and Ellie. I mutter something to the paramedic as he preps me for an IV line.

'What's that, love?'

'Will Michael be there too?'

22

I spend two nights in hospital with severe concussion. When I'm finally discharged, both Adam and Grace come to collect me. I'm just folding my dressing gown when I hear them approach. The look on their faces is odd, almost conspiratorial, as if something has passed between them that I am not party to. Grace sits on the bed and pats the space next to her. I sit down and await her instructions.

'Adam and I have been talking,' she begins.

Adam is beside me now. I can feel the hairs on his arm tickle my wrist.

'Kate,' his voice is soft. 'The doctor says that because you were unconscious for a time there is a possibility that you could experience some side effects from your head injury.'

'Side effects?'

'Post-concussion syndrome,' says Grace, taking the baton. 'Fatigue, disorientation, depression.' *Ah, the magic word*. 'The doctor has recommended that you're not alone, that you've got someone watching over you for at least a week. That's why I was thinking you could come and stay with me. That way I—'

'The doctor also recommended that you're somewhere familiar and comfortable,' interrupts Adam, a slight edge in his voice. 'With no stress.'

'There'll be no stress at my place,' says Grace defensively.

'It's not fair on Ellie,' Adam counters. 'She needs you right now.' *Clever one, Adam*. He leans past me to look at my sister. 'You've been a fantastic support, Grace, but I'm her husband. She needs to be at home with me.'

I wonder if either of them has even thought to consult me about what I might want.

'Look Adam, it's not that I . . .'

Their voices fade into the background and I watch in amazement as the pattern on the wallpaper in front of me begins spinning and swirling. It becomes an enormous whirlpool, threatening to suck me in.

'I want to go home,' I say, extracting myself from the vortex. The thought of travelling all the way to Cambridge feels unbearable. If I can't go back to my mother's place, then at least I want to be somewhere familiar. *Choose your battles, Katie*.

'Well I guess it's settled then,' Adam says. 'I'll take you home and either Grace or I will go to your mum's and pick up your things.'

'I need to speak to Doris,' I say, 'about the cat.'

'I can do that,' offers Grace.

'No!' I hadn't meant to yell. 'I need to speak to her myself.'

'Okay,' says Grace, exchanging a look with Adam.

'I'll be taking leave for the next week,' says Adam. 'So you won't be on your own. We'll see how it goes after that; maybe get someone in if we need to.'

All settled then.

I nod, grateful for not having to think too much. Thinking at the moment seems difficult, elusive, like trying to capture a flower petal in water.

'I'll tell the nurse,' says Adam, marching off.

I turn to Grace. 'What about Ryan?' She looks uncomfortable and even though my brain is foggy, I understand at once. 'I get that you and Adam agreed not to talk to me about him, but I have a right to know.'

Grace glances towards the nurse's desk. 'He was pretty upset. Adam didn't help by going completely ballistic.'

'What?'

'Honestly, Kate, be glad you were unconscious. The pair of them caused such a scene. Ryan was crying and apologising, and Adam was threatening to beat the crap out of him. I thought we were going to have to call the police.'

'Jesus.' The next question proves difficult, but I have to ask. 'And where is he now?'

'Home, I think,' says Grace, 'in the West Midlands. He did ring me to see how you were, but Adam said if he tried to show up at the hospital he'd kill him.'

'What a mess,' I mumble.

201

'It's not your fault, Kat.'

I think of the lies, the manipulation, the payoffs; the devastation that I have left in my path. All I want to do now is bury myself under the covers and never come out. My head starts thumping and I'm forced to lean back onto the pillows to stop the vertigo.

'Is she all right?' says Adam, now returned to my side. 'Do we need a consult?'

I wave my hand in reassurance. 'Just a little dizzy, that's all.'

Adam strokes my hand. 'It will be fine, darling; everything will be fine.' Leaning closer, he whispers, 'We can start again; forget the past.'

'Yes,' I reply, but I wonder to myself whether by forgetting the past, he means Michael.

The first few days are a blur. I sleep most of the time, finding reading and even watching television too tiring for my rattled brain. Adam is attentive, bringing me trays of food and helping me in and out of the shower. By the end of the week, and with Adam needing to return to work, I am allowed to be home alone, although he does enlist the help of the neighbours to check on me throughout the day. Each morning he makes me a packed lunch, downloads a new audio story on my tablet and tapes a list of dos and don'ts on the refrigerator.

Do go for a walk around the block.
Don't forget to lock the front door when you do.
Do be careful using the kettle.
Don't forget you like one sugar in your tea.

Most of the time I either sleep or sit in the garden watching the squirrels stealing nuts from the bird-feeder. Even the simplest decisions seem beyond me. When one Saturday Adam convinces me to go to the beachside café for fish and chips, I can't remember if I like vinegar on my chips. Adam starts laying out clothes for me in the morning as I am often unable to decide what to wear. I feel as if I am slowly shrinking, dissolving into myself, and I imagine ending up as nothing but a tidy pile of dust on the bedroom carpet. It's a telephone call from Grace that changes all that.

'I've booked us on a spa weekend,' she announces, a few weeks after my accident. 'Massage, reflexology, sauna, the whole hog.'

'I – I'm not sure . . .' I stutter. I'm not sure about a lot of things these days.

'We'll go at your pace,' says Grace, 'no pressure.' Almost as an offhand comment, she adds, 'and Adam could probably do with a break too.'

When we arrive, I discover it isn't just a beauty spa; there are physiotherapists and osteopaths on site as well. I give my sister a searching look.

'I know, I know,' says Grace. 'You're the expert, but I did a bit of research on recovering from concussion and thought—'

'Thank you.' I can say no more.

After checking in and giving a detailed medical history, all I can do is lie on a sun lounger and sleep. When I wake, I feel a tiny bit better. Escaping the stifling atmosphere of home has done me good. We have lunch, a body massage and then an 'Introduction to Meditation' session, where it feels as if bits of my brain are slowly beginning to slot back into place.

After lunch, Grace slides a newspaper across the table towards me.

'You know I don't read the *Daily Mail*.'

'Not the paper, silly.' Grace opens the page to the crossword section. 'I read somewhere that doing crosswords and sudoku helps the neurons start firing again.'

I smile and take the newspaper gratefully. As a nurse, I know that the most successful recovery takes place within two months of a concussion. I haven't been doing much to aid my recovery except to stare at the begonias in my garden. Maybe Grace was right. Maybe it is time to put in a little effort.

We sit in the solarium doing the crossword together until I grow tired. Then there is a gentle yoga session where I am thrilled to discover some renewed strength in my body.

'You've finally got colour in your cheeks,' Grace says at dinner that night.

'I don't quite know how to explain it,' I reply. 'Except to say that I feel a bit like my body is rebuilding itself.'

'Hallelujah!' Grace cries, lifting her glass of sparkling water in celebration.

I do the same, and then reach across the table to squeeze my sister's hand.

'Thank you.'

Grace's smile seems to falter. 'It's nothing more than you deserve, Kat.'

'Shame we have to leave tomorrow.'

'Not we.' Grace's smile has returned. 'Just me.'

'What?'

'I've booked you in for the rest of the week.'

'You've got to be kidding!'

'Look at the progress you've made in three days. Imagine what a week will do?'

'But the cost!'

'I've put it on my card,' says Grace, and then almost sheepishly adds, 'It may have to come out of the sale of Mum's house though.'

'Agreed!' I wish there were no table between us so that I could reach out and give her a hug.

By the end of the week I'm not cured, but better. My mind is clearer, my motor functions more precise. There's still more work to do, but with a list of therapeutic exercises and a stack of completed crosswords I feel as if I have come a long way. It's only when Adam comes to collect me, and I decline his hand to help me into the car, that I realise just how far I have come.

Back at home I begin to integrate myself back into my pre-concussion routine.

Thank you for the sandwiches, darling, but I don't really like pastrami.

I've got plenty to wear in the wardrobe, sweetheart. No need for you to choose.

I never had sugar in my tea in the first place!

I observe his reluctant acceptance of my newly regained independence and wonder if he preferred me as I was.

The one thing we don't address is the diary. I imagine both he and Grace had a good look through my mother's house for it when they were collecting my things. Clearly they haven't twigged that my call to Doris while in hospital wasn't about the cat, but about the diary and laptop; I asked her to keep them somewhere safe, and under no circumstances to give them to anyone.

I try not to think about it all too much – the diary and everything I have discovered. I just don't have the energy, courage or ability to go there at the moment. I can't even remember that much about the month leading up to my injury. How can I possibly resume my research? I have decided that I will try and put everything to do with Lisa and Susan O'Neill in the background for a little while, while I recover.

There is one person, however, that I do need to see.

I wait until Adam has left for work, and knowing full well that he'll be tied up in meetings all day, I make the call. When the doorbell rings a few hours later, I flick on the kettle and lay a plate of biscuits on the kitchen table.

'Doris!' I say, waiting until she's inside before enveloping her in a huge hug. 'I'm so glad you could come.'

'It's lovely to see you, Katie,' she says, dabbing at her eyes with a tissue. 'My, you look well. How are you feeling?'

I tell her about the hospital, my recovery at the spa, and my commitment to *moving forward*. I also tell her about Lisa. There's something I have to ask her before I can really start to put this all behind me.

'Do you think it's my fault, that she killed herself?'

Doris looks at me sternly. 'I thought you said you were having a break from all that?'

'I wish I could,' I reply, 'but having all this time to think, well . . . I just can't escape it.'

Doris sips her tea, clearly considering how to respond. 'From what you've told me, that poor girl was clearly disturbed. Her personal situation with her house, her marriage . . .' she shakes her head sadly. 'And with losing her job and all – well, to be honest, you seemed like the least of her worries.' She puts her cup down. 'Are you really going to give it up, Katie? The investigation I mean?'

That woman knows me almost better than I know myself.

I tell Doris my suspicions about Susan O'Neill, but it still seems so unlikely. Michael having an affair with his twenty-something swimming coach.

Doris raises an eyebrow. 'I hate to jump to conclusions, just because she was his teacher;' she absent-mindedly toys with the silver crucifix that dangles from a chain around her neck, 'but let's be honest, Katie; it's not unheard of.' She Googles something on her phone and within minutes comes back with a story of a thirty-five-year-old Maths teacher in Sussex having an affair with one of her fifteen-year-old pupils. 'This only happened a few months ago.'

'I can't believe it,' I say. 'Michael would never be interested in someone my age.'

There is a moment of telling silence from Doris. 'Are you sure there was no mention of Diving Fish being a fellow student in the diary? A sixth former perhaps?'

'I'm sure.'

Doris reaches into her Cath Kidston tote and removes Michael's diary, which she lays on the table in front of us. 'And the sketch? Do you think there could be a clue there?'

I turn to Michael's drawing of the nude woman on the bed. In pencil, with rough, undefined features, and feet that look like paddles, it's hard to distinguish anything about the figure other than the fact that it is female.

'Michael had many talents,' I murmur, 'but art wasn't one of them.'

'So,' continues Doris, 'aside from the very real concern that someone – someone perhaps older – may have been taking advantage of Michael and may have been with him by the lake the night he drowned, there is also another serious matter.' I look up from the diary in surprise. Is there something I've missed? 'The fact is, Katie, that this person, whoever they are, may still be taking advantage of other young people like Michael.'

So obsessed have I been with solving my own mystery that I haven't even thought about the wider implications; the other innocent victims.

'Oh God.'

'Indeed,' replies Doris. She clears her throat and sits up a little bit straighter. 'So there really is only one thing to do isn't there?' I know the answer, but I need Doris to say it. 'Find Diving Fish and get to the bottom of it.'

Along with Michael's diary, Doris has brought my files and Michael's laptop with her. I make a second pot of tea and we begin the familiar task of searching online.

An hour or so into our fruitless investigation, Doris glances at her watch.

'Adam will be home soon,' she warns. 'You'd better start putting those things away, and I'd better be going as well. I'm not sure he'd appreciate my being here.' She gives me a conspiratorial look. 'Especially if he knew what we've been up to.'

I rub my aching temples. What exactly *have* we been up to? We've got names, conjectures and suppositions, but no concrete evidence, no living witnesses, a police force that doesn't seem to want to take any of this seriously, and most of all, nowhere left to go.

Sensing my despair, Doris takes my hand and squeezes it.

'Lost causes are the only ones worth fighting for.'

Adam returns home that evening buoyant. I try to keep up with his upbeat mood, but by teatime I'm flagging. The afternoon spent with Doris has tired me out. It's left me feeling determined but downhearted. Could Michael really have been having a sexual relationship with a woman nearly twice his age? Doris has shown me stark evidence to prove it isn't unprecedented. I even looked up the story myself: some sordid tale about the teacher sending the boy topless photos and having sex with him in the back of her car. There was also testimony about threats to the boy if he told anyone. I think back to one of Michael's diary entries.

I told her I loved her, would love her forever. She just smiled. I told her I wanted the world to know. That's when it all went ka-boom!

Even though I'm still finding it hard to believe, Susan O'Neill is the only clear link I have to Diving Fish. Is that what Lisa was trying to say when she thrust the photograph at me and said, 'You figure it out!'

I could try calling Siobhan to try to gain some insight into Edgecombe's former PE teacher and swimming coach, but I know from her Instagram posts that's she's already on the Gold Coast, snorkelling on the Great Barrier Reef. What about another online search? I can't really imagine finding anything more than Doris and I did this afternoon. I wonder about looking through her HR documents once again, but it's getting late and Adam will be expecting his tea.

I prepare something simple – grilled salmon and asparagus – and we eat our meal in the garden, enjoying the fading sunlight and cool evening breeze.

'I've booked a weekend away for us in Dorset,'

Adam announces, biting through an asparagus spear. 'I could do with a break. What do you think?'

I sense that what I think is irrelevant to Adam, but if I'm really going to make a go of rebuilding our marriage, I'd better do my part.

'Sounds great.'

We travel to Lyme Regis on the following Friday evening and arrive to indigo skies and a moon so bright I can see every cobblestone on the pathway to the pub.

'Just tonic for you,' Adam says, as he sips the thin layer of froth from the top of his Guinness.

I hadn't fancied something alcoholic, but the thought of it being forbidden suddenly makes it more appealing.

'And add a shot of vodka,' I whisper to the barman, as I watch Adam negotiate a table near the fire.

The sex that night is successful insomuch as Adam is asleep long before I am. I stand and gaze out of the open French doors, watching as moonlit waves disappear into the shadows. Try as I might to avoid it, water makes me think of only one thing.

'What happened to you, Michael?' I whisper, before closing the doors behind me and returning to bed.

We spend the morning at a ruined castle, and then at a fossil museum where Adam scours the gift shop for the perfect ammonite.

It is late afternoon by the time we make it back to the hotel; still hours until dinner. Adam's excess energy seems to flood the room. I find watching him completely draining. The solution pops into my brain so quickly that I know my recuperation is complete.

'Why don't you go to the gym and then have a nice long sauna?'

He easily agrees, and I find myself alone in the lounge with a chilled glass of Chablis and a stack of daily newspapers. With so much on my mind I'm finding it hard to relax. I need a distraction.

'Crosswords, crosswords,' I mumble as I rifle through the nationals. I tut in frustration as I realise that the other guests have already beaten me to the best ones. All that's left is the Quick Quiz and Word Match in the *Lyme Regis Echo*.

I race through the quiz and word match in record time. Now pleasantly bored, I begin reading the paper. I work my way through stories about TB-infected cattle and the Dorset Super Slimmer of the Year before chancing upon the recent marriages section. *The bride wore a strapless gown of ivory silk, finished with hand-sewn freshwater pearls.*

My wedding to Adam was a straightforward affair; an off-white designer dress and a civil ceremony at Exeter County Hall followed by lunch at a posh hotel. I check the *Echo* for any more reports of joyous celebrations, and something catches my eye. In the bottom corner is a recent write-up about a local society wedding.

Professor Duncan Masters and Mrs Maureen Masters were delighted to host the wedding of their daughter

Matilda Josephine to Captain Gerald O'Neill of the Royal Navy, from Portsmouth Hants. The ceremony was held at St Mathias Church in Bridport. In attendance were the bride's younger sister and bridesmaid Lucy, and her older brother Niall, who also acted as best man to Captain O'Neill. In a departure from tradition, the groom was also attended by a 'best woman', his sister Mrs Desra McKinley of Perth, Scotland.

Next to the write-up is a photograph of the bridal party. I can feel the blood pumping through my head so fiercely I think I'm going to faint. Had my mouth not been so dry I may have cried out. The woman in the picture – the best woman to Captain Gerald O'Neill – is Susan O'Neill. The woman from the photo.

I have to look at the photograph a few more times to make certain. I even think about asking the woman at reception if she has a magnifying glass, but I know that isn't necessary. The hair is different, but the face is the same: sharp-featured, unsmiling – even at a wedding – and with an air of adolescent sulkiness that clearly identifies her as the same person in the photograph with Michael and Lisa. I order another glass of wine and stare at the picture in front of me. Only moments before the path to finding Susan had seemed so unclear, so undecided. Finding this photograph, in the most unexpected of places, is a sign. An omen. There is no going back. My journey is set.

I trace my finger around the small, dark spot that

Susan O'Neill, now Desra McKinley, has left on the page. She has obviously married; but why the change of first name?

Then I remember. On her HR file she was listed as *Susan D O'Neill*. Did Desra seem more exotic? Or more anonymous for her new life in Scotland? Does it matter?

All this time I have been investigating, all the questions I have asked, all the phone calls and visits I have made. Now, out of the blue, without forethought or design, they are being answered, and the one person who has the answers to the questions I have been so desperately seeking is staring right back at me.

'Got you,' I whisper, my smile vicious and victorious at the same time.

When Adam returns from the gym, I have replaced my glass of wine with herbal tea. The newspaper article is carefully tucked away in my pocket.

'I'm feeling really good,' he says, giving me a kiss on the cheek. 'I'm really glad we came away this weekend.'

'Me too,' I reply, 'me too.'

23

We have dinner in the Spinnaker Room where Adam devours a fillet steak and I pick at a vegetable risotto.

'How would you feel about moving to Bristol?' he says.

'Bristol?'

'I've been offered a job as a senior A&E consultant at the BRI.' He holds my gaze. 'The money's good and it's a fantastic opportunity.'

So that's the reason for the surprise weekend away.

'When did this happen?'

Adam sucks a piece of meat from between his teeth. 'I've been keeping my eyes open for opportunities; you know, fresh start and all.'

By *fresh start* I expect he means getting me away from any memories of Michael.

'When do you have to let them know?'

'I already have. I've accepted.'

I drop my fork and feel all eyes on me as it clatters noisily against my plate. 'Without asking me?'

'Oh, come on, Kate. For the last month I've had to make every decision for you. What food to eat, what clothes to wear, what pills to take.'

'I'm not sure I—'

'Look.' He's chewing quickly, and a tiny splash of gravy has settled on his chin. 'I'm sorry if I didn't consult you about this but considering your physical and mental state, I thought it best not to burden you.'

'*Burden* me?'

'Keep your voice down,' he hisses, and then in a sudden shift his face softens. 'I was just thinking of you. I mean if we're serious about making a go of it, why not wipe the slate clean and start somewhere new?'

Wipe the slate clean of Michael, he means.

The risotto feels like pebbles in my throat. 'I need to think about this. I mean I'm due to start back at the surgery next month.'

Adam gives a little snort. 'With this new job, I'll be paying more in tax every month than you'll be earning.'

He might as well have plunged his knife straight into my heart.

'I'm just not sure.'

Adam takes a sip of wine. 'I've accepted the job, Kate. I start next month.'

And that is that.

'It's a lovely evening.' Adam's tone suggests the discussion is over. He takes his last bite of steak and then lays his knife and fork on the plate. I've barely touched my food, but he doesn't seem to notice. 'Shall we have our coffee on the terrace?'

I stare at him in wonder. It's as if recent events have stripped back his skin. I'm now starting to see the real man I married.

'I'm doing this for both of us,' says Adam, wiping his mouth with a napkin. Rising from the table, he takes my hand and leads me outside.

It takes some effort to tire out an enthusiastic Adam, but when he is finally asleep I slip out onto the balcony with my mobile and begin searching the internet for more information, armed with a new name: Desra McKinley. The first hit is linked to the wedding report I have already seen in the *Echo*, but the second is much more interesting. It's a newsletter from last year from a private boarding school in Scotland. Apparently Lennoxton Academy is amongst the most progressive and exclusive private boarding schools in Great Britain. Alongside a list of recent achievements in sport and the arts is a brief notice welcoming the new Head of Sports Performance. That's not the most interesting bit, however. As I read on, it feels as if some of my questions are finally starting to be answered.

Lennoxton Academy extends a warm welcome to Dr Desra McKinley, formerly of Lakeview College in Ontario, Canada. Not only is she a highly regarded sports performance expert, who has coached young swimmers moving on to the Canadian Olympic team, but Dr McKinley also recently completed her PhD in Contemporary British Poetry, and was shortlisted for Canada's most preeminent poetry prize, the Governor General's Award. We look forward to her contributions to the vibrant sports and creative programmes at Lennoxton.

There are several other postings listing her steady rise from teacher and coach at Edgecombe Hall to Sports Performance Coach and Creative Writing Tutor at the famous Canadian private school. A bit more Googling informs me that she was married to Lakeview's headmaster Elias McKinley, albeit briefly, and during that time also published two anthologies of poetry. There are plenty of articles and reviews of her poetry, including a short YouTube video of her reading at the Canadian Festival of the Spoken Word. After that, however, there is a surprisingly limited online presence.

'Canada,' I mutter. 'That explains my not being able to find her.' I stare at the moonlit horizon, realising that for the first time in weeks I feel vibrant, alive again. My brain is buzzing with possibilities. Gone is the doddering shut-in who couldn't remember if she liked vinegar on her chips, replaced now with a newly confident and determined woman. Had I ever really been that helpless, or had I simply let everyone else take control and make me feel that way?

None of that matters any more. My mind is crystal clear and focused. I know what I must do.

We arrive back home in Exmouth on Sunday just after lunch. Eager to get on with preparing for his new job at the Bristol Royal Infirmary, Adam retreats to his study. I'm grateful for a few uninterrupted hours alone with the internet.

I find out everything I can about Lennoxton Academy. Founded in 1842 by the social and educational reformer Sir Richard Woodley Johnston, it offers a 'new and compassionate approach to higher education'. Located less than an hour from Edinburgh, it consists of over fifty acres of woodlands, orchards and playing fields. There is even a golf course. Nurturing a philosophy of 'individuality, initiative and an enquiring mind', it has a long history of prestigious alumni including a Prime Minister and numerous members of European and Middle Eastern royalty. From the blog and other online posts, it now appears to be the private school of choice for the children of the super-rich. Actors, oligarchs, footballers: you'd better have connections to get into Lennoxton. I search the website pages for any other news about Desra McKinley. It isn't until I click on the upcoming calendar of events that I spot it.

Events in August

Lennoxton will be opening its doors once again to poets from around the United Kingdom as part of our annual residential poetry summer school (in conjunction with the Lennoxton Summer Lecture

Series). Geared towards emerging poets, the summer school will comprise a five-day residential experience to include group workshops, one-to-one tutorials, and plenty of time to write. Included in the price is room and board, and WiFi. No experience necessary, just a desire to explore your creative side and a willingness to learn. For more information contact . . .

I scroll down further.

*Note: Due to unforeseen circumstances, local poet Maire Donaldson will no longer be leading the residential experience this year. However, we are pleased to announce that celebrated Canadian-British poet Desra McKinley will be directing the week. Click **here** for more details. We are also delighted to announce that acclaimed Scottish poet and Saltire Society Scottish Poetry Book of the Year Award winner (2003) Professor Findlay Cardew will be presenting the final address as part of the Lennoxton Summer Lecture Series on the last night of the summer school.*

It's time to send an email.

My enquiry about the poetry summer school receives a response the following morning.

Thank you for your enquiry regarding the poetry residential summer school at Lennoxton Academy. Due to a last-minute cancellation there is a single place left on the course. We will require a non-refund-

*able deposit of £75 within the next 24 hours to secure your place. As per instructions on the website, all travel arrangements and associated expenses are the responsibility of the guests. Please click on **this link** to secure your place.*

I don't hesitate. Grabbing my credit card from my purse, I book, uncertain if or how I will get there. Running it by Adam will be quite a challenge. I can't see him being thrilled about my going to Scotland for a week. Trying to sell him on the fact that I have suddenly developed an interest in writing poetry will be my biggest challenge yet. All I know is that *if* I'm going to find out the truth about Michael's death, I need to get to Scotland and ingratiate myself with Susan O'Neill – I mean Desra McKinley. This is now bigger than Adam and bigger than me. Maybe I can use the move to Bristol as leverage; a negotiating tool. I'd better think of something fast though. It's just over two weeks until the course begins.

24

'You realise that the estate agent is coming to look at the house tomorrow?' Adam is standing in the kitchen, noisily slurping his tea; a sure sign that he's angry. 'We've still got a lot to do.' He puts his mug down on the table with a thud. 'There are rooms to clear; the loft to empty.'

I wait for my bagel to pop up from the toaster before replying. 'Don't worry, darling – I'll sort it all out.'

'When will you *sort it all out*?'

I look over at him, smile, and say calmly, 'When I'm bloody well ready.'

Occasionally, when I have drunk too much wine or indulged in one blue pill too many, I have a private moment of courage or resolve. Something, however, has shifted since the return from our weekend in Dorset. Maybe it's my renewed sense of purpose; or perhaps it's the thoughtless blatancy of Adam's behaviour, accepting that job in Bristol without even asking me, that has made me so angry and so bold. Most likely it's the sixty-thousand-pound legacy my mother left for Grace and me, as well as the estimated value of the house with its 'original Georgian features' and 'exquisite riverside location', at nearly two hundred and fifty thousand pounds.

'What the hell has gotten into you?' Adam yells, but there's something different in his tone. It's as if he knows that I can't be intimidated any more; that I don't care. The freedom offered by my mother's legacy, along with my decision to register for the summer school, has given me a giddy sort of confidence.

'You'd better get to work,' I say dismissively, 'or you'll be late.'

I spend the day sorting out the house in preparation for viewings and doing more research.

Adam arrives home and I find myself carefully tiptoeing around his sullen mood and trying to cheer him up. I still must tell him about Scotland after all.

'Why don't I get us a curry?' I say, handing him a glass of wine. 'We can watch a film and maybe have an early night?'

Relaxing on the settee, Adam gives an indifferent shrug, but I can tell that the chill is beginning to thaw. I drive the few miles to our local curry house, humming to music along the way. I return home a half hour later to find the sitting room empty.

'Adam?' He's not in the kitchen or dining room. I go upstairs to check the bedroom, thinking that maybe he's having a nap. I hear a noise at the end of the hall, from my office. I approach cautiously, dreading what I might find.

'Adam,' I whisper, pushing open the door. 'Is that you?' Inside, I find the drawers of my filing cabinet have been thrown open. There are papers strewn across my desk. My husband looks up at me from where he's sitting. On the desk in front of him is Michael's laptop.

'What's the password?' he says.

It takes a few seconds before the anger kicks in. 'What the hell do you think you're doing?'

'I knew there was a reason for all that *attitude*,' he says, pointing a finger at me. 'You've never stopped looking into Michael's death, have you?'

'How dare you break into my files?'

'What, these?' he says, picking up one of the folders. 'Investigations of possible police corruption?' He points to another. 'Or research on how funding cutbacks have compromised forensic investigations?'

'You have no right!'

'I have every right,' he counters, 'especially if my wife is losing her fucking mind!'

'How dare you!'

'How dare *I*?' Adam yells. 'I'm not the one who promised to put this all aside to try and rebuild our marriage. I'm not the one who agreed to—'

'Move on?' I cry. 'When I said that, I didn't think it would mean you forcing me to move *away*!'

'Oh, that's it, is it?' Adam laughs patronisingly.

'The old passive-aggressive *it's fine Adam*, but underneath you're just festering away.'

'I never said it was fine! I never had the chance!'

'You're crazy, do you know that? Completely and absolutely crazy!'

I have never seen Adam like this before. His intimidation has always been subtle, understated; never as unredeemable as this. 'All your bizarre theories about Michael's death not being an accident.' He stands up, his fists clenched. 'All this bloody *research* on miscarriages of justice and police incompetence.' He picks up a folder full of articles I've collected and throws it across the room towards me, the corner catching me on the side of the face. 'I knew about it all, of course,' he says, smiling as he points to the filing cabinet. He hasn't noticed the blood on my cheek. 'Knew where you kept your little key hidden.' My eyes widen in disbelief. 'Well I had to keep an eye on you, didn't I?' He takes a deep breath to try and calm himself. 'What the hell did you think you were doing with all your *secret dossiers*? Is that what you're up to now, still investigating Michael's death? You're determined to prove that your doped-up son didn't die in some stupid, pointless accident, or – even better – off himself on purpose, aren't you? Who the hell do you think you are?' He steps from behind the desk towards me. 'Some sort of fucking Miss Marple?' Then Adam does something funny with his head, shaking and twisting it as if his brain is trying to reboot. I can see patches of sweat under his arms. His eyes are a stunning, bloodshot red.

'Where's the diary, Kate?'

'What?'

'Where is Michael's diary!' His voice is so loud it feels as if the windowpanes are trembling. 'I'm going to take that bloody thing and destroy it once and for all!' It's only then that I notice the smoke from a bonfire in the back garden drifting past my office window. Thank God I asked Doris to take the diary back to Calstock with her.

'He's been dead for six years,' Adam yells, moving towards me, 'and still that little shit is messing up our lives!' I find myself searching the room for some form of defence. On top of the filing cabinet next to me is a hand-painted paperweight Michael made for me in primary school. Lovingly created from a fist-sized piece of granite, Michael had painted a bright yellow smiley face on it. *So you will always be happy Mummy.* I pick it up and weigh it in my hand. If Adam takes one more step towards me, I will hit him. He looks at me, to the rock in my hand, and his expression changes, almost melts. He stumbles backwards, sits on the edge of the desk, and buries his face in his hands.

'What are we doing?' he sobs. 'What are we doing?' I stare at him numbly. After a few minutes he wipes his eyes and sits up straight. 'Let's talk about this, Kate.' His voice is soft now, gentle. 'Let's just sort things out.'

I reach into my back pocket for my mobile phone. 'I suggest you pack some things and find a place to stay.'

Adam's face registers surprise. He stands, spreads his arms wide and whispers '*Kate.*'

I push the number nine on my mobile, ensuring he can hear the soft bleep. 'If you don't, I'm going to call the police.'

I wait until he's gone before I let the tears come, and after a few minutes I pull myself together. I'm bored of crying; bored of being afraid. No matter what Adam says or does, this marriage is over. I take photographs of the small cut and the bruise on my cheek from where Adam threw the file folder at me. If he tries any further intimidation or manipulation, I have the evidence.

Wired on adrenaline, I tidy my office. I empty the filing cabinet, drawers and bookcases of their contents and place everything in a large box with the paperweight sitting proudly on top. Then I systematically begin moving through every room in the house.

First, I make my way into Michael's bedroom. After his death I had wanted to preserve it, keep it untouched; a living memorial. Adam, however, convinced me to remove the Che Guevara flag and paint over the lime green walls with a more suitable magnolia. Opening the wardrobe, I remove a stack of A3 photo albums from the top shelf and slip them into my suitcase. Next is a tea-tray-sized hand-polished oak box. Contained within it are Michael's swimming medals. I handle it as if it's made of gold. Then I reclaim an old primary school jumper and a favourite baseball cap. Closing the wardrobe door, I turn to a nearby shelf. A battered teddy wearing a union jack t-shirt smiles its wilted smile. Billy. Next to that sits a small mountain of picture books. There's a notebook I've kept from his primary school in which he had written and illustrated a story about a shy dragon named Ollie. His guitar is there, too; a reproduction of a Fender Stratocaster he found in a pawn shop and bought with his birthday money. I run my fingertips across the frets, remembering Michael doing the same. He was a competent guitarist, not brilliant, but he had a lovely voice.

Heading into my bedroom I collect clothes and shoes, adding them to my catalogue of escape items. I rummage through my jewellery box, taking the pearl earrings that Michael gave me one Christmas, but not the diamond studs from Adam. From the bathroom I take makeup, creams and lotions, and a faded rubber duck. I remove the box of Michael's baby clothes from the loft and place it next to my suitcase.

At the top of the landing I stop and look around. The house, once Adam's pride and joy, now seems just a shell; empty and unloved.

Something is missing.

Spinning around, I am shocked to find that a framed photograph of Michael which has hung on the wall at the top of the stairs ever since we moved in has been removed.

'Bastard,' I whisper, and I spend a frantic half hour searching before I finally discover it in the airing cupboard. I carefully wrap it in a towel and bring it downstairs with the rest of my things.

My final stop is the kitchen for the fridge magnet with the picture of Michael on it. Funny how the most apparently insignificant things seem to have the most meaning. Loading up the car, I lock the front door and drive away.

25

When I arrive in Calstock, Doris is waiting for me with a smile and a hot cup of tea.

'Are you sure you don't mind keeping these for me?' I say, after helping her store the paintings, framed photograph, and box of artefacts in her loft.

'Not at all,' she replies.

'I'm sorry to ring you at short notice like that.'

'Don't apologise, my love.' Doris is toying with a piece of shortbread on her plate. 'When Adam came by to collect your things after your accident, he did ask me about the diary. If I knew anything about where it might be. He was most insistent.' She shudders, and I pray that he didn't do anything to intimidate her. 'Michael was your son. He was and will always be an important part of who you are.'

I find myself so touched by Doris's kindness that I can barely speak. 'I really don't know what I would do without you.' I pause, trying to decide just how much I should tell her. 'But if you don't mind, I think I'll collect the diary now.'

'Of course. It's still safely locked away in the filing cabinet.' Doris gets up, stops, and then turns. 'Aren't you worried that Adam might find it if you take it back with you?'

I decide then that I can't keep the truth from my dearest friend any longer. 'I'm certain he won't find it, Doris, because I'm taking it with me to Scotland.'

'Why in heaven's name are you going to Scotland?'

'I think I've found someone who can lead me to Diving Fish.'

'Sweet Jesus.'

I spend the next fifteen minutes relating the story of our weekend in Dorset and finding the article about Susan O'Neill. I even show her the wedding photograph from the newspaper. I don't mention the scene with Adam though.

'So you'll be off to Scotland,' says Doris. 'But what are you going to do when you get there?'

'Try and find out what really happened,' I reply with chilling determination. 'Find out if Susan O'Neill, or Desra, or whatever she's calling herself now, was having a relationship with Michael and if she was with him that night at the lake.'

'So you do think that she's Diving Fish?'

'I don't know, Doris. All I do know is that the moment Lisa thrust that photograph at me there was no going back.'

'And you still believe what she told you, after everything that happened?'

'I've got to. I've got nothing else to go on.'

The next few days are agony as I settle back into my mother's house and try to concentrate on my journey to Scotland. There are numerous calls from Adam, all unanswered, and then finally, one morning, an angry text suggesting I should think about getting a solicitor. Done that already. I'm determined to be legally separated before my mother's estate is finalised and her house is sold. I decide not to pack until the very last minute, but I have arranged the clothes I will be taking with me into tidy piles. I have gathered most of my personal documents, including my passport, birth and marriage certificates, and I've secured them in a safe deposit box at a bank in Tavistock.

There's only one thing left to do.

'Hi Grace, can you talk?'

'Kat, is everything all right?' My sister knows me well enough to sense when something is up. 'Simon and I just got back from a few days away and I tried calling you at home. Adam was . . . *weird*. Has something happened? Are you okay? Do you need me to drive down?'

'Give us a minute,' I reply. 'Everything is all right.'

'You can pretend as much as you like, Kat, but I can tell when something's wrong.'

I find myself smiling grimly. 'Depending on how you look at it, something could be wrong, or something could be right.'

'What?'

I tell her about Adam's decision to move us to Bristol without asking me.

'Bastard,' she replies, with barely contained vitriol.

I also tell her about our argument and my decision to leave him.

'Did you call the police? Report him?'

'I'm sure he didn't mean to hit me with the folder.' I can sense Grace shaking her head at the other end of the phone. 'I just wanted him out of there.'

'But that's assault!'

'I've taken photos.'

'And you're safe at Mum's? He won't try anything will he?'

'I've been in touch with a solicitor and a friend from the Domestic Violence Unit at Devon and Cornwall Police.'

'But you should—'

'Adam knows full well that an assault charge will end his career. He won't dare approach me.'

'That doesn't mean he shouldn't be punished.'

'I think I have quite enough on my plate for the moment.'

There's a long pause as Grace clearly struggles with my decision-making process. Finally she speaks. 'So what's next?'

'I was hoping I could stay here for a while when I get back from holiday. I thought I could do the place up, redecorate, you know, get it ready for selling. Then I'll find a place of my own.'

'And your job?'

'I've handed in my resignation.'

'Okay,' says Grace, sounding supportive but uncertain.

'I don't fancy the two-hour commute to Exeter every day and until I know what I'm going to do next, where I'm going to live, I thought I'd sort of just go with the flow.'

'Go with the flow?' she says. 'You?'

'Yes, me. And I'm even going to have a little holiday.'

'You are kidding me!'

'I'm attending a poetry-writing summer school in Scotland.'

'Poetry!' Grace sounds astonished. 'I never knew you liked writing poetry.'

'I didn't either,' I confess, 'but I guess reading Michael's stuff has sort of made me want to give it a try.' I pause before carrying on. 'And I definitely won't be going back to Adam when I return.'

'Well, thank God for that!'

'It's over, Grace. Time to move on.' I hadn't realised how satisfying it would be to finally say those words aloud.

'Well, you're welcome here anytime, and for as long as you need.'

'Thanks sis, but you know, for once I actually think I might be all right.'

'Oh, Kat.'

'You're not crying, are you?'

'Of course I'm crying,' she laughs. 'All I ever wanted is for you to be happy.'

I'm not sure *happy* is something I'm aiming for. Not quite yet anyway.

26

I leave Cornwall at six a.m., travel all day and arrive in Perth at five. I considered stopping over at my sister's house in Cambridge, but the thought of having to go over my marriage break-up with her in minute detail is too depressing. I just want to move on.

In a moment of indulgence, I've booked myself into a posh manor hotel with a glorious view of the Tummel Valley. Though tired from my long drive, I still take time to walk off my fatigue. The heather is a vibrant, ready-to-burst purple, and the valley stretches out before me like a lush, green carpet. I watch in wonder as a falcon punches a wood pigeon from the sky, before vanishing into the treetops. It's as if nature itself is a sealing wax to my wounds.

I swim in the outdoor pool until my arms ache. Dinner is venison loin with blackberry sauce. I drink only sparkling water. After a hot bath in peat-infused water, I slip on a pristine white bathrobe and step onto the balcony. The sky is swathed in stars and a cool breeze gently lifts my fringe. I pull my bathrobe tightly around my body and stare into the wide gulf of darkness, striving for a focal point, something to fix on to. I thought by now the feeling of adventurousness that has recently seemed to infuse me would have settled my uneasiness, but in truth I still feel lonely and afraid. My desperate search for answers has become so much harder than I ever expected, the sacrifices greater than I ever could have imagined.

I sleep soundly and I don't dream. I wake to the ping of an incoming text, and seeing that it is from Adam, delete the message without reading it. Then I block his number.

'A whole new life,' I whisper; then I turn over and go back to sleep.

The three days at Beginsy Hall have somehow finally grounded me. Whether it's the homemade porridge, or the daily five-mile hikes, I can't say. All I know is that the anxiety that has dogged me since leaving Cornwall is starting to fade. There's still the uncertainty of what I will do once I get to Lennoxton and finally meet Susan O'Neill – or rather Desra McKinley – I must call her that from now on – but there is also a new sense of assurance, of resolve.

On my final morning I follow the footpath from the hotel to the water's edge. I gaze into the distance, past the pine trees and rocky outcrops, over glistening water to where Lennoxton Academy sits waiting.

'Not long now, Desra,' I whisper, before turning and heading back to the hotel.

I check out early the next morning and drive the twenty-six miles to Lennoxton, arriving just before nine. Check-in time for the summer school isn't until eleven, so I find a café and nurse my way through a cappuccino while reading a local tourist information brochure. At ten o'clock I drive the last few miles and park in a lay-by opposite the school's front entrance. Towering stone walls are drawn together by an ornate wrought iron gate. On top of a stone plinth sits a large bronze statue of a stag. Clouds steal in from the nearby loch and within seconds my windscreen is pelted with hailstones.

I wait until I see three cars pass through the gates before I start my engine. I follow a long gravel drive that bisects the school's private golf course and then gently curves past the riding stables. A low mist has settled, but as I near the school, sunlight dissipates the vapour and I get my first proper view of Lennoxton Academy.

The first thing I notice is the long, gabled facade of the main building.

'Looks like something out of *Jane Eyre*,' I mutter. I follow the drive as it loops past the main entrance and around to a parking area. I pull up under a row of sticky pines and pause to take in the world around me. To my left I can see an expanse of cricket and rugby pitches, and beyond that a wide curtain of leylandii. To my right is the main building, and behind that I get a glimpse of what appears to be a chapel.

237

I take the site map from the glove box and study it closely.

'The Rep,' I say, referring to the main building and reception area. I trace my finger along the wide arch of buildings that spread out behind it. 'And there's the quad with all the teaching rooms.'

Beyond the quad are the boarding houses and sports centre, and in recognition of a key Eastern European patron, The Arkady Ishutin Business and Enterprise Centre.

'What the hell am I doing here?' I whisper, overcome by doubt. There is a soft tap on the car window which makes me jump. I look up to see the smiling faces of two young women.

'Are you here for the summer school?' asks one as I open the car door and get out.

'Yes.'

'We're terrified,' says the other. By the open, welcoming looks on their faces it is clear they are inviting me to accompany them. I consider their offer with caution. It would be nice to have the time to prepare myself for my first meeting with Desra McKinley, but then again, what better way to appear inconspicuous than to arrive in a group?

'I'm Marie-Claire.' The woman closest to me holds out her hand.

'And I'm Julia,' says the other.

Both women are in their late twenties. Marie-Claire is tall and whippet thin, with tidy dreadlocks and the most luminescent brown skin that I have ever seen. Her soft French accent hints at someone who's lived in the UK for several years. Julia, on the other hand, is short and round with striking blue eyes, a mass of blonde curls, and a face that seems made for smiling. Her accent is pure Yorkshire.

'I'm Kate,' I say, returning their handshakes. 'I'm pretty nervous too.' I grab my suitcase from the boot and follow the two women towards the main entrance of the Rep where a small group of people are already waiting. I scan their faces, looking for Desra.

'Welcome,' says the receptionist, ushering us into the entrance area. 'If you would be kind enough to sign in,' – her voice echoes amongst the high stone arches – 'it would be most appreciated. You can leave your bags in the cloakroom just to your left for now, and then proceed to the meeting room on your right where tea will be served.' As if by magic, two attractive, healthy-looking teenagers appear beside her. 'Some of our students stay on campus over the summer months to continue their elite sports training. Nearly twenty of our alumni have made it onto Olympic teams,' she adds proudly. 'They also are often kind enough to help with other events that fund our sports scholarships.' She turns to the two young people standing beside her. 'Becky and Turner here are both hugely talented athletes who have their eyes on the next Olympics. They are also kind enough to be acting as Student Ambassadors over the next week, helping our regular staff with any issues or queries you may have during your stay.'

The guests form an orderly queue, sign the register

as instructed, and dutifully follow their guides to the meeting room.

'Good afternoon everyone,' says Becky, whose accent is definitely more East Coast American than Scottish. 'My name is Becky Wilson, and I'm a Student Ambassador here at Lennoxton.' She points to the young man standing next to her, who has the healthy good looks of someone from privilege. 'This is Turner. We're here to ensure your stay at Lennoxton is a pleasant one and that everything runs smoothly for the next five days.' *Perfect*, I think. *Perfect teeth, perfect face, perfect life*. Then I feel guilty for being so ungenerous. 'I'm about to take you into the Headmaster's outer meeting room, which at Lennoxton is affectionately known as the Crucible. As many of you may know, a crucible can be defined as a situation of severe trial.' Becky gives the group a glowing smile. 'Any Lennoxton pupil invited to meet with the headmaster or deputy headmaster in this room would be familiar with that experience.' There are a few polite chuckles from the group.

Pushing open the heavy wooden door, Becky leads us inside. The room is rather less imposing than suggested; a large, Georgian style sitting room with a stone fireplace and high-backed chairs covered in tartan material. In the far corner a large table is set out with coffee and tea urns, as well as plates of scones, cakes, and shortbread.

'Your first task,' says Becky brightly, 'is to help yourself to a cup of tea or coffee and a snack and relax.' She glances at her watch. 'I believe we are expecting a few more arrivals any minute now. As soon as they get here, we will take you all on a tour of the facilities before allocating you your rooms.' She gives the group another glowing smile. 'Are there any questions?'

For some reason I am beginning to find her rather annoying.

I sip my Lapsang Souchong and make small talk with the other students. It's oddly disconcerting how normal this all feels, as if I was just attending a short break for indulged, artsy folk, instead of a determined investigation into my son's death. I note that my fellow students range in age from late twenties to early sixties, and that by the make of their clothes, shoes, and luggage, are all solidly upper middle class. Even Marie-Claire and Julia, the two more studenty members of the group, still sport expensive water-proofs. As I drift in and out of polite conversation, I can't help but wonder how I will manage the next five days. It was in secondary school over twenty years ago that I made my first and only attempt at writing poetry. That experience had been an unsuc-cessful and embarrassing one. The small group presently ensconced within the nineteenth-century walls of Lennoxton Academy appear to be committed, experienced – some are even published – and deter-mined. I can only attribute one of those qualities to myself, and that has nothing to do with poetry.

There is a gentle knock and then the cathedral arch door is pushed open.

'Ah,' says Becky. 'That must be our final two.'

A small, bird-like woman steps forward and smiles. She has bright pink hair and is wearing what can only be described as a tie-dye patchwork-type dress.

'Sorry we're late,' she says in bright Geordie. 'Accident on the B846.'

'No problem,' replies Becky politely, adding a tick to the sheet of paper on her clipboard. 'Please help yourself to a drink and something to eat.' The bird woman nods and makes her way towards the refreshment table. She is followed close behind by our final member. He is so tall he ducks to avoid hitting his head on the door arch. It feels as if sunlight is entering the room. He smiles shyly at the group but doesn't introduce himself.

'Please do mingle and say hello to the other guests,' says Becky. She glares at Turner, who is helping himself to a miniature Victoria sponge, but blushes charmingly when he returns her look with a wide grin. 'In approximately twenty minutes, Mrs Roe, who checked you in when you first arrived, will be giving the health and safety briefing, and then we'll begin our tour. Turner and I will be here to answer any questions you may have. I will be just outside finalising a few details, and I'll see you in about thirty-five minutes.'

'Give or take,' I mutter.

'Damned efficient I'd say.'

I turn to see a smiling Marie-Claire dusting icing sugar off her chin.

'Can anyone really have teeth that white?' adds Julia, sidling up on my left and giving me a cheeky smile.

I smile in return. 'Exactly what I was thinking.'

'And who is *he*?' says Marie-Claire, pointing discreetly towards the man who arrived with the bird woman.

He must be over six feet tall, with the long, lean physique and tanned skin of someone who's used to working outdoors. His pale blond hair and striking green eyes give him a fairy-tale quality.

'A Viking god,' Julia whispers.

'If only I fancied men,' Marie-Claire sighs.

'I get the feeling that you two are going to be a *bit* of a handful,' I say, in a playful tone I haven't exercised in months.

'We probably *will* need keeping in check,' Julia replies, flashing huge, innocent eyes.

We've barely gotten around to introducing ourselves when Becky re-emerges and begins handing out health and safety checklists. I am more than happy to be relieved from my discussion with Marvin and Roz, a middle-aged couple from Sussex, regarding their self-published anthology of poems about their pet cats Byron and Will.

'Byron is named after Lord Byron,' Roz says.

'And Will is named after Shakespeare. William Shakespeare,' Marvin adds.

I have never welcomed a health and safety briefing more in my life.

'Thank you, Mrs Roe,' says Becky, after what seems like an interminable session on fire alarms, not smoking in one's room, and even an overview of how to safely use a kettle. 'If you all follow me back into the reception area, we'll begin our tour.' I exchange glances with Julia and Marie-Claire before following the group back to the main reception area. 'Welcome to Lennoxton Academy,' Becky begins. Turner has mysteriously vanished, replaced by a day boarder named Malcolm, who is also employed as a Student Ambassador for the summer. 'Founded in eighteen forty-two, Lennoxton Academy is one of the most prestigious and well-respected boarding schools in Europe, with students from around the world including the United States, United Arab Emirates, and South East Asia. Lennoxton prides itself on its multicultural approach to teaching and learning. This approach is reflected in the success of our alumni, who include European and Middle Eastern royalty as well as numerous heads of industry including those in Thailand, China, Nigeria, and Kenya. The Lennoxton philosophy of . . .'

I had read it all on the website and so I let my attention drift to the countless coats of arms that speckle the grey stone interior.

'McIntosh, McKenzie, Buchanan, Boyd,' I mumble, and swivelling my head to the left, find myself intrigued by a less traditional inventory. 'D'Annunzia, Rossa, Muscatolli.' I twist further and am delighted to discover some more modern additions. 'Abadi, Barkutwo, Huang, Malouf.'

'And if you'll just follow me.' Becky's determined nasal twang pierces its way into my consciousness. 'As you all arrived via the main gate and drive,' she continues enthusiastically, 'I wonder if any of you noticed the CCTV cameras outside the gate, as well as those that would have tracked your journey along the road to the Rep?' The twelve guests exchange uncertain looks. 'Just as it should be,' she declares triumphantly. 'Our security procedures are top notch and designed to protect Lennoxton students at all costs.'

'Which would indicate,' whispers Julia, 'that some may come from more questionable origins than the pretty shields above our heads would suggest.'

'Now come on chérie,' replies Marie-Claire, wagging a finger at her girlfriend. 'You're not implying that this school is a safe house for the children of well-to-do criminals, are you?'

'As an additional safety measure,' Becky continues, 'access to the student-centred areas of the school, including boarding houses and teaching areas, is via secured entrances and exits. Doorways and gates are operated by a keypad system. For the purposes of this week you will all have one code for all entrances. Now, if you follow me along this hallway to the rear of the building, we will pass some of the other areas, including the main hall, canteen, and library. I will also show you how to use the keypad system.'

'Oh, for Christ's sake,' Julia whispers.

'Do you think she's always like this?' whispers Marie-Claire.

'Always,' comes the response. We turn to see a dour-looking Malcolm standing next to us.

'Oh, you poor thing,' says Julia, patting his arm sympathetically.

We tour a series of buildings, which are laid out in a tidy quadrangle behind the Rep.

'And finally,' declares Becky, 'behind the quad and just to our left we have the boarding areas. These have been recently upgraded thanks to a generous donation from one of our benefactors. In front we have the junior and middle school residences, which can house up to one hundred pupils each including house masters and matrons, and a little further back are the sixth-form residences where you'll be based.'

I stop to admire the beauty of it all. Edgecombe Hall, with its damp, squashed, crumbling halls of residence, and the more recent addition of an ugly prefabricated group house for the swimming team, has nothing on this. Lennoxton's two-storey dormitory, with its surrounding landscaped gardens, looks more like an upscale adult apartment complex than private boarding halls. While Becky drones on about *eco* this and *sustainable* that, I wander off, heading towards the chapel: a bright, triangular building notable for its glass and steel facade. The afternoon is blazing, and the chapel doors are wide open and inviting, but I resist crossing the threshold into what I suspect is a cool marble and polished-teak interior. I can't bear the endless memorials that I know will be pinned to those shiny stone walls. Passchendaele, Normandy, Gallipoli, Ypres, Korea, Northern Ireland, The Falklands, Afghanistan. Would there even be any space remaining? Instead I gravitate further west to a stunning Cubist structure accented with a large vertical water wall.

The Arkady Ishutin Centre, reads the brushed silver plaque. I settle myself on a bench and let my hand drift in and out of the cascading stream of water before gently pressing it against my blazing forehead.

I look up to see Malcolm approaching. 'There you are.'

'I'm sorry,' I say. 'I was just rather hot, and Becky's induction was—'

'Making you lose the will to live?' he replies. 'She takes her Student Ambassador role very seriously.' His face creases into a roguish grin. 'This summer we've already had an art residential school, three faith groups, and a team of IT consultants for an away day, and they all needed tours and information sessions from the rather long-winded Becky.'

'Oh, you poor thing,' I laugh, echoing Julia's sentiment. Realising that my words may sound more critical than light-hearted, I add, 'Are you two together?'

'God no!' exclaims Malcolm, and reaching out, he helps me to my feet. 'She and Turner have been a thing since the start of term, poor chap.'

'Well, I'm sure everyone appreciates her diligence.'

'The income from our summer schools contributes significantly to our scholarship fund,' he says, his tone softening.

The words *scholarship fund* bring me tumbling back to reality; to the photograph of Michael, Lisa, and Susan. Not for the first time do I wonder what I'm doing here. Maybe I should just go to the local police and tell them everything I know.

But what *do* I know? Michael's diary could easily be construed as adolescent fantasy, the texts and emails just the same. I can't go to the police on a gut instinct. The information that Lisa gave to me is unsubstantiated, inconsistent, and to some eyes would appear as nothing more than fabrication and fancy. I still berate myself for forgetting to turn on the voice recorder on my phone during our conversation.

I think back to my discussion with Doris, how instead of dismissing my concerns as an overly emotional response to unresolved loss and grief, she had suggested instead that my journey here might be an opportunity for truth, and even some form of resolution.

What you're going to need, Katie, is good, solid evidence.

'And that's what I'll get.'

'Pardon me?' says Malcolm.

'I said I'd better get back. Before Becky gets cross with me.'

'Believe me,' he replies, with a knowing look, 'you won't be wanting that.'

The small group are just emerging from the chapel when I rejoin them.

'Are you okay?' whispers Marie-Claire.

I nod and discreetly slip back into line.

'So, as you can see, Lennoxton spreads out in a series of teaching and living spaces behind the main building. First the boarding houses, then the chapel, and finally the Ishutin Building from which Mrs

Hardy has just returned.' Next to me Julia gives a huff of amusement. 'Your induction lecture will be held there after lunch so there is no need to visit at this time. If you'll follow me, we'll continue along the Cobbles.'

'Why does everything in this place have to have a boujie nickname?' Julia whispers.

The group follow Becky along the cobbled path that runs behind the chapel and boarding houses.

'Finally, we have the leisure area – or Free, as we call it – which includes the sports and outdoor activity centre. As you may know, alongside its outstanding academic curriculum, Lennoxton has a vibrant sports programme including golf, rugby, and equestrianism. If you glance just to your left, you'll see the sports centre, and just beyond that Loch Haugh where most of our water sports take place.'

The relentless self-promotion is giving me a headache. All I want is to get to my room, have a shower and take a nap.

'My, hasn't the time flown,' says Malcolm, and, making a show of looking at his watch, he adds, 'I believe chef was very clear about lunch being served at one, and as it's nearly twelve, I wonder if it's best we get on with settling our guests into their rooms?'

I'm not certain, but I think I hear a collective sigh of relief from the group.

Becky's cheeks redden.

'Yes, Malcolm, I'm aware of that – but there *are* a few more points I need to cover.' And without breaking stride, she carries on. 'There are no boarders on campus during your residential stay; however, there are still a number of admin staff on site, as well as Student Ambassadors including myself, Malcolm, Turner and Nikki, who have all remained here over the summer months.'

Turner approaches carrying a fibreglass canoe above his head. 'Nice to see you all again,' he says, in a clipped Home Counties accent. 'I'm just setting up for tomorrow's canoeing lesson – so if you'll excuse me.' He gives Becky a wink and carries on towards the loch. The self-assured young American suddenly seems flustered.

I turn to Julia and Marie-Claire. 'Canoeing lesson?'

'Oh la-la,' grins Marie-Claire. 'You haven't read the programme, have you?'

'Thank you, Becky,' says Malcolm, stepping forward, 'for what I'm sure our guests have found to be a fascinating and most comprehensive tour.' He gives me a cheeky sideways glance. 'I've just received a text from Mrs Roe saying that the guests' bags have been delivered to their rooms. I suggest we break up so that they can unpack and get settled. Lunch will be served at one precisely.'

'But I—'

'Cook doesn't like to be kept waiting,' Malcolm scolds, his Highland burr tinged with a dash of bold humour.

27

My room is fit for purpose and comfortable, and best of all it has a wonderful view of the loch. For a moment I forget what I've come here to do and simply drink in the beauty; the abundant green of the woodland and the sound of waves gently lapping at the shore. As hard as I try, however, my thoughts drift back to Devon: to Adam and his incessant attempts to get in touch with me. I blocked his mobile and our old landline number, but he still managed to sneak his way through to my Facebook page via a mutual connection. He even used his mother's mobile to try and speak to me, pleading for me to hear him out before I hung up. Why won't he just leave me alone?

I unpack my bag, shower, and then lie on the bed, the soft breeze cooling my naked body. Had this been a normal day in someone's normal life, perhaps some of the other students and I might become friends. But

I'm starting to recognise that while it is important for me to blend in, I also need to keep myself to myself. This whole exploit has occurred in a mad, frenetic rush. In less than two hours I will be meeting the woman I'm certain knows what really happened to Michael on the night he died.

Focus on the present. Easy to say, but the past, present and future all seemed to be mingling into one colossal confusion. *Deal with the task at hand.* But what is the task at hand? I take out my notebook and begin writing.

1. *Try to get in with Desra McKinley, get close to her/ find out everything I can about her*
2. *Try to get her to talk about her past, about Michael*
3. *Confirm that she is Diving Fish*
4. *Find out if she was on the beach that night, and what really happened*
5. *If none of the above works – confront her!*
6.

Point six remains blank, even though there is only one thing I really want to do.

Glancing at the clock on the bedside table, I get dressed and make my way to the common room on the first floor. The room is empty apart from the pink-haired Geordie lady who is quietly sipping a cup of tea.

'Hi, again.'

'Kate, isn't it?'

'Yes,' I reply. 'And you are?'

'Sally,' she replies, and, studying me carefully adds, 'not local, are you?'

'No,' I say. 'I've lived in Devon for the last fifteen years but born Cornish through and through.'

'More power to you,' she replies, raising her cup of tea in salute.

The door to the common room opens. A man in his early sixties enters. He has curly grey shoulder-length hair and deep brown eyes. He gives us both an open, engaging smile.

'I'm Dave,' he says, making his way unashamedly towards the plate of biscuits on the table.

'I'm Sally.'

'And I'm Kate.'

'Very nice to meet you,' he mutters through a mouthful of ginger nut. 'I know lunch is in fifteen minutes but I'm starving.'

'Newcastle?' asks Sally.

She's clearly interested in where people come from.

'Durham,' replies Dave, dusting the crumbs off his shirt. 'Via Musselburgh to see my granddaughter. I left at six this morning and I'm exhausted.'

We nod sympathetically. A gentle gong begins reverberating throughout the room and I find myself looking around in confusion.

Both Sally and Dave begin to laugh.

'You haven't read the programme, have you?' says Sally. 'That gong indicates either mealtime or the start of classes.' She points to a small speaker bolted on the wall near the ceiling. 'During term time I think there's also a gong for lights out. As liberal as the school likes to present itself as being, I still get the impression the routine is pretty regimented.'

'Which is great news for me,' says Dave, holding the common room door for us. 'Because I like my meals on time.'

I meet Marie-Claire and Julia in the hallway and we're all making our way outside when I hear a door close behind me. I turn to see the tall, fair-haired man who arrived with Sally. He smiles and follows.

Lunch is a buffet that includes smoked salmon, homemade cheese scones, salad, and a tower of cakes and biscuits. A special area has been set up for the group in the conservatory that adjoins the dining hall. The French doors have been opened and a cooling breeze drifts in from the loch, bringing with it the scent of pine and fresh lavender. I'm just debating as to whether I should have another shortbread round when Malcolm appears.

'Good afternoon everyone.' He seems to have come to life now that Becky isn't present. 'I hope you all enjoyed your lunch. If we can all make our way to the Ishutin Building, your afternoon session will begin.' I try to stifle a yawn. 'We realise that many of you have travelled some distance and may be feeling a little tired, but we also want to make sure you get the most out of this week. There will be plenty of free time for you to relax later this afternoon.' He gives a nod and, indicating towards the open French doors, adds, 'So if you'll kindly all follow me.'

28

As we make our way along the Cobbles, I am filled with anticipation, apprehension, and, most strangely of all, a sense of acute exhilaration. I am finally going to meet the person who will give me the answers I need. This is where it will all begin; and hopefully all end.

The foyer area of the Ishutin Building is light and airy. There are displays of student work, open-plan work areas, and to the rear, a large auditorium-cum-theatre. There are posters on the walls announcing the Summer Lecture Series, including Professor Findley Cardew's address on Friday. I follow the group into the auditorium and cross into shadow. It takes a few minutes for my eyes to adjust. The seating area descends gently to the stage, where twelve chairs are laid out in a wide semi-circle and face a large drop-down screen. Facing the audience is a stool, a lectern, and a flip chart. The chairs are in muggy gloom, but I can see that a spotlight has been carefully focused on the lectern area.

Becky's perky twang cuts through the gloom.

'If you'll all just take a seat,' she says, 'Dr McKinley will be with you shortly.'

I make my way onto the stage and find an empty seat next to Sally.

'How are you feeling?' she asks.

'A bit nervous. You?'

Sally nods. 'Very dramatic,' she says, indicating the seating arrangement.

The lights dim and the screen in front of us bursts into colour. Vibrant blue images of sky; clear water and a basket overflowing with ripe purple berries. It pales back to white before erupting into a sunrise of golden tones that flicker before shifting into innumerable variations of verdant green. The kaleidoscope of colours swirls into one before fading back to white.

'What *is* poetry?' A voice echoes from behind the screen. I watch as Desra McKinley emerges from the black and steps directly into the light. There is an audible intake of breath from the observers, and I note McKinley's smile of satisfaction. 'The need to define, quantify, classify what poetry is has challenged scholars throughout history.' Though tiny – she can't be over five feet two – McKinley's deep voice seems to fill the auditorium. 'James Fenton, in his introduction to English poetry, puts forth the idea that poetry is what happens when we RAISE OUR VOICES.' To make her point she yells out the last three words. 'Others suggest that poetry is what happens when we *lower them.*' Again, to emphasise her statement she drops her tone to a whisper. 'Ultimately, poetry isn't about volume, neither sound level nor quantity; poetry is about ideas, feelings, emotions.' Behind her, the screen displays images to highlight her statements. 'Good poetry, however, is more than all of that,' she pauses dramatically. 'Good poetry is all about words, words, words. It is language that makes emotions, ideas and feelings come into being.' Selections of McKinley's own work appear on the screen behind her. 'For example, in my poem, "Feed the Good Wolf", based on a Cherokee tale about nurturing the positive side of our natures, I use wordplay to explore the nature of kindness. The Cherokee word for kindness is "nudanvtiyv", and so I began this poem with the line "The naivety of kindness", using wordplay both figuratively and literally to explore ideas through language.'

I discreetly glance at my fellow students. They appear to be spellbound. I, however, am less than impressed. As far as I can tell – though I'm no expert – Dr McKinley's introductory lecture is simply a series of dodgy soundbites linked together with some self-aggrandising IT. I study the dark blot of a woman on the stage in front of me. O'Neill doesn't look very different to the photo I carry in my shoulder bag. She's wearing a chic denim shirt dress and white plimsolls. Her calves are lean and muscular, and her chestnut-coloured hair is parted down the middle, falling in a perfectly straight line to just above her shoulders. I catch the glint of diamond studs in her ears. She seems hugely confident, but even with all the designer wear and expensive jewellery there's still the sense of a child fighting to look grown up.

'In order to learn how to write poetry, you need to *read* poetry!' I resist the urge to roll my eyes, particularly as the rest of the group clearly seem impressed by the diminutive poet. 'We'll talk more about structure and metre later,' she continues, 'but for now I'd like you to spend a few minutes with the person next to you discussing your own personal definition of poetry.'

'Isn't she wonderful!' Sally whispers, before embarking on a five-minute monologue of what poetry means to her. I echo a few of Sally's thoughts, but contribute few of my own. Not that Sally would have noticed. The truth is, because of the Brethren ban on reading anything but approved texts, I knew little about poetry until I started university. One of my fellow nursing students was a huge Ted Hughes fan – '*he was so good looking!*' – and forced her *Oxford Book of Twentieth Century Verse* on me one weekend. I devoured the poems as if starving. All those words, all that feeling, denied to me for so long, filled me with a deep and furious longing. Discovering that Michael was writing poetry, doing something I never had a chance to, makes me feel both sad and thrilled at the same time.

'Now,' says McKinley, cutting through the chatter, 'I'd like you each to introduce yourself to the group. Tell us where you're from and, in one word, tell us what poetry means to you.'

Everyone looks around in terror at the thought of having to condense their views into a single word.

'Shall we start at this end?' She points to the good-looking fair-haired man who arrived late.

He clears his throat, and without looking up, says, 'My name is Caleb Henson, I'm from York.' He clears his throat again. 'Well, *was* from York. To me, poetry means escape.'

There are supportive nods all around.

'Thank you, Caleb.' O'Neill points to Julia.

'I'm Julia. I'm originally from the Isle of Wight, but now I live in St Andrews with my fiancée Marie-Claire.' Julia reaches over and squeezes her partner's hand. 'I think poetry means . . .' she pauses and nibbles on her lower lip. 'Expression.'

'Thank you, Julia. Next . . .' McKinley gestures to my left.

'I'm Sally and I'm from Newcastle and, for me, poetry means . . . well, the opportunity to explore my inner life.' She gives a little giggle. 'Oh, that's more than one word isn't it?' McKinley's smile hardens. 'Let's see . . . I guess my one word would be to explore. I mean just explore. Explore.'

As my turn approaches, I find myself becoming increasingly anxious.

'Thank you,' says O'Neill, and then turns to me, 'I believe you're next.' I find myself staring into the face of the woman who I believe knows what happened the night my son died. It is the first time we've made eye contact. I can't tear my eyes from hers and McKinley's confidence seems to falter. She looks away, apparently to adjust the sound bar on her laptop.

'My name is Kate. I'm from Devon, and for me poetry is about *truth*.' I hadn't meant to speak so loudly, but for some reason my voice has risen, and the word reverberates around the lecture theatre.

'Truth,' repeats McKinley. 'Interesting . . . but what is truth?'

'Oh, for Christ's sake,' I hear Julia mutter.

Marie-Claire puts up her hand. 'Well, for me being truthful in terms of my poetry means trying to express my thoughts and feelings no matter how difficult that might be.'

'Excellent,' says McKinley. 'But I would ask you to consider that *personal* truth, whatever that may mean to you, is in fact a construct built on shifting sands. The feelings, thoughts, and emotions we feel when we are head over heels in love can be much the same as those we feel after being rejected: a speeding heart rate, a lack of appetite, all-consuming thoughts. Each is based on our own personal truth, but each is also different.' She stops to take a sip of water. 'And what about that old gem poetic licence? Literally the freedom to deviate deliberately from normally applicable rules or practices? One could argue that it implies that poetry is inherently *un*truthful.' There are nods and whispers of agreement. 'In fact, I would suggest,' she says, holding her hand up to silence the group, 'that each of us has our own personal definitions of *truth*. What one person feels is truthful, another may find not so –

which takes me back to my original statement: what *is* truth?' McKinley smiles triumphantly, and I feel the people around me being sucked into the lecturer's discourse like guppies into a whirlpool. Something about her overly simplistic reasoning makes me cringe, but I don't challenge her. I want to remain inconspicuous for as long as possible.

We finish up the introductions and have a break. How I am going to get through this week I do not know.

29

We spend the rest of that afternoon doing a series of exercises to 'free the poet within', whatever that means, with McKinley instructing us to run around the stage shouting our favourite words at each other, followed by ten minutes of lying on the floor with our eyes closed listening to the sounds around us and imaging innovative ways of describing them.

'It's nearly three o'clock,' announces McKinley as she makes her way around our prostrate bodies. 'In your own time I would like you to get up and find a quiet place to work on your own. I would like you to jot down some of the thoughts, feelings, and emotions you have experienced this afternoon. I do not want a poem. What I want is the unedited record of your experiences. You can mind-map, bullet-point, write in prose, make a list, draw pictures; it doesn't matter. All that matters is that it is pure, uncensored and comes from a place of truth.' Through half closed eyes I watch as she checks the messages on her iPhone before continuing. 'There are large sheets of paper, notebooks, and coloured pens on the tables in the foyer. Feel free to use your tablet or mobile phone if you wish; you can record or film your responses if that's your preferred mode. It's all up to you. All I ask is that they are not in poetic form. That comes later. When you feel satisfied with your work you are free to go and spend the rest of the afternoon as you please.' She slips a small mirror out of her handbag and begins applying lipstick. 'I believe a welcome barbecue has been arranged at the old boathouse at seven tonight. Unfortunately, I won't be able to join you, but I will see you here tomorrow at nine a.m. prompt.' She presses her lips together firmly, and then gently runs her fingertips across both eyebrows. 'Have a good evening.' With that, she walks up the steps and out of the theatre. Slowly people begin to yawn, stretch, sit up, and, without a word, follow her out. I sit on the floor, waiting for everyone to leave.

When at last the theatre is silent, I give a deep sigh of relief. Maybe it is the fatigue, or the residual effects of leaving Adam finally catching up with me, but I suddenly feel like crying. The thought of having to try and chronicle my thoughts and feelings over the last few hours seems both terrifying and absurd. What was I thinking? I don't belong here any more than bloody Desra McKinley does. Reluctantly, I open my notebook. I have never thought of myself as the least bit creative. As a nurse, I spent years training to be practical, observant, efficient; I know how and when to put emotion aside to do my job. That, and the death of my son, means that I have actively refrained from 'exploring my inner world', as McKinley so insipidly suggested.

Still, I will have to try and write something, won't I?

The room is very dark. I can barely see the page in front of me. There are sounds all around: a projector cooling, the ventilation turning on and off. They fill the space like a shadow.

I throw my pen down and watch as it clatters across the floor. There is no way this is going to work. Feeling frustrated, I head back to the hall of residence to make myself a cup of tea, doubtful that a hot drink will produce any inspiration.

The common room is empty; the group is clearly taking advantage of the late afternoon sun. I make myself a drink, shut the bedroom door tightly, and settle on my bed. I need to come up with something. I don't want McKinley to become suspicious or recognise me as a fraud; not until I can find out what she knows. I re-read my first few lines, wincing in disgust at my ineptitude. How did Michael do it?

My brain flares with sudden recall. I remove Michael's diary from my suitcase, flipping the pages to one of his early, unfinished works.

Black in a coloured space

Darkness, eternal, unending
Darkness, eternal night
Soaks into my already wet heavy saturated skin
Soaks out of my saturated skin
puddles beneath spreading misery
A spectre across the sky.
Drowning light,
submerging shadow
engulfing/gorging on colour?? Murderer of light? Am
I the murderer of light?

I begin to write.

The darkness is everywhere, shadows merging into shadows. It spreads across the room, out of the door into the fields, into the water and across the sky, drowning light, murdering calm, engulfing the colour all around me. It is a huge, hungry monster gorging itself on colour and light, never satisfied, always hungry.

The sound of a screeching gull catches my attention, and the moment is lost. I stare at the words in front of me. Part Michael's, part my own, they seem to have transformed into something different, something new. I feel at once sad and elated. Michael is with me in ways I never could have imagined.

Just before seven, I decide to wander down to the loch. The old boathouse, now a comfortable meeting space, is decorated with brightly coloured bunting. Nearby, a rustic wooden jetty stretches twenty metres into the water. I wander along it over the loch, breathing in the beauty that surrounds me.

The sound of cheerful voices brings my attention back to the boathouse. As much as I want to be alone, I know that mixing in is integral to my plan to go unnoticed and gain Desra's trust. I exhale deeply and make my way back along the jetty towards civilisation. It's a warm evening and the doors are wide open. Inside is a study space with tables and, closer to the front, a communal meeting area with settees and cushioned benches laid out in a wide U shape, facing the loch. On the grass, a long table has been set up, covered by a large awning and with softly glowing chimineas at each end. A procession of citronella candles stand guard around the dining area in a futile attempt to keep the midges at bay. Nearby, the chef is busy stoking the barbecue and next to him a table is laden with salads, cold meats, and bread of every description. The smell of burning charcoal fills the air. I find a quiet spot, open my notebook and stare at the large, blank space in front of me.

'I looked for you in the common room.' Sally takes a seat beside me on the wooden bench.

'I was struggling a bit, you know, feeling tired and—'

'I wrote loads,' she says, displaying three pages of work, most of which look suspiciously like completed poems. 'Desra's just so inspirational, isn't she?'

I reply with a polite smile and then give a huge sigh of relief when I see Marie-Claire and Julia approaching.

'We weren't sure if you preferred red or white,' says Julia, handing me a glass.

'Wet is all that is required,' I reply, taking a long, grateful sip.

We fill our plates with salad, homemade bread, and choose from a platter of grilled fish, chicken, and beef, before joining the rest of the group at the long table. There are a few snippets of conversation, praising the food, the fine weather, but mostly we eat. Becky, Malcolm, and another Student Ambassador, Nikki, a local beauty who is attending Lennoxton on a golfing scholarship, are on hand to ensure everything runs smoothly. Turner, we are told, has been given the night off to go to dinner with a visiting aunt.

Finally, when we have had our fill of freshly made cranachan and the meal is over, we make our way into the boathouse. To the left of the seating area a fire blazes in the open hearth. Any remaining bottles of wine and beer have been placed in a large plastic tub filled with ice. A smiling, red-cheeked Malcolm greets us.

'Hello again,' he says, taking a sip from a bottle of cider at his side. 'I hope you have all had a pleasant first day at Lennoxton Summer School.' There are general hums of approval. 'Normally your tutor would lead an informal get-to-know-you session, but unfortunately Dr McKinley is in Edinburgh this evening at a poetry reading.'

'How nice for her,' mutters Julia. I turn to her in surprise. 'Well come on,' she whispers. 'She's being paid for this isn't she? The least she could do is be here on the first night.'

I nod in agreement but say nothing. Evidently, I am not the only person who feels distinctly underwhelmed by Dr Desra McKinley.

'While our lovely Becky did volunteer to facilitate the session,' Malcolm gives an impish grin, 'I suggested to her that you are all quite capable of doing so on your own. If agreeable, I would like to suggest that you spend the next hour or so introducing yourselves, enjoying another glass or two of wine, and helping yourselves to coffee and tea.' He indicates towards a small kitchen area at the back of the boathouse. 'Becky, Nikki and I will be in the room just next door preparing for tomorrow's outdoor session. Even though the path from here to the boarding house is well lit, I would ask that none of you venture back on your own, at least until you're more familiar with the grounds. As you can see we are close to the loch and I wouldn't want any of you to lose your bearings and possibly end up going for a moonlight dip.' There are a few giggles; someone, possibly Sally, yells out something about skinny dipping which Malcolm ignores. 'We'll be back at ten to escort you to your rooms, but should any of you wish to return earlier, please just pop your head in next door and we'll be happy to take you back whenever you wish. Relax, get to know each other and I shall be back in an hour or so.' He raises his bottle to the group and declares, 'Mìle fàilte, which to the uninitiated means *a thousand welcomes* in Gaelic.'

I, and the rest of the group, raise our glasses in response.

'*Mìle fàilte!*'

It doesn't take long for the twelve aspiring poets to get settled. I find myself seated on a large settee next to Dave.

'More wine?' he asks.

I nod and watch as he tops up my glass, the ruby liquid shimmering in the firelight. I recline, rest my head on the back of the settee, and close my eyes. This is not at all how I expected it would be. I had planned to be detached, even methodical in my dealings with the other students. They are simply a means to an end; no need to be friendly. What I hadn't anticipated though, was how nice they would be, and even after just a few hours together, how much I would like them. The maternal Marie-Claire and puckish Julia have been warm and friendly, already offering to host me at their flat in St Andrews after the course. Dave has demonstrated a wise benevolence to balance the highly competitive natures of some of the other students.

'Not all of us are published,' he had said quietly at dinner to four twenty-somethings who had broken off into an elite group and were debating whether to have a private meeting in the common room instead of attending the evening session. 'Sharing your experience with the rest of the group could be very beneficial.' With a tone of wry humour, he added, 'And we may even teach you a thing or two.'

Even Sally kept the table laughing with tales of

her recent and short-lived foray into the world of golf.

'God forbid you try and bag a table by the window,' she says, regaling us with the complexities of club house etiquette. 'They're only for the *established* members. You can imagine their faces when I told them to stuff it and walked out, never to return.'

I find my cheeks aching from laughter, something I haven't experienced in years. I feel the settee next to me give, and opening my eyes, am surprised to see Caleb sitting down beside me.

His voice is deep, hesitant. 'You don't mind?'

'Of course not.' He smells of fresh air and sandalwood and I find myself discreetly studying his profile. He must be in his early thirties; fair-haired and with eyelashes so pale they are nearly invisible. Though quiet, he has an intense, almost anguished air about him. He catches my eye and I recognise something in his uncertain, yet open, expression. He looks nothing at all like Michael, yet . . . I shake my head clear. I have made a deliberate decision not to impose my experiences and the pain they have caused me on others. Caleb may just be shy, or even uninterested. It isn't for me to decide.

'There's a note here,' says Sally, reading from a laminated card on the table, 'that suggests we go around the room and say a little bit about ourselves and what we hope to get out of the week.' She looks around the room. 'Is that okay with everyone?' There are a dozen nods of assent. 'Well, if we're all happy to go, I guess I'll start. As you know my name is Sally. I'm an accountant. Well . . . I was an accountant. I wasn't very happy in my job or my marriage, and after my two sons left home, I decided to leave my suburban bungalow with its fading wallpaper and infidelities – his not mine – and try something new. That something new involved going into partnership in an organic restaurant in Gosforth which just recently has been bought out by a national chain.' She raises her shoulders in a *who would have ever believed that* gesture. 'So, what do I do now?' she concludes. 'Well, I go on a fabulous residential poetry retreat!' There are low cheers from everyone around the table. 'As for what I want from the week, well . . . really I just want to improve my technique and maybe get a good sense of how to prepare for publication.' She turns to Marie-Claire who is rolling a cigarette. 'Are you okay to go next?'

'Of course,' she replies, licking the cigarette paper and sealing it tight. 'My name is Marie-Claire and I'm originally from Montreal. I studied Urban Design at McGill where I fell in love with a poet.' She takes a sip of her wine and continues. 'The relationship didn't last, but my love of poetry did. I was completing my masters at the University of Toronto when I met my lovely Julia, who was doing her PhD in Global Health Studies.' She takes Julia's hand. 'It was love at first sight, so here I am in Scotland planning our wedding.' There is a round of applause and cries of congratulations.

Julia, it turns out, is a lecturer at the University of St Andrews School of Medicine, and is slightly ambivalent about writing poetry, but as both she and Marie-Claire have decided to write their own wedding vows, thought the summer school was a good idea.

'Hi, everyone,' says Dave, continuing the round-robin introductions. 'I'm a retired solicitor from Durham who has always enjoyed dabbling in a bit of poetry.' He clears his throat and seems troubled. 'I was due to attend the course last summer as a sixty-fifth birthday present from my daughters,' he adds, smiling, 'but unfortunately my wife Alice was diagnosed with dementia a few months before, so, well, you can imagine.' The room is silent. 'Alas, her condition has deteriorated to the stage where she now requires residential care.' His sad eyes glisten in the flickering firelight. 'And my children, they, er, insisted I have a break and do something for me. So here I am.' He gazes around the room, seemingly surprised by his fellow students' reaction. 'Oh now, come on everyone, don't look so glum. I've had a great life, a great marriage and I'm really looking forward to a week I hope will be challenging, invigorating, and life-affirming.' He reaches for his glass and raises it high. '*Mìle fàilte!*'

Everyone responds in kind and the boathouse echoes with affection and good wishes.

Now it's my turn.

'I'm Kate,' I begin, and then my well-planned monologue evaporates like rain on hot pavement. I had planned to be dignified yet warm, open yet guarded, and I have constructed an elaborate backstory so impenetrable that no one would dare ask me any

272

personal questions. I feel all eyes on me, and a sense of awkward yet intense expectation. There is only one thing to do. 'My marriage has very recently ended,' I continue. 'In fact, I left my husband only a few days ago.'

There is a gaping silence. I experience that familiar gut-clenching reaction, one that seems to make my body rebel and my brain stop functioning. I can easily handle a compound fracture or open head wound; I can dab away unselfconsciously at leaking cerebrospinal fluid; but ask me to manage emotional honesty, confrontation or conflict, and well, that's the challenge I've spent most of my life avoiding. Even now, as I feel the silence harden around me, all I can think of is escape. The bulge of car keys in my back pocket presses furiously into my sacrum.

Leave quietly, no apologies.

Bag is packed and ready, always ready.

Don't forget the diary.

Call Grace.

'Well good for you pet!' says Sally with a hearty chuckle, and suddenly the room erupts in riotous, supportive laughter.

I look around in wonder at the bright, smiling faces that surround me. Strangers, all of them, yet somehow new friends.

'So,' I fix my gaze on a small chip on the lip of my wine glass. 'I've been experimenting with poetry as a way of . . . sort of . . . *dealing* with it, the breakdown of my marriage and all that. I have absolutely no idea if I'm any good at it and to be honest I don't really care.' I can feel the warmth of Caleb's arm against mine and I am having trouble concentrating.

More silence. Now I feel embarrassed; foolish for exposing myself so openly. I look up, hoping, praying that the group's attention is already focused elsewhere. Instead I find myself looking into a circle of smiling faces. Some part of my brain reminds me to breathe; and then it is over. I sit back and drain my glass.

Caleb speaks eloquently of his recent expulsion from the Jehovah's Witnesses. 'Wine, women and song,' he explains, but I know just by looking at him that the reasons are probably far more complex and far more painful. He speaks of isolation, of being disfellowshipped by his congregation, meaning that some of his former friends and even family members won't speak to, or even acknowledge, him. I long to touch his hand and whisper *I know*, but instead I simply nod and say, 'well done,' when he is finished.

It's just gone ten when all the introductions and conversations are finished. Malcolm arrives to escort us back to the boarding house.

'Breakfast is at eight,' he says, leading us along the path, 'and then back to the Glasshouse – that's what we call the Ishutin Building – for a ten-a.m. start. Lunch will be at one, and then of course there's a canoeing lesson at two.'

I feel my heart sink. I had forgotten all about the canoeing lesson. I'm going to have to find some way of getting out of it. There is absolutely no way I am getting into the water.

* * *

I am just preparing for bed when I hear a soft tapping on my door.

'Yes?'

'It's only us.' The door eases open and I can see Marie-Claire and Julia's smiling faces, as well as the fact that they have managed to commandeer a couple of bottles of wine from the barbecue. 'Fancy a nightcap?'

30

I wake early, surprisingly clear-headed and hangover-free. 'Must be the adrenaline,' I whisper to myself as I push open the bedroom window. There is a steady breeze which cools my cheeks. Brightly coloured sailboats dot the loch.

I feel a sudden tightening in my throat. Marie-Clare, Julia, Sally and I had sat in the common room until the early hours, chatting, exchanging stories, and laughing until we cried. They had also convinced me to take part in the canoeing lesson, suggesting it would be an excellent way to challenge my fear of the water. I had smiled and acquiesced, feeling as if I was part of the group and yet separate, all at once. My life of obedience, first as a Brethren, and then as a wife, has robbed me of so many opportunities: so much joy. At least I'd had Michael.

I remind myself once again that I'm not here to be happy or to make friends; I'm here for the truth, no matter the beautiful surroundings or the people I meet.

I have never felt so alone.

I shower and make my way down to breakfast, desperately relieved to see Julia and Marie-Claire beckoning me to join them. A moment later, Sally and Dave join our group, delighting us with their tales of trying to negotiate the 'high-security' keypad system.

'Really,' rants Sally. 'Could they not think of a better passcode than 1-2-3-4?' As she takes a seat beside me, I catch the scent of hairspray, deodorant, and Chanel Number 5, and I feel an inexplicable urge to reach out and hug her. I've always hated sitting alone; seminar tables, dinner parties, hotel bars, I still find negotiating the unspoken rules of who to sit next to an excruciating task. Even though I went to a C of E primary school, I was still forbidden from sitting with non-Brethren children during lunchtime. The Doctrine of Separation dictates that Brethren can only eat or drink with fellow Brethren and not outsiders. A small table was set aside for me and the few other Brethren children in the village. I remember gazing across at the other tables, in awe and envy at the girls with their colourful hair bobbles and pierced ears.

'You just missed Caleb,' says Julia, buttering her toast. 'He was actually quite chatty this morning.'

'Where's Desra?' I say. 'Isn't she joining us for breakfast?'

'From what I gather, Dr McKinley isn't the mixing

type,' says Julia coolly. All eyes turn to her. 'I'm told she was forced to take over the summer school from Maire Donaldson at short notice and wasn't too happy about it.' She takes a sip of tea. 'But I gather Lennoxton gives her a lot of leeway to do her *poetry* along with all her sports stuff, so when the headmaster insisted . . .'

'How do you know all this?' I say, my eyes wide.

'I was chatting to one of the cleaners this morning.'

The table erupts in laughter.

'Maybe you should consider writing detective fiction instead of poetry,' Marie-Claire says, leaning over and giving her fiancée a peck on the cheek.

The morning begins with a feedback session on yesterday's efforts, in which McKinley slates just about every effort by announcing it to be *contrived*, *derivative* or *cliché*. All I can think of is her horrendous poem about feeding the wolf that she displayed to us the day before. While I reluctantly agree with McKinley that Marvin and Roz's contribution about their two cats is somewhat underwhelming, I am adamant that her criticism of Caleb's stream of consciousness piece about growing up as a Jehovah's Witness is completely off the mark.

'How can you say that sounded contrived?' I say, deciding to challenge the reverential silence that tends to follow each of McKinley's diktats. 'Of course it's contrived. Everything we're doing is contrived, but, as far as Caleb's piece goes, I think it's not only beautiful but completely authentic – because that's exactly how people from those sorts of communities behave.' I can feel myself getting increasingly angry with what I feel is the tutor's readiness to criticise from a position of little understanding. 'My child-hood in a fundamentalist household was closed, isolated, suffocating; every move I made was over-shadowed by acquiescence and fear.' I am giving away more than I intend to. 'Fear of sinning, fear of dishon-ouring our parents, fear of dishonouring our brethren. Fear that distorted and disabled you until you became nothing more than an outline – someone who walks in shadow.' I look around to see the rest of the group watching me, and Caleb's green eyes fixed intently on my face.

'Bravo!' cries McKinley, clapping her hands. 'Kate here has just perfectly demonstrated how I wanted you to attack the first exercise. Her response was truthful, emotional, full of feeling, but not yet a poem. Kate's even incorporated subtle imagery in her idea of an empty outline of a person, which points to the exploration of language I've been talking to you about.' I feel McKinley squeeze my shoulder and for the first time that morning, hear her say the words, 'well done!' There is a splatter of applause from my fellow students, but I shake it away. I wasn't trying to be clever, poetic or emotional. I just wanted to put Desra McKinley in her place.

'The next stage is to start thinking about imagery, rhythm, meaning.' McKinley glances at her watch and starts to pack up her things. 'I gather you've got a sandwich lunch at the boathouse and then the

279

canoers are to meet at two. Use this opportunity to explore landscape as meaning. Think of perspective: how the lake looks from the shore, and vice versa. Is there some greater meaning you can find there? We'll be looking at that tomorrow.' She gives the group a smug grin. 'I'm afraid I won't be partaking, as I'm meeting my agent this afternoon to discuss the publication of my new anthology.'

'Anthology?' says Sally with wide-eyed interest. 'How exciting. What's it called?'

McKinley places a finger to her lips. 'Not until the deal is signed,' she says. 'Don't want to be jinxing it, do I? What I can tell you is that it's a fusion of works both old and new.'

I bite back a sigh. I'm finding Dr Desra McKinley increasingly unbearable, which is already making it difficult to put the first bullet point of my action plan into play:

1. *Try to get in with Desra McKinley, get close to her/ find out everything I can about her.*

'I should be back in time for our after-dinner session in the boathouse,' she says. 'I'll tell you all about it then.' Next to me, I hear Julia muttering something under her breath. 'I would ask that all of you leave the work we discussed today until after dinner; or at least later this afternoon. It needs time to grow and develop both in the conscious and unconscious mind. Overworking it can lead to stagnation. If you feel you must write, try some diary or journal writing, but just as you would do with bread dough, or finely cooked steak – let it rest.'

There are a few chuckles, but if anything, I find McKinley's metaphors to be more clichéd than those of her students. I feel edgy, uneasy. My disclosure this morning has rattled me more than I can say. The whole point of the week had been to integrate with the group and ingratiate myself with McKinley. That means keeping my life and my past a secret. Exposing myself means exposing weakness. I can't afford for that to happen.

31

After lunch I am reluctantly coerced by Julia and Marie-Claire into a wetsuit and life jacket and then find myself stepping into a large, open Canadian-style canoe.

'It's not as bad as I thought,' I say, gripping the oar. Sitting behind me, Becky provides support.

'Blade in the water at ninety degrees, Kate. Imagine yourself slicing through the water like a knife through butter.'

We have only travelled a few metres offshore when Nikki and Malcolm approach in another canoe.

'One of the most important parts of this training session is learning the capsize drill,' Malcolm calls, as he slips out of his canoe and into the water.

'In a minute, Malcolm is going to tip our canoe over,' says Becky. 'We'll be inside.' Her voice sounds far away. 'It will be our job to right it.'

'What?' I can feel the panic rising in my throat.

'It's all right,' Caleb calls from the shore. 'You can do it! You know you can.'

I gaze around in terror.

'It's just like we practised earlier,' says Becky, and I feel her grip my shoulder reassuringly.

'But I didn't practise, I was late for—'

Becky, it seems, hasn't heard me.

Before I can finish my sentence, I find myself face-first in the water. Something wet and stringy covers my face and slips into my mouth. Is it algae or seaweed? It's pitch-black and claustrophobic inside the overturned canoe, and I find myself struggling, jerking and flailing like a landed trout. Panic overwhelms me and I feel my lungs screaming for air. Is this what it was like for Michael?

From somewhere in the watery darkness comes a voice.

'Calm down, Mum. It's just water. You've lived beside it your entire life. Grew up in it. Taught me to love it just like you do.'

Michael?

'Kick, Mum. Just kick.'

I can't.

'Don't give me that bullshit. Do you remember the time I bet you that I could swim upriver to Cotehele?'

The tide was turning, and I was frightened there was no way you could make it all that way.

'But I did.'

You were so determined.

'I wanted to win.'

I could see how tired you were, and the current was so strong.

'And there you were, puttering alongside me in granddad's old dinghy.'

You were only eight. I wanted to pull you out.

'But I wouldn't let you.'

You were so stubborn.

'Determined.'

Yes, determined.

'I was a bit afraid.'

You didn't show it.

'What good would that do?'

How did you ever get to be so clever?

'I had a good teacher.'

I miss you, Michael.

'I miss you too, Mum. But now you've got to kick, okay?'

Suddenly, I am kicking. I surface to sunshine and the sound of laughter.

'Kate, grab the side of the canoe.' Becky is beside me. 'I'm going under. When you hear me knocking on the inside, you need to flip the canoe over. After that, we'll work on getting ourselves back in.'

Things are happening so fast I don't have time to think or feel frightened. Becky was beside me, and now she is gone, ducking into the water and under the overturned canoe. I can feel it lifting and then grab the side and push with all my might so that it flips the right way up.

It takes a few attempts, but finally, with a bit of

help from Becky, I'm pulled into the canoe. I hear cheers from my classmates on the shore.

'I can't believe I just did that.'

'You were great, Kate,' says Becky. 'Really great.'

'How long were we under?'

'Under?'

'When Malcolm tipped us into the water. How long?'

'Just a few seconds,' Becky seems confused by the question. 'In fact, you were up before me.'

'Was I?'

'For someone afraid of water,' says Becky, 'it really was the bravest thing.'

I turn and smile gratefully at her. Throughout our twelve years of marriage Adam had often berated me for my lack of self-assurance. I think back to our first meeting, of sitting next to him at a colleague's dinner party. It was so obviously a setup that it was almost embarrassing.

'Divorced three years ago, no children.' His summary during the pudding course was concise. 'I suppose I spent too much time at work and not enough on the marriage.' I remember thinking at the time how confident he appeared; his sense of absolute certainty. With Adam I had a strong, confident partner who could offer security and support, as well as being a good role model for Michael. Long gone were the days when I made decisions based on emotion. Look where that had got me: pregnant at fifteen.

My thoughts turn to Ryan on the afternoon of my

mother's funeral. *Forgive me, Katie. Please say you'll forgive me.* With Adam I was strategic, clever; or so I thought. The marriage was good at first. Yes, it was true we didn't share a joint bank account, and he did like the house – *his house* – to be kept *just so*, but I found myself easily adapting; reworking my personal habits to ensure his approval: Michael had called it *keeping the grumpy monster at bay* in his diary. There had been that brief separation when we escaped to my mother's house. When I returned, I had been unequivocal.

'If you ever try to pressure me into giving Michael prescription medication again, I will leave you for ever,' I whispered to Adam, the first time we had sex after my return. He had looked at me in stunned silence – or perhaps grudging respect. Whichever it was, there would be no more doubt in my husband's mind who came first.

A year later, Michael was at Edgecombe to start his GCSEs, his application supported by Adam's friendship with a member of the Board of Governors. *You got your way in the end, Adam, didn't you?*

Feeling tense and uneasy after my experience that afternoon, I need to walk. I avoid the Cobbles and any chance of running into my classmates, and instead take a grassy path that leads behind the halls of residence and into a large, wooded area that borders the loch. I walk quickly, forcing my body onwards, hoping that the heavy exertion will steady my shallow, anxiety-driven breathing. There is nothing but body, breath and my mind gently unravelling itself. I put aside my thoughts to negotiate an enormous fallen pine, the sticky sap still bleeding from its splintered trunk. Was it a lightning strike? A windstorm? I run my fingers across the Goliath's honey-coloured rings. I feel my breathing still and let my mind unfold into the soft green that surrounds me. I hear the crunch of a twig and, turning, see a figure emerge from behind a row of spindly pines.

'Caleb.' Beams of late afternoon sunlight stream in through the pine canopy, bathing him in a curtain of gold.

'I was walking,' he says in his usual straightforward manner.

'Me too.'

He steps forward, and I find myself walking alongside him in silence, neither of us awkward or uncomfortable.

'Thank you,' he says, as we reach the fork in the path that will lead us back to the Cobbles.

'What for?'

'For your defence of my work this morning.' He smiles shyly, and I see just how handsome he really is, his narrow face and high cheekbones giving him a slightly haunted look. 'The way you challenged Dr McKinley was very . . .' he ruminates over his next word, '*impressive*.'

'I thought your piece was sensitive and extremely well written.' I find myself becoming both angry and slightly tearful. 'She was wrong, Caleb. Completely wrong.'

Now he is openly grinning, exposing perfect white teeth. 'And you know something about living in a religious community?'

'Pardon?'

'This morning you mentioned brethren?'

'Oh, that,' I reply, wishing that I hadn't let my emotions get the best of me. 'It was nothing.'

The look of disappointment on Caleb's face makes me reconsider.

'Plymouth Brethren,' I say, and, seeing his lack of comprehension, I continue. 'Exclusive Brethren, which meant we weren't allowed to mix with any non-Brethren, read non-religious material, watch telly, listen to the radio; even have a pet.'

'Sounds tough.'

'They were hugely controlling, and unfortunately my family had a particular fondness for corporal punishment.'

Caleb sighs. 'Now that I understand. Why did you leave?'

'We were cast out when I was fifteen.'

'Cast out?'

'Sort of like being disfellowshipped.'

Caleb gives a grimace of understanding. 'And why?'

At first I wonder why he would ask such a personal question, but something about the way he is regarding me – open, honest, and clearly interested – makes me trust him.

'I got pregnant.'

Caleb is silent, but his eyes never leave my face.

'Ah well,' he says after a moment, a gentle smile playing at the edge of his mouth. 'That's one way to free yourself.'

I find myself smiling too. 'It was the best thing that ever happened to me.'

His expression grows serious. 'Then why are you so sad?'

I freeze, shocked by his insightfulness.

'I'm sorry,' he looks away. 'That's far too personal a question. I apologise.'

'It's all right,' I say, and I mean it. 'It's nice to meet someone so open.'

'A blessing and a curse,' he replies sheepishly.

We walk on, speaking only occasionally, but enjoying the tranquillity of each other's company. As we approach the halls of residence I stop and put my hand on Caleb's arm.

'I would really appreciate it if you don't tell anyone about what I've shared with you today.'

'Of course.'

'Nothing about my past, my pregnancy.'

He puts his hand on mine. 'You have my word.'

Feeling both awkward and content I slip my hand from his arm. Not wishing to be seen arriving together, I hold back. Caleb clearly understands my anxiety, and without a word, carries on without me. I note his long strides as he walks onwards, and his well-muscled arms as he pulls the metal gate shut.

'Caleb?' He turns towards me. 'I think you are an extraordinarily talented poet.'

289

32

Dinner that evening is fillet steak with mash, and some sort of nut roast for the vegans. The burgundy is flowing, and my glass never seems to be empty. McKinley, at once effervescent and smug, arrives just as the cheese course is being served. Parking herself next to me at the long dining table, she fills a wine glass and then helps herself to the cheeseboard.

'How did it go?' Sally calls from across the table. McKinley responds with an enigmatic smile and a bite of brie.

As we make our way towards the boathouse, I find myself listening to McKinley's cheerful chatter with growing confusion. The tutor is on form, listening intently to the students' concerns, offering advice, reassuring them. Maybe it's her recent success, or perhaps the course administrator has had a word with her – whatever it is, it seems to have transformed her from a self-centred idiot into someone with an energy and charisma that is undeniably compelling.

When we reach the boathouse, a large space has been cleared in the middle of the room and Malcolm and Becky are attempting to teach the group Scottish country dancing. Before I know what is happening, I have been dragged from my chair and into the throng. The wine and music, along with the cool breeze from the lake, seem to have imbued the room with a sense of gentle hysteria, and before long I find myself overcome with laughter.

After a particularly robust promenade in which I step on Dave's toe, I excuse myself to get some fresh air. Above me, the evening sky has shifted and nearby a bonfire blazes on the sand. I remember what it feels like to be happy. I feel a hand on my arm and, thinking it is Caleb, I turn.

'No need to be out here alone.'

'Desra.'

'You're far too hard on yourself, you know,' she says. I am speechless. 'I realise you're a novice, but I was impressed by your work today.' She sways slightly and then grips my arm to steady herself. 'Your openness and vulnerability are very appealing.' I feel my throat constrict but say nothing. 'So, tell me Kate, where does it all come from?' She moves closer and I resist the urge to push her away. Now is the moment to ingratiate myself, gain her trust.

'My marriage breakdown I suppose. It's been difficult.'

'And the kids? You have children, don't you?'

I count to three. 'No.'

'Oh, I was certain you . . .' she shakes her head as if to clear away a thought. 'Never mind. What's important is that you're using that pain as a means of expression.' She pats my shoulder, nearly touching my neck. 'I'll be starting one-to-ones tomorrow. I think you and I will work well together.'

My close-mouthed smile conceals gritted teeth. 'I'm sure we will,' I say finally. 'I'm looking forward to it.'

'Desra,' Sally's voice rings out. 'I need a partner for the Acadian Jig.'

McKinley leans forward, so close I can smell the wine on her breath. 'Duty calls,' she whispers, and for a sickening moment I think she is going to kiss me.

'She was definitely making the moves,' says Julia, topping up my glass of wine.

The three of us are sitting on the jetty, watching the crimson embers of the bonfire flicker and pop.

'I'm sure it wasn't as bad as all that,' says Marie-Claire with little conviction.

'Oh, come on,' snaps Julia. 'She's been making the moves on every good-looking piece of flesh, male or female, since the moment we got here.'

I feel that deep wrench in my gut but force myself to remain calm. 'Did you not see the way she *consoled* Caleb after this morning's session?' continues Julia. 'Interesting, too, how it was after she trashed his work?' Julia's face is pinched in disgust. 'Honestly, she was all over him. And the way she fawns over that Turner boy.'

292

I want to reply, but my throat is tight. 'I thought she only fancied blokes,' continues Julia, and, turning to me, adds, 'but after that play she made for you? Well now I'm not so sure.'

My mind is reeling. How had I not seen it before? Her 'consoling' Caleb, her 'fawning over' Turner?

'She's drunk,' I reply, finally finding words. 'We all are.' I ignore Julia's questioning look. If sucking up to McKinley means I can find out more about her and what she knows about that night, then so be it.

As if reading my mind, Julia says, 'You just be careful. I get the impression that Desra doesn't do anything without a reason, and a self-serving one at that.'

The clanging of the ship's bell alerts us all to the end of the evening. We all head back to the boathouse for our final instructions.

'Thank you all for a wonderful evening,' says Desra. 'It was a great opportunity to get to know you all a bit better.'

'Which should have happened on day one,' Julia grumbles next to me.

'Now before you all head off, I've got an announcement – and a special surprise for you.' The room quiets to a hush. 'As you know, I met with my agent today and I'm pleased to confirm that my collection of poems will be published in both the UK and North America by Epiphany Press in the new year.' A few members of the group began to offer their congratulations, but Desra raises a hand. 'But the surprise I mentioned is to do with you, not me.' She is so puffed

293

up I'm surprised she doesn't float away. 'As you're all aware, I've been a key player in the planning of the Lennoxton Summer Lecture Series, the final event of which will take place this Friday. Poets, scholars, and poetry enthusiasts from all over the United Kingdom and Europe will be attending, and I'm delighted to say that I've arranged for the guest lecturer Professor Findlay Cardew to host a special poetry masterclass on Friday morning. As part of this masterclass you will also be reading your work to Professor Cardew for feedback.' The group's earlier excitement has now dimmed to a mixture of terror and awe. 'Because of time limitations it will need to be a short piece of three to five minutes. Professor Cardew will then take a few minutes to give individual feedback.' She presses both hands together as if in prayer. 'This is an extraordinary opportunity to work with one of the best poets of a generation.' Gazing around the room with a laughable attempt at gravitas, she adds, 'Don't waste it.' There is a smattering of applause and a few whoops of excitement. 'Now get to bed everyone. I'm sure tomorrow's going to be another exciting day.'

'Desra!' Sally calls, her cheeks pink with excitement. 'What's it going to be called? Your collection of poems, what's it going to be called?'

Desra gives the group a triumphant smile. 'As it's a collection focusing on innocence and experience via the natural world, I've decided to title the anthology after the central poem.' She pauses to ensure that all eyes are on her. 'It's entitled *Carnation*.'

It's as if all my senses, all my motor functions are slowly shutting down. My heart slows to a hibernation state. My brain, at first fired with supposition, now seems sluggish, unable to reason.

'Carnation' is the title of Michael's poem. The one in his diary.

'It also touches on themes of sexual obsession and forbidden love,' Desra continues cheerfully.

I watch, frozen, as the tutor makes her way through the small throng, accepting congratulations and commendations with a false modesty that is sickening. As she grows closer, I find myself wanting to shove her back into the darkness where she belongs. Suddenly she is standing next to me.

'Congratulations,' I whisper. I force a smile, but in truth I feel shaky; sick. Desra squeezes my arm, smiles, and moves on. I take a deep breath and force back the bile. Everything is upended.

At least I know for certain now that Desra McKinley is Diving Fish.

33

I spend a sleepless night brooding over Desra's announcements, of her publishing deal, her anthology, and her wonderful, wonderful life. How is it that her anthology, *Carnation*, has the same title as Michael's poem? I glance to where Michael's diary lies open on the bed next to me, to his own 'Carnation'.

> *Moonlight lingers on*
> > *the pale abandon*
> > > *of*
> > > > *your*
> > > > > *skin.*

I go through all the diary entries again and again to try and find some hint, some clue as to what this all means. There is only one answer. Desra McKinley stole Michael's poetry, his innocence, and his life. I feel sick, but more than that I feel driven.

Driven for truth, driven for justice, and driven for revenge.

I review Desra's behaviour over the last few days: the toying with Caleb, her suggestiveness with me last night, and of course that bombshell from Julia about her flirting with the young Student Ambassador, Turner. Resentment burns in me like poison, sullying even the tiniest flavour of hope. Forcing myself from bed, I sit in the cold glow of dawn, desperately trying to think of what to do. My plan had always been so clear: use Desra McKinley to find out more information about that night. Now, however, as I find myself virtually face-to-face with Diving Fish – with the person who groomed, seduced, and corrupted my teenage son – I feel rudderless. I return to the action plan I scribbled in my notebook earlier in the week. Point six is blank. I add a sentence, short and to the point.

6. Get the truth and make her pay!

There's work to be done on the last one, but I've still got three days of summer school left to prove my suspicions. If Desra really was making the moves on me tonight, as Julia suggested, then maybe I can use that to get close to her. I have to try to find out more about her and Michael and if she was on the lakeside with him that night. Whatever happens, by the end of the week I will go to the Headmaster and Board of Governors with a copy of Michael's diary, details of Lisa's story, and a clear accusation that

Desra McKinley has a history of becoming sexually involved with her students; and she may in fact be grooming one of them right now. Until then, I'm going to have to play it very carefully.

I take a moment to lie back on the bed, close my eyes and breathe. Maintaining this pretence requires a level of energy and diligence that is difficult and draining.

Revenge is a lonely thing.

The morning's session begins with one of Desra's typical self-promoting declarations.

'I want to make a really good impression on Professor Cardew,' she says, sipping from a Thermos mug that reads *POETRY ROCKS*. 'So, to help prepare for your reading on Friday, I've planned a truly inspirational morning of exercises.' She removes a small pouch from her rucksack and hands it to Sally. 'Take a marble from the pouch and pass it on,' she instructs. 'Then I'll ask you to find the person with the same coloured marble as yourself. That's who you will be working with this morning.'

I pick a red marble and gaze around the group to see who might have collected its twin. Piercing green eyes meet mine, and I smile awkwardly as Caleb holds up his matching stone. Next to me I hear Julia's intake of breath as she realises that she is paired with Marvin, and Marie-Claire's sigh of relief when she learns her partner is Dave.

'Today we're going to be working on haikus,' Desra announces. 'Is everyone familiar with haikus?' The other students nod, and I find myself wracking my brain trying to remember anything from GCSE English. 'Just to refresh your memory, a haiku is a Japanese verse form that uses just a few words to capture a moment and create a picture in the readers' minds. It is like a tiny window into a scene much larger than itself.' She takes another sip of coffee. 'Due to its brevity, and yet the skill involved, I thought this would be the perfect format for your readings at the masterclass on Friday morning. Your piece doesn't have to be a haiku in itself, but it needs to take on board that level of brevity and meaning.' The mention of the masterclass sends murmurs of excitement throughout the room. 'Keeping in mind the theme of my soon-to-be-published anthology, I have decided that our explorations this morning will focus on nature, the natural world and your physical and emotional responses to it.' She places a pile of white envelopes on the floor in front of us. 'In each envelope you'll find a series of questions I want you to ask each other about your impressions and experiences. I don't want you to settle for stock responses. I want you to challenge each other to go beyond the commonplace.' She checks her watch. 'I want you to wander around the campus, seeing, smelling, touching, experiencing nature in all its incarnations. It's nine fifteen now. I'd like us to meet back at the theatre for eleven. I'll be wandering around checking in on you, so feel free to ask me any questions.' She picks up her Thermos and leaves the theatre.

'It would be nice if there was some actual *teaching*

going on,' Julia mutters, before reluctantly joining Marvin.

Caleb and I decide to spend some time in a maple grove, examining the intricate tributaries in each leaf, rubbing earth through our fingertips. Caleb reads from the instructions in the envelope, challenging me to push myself further.

'It smells like earth,' I say.

'What does earth smell like, Kate?'

'Wet; damp. Earthy.'

Caleb smiles. 'What else?'

I shake my head.

Caleb takes a handful of earth and lets it trickle into my open palm before taking my hand in his and holding it to my face.

'Close your eyes, Kate. Relax.' I can feel the warmth of his body against mine. 'Now tell me: what does it smell like?'

I close my eyes and breathe in deeply. There is a musty smell, dank but fresh, like the garden after a rain shower.

'It smells like vegetation, rotting for centuries in cool obscurity. It smells like the beginning and the end. It smells like life.'

I open my eyes to see Caleb smiling at me.

We carry along the forest path until we come to a small beach surrounded by silver poplars. Caleb takes off his shoes and socks, rolls up his jeans, and walks ankle deep into the water.

'It's cold!'

'How cold?'

'Freezing cold.'

'And?'

'So cold the blood flow is halted.'

'Like?'

'Like an image frozen in time . . . no! Like a statue after a heavy snowfall. The features are blanketed, undefinable, forgotten.'

I find myself clapping in appreciation.

'Come in,' calls Caleb. 'You don't feel the cold after a while.'

I step forward onto the sand, but no further.

'You don't like the water?'

I shake my head.

'But you went canoeing?'

'Never again,' I reply, remembering the feeling of wet, slimy leaves on my face and the inexplicable sound of Michael's voice.

Caleb walks out of the water and sits on the sand. A cool breeze blows in from the loch and I find myself sitting down beside him.

'Have you always been afraid of the water?'

'No. Just the last few years.'

'Something happened?'

I nod and look away. 'My son, Michael.' The words cling in my throat. 'Six years ago.'

Caleb takes my hand in his. We hear splashing and I look up to see the water silver and frothing.

'A shoal of stickleback,' Caleb explains, seeing the confusion on my face. 'Trying to escape from predators. Pike I reckon, maybe carp. The fish tend to come up to the surface like that in a panic before diving down again.'

Diving Fish.

'We'd better get back,' I say, removing my hand from his. 'We don't want to be late.'

We arrive to hear Desra addressing the group.

'An important part of this course is ensuring that you have the time to write,' she says, 'so I'm wrapping things up early today.' She reaches into her bag and puts on a slick of lip gloss. 'Final drafts for your readings are due in tomorrow lunchtime at the latest. I would suggest you spend the rest of the afternoon working on that, and maybe even arrange a group critique session. I'll have a clinic this evening in the boathouse for anyone who wants feedback, but for now,' she says, her cheeks creasing in a self-satisfied smile, 'I'm off to meet with Professor Cardew.' With a final smack of her lips, she leaves.

The rest of us disperse slowly. I make my way out of the building, watching as Desra climbs into the passenger seat of the school transport, a shiny Mercedes people carrier driven by Turner.

Julia, Marie-Claire and I exchange looks and then glance towards Becky, who waves determinedly as the car drives away. The schoolgirl looks momentarily troubled, and then, almost as quickly, her expression returns to one of cheery professionalism.

'Just a reminder, everyone,' she calls. 'Picnic lunch by the loch. If you'll all follow me . . .'

'Is Turner old enough to drive?' Julia asks.

Becky turns. 'Of course,' she replies brightly. 'He's nearly eighteen.'

'What I really meant was *safe* to drive,' says Julia under her breath, 'with *her* in the car.'

I'm not sure if Becky has heard, but her demeanour seems to change. She stands straighter, flicks back her ponytail, and marches onwards with a firm 'Come along now everyone.'

'I'll join you a little later,' I say to Julia and Marie-Claire. 'I have to phone my sister.'

I wait until the others have made their way towards the loch before taking the cobbled path towards the quadrangle. The Rep, I have discovered, has a rear entrance facing the woods that is not overseen. I enter the generic passcode and the door opens with a soft click. Once inside, I make my way along the narrow corridor. The offices are interspersed with study areas, labs and small classrooms arranged in subject order. I pass an office with a skeleton on a stand and a large fish tank, then find myself glancing into the map-lined office of the head of Geography, before finally reaching the PE department. There is a teaching room plastered with posters of sports stars urging viewers to *Just do it!* Beyond that is a dark wooden door with a brass plaque that reads:

Dr Desra McKinley PhD, Head of Sports Performance

The door is locked.

I'm just wondering what to do next when I hear the hum of a hoover. Making my way down the corridor, I find the cleaner doing her rounds. A plastic badge on her lapel reads 'IRIS'. She gives me a friendly nod.

'I'm normally long gone by this time,' she grumbles. 'But there was a governors' meeting this morning.' She shakes her head. 'Who'd have thought they could make such a mess with a few shortbread rounds and a couple of flasks of tea?'

Struggling to decipher her thick Highland brogue, I nod in sympathy. I reach into my shoulder bag and remove a small book of poetry I brought from home.

'I'm sorry to bother you when you're so busy, Iris,' I bend down to retrieve a sweet wrapper that has fallen from the wastepaper basket she is emptying, 'but I promised Dr McKinley I would return this book I borrowed to her office before the end of the day.'

Iris gives me a sharp look. 'You don't want that hen cross with you,' she mutters, and, sighing, glances up at the clock on the wall.

'If it's any help I'll do it myself. I mean I can see how busy you are,' I say. 'I'll just be a second.'

Iris deliberates for a moment before unclipping the large keyring from her belt. 'It's the one with the square top,' she says, handing me her keys. 'Just bring them back when you're done. No need to lock up as I'll be along soon.'

I give my thanks and hurry along the corridor to Desra's office. The key slips into the lock without hesitation, and the door opens smoothly and silently. The room is long and narrow, with a built-in desk and shelving unit along the right wall and free-standing bookshelves along the left. At the far end is a narrow window permitting a thin shaft of sunlight. Below the window is a small two-seater settee: the only place for students to sit. I wonder if Desra eschewed the sturdy desk chair in favour of more pleasurable contact with her students on the settee.

I give myself an inward shake. There isn't time for this. Iris will be expecting her keys back any minute now. I glance around the office trying to take everything in. On the desk sits an Apple Mac, a small printer and a desk tidy with pens, paperclips, and push pins. To the left of the computer is a large leather day-by-day diary opened to today's date. On the shelf above are two handcrafted mahogany bookstands, both displaying thin volumes of poetry. The first – an in-house publication from a UK university – is drab and uninspiring. The second, a more artfully put-together prospect, has a glossy cover and a sticker on the front that reads:

Shortlisted for the Governor General's Award for English-language Poetry

It is a Canadian publisher, which I assume means it was written during Desra's five-year sojourn at Lakeview College in Canada. What occurred, I wonder, to take her from the highest echelons of Canadian society to this prominent but backwater Scottish prep school?

'You messed up, didn't you, Desra?' I mutter, as I trawl through the tutor's in-tray. I freeze when I see an A5 envelope with a return address that reads *Epiphany Publishing*, and with a note in the bottom right-hand corner that reads *copies x 1*. Inside is a galley proof of McKinley's newest anthology, *Carnation*. The thick, unrefined paper cover is a muted cardboard grey. There is a simple, uncompleted drawing of a carnation, and within that outline another image of two figures, male and female, their bodies entwined. I flip through the pages, still marked in red pen, to the title poem.

> *Moonlight lingers on*
> *the pale abandon*
> *of*
> *your*
> *Skin.*

My heart is beating so fast I have to sit down on the edge of the desk. The first line of the poem is set out exactly as Michael had done it, word for word. 'Bitch!'

I carefully work my way through the remaining pages, when all I really want to do is tear them into shreds and hurl them into the loch. I think of Lisa, of the poor broken girl whose life was ruined by exploitation and abuse, whose future was over even before it had started. I drop the proof copy on the desk, where it lands with a soft thud. There follows a soft jangle of metal. I look down to see the keys to the top drawer of Desra's desk gently swinging back and forth.

The first thing I spot in the drawer are pages of job descriptions from American private schools, clearly printed off from their websites. Parts of the personal specifications have been highlighted, and there are handwritten notes: *use example from the teaching conference at Lakeview!*. There is also an email from a school in Rhode Island inviting Desra to attend an online interview a few weeks before. Scribbled on the page are preparatory notes for her interview – *make sure to mention work on the lecture series, and particularly with Cardew* – and tick marks or happy faces next to her planned responses suggesting she had answered the question successfully.

'On the move already are we, Desra?'

I riffle through the paperwork, school newsletters and staff rotas, before finding an A4 leather document folder. I gently ease it out of the drawer and unzip it. Inside, there are newspaper clippings from Desra's time at Edgecombe Hall, including an event she hosted for National Poetry Day, and a short interview with her in the *Swimming Times*, where she talked about how the arts have real value in sports education. I also find a photograph from a school swimming gala at Edgecombe Hall. I am becoming increasingly impervious to shock, but the image still drains the colour from my cheeks. In the photograph are Michael and Lisa. Both are in their swimwear. In the middle stands Desra, her arms linked through theirs. I contemplate tearing the image to pieces, but taking it would give the game away, and I won't do that yet.

I'm carefully returning the contents to the folder when I see something poking out from one of the side pockets. I slip my hand in amongst the soft calfskin and remove the final item. Another photograph. It's of Desra with a handsome, auburn-haired boy about Michael's age when he died. It's clearly been taken at a swimming competition, because he's wearing a Speedo and has a medal around his neck. It's not at Edgecombe, though, and I don't recognise him from the countless swimming events I attended over the years. His proudly smiling face and bare chest are dotted with freckles. She is standing next to him, a hand on his shoulder. I turn it over. On the back is written a single name. *Alistair*. Was Alistair another Edgecombe student taken in by Desra?

I turn the photo back over and study it closely. On the wall behind the boy is a banner. There is an image of a swimmer and above that a maple leaf. I strain to read the lettering below.

Swimming Canada – Junior Championships – Parc Olympique – Montréal

I strain further to read the date and my breathing stills, almost stops. This picture was taken three years after Michael's death. Three years after Desra's involvement with Lisa. God help me; was this poor boy another one of her victims?

I take my mobile from my back pocket and photograph the image front and back, as well as the one of Michael and Lisa, then return all the items to the folder before carefully putting it back in its hiding place in the drawer.

'Everything all right?'

'Iris.' I turn to see the cleaner standing in the hallway outside the door. Feeling guilty, I grab the anthology from the desk, slip it back into its envelope and return it to McKinley's in-tray. 'I couldn't resist a little peek,' I say sheepishly.

'Crap isn't it?' she replies, holding her hand out for the keys.

34

I spend the next few hours restless and uncertain. Confirming that Desra has plagiarised Michael's work, and most likely has manipulated a third young person, corroborates my suspicions in the worst possible way. If this immoral woman would steal a dead boy's poem, or abuse a young person and then write about it, then what else is she capable of? It's a good thing she's in Edinburgh or I would take that damn anthology, march into that damn theatre, and, in front of everyone, shove it in her pinched little face, exposing her as a liar, a thief and paedophile.

But what good would that do? I need proof, and, if she's been getting away with it for this long, that isn't going to be easy.

After my late lunch, I grab a cup of tea and escape to my room, explaining to Julia and Marie-Claire that I'm planning to spend the afternoon in my room, writing. I don't think I could face a group critique session, no matter how friendly.

Taking out my laptop, I decide to see if I can find out anything about that boy in the picture, Alistair. If Desra was having a sexual relationship with him as well, then maybe he could corroborate . . . I don't allow myself to think any further. There have been too many disappointments already.

I go first to the photograph on my phone I took of the photograph of Alistair and Desra. *Very meta, Mum*, Michael would have said. I stare at the image, of an innocent smiling young man with everything in the world to hope for. My eyes shift to the woman standing next to him, her hand possessively gripping his shoulder. I have never truly felt hatred for another human being, but now I am bloated with it; overcome. I tiptoe to the common room, grab a half-bottle of wine, the remnants of our drinking session from a few nights before, then head back to my room and lock the door.

I start with the *Swimming Canada* website and the results for the junior championships in Montreal in 2018.

Even after years of following Michael's competition results, I still find the website confusing. There are fifteen heat sheets for both men and women, which include 'prelims' and 'finals', including races in age groups ranging from eleven to twenty, and in categories including breaststroke, backstroke, butterfly and freestyle. The lettering is small, the sections poorly formatted, and clearly a scan, as someone has scrawled *PB* in large letters throughout. After a half hour of searching my eyes are sore and my head aches. Maybe the wine wasn't such a good idea after all. I decide to shift my search wider than just the men's competitions.

That's when I find it.

Event 33: Mixed 400 Meter Medley Relay.

In amongst a catalogue of surnames and initials, I come across one that stands out. *Team LCSWIM. March, A.* I lean back, place my head in my hands and breathe. Could this be him? Then I realise this is a mixed relay; boys and girls. A March could be Alison, not Alistair. I look for the psych sheet: a list of swimmers, their best times, and where they are seeded in the competition. Coaches and athletes use psych sheets all the time to check out their competitors. Under *Event 33*, and in the middle with a very decent time, is *LCSWIM*, and under that, just what I've been looking for: *March, Alistair (15).*

'I've found you.'

I scribble the words *Alistair March, Lakeview College swimming team* in my notebook, and begin searching through the social media sites with renewed vigour.

It's nearly five when I leave my room. Initially downhearted, I finally uncovered a significant lead as to Alistair's current whereabouts. According to the Lakeview College alumni page he was granted the McKenzie Corbett Memorial Scholarship and is currently studying International Relations at

312

St Andrews University, less than fifty miles away. This can't just be a coincidence. This was meant to be. All I need now is a bit of help to bring this all to life.

I find Julia and Marie-Claire sitting on a picnic bench in the courtyard. I hold up a bottle of wine and some plastic cups. 'Fancy a drink?'

'You must be a mind reader,' says Julia, pouring her cup of herbal tea onto the grass. 'Where have you been all afternoon?'

'No Sally?' I ask, trying to change the subject.

'She's been working on her piece for Friday,' replies Marie-Claire, and, with a wink, adds, 'We thought you two might have gone off together.'

'She's taking it all very seriously,' I mutter.

'And you?' Marie-Claire scrutinises me closely. 'Have you been taking this all very seriously too?' At first, I think she is being critical, but the kind, questioning look on her face tells me something different. 'It's just the way you challenged Desra about Caleb's piece – it made me think—'

'That Dr Desra McKinley is a complete, bloody idiot!' says Julia. She takes the glasses from me, opens the wine, and pours us all a drink.

'I didn't quite mean—'

'Oh, come on,' says Julia taking a furious gulp. 'That ridiculous PowerPoint presentation on the first day? The rudimentary exercises that wouldn't even challenge a secondary school student?'

'I must confess – that poem about the wolf,' says Marie-Claire, trying her best not to sound unkind, 'well, it was pretty—'

313

'Horrendous. Shit! And she didn't even know who Martha Sprackland is!' Julia seems genuinely affronted. 'How could someone who *supposedly* did their PhD on contemporary British poets not know who Martha Sprackland is?'

I wait a moment before speaking. 'What do you mean by *supposedly*?'

Julia glances at Marie-Claire. I pour us all another glass of wine.

'I tried to ask her during the coffee break this morning where she did her PhD.' Julia shakes her head and makes a little tutting sound. 'She refused to answer. Changed the subject as quickly as possible and then ran off to make a phone call. Something about her just doesn't ring true.'

'Do you really think she's faked her PhD?' I ask. Julia shrugs, as if unwilling to be pinned down. 'What difference would it make if she did?' The two women look at me, perplexed. 'I mean whether or not she's got a PhD. It's not actually a requirement to teach this course is it?'

'The course, no,' says Marie-Claire through a mouthful of wine, 'but for this school, and using the title. Lying on her application. Academic misconduct.' Her eyes widen dramatically. 'It would be very detrimental to her career as a teacher, and I suspect as a poet, if someone were to learn she lied about her credentials.'

Speaking of hungry wolves, I think. Both women are watching me intently. There is so much I want to say; so much I *could* say. Julia's barely concealed

314

animosity towards McKinley is palpable, like the taste of smoke on bonfire night. Marie-Claire, slightly more forgiving, is still clearly suspicious. I would probably only have to say a few words to either of them, and Desra's career at Lennoxton – and possibly at that posh private school in Rhode Island – would be over.

That, however, wouldn't get me the information I need. Once I find out about Desra's involvement with Michael, I will happily feed her to Julia and Marie-Claire; but not just yet.

'I couldn't really comment on her academic merit,' I say, feeling like I am tiptoeing through a minefield. 'I mean I come from a healthcare background. But she does seem a bit slipshod.'

'Slipshod!' says Julia. 'That's an understatement. Arrogant, incompetent, unprofessional more like.'

'Maybe she's just getting warmed up,' counters Marie-Claire. 'I mean she did have to step in at short notice.'

For a moment Julia looks as if she is going to lose her temper, but almost immediately her face softens.

'It's one of the things I love about you most,' she whispers, leaning over and giving Marie-Claire a kiss. 'You always give people the benefit of the doubt.'

'Well we've got to try to make the best of things I suppose. I mean we're in a beautiful location, with good wine and good friends.'

'Why didn't you both just cancel when Maire Donaldson backed out?' I say. 'I mean it's not like this course is really going to help you write your wedding vows, is it?'

315

'They didn't let us know until a week ago,' replies Julia. 'I'd already booked the travel, taken time off from my job, and we got a discount when they told us she had cancelled. Maybe you should ask for one too?'

'Maybe,' I say, unwilling to tell them that the sole reason I have come all this way wasn't for the noted Scottish poet, but for the suspect Desra McKinley. 'Is there any way that we could find out about her PhD? I mean if she actually does have one?'

'Well aren't you the little detective,' says Julia, with a wicked smile. 'Normally a PhD will be registered with the university where the person completed it. Trouble is, Desra refused to tell me which one that was, hence my wondering whether maybe she's telling porkies.'

'Alors,' cries Marie-Claire, clearly excited by the mystery. 'If she did her thesis in the UK it wouldn't just be registered with the university . . .'

'But with the British Library as well!' says Julia, rubbing her hands together in glee.

'The British Library?'

Julia's expression becomes catlike. 'Standard,' she purrs. 'Provided she did her PhD in the UK, it will be registered.'

'What if she did it when she was in Canada?'

Julia is not daunted. 'We could do an author search on the Theses Canada website.'

'Shall we go up to my room?' I say. 'My laptop is fired up and ready to go.'

*   *   *

It doesn't take long to find the British Library's electronic thesis online service, as well as the Theses Canada Portal.

'Des-ra Mc-Kin-ley,' says Julia, typing the name into the search engines for each site.

There is no result.

'Are you spelling it right?' Marie-Claire asks.

'Of course I am.' Julia points to the screen. 'I've tried it three times, and nothing.'

'I think you'd better try Susan O'Neill,' I whisper.

Julia looks up from the keyboard. 'What?'

'Susan O'Neill, try Susan O'Neill.'

Marie-Claire moves closer. I can smell the musky scent of her perfume. 'Is there something you're not telling us, chérie?'

'So, you've come all this way to try and prove that Desra McKinley, or Susan O'Neill, is a fraud?'

Julia and Marie-Claire are sitting on the bed staring at me. I'm not sure if they buy my story of my fictional niece's poetry being stolen by McKinley when she was one of her students. I may need to hint at more.

'I know it sounds trivial,' I say, 'but Lisa was only a sixth former. She was seventeen years old, incredibly talented, and she trusted her.' Holding out my phone, I show them the image of Michael and Lisa at the school fundraising event. 'Afterwards, she became very depressed and gave up her place at university.'

'But why now?' Marie-Claire asks. 'Six years later?'

'Lisa eventually did go to university,' I reply, 'she

317

graduated last month.' The lies are like liquid on my tongue. 'She stayed with us for a few days afterwards. One night we were celebrating and got a bit drunk.' I imagine all those hoped-for conversations I should have had with Michael, and I find myself blinking back tears. 'That's when she told me what Desra – or Susan, as she was known at that time – had done to her, and how she had completely destroyed her self-confidence and faith. Then she told me that she had heard that O'Neill was back in the country, was now calling herself Desra McKinley, and was teaching at Lennoxton.' I take a crumpled tissue from my back pocket and blow my nose. 'Lisa was determined to come here to seek her out, but I convinced her not to as I knew it wouldn't be good for her mental health. She only relented when I promised to do it myself.'

'Doesn't surprise me about McKinley stealing her work,' says Julia. 'A mediocre undergraduate's work would be better than most of the stuff of hers I've seen so far.' She glances at me. 'No offence to your niece of course.'

'I hate to be the only dissenter,' says Marie-Claire softly. 'But do you have proof that she stole your niece's work, or that it wasn't all some sort of fantasy?'

'Marie-Claire!'

'Oh, come on, Julia. If the young woman had a fixation for her teacher, which is not unheard of, she could have constructed this entire story and pulled poor Kate into it.'

'She said she wrote a poem on a piece of paper

318

when she was at Desra's flat.' I feel the flush of guilt as I shamelessly plagiarise and distort Lisa's story.

Julia raises an eyebrow. 'She was at her teacher's flat?'

'That's what she told me.' I continue. 'But you're right, Marie-Claire; of course you're right.' I can't contain the emotion in my voice. 'I have no solid evidence, and no proof; only Lisa's word, and unless she decides to take it forward, there's really nothing more I can do.' I shake my head in self-reproach. 'You probably both think I'm a complete idiot for coming all this way.'

'Of course not.' Marie-Claire gets up and takes my hands in hers. 'Just a loving aunt.'

'For God's sake, Kate, why are you apologising?' Julia is furious. 'We've all seen the way she carries on with that Turner lad!'

'I'm not sure,' says Marie-Claire, uneasily, 'that her *friendliness* with Turner can be construed as anything other than that.' She gives Julia a gentle warning look. 'You know how you tend to jump into things, and not always with all the facts.'

There is a silent exchange between the two women, and I wonder if Julia's headstrong sense of justice has gotten her into trouble before.

'But if we could find out about her PhD,' says Julia, seemingly not having heard Marie-Claire's warning.

'For all we know she may have completed her PhD,' said Marie-Claire, 'but didn't sign the licence agreement to have it published online.' I can tell which of the duo is more cautious.

'Marie-Claire may be right,' I say, hoping to stop an impending argument. 'There seems to be no definitive way we can prove—'

'Is she published in any academic journals?' says Julia, returning her keen eye to the computer screen. 'Does she have a LinkedIn profile?'

Marie-Claire places a hand on her fiancée's. 'This is not our battle, Julia.'

'If she's guilty of academic misconduct, it is!'

'*Please don't argue*,' I beg. 'I never planned to get anyone else involved, and I certainly don't want you to do anything that might get you both into trouble.' I'm going to have to extricate at least one of these women from any further involvement if I'm going to get the answers I need. It was all becoming too messy and too dangerous. 'I'm sorry for dragging you both into this. I hope it hasn't ruined the summer school for you both.'

'Ruined it?' Julia yells. 'It's the most exciting thing that's happened all bloody week!'

Smiling tightly, Marie-Claire gently prises the empty bottle of wine from Julia's hands. 'I think we've all had enough to drink, don't you?' She opens the bedroom door. 'I'm going outside for a quick smoke, and then perhaps afterwards we can all make our way to the dining hall for something to eat.' She turns back to her fiancée. 'And maybe no more wine for you, eh chérie?'

I watch in relief as the bedroom door slams shut behind Marie-Claire.

'Julia,' I say softly, and blatantly contradicting my

320

earlier statement about not wanting to get either of them into trouble add, 'I really, *really* need your help.'

I wait until I see the smoke rising from Marie-Claire's cigarette in the courtyard below before telling Julia the full story.

'I found another of Desra's students,' I begin, 'from when she was a coach in Canada.' Julia's eyes widen, but she says nothing. 'It just so happens that he won a scholarship,' I show her the Lakeview College post, 'and he's studying here, at St Andrews.'

Julia face is unreadable. 'So this isn't just about her stealing your niece's poetry, is it?'

'I wondered about her being in her teacher's flat as well.' This is getting dangerously close to the truth, but I must carry on. I point to the image of the handsome, smiling Alistair on the Lakeview College alumni page. 'He's a lot like Turner, don't you think?'

'*Shit*,' whispers Julia. 'You think she might have . . .' she stumbles for the words, '*you know*, with this Alistair person, when she was a teacher in Canada?'

'That's what I want to find out.'

Julia stands up and walks out of the room. Is this all too much for her? I glance out the window to see if Marie-Claire has finished her cigarette, and I am relieved to see her chatting animatedly to Dave. Just when I'm certain she won't be coming back, the door opens, and Julia enters clutching a bottle of vodka. 'For courage,' she mutters.

It takes a few minutes for Julia to settle; first a sip or two of vodka, and then a return to the Lakeview website to re-read the entry about Alistair's scholar-ship at St Andrews. Finally, she speaks.

'What exactly do you want from me, Kate?'

'If you could just help me to find out if he's arrived in Scotland—'

'No way,' says Julia, shaking her head.

'The new university term starts in a few weeks. He may be here already.'

'And if he is?'

'I can do something about it.' I know I'm giving away far too much, but it's Wednesday, and there's only two more days left of summer school. I've got to push. 'If Desra did try something on with Alistair, like she may have with Lisa, like you think she is with Turner, then we need to do something about it.'

Julia lets out a long, deep sigh. 'You really are obsessed, aren't you?'

I hold her gaze and know exactly what to say next. 'All I want is justice.'

'What did you say his surname was?'

Julia is sitting at my desk, her eyes focused on my computer keyboard.

'March,' I reply. 'Alistair March. He's a first year International Relations student.'

Julia leans back from the keyboard and turns to look at me. 'You must never *ever* tell anyone I did this,' she whispers, 'especially Marie-Claire.' I nod. 'Not only is it illegal; if I'm found out it could cost me my job and incur a huge fine for the university.'

'Of course not,' I say softly. 'It's our secret.'

I watch as she enters her password to access the student database, then enters *March, A.* A photograph appears. It's him. Then a list of subheadings, including *enrolment*, *assessments* and *personal information*.

'Here we are.' Julia squints to read the small text. 'Alistair March. Agnes Blackadder, eh?' she mutters softly to herself. 'He must have a bit of dosh.' I make a mental note to remember that name and look it up later. She turns to me. 'It looks like he's requested an early check in.'

I give her a quizzical look.

'He's here,' she replies. 'Alistair March is in Scotland.'

I force myself to exhale, slow and steady. 'Where?'

'What?'

'Where is he staying?'

'No, no, *no*,' says Julia, holding her hands up in protest. 'Confirming he's in Scotland is one thing, but giving you his personal details, that's another.'

'But how am I going to speak to him?'

'You won't,' says Julia sharply. 'If you really believe Desra has been having inappropriate relations with her students then this is not just about your niece and this boy, but a wider safeguarding issue. You have to go to the authorities.'

It feels like my carefully constructed facade is crumbling.

'It's just supposition Julia. I have no concrete proof. How can I go to the authorities without proof?' I remember trying to convince a reluctant Lisa to come to the police station with me – *I won't go back there* – and I add, 'That's why I need to speak to him.'

Julia downs the last of the vodka from her plastic cup, crumples it and throws it in the bin. 'I'm sorry, Kate, but I can't help you with this.'

I attend dinner with a pasted-on smile and a plan in mind. I let Julia and Marie-Claire get far too close. Now I need to step back and make sure they do too.

During the starter we talk about the weather, and throughout the main course I persuade the couple to tell me all about their wedding plans.

'Bali,' says Marie-Claire with a sigh. 'Sun, sea and no family.'

'Are they a problem?' I ask, after a bite of cod wrapped in prosciutto.

'No,' responds Julia brightly, 'just annoying.'

She seems to have put our earlier conversation aside, satisfied with my promise that I will go to the police on Friday with what evidence I have.

By the pudding course, we are on to our pieces for Friday's masterclass.

'It's about love, fidelity and honesty,' says Marie-Claire, describing a sestina she has been working on.

'Sunsets,' mutters Julia, when asked about hers.

Claiming a headache, I beg out of the literature quiz in the boathouse, and retreat to my room to prepare. I have put together as much evidence as possible, including the diary; the photograph of Michael, Lisa and Desra; the photograph of Alistair; and a screenshot of the poem 'Carnation'. I've also written up everything Lisa told me.

'It's not enough, though, is it?' I throw the documents

324

on the bed in frustration. I know now more than ever that what I need is an eyewitness; or even better, a victim.

I get through the next morning's session like an automaton; smiling and nodding when necessary, when really all I can think about is this afternoon's free time. The minutes seem to tick by with intolerable lethargy. Desra manages the session, based on how to read poetry aloud, with her usual minimal attention combined with an infantile self-centredness. '*Watch how I do it.*' By twelve o'clock I am ready to scream.

'Okay, everyone,' she says, finally. 'I'm impressed with the work you've done today and I'm confident none of you will embarrass yourselves tomorrow.'

'Cheers,' mutters Julia.

'What's he like?' asks Sally. 'Professor Cardew. I've heard so much about him.'

'All will be revealed tomorrow,' Desra replies, clasping her hands together. I wish I had the courage to step up onto the stage and punch her right in her self-satisfied face. 'I've still got a lot to do to prepare for tomorrow's reading, so as a surprise I've brought in a guest who will be leading a session after lunch on editing – the most important skill of all,' she adds glibly. 'That will finish at two, and afterwards you can spend the time writing, practising, or using some of the sports facilities on site.'

Everything seems to be fitting right into place.

35

After the editing workshop I tell the group that I'm planning to go hiking and probably won't be back until dinner.

'Don't forget to let reception know your route,' says Becky cheerfully. 'In case you get lost, or break a leg or fall into a bog.'

'Yeah, thanks.'

I put on my hiking boots, but instead of taking the path that leads to the loch, I double back to my car. Then I make the forty-five-minute drive to St Andrews and Agnes Blackadder Hall, the hall of residence Julia inadvertently let slip earlier.

When I arrive, I'm surprised to see it's not the damp, crumbling Georgian building I'd expected, with poor security and blocked-open back doors. It's a modern structure with over three hundred rooms. It looks more like a conference centre than student digs.

I berate myself for my carelessness. I must have clicked on the wrong link when I was looking it up on the website. How on earth am I going to find Alistair in this labyrinth? I wish now that I had paid more attention when Julia was entering her login details to the student database.

I drive to a nearby Starbucks for a coffee and a chance to think. I'm struggling with what to do next when I see a small group of people emerging from the superstore next door. They're carrying cartons of wine, boxes of beer, and what appears to be the makings of a barbecue. I throw my cup of coffee in the bin and head into Tesco.

I wait outside the key card entrance into Agnes Blackadder Hall with my bottle of Jack Daniels, bag of snacks, and bale of towels.

'Excuse me?' I say to the first studenty-looking girl I see approaching. 'I'm here to see my nephew.' I hold out my offerings. 'I've brought him a little something to settle in, and, well, I wanted to surprise him.' The student – young, pretty and trusting – smiles politely. 'I wonder if you might know him. His name is Alistair. He's Canadian. He arrived early.' She shakes her head, mutters an apology, and moves on.

I could buzz reception and try the same approach, but I decide it's too risky. Instead, I wait patiently for the next student, and the next. Finally, three well-built young men, clearly athletes, approach.

'Excuse me,' I say, and begin my deception once again.

'Alistair!' says one of the lads, after I finish. 'Canadian chap. Nice. Arrived last week. Third floor by the fire escape.' The other two nod in agreement. They smell of fresh air and beer. 'If you want to surprise him, we'll have to sneak you past reception,' he says with a grin.

This is working out better than I had expected.

I make it to the third floor, grateful that my accomplices got off the lift on the second, then make my way to flat 3F, the one next to the fire escape. I take a breath and knock on the door. From inside I hear a deep voice call, 'What do you dickheads want now?' and then the door is pulled open and I am staring into the eyes of Alistair March, the one and only person who may be able to prove my suspicions about Desra McKinley.

'Yes?' he says. Now that I am closer, I can see that this is definitely the same person in the photograph with Desra. He's wearing jeans and a t-shirt. The outline of his muscular torso is clearly visible through the thin, white cotton.

'Alistair?' My voice sounds small. 'Alistair March?'

His eyes narrow in distrust. 'Who wants to know?'

I attempt a smile. 'My name is Kate Hardy. My son Michael was a swimmer like you.' I take the photograph of Michael, Lisa and Desra and push it towards him. 'Six years ago, to be precise.'

I watch as he scans the image, his expression changing from suspicion to shock when he spots Desra. His face goes very pale.

'May I speak with you, please?'

'I, ah, don't—'

'Please,' I beg. 'Something happened to Michael six years ago.' I tap my finger on the image of Desra McKinley. 'Something she did. I need to find out what.'

I can see his struggle; his fear. Finally, his expression softens. 'You'd better come in.'

He steps back, allowing me to pass through the doorway and into the room beyond.

I wait for him to place the cup of coffee on the desk next to me before speaking.

'Thank you for seeing me.' I take a small sip from a mug that reads *Life is for the Living!* 'I realise it must be a bit odd, my showing up like this.'

Alistair regards me with a mixture of caution and curiosity. 'What exactly do you want from me, Mrs Hardy?'

'Just to ask you a few questions.'

He points to the photograph I've put on the desk in front of him. 'About her?' I nod. He runs his hand across his freckled jawline. 'You said something about your son?'

'Michael,' I reply. I indicate to the photo. 'That's him sitting next to her.'

'Any good?' he asks.

'Pardon?'

'You said he's a swimmer. Any good?'

'Decent,' I smile. 'But not up to your standard.' He knows why I'm here, I'm sure of it; but I have to proceed very cautiously. I don't want to scare him off.

'The thing is,' I clear my throat. My mouth is so dry. 'Michael kept a diary.' Alistair looks at me in surprise, but I carry on. 'And in this diary, he indicates that he had a relationship with Desra McKinley. A sexual relationship.'

'Woah!' Alistair jumps up as if stung, knocking against the coffee table, and sloshing half the contents of my coffee mug onto the carpet. 'Shit!' he cries. 'I'll lose my damage deposit.'

'Get some loo roll,' I say, cupping my hands at the end of the table to stop more coffee dripping on the carpet, 'and wet wipes if you've got them.' Alistair escapes to the en suite, returning seconds later with a loo roll and a packet of wipes. 'Let me,' I say, kneeling on the floor. 'The trick is to dab, not rub.'

'Thank you,' Alistair mutters after I've cleaned up. 'I've only just moved in and I'm already trashing the place.'

'I didn't mean to shock you,' I say, suddenly aware of his vulnerability. He's standing by the window, his broad torso partially blocking out the light, 'but there's something I need to show you.'

Overcome by curiosity, he steps forward. I show him the photo of him and Desra at the swimming competition. There is a pause: time stills like a dying helium balloon, suspended between floor and ceiling.

'Shit!' Alistair cries. 'Shit!'

'I'm so, *so* sorry,' I whisper. 'The last thing I wanted

330

is for anyone else to go through what Michael did.'

'So why are you?' he whimpers. 'Making me go through it!'

'She's still around,' I say, forcing myself to stay calm. 'Desra McKinley is still around, and still teaching. In fact she's a teacher at Lennoxton Academy less than fifty miles from here.'

Alistair seems embarrassed, ashamed, and for a moment the six-foot-two athlete looks like the fifteen-year-old schoolboy who was taken advantage of all those years before.

'You knew,' I whisper.

Alistair lifts his chin, and his expression hardens. 'What if I did?'

'People like her don't stop, Alistair. They just find fresh prey.'

'You don't know anything about her!' he yells, and stomps his way past me to the en suite, where he splashes cold water on his face, before returning to face me.

I know just about everything about her.

'Not only did Desra have a sexual relationship with Michael,' – my voice has a cool assurance that surprises me – 'which is an illegal act in this country by the way; she was also with him the night that he died.'

'What?' Alistair's face takes on the pale countenance of a death mask. 'He's dead?'

'He drowned, six years ago.' I bite back the tears. 'He was only fifteen.' Alistair shakes his head, seemingly unable to comprehend. I hold up the

331

picture. 'Look at him!' I watch his gaze shift to the image, then away.

'I – I don't . . .' His eyes are shiny, and he hastily swipes a tear from his freckled cheek.

In a moment of unconscious compassion – I'm a mother too after all – I lay my hand on his. 'I'm so sorry this happened to you, Alistair.'

'Why are you doing this?' He pulls his hand away so fiercely that I nearly lose my balance and topple backwards. He grabs my wrist to steady me, and the simple act of kindness, of care, seems to drain him of all anger. He begins to cry. My heart breaks. 'Why couldn't you just leave it all alone?'

'Leave it all alone?' I take a few steps to the window. On the bedside table is a tidy arc of framed photographs. I lean forward to study them more closely. 'I only found out a few months ago myself, about Michael and Desra.' There is an image of Alistair as a youngster with his parents, and someone who I assume is an older sister; pale like her brother and with the same bright auburn hair.

'Your sister?' I ask, pointing to the photograph. He gives a curt nod. 'They must be proud of you winning a scholarship and coming all this way to study.'

'My sister thinks it's cool that I'm studying at the same uni Prince William did, but my parents . . .' he trails off and looks as if he's going to cry again.

'They didn't want you to come?'

He doesn't reply but the look on his face says it all. I wonder if they had any inkling that their son was coming to study in Scotland so he could be near Desra. Once again I am reminded of the enduring damage that woman has left in her wake. I return my attention to the photos, to the flame-haired sister, now grown up, married, and standing with her husband in front of a baptismal font holding a baby dressed in a cream gown with pale blue piping.

'Your nephew?' Alistair nods. I place my hand on the bedframe for support. 'I want you to come with me to the St Andrews police station. To report Desra McKinley for the historic grooming and sexual exploitation of minors.' The time to play it safe has long since passed. I return my gaze to the image of the sleeping baby at the font, run my fingertips across the ornate frame. 'Would you want *him* to have to go through something like that?'

Alistair's complexion turns crimson.

'How fucking dare you!' he roars. I find myself cowering against the wall. 'You come here, out of nowhere, to emotionally blackmail me!' He's in front of me, his large frame looming. 'I'm doing a work placement next summer with a top firm in Japan. How do you think it would look if I'm involved in some sort of sex scandal? How do you think it would affect my career?'

My mouth drops open. 'Your *career*? Innocent people have died, more are at risk, and all you can think about is your career?'

Alistair steps back as if struck. Stumbling towards the desk he grabs the bottle of Jack Daniels from the gift bag, then two shot glasses from the shelf above. He cracks open the bottle and pours two shots. He downs one and places the other on the desk. 'Drink it,' he snarls, 'and then get out.'

36

It is dusk by the time I reach the stag-framed gates of Lennoxton. I have spent most of the afternoon sitting in an anonymous car park, overlooking an anonymous beach, sipping endless cups of lukewarm coffee. With no Alistair, there is no concrete proof. With no concrete proof, there is no conviction. With no conviction, there is Desra with a publishing deal, a possible teaching post at a prestigious private school in Rhode Island, and a catalogue of discarded innocents behind her with no avenue to justice or recompense. Michael is just dust – collateral in Desra's relentless rise to glory. The truth is like a dart in my vein, spreading poison to every tributary, accruing in my heart.

I fake my way through dinner, but I can only manage the final night's celebrations with wine, wine, and more wine. As the group moves outside for a singsong by the bonfire, I escape to my room. The dormitory is silent and unpeopled. I sneak into Julia and Marie-Claire's room and slip the bottle of vodka from the desk drawer where I know Julia keeps it. In a moment of despair and disgrace, I search through the lining of my bag for a blue pill. With a gasp of relief I find one, nestled in amongst old shopping receipts and a lost stamp. I gulp it down with a slug of vodka and retreat under the bedcovers. Later, when I hear a knock on my door and Marie-Claire's worried voice, I turn my face to the wall.

I sleep badly, dreaming I am walking hand in hand along a forest path with Michael. Water oozes from his every pore, trickles down his body and pools at his feet. He opens his mouth to speak but something blocks his breath. I reach into his mouth, past his blackened tongue and deep into his throat. I feel something thin and slimy. It squirms beneath my fingertips. I pull it free and fling it to the ground. An eel. Its greasy body swivels and squirms as it wraps itself around my feet. Grabbing a large stone, I pound it against the creature's head, smashing its tiny bulb-like eyes into oblivion. Slowly the creature transforms into something different; something human. When I look closer, I see Desra McKinley's ruined face on the ground in front of me.

I wake bathed in sweat, with a terrifying sense of the walls closing in. Throwing on my clothes, I race from the dormitory and into the night.

Moonlight has transformed the loch into an undulating silvery blanket. A breeze blows in from the east, drying the perspiration that dots my forehead. Open water had once been my salvation: a place where I could find peace. From the moment I could sit up, I would go out with my father in his rowing boat. Later, there were canoeing trips along the Tamar with Brethren friends, and in my early teens, clandestine wild swimming with Ryan on moonlit nights. I would sneak back into the house soaking wet, teeth chattering, pulling at the thin tendrils of wet hair curled around the nape of my neck. The next morning my mother would sniff loudly and claim the house had damp.

I slip off my trainers and dig my toes deep into the freezing sand. The scent of pine drifts on the cool night air. I find myself walking towards the water. I shed my jeans, my t-shirt, and lay them on a mossy boulder. I stare out at the loch; feel the night's cool breath on my skin. Water calls to me: hypnotic; deceitful.

Dressed only in a bra and pants I take a few tentative steps and splash water on my knees, thighs, stomach. It's like ice crystals on my skin. I'm up to my waist now and moving deeper. It's so very, very cold. I feel my nipples tighten and a pleasant numbness in my feet. Stretching forward, I reach out my arms and begin to swim. On and on I go, farther and farther from the shore. Some unseen force is driving me onwards. I think of Michael and our practice sessions in the river, of our unspoken understanding of the power and serenity of deep water. I haven't felt so peaceful in months. Maybe I'm asleep.

I feel a searing pain: shards penetrating my skin. As if lifted from a trance, I find myself awake to the world around me. What I see fills me with horror. I am at least a hundred metres from the shore. A breeze has picked up, forcing the inky waves against my numb body, and pushing me even deeper into the loch. I struggle forwards, but my arms ache and my legs are like lead. Beneath me, a swirling current drags me on. I kick, fighting against my enemies, wind and tide. I make it a few metres closer to shore before my muscles seize.

I should scream for help; wave my arms like that hapless hero in that GCSE poem, but why bother? No one is around: no one will care. I attempt one final push, but I'm tired, defeated. Was this how Michael felt? I imagine myself sinking; my pale, bloated body settling amongst the silt, my flesh food for zebra mussels. I hear a sound – splashing – and then, astoundingly, I feel an arm slip beneath mine.

'Kate!' It's a male voice: deep; resonant.

'Caleb?'

'Hang on to me, Kate – don't let go.'

I hook my arm around Caleb's neck. He swims with one arm, the other supporting my back. I can feel the power of him as he kicks, and hear his laboured breathing as he pounds his way towards the shore. With one final, agonising effort he lifts me onto the sand. We both lie exhausted, coughing and panting. He covers my shoulders with his dry shirt.

'Are you okay?' he asks, rubbing my hands between his. 'You're freezing.'

'I didn't mean to go out so far,' I whisper through chattering teeth.

'Water at night is always deceptive.'

'If you hadn't been here . . .'

'I was,' he says; and he puts his arm around me to warm me further. In the moonlight, his face is marble.

'I thought I could do it,' I say, biting back a sob.

'You did.' There's something like admiration in his voice. 'You were.'

'Hardly,' I reply. Then, in confusion, I ask, 'How did you know I was here?'

'I'm not a great sleeper,' he replies. 'I often go out at night. I was walking past the outdoor adventure centre when I saw you race past. You seemed upset. Disorientated.'

'It's all such a mess,' I say, no longer bothering to hide my tears. Caleb says nothing, just holds me tighter. 'I wanted to prove to myself that I could do it; that I could conquer the water, for Michael.'

He pulls back and studies my face, trying to put two and two together; making assumptions.

'Well, the first thing I would say to you is that water is generally unconquerable.' His voice is kind. 'And the second is that you certainly gave it your best go. You were swimming so quickly that by the time I reached the shore you had nearly disappeared.' He gets up and collects my clothes from the rock where I left them. My fingers are so cold and stiff he has to help me to get dressed.

'I'm such an idiot!'

'You're in pain.' Caleb leans forward and takes my face in his hands. 'There's nothing wrong with admitting that.' He is so close that I can feel the warmth of his breath on my cheek. He kisses me. I feel the strength in his body; the question in his lips. I respond with an intensity that surprises me. His hand slides under my shirt and circles my waist, pulling me in. My body is molten. Taking me by the hand, Caleb leads me back to the dorms.

37

I wake to the beginnings of sunlight and the murmurs of a collared dove. Next to me, Caleb dozes contentedly. I kiss his neck and delight in the simple pleasure of watching him sleep. In a few hours, the bustle of our fellow students will force us into wakefulness and secrecy, but for now, there is just his warm body against mine.

I drift in and out of consciousness, waking finally to an empty space in the bed beside me. There is a knock on my door and seconds later I feel someone tickling my toes.

'Wake up, chérie,' murmurs Marie-Claire. 'You don't want to miss the opportunity to read your poem to Professor Cardew, do you?'

I turn over and look into her smiling face.

'Where's Julia?'

Marie-Claire's expression hardens. 'Hungover,' she sighs. 'I'm not sure this summer school was such a great idea.'

'I hope I didn't ruin it for you both.'

'It's nothing to do with you, my darling,' says Marie-Claire with an embarrassed smile. 'This is perhaps just a little bit too far out of her comfort zone.' She points to my bedside table. 'A cup of tea for you, and I will expect both you and my fiancée in the canteen for breakfast in fifteen minutes.'

'Yes, ma'am.' I attempt a feeble salute. 'And thank you.'

'*De rien.*' Marie-Claire smiles and taps a finger against her watch. 'See you downstairs.'

I quickly shower, dress, and apply makeup, concentrating on the dark circles under my eyes. I make a concerted effort to be bright and cheerful at breakfast. I haven't spoken to Julia since we accessed the student database at St Andrews University. I suspect that she has already worked out the reason for my absence most of yesterday evening, because there is a new frostiness in her demeanour. Caleb, I am told, has already come and gone.

'Everything all right?' Julia enquires, not looking up from where she is buttering her toast.

'Fine.'

She glances up and our eyes meet, a silent exchange of both knowledge and guilt.

'I'm glad you both managed to drag yourself from your beds,' says Marie-Claire, placing a large cafetière on the table in front of us. She studies my face, her eyes creasing in concern. 'You look very pale. Did you get any sleep last night?'

342

'I'm fine,' I reply and force a smile. 'Really.'

Marie-Claire places a splash of warm milk into a mug, adds coffee and slides it towards me. 'And the situation with your niece?'

'Sorted,' I reply. 'I spoke to her yesterday.' I sneak a peek at Julia, but she is studiously checking emails on her phone. 'I'm grateful to both of you for all your patience and support.'

Bright and cheerful. Bright, and cheerful.

'Just glad it's all sorted,' says Julia, with little conviction.

Marie-Claire gives us both a curious glance. 'Speaking of being sorted,' she says, 'we'd better hurry up and finish our breakfast. I don't know about you, but I don't want to miss a moment of our masterclass.'

'Not like I care.'

'Julia!'

'Well, it's not like I've ever disguised my dislike of this whole ridiculous exercise.'

There is a moment of silence as Marie-Claire takes in her fiancée's words.

'Ridiculous exercise?'

'A shambles,' Julia mutters, and I watch as Marie-Claire's ebony cheeks slowly grow rosy. 'That ludicrous McKinley woman with her flagrant self-promotion and arrogance. A domestic drama that I didn't really want to have any part in.' She avoids looking at me, but the implication is clear. 'And now a so-called *masterclass* in which we're supposed to be grateful for being given the opportunity to read our mediocre work aloud to some poetic has-been!'

'What has gotten into you!' I can see that Marie-Claire is close to tears.

'I'm tired of the bullshit,' her fiancée replies, and throwing her napkin down, pushes back her chair and storms from the dining hall.

'I'll talk to her,' I say. 'Why don't we meet you at the theatre in a bit?'

Marie-Claire nods and blows her nose. 'She always gets like this when she drinks too much.'

I rush to follow Julia out into the quad where she is lighting a cigarette. 'I didn't know you smoked?'

'I don't,' says Julia, taking a deep drag. 'I nicked one of Marie-Claire's.'

'You're angry with me, aren't you?'

'Furious.' Julia's jaw tightens. 'I saw you yesterday afternoon leaving, in your car. You went to St Andrews, didn't you?'

There's no point in denying it. 'Yes.'

'And did you find him?'

'I did.'

Julia takes another drag, angrily blowing smoke out through her nostrils. 'What if he complains to the university? What if they check who logged into the student database and put two and two together?'

'He won't.' I think of the look on his face when I told him that Desra was in Scotland, and that he clearly knew. 'You've got nothing to worry about, Julia. There's no reason for him or anyone else to suspect your involvement.'

'That's not the point, though, is it?' she says.

'I should have never done it in the first place, and you should have never asked me to.'

This isn't the first time I am being forced to question my conduct, and probably won't be the last. 'I'm sorry, Julia, I really am, but McKinley's got away with too much for far too long.'

Julia drops the cigarette, taking her time to grind it into the gravel at her feet.

'What did he say?'

I know what she means, but I take my time answering. 'It's clear they were together at Lakeview.' I breathe in deeply, desperate for any last remnants of her cigarette smoke. 'And he knows she's here, in Scotland.'

'Jesus.' She sighs, then, studying me with fierce intensity, she says, 'What's the big *but*?'

I look up at the clear blue sky above. 'He got a work placement lined up next summer with a *top* company in Japan.' I feel the tears falling. 'Says a *sex scandal* could ruin his future career.' I'm glad of a nearby bench and I stumble my way towards it. I feel it give as Julia sits down beside me.

'You never said if your niece mentioned any inappropriate behaviour.'

'What?'

'From McKinley.' Julia's expression is flint-like. 'You said Lisa visited her flat.'

'Yes, but—'

'And did McKinley do anything? Try anything?'

'I don't know,' I reply. 'Why are you asking me this?'

Julia sighs again and runs her fingers through her thick, blonde curls. 'I'm sure there's something going on between her and Turner. She's hardly discreet, is she? Getting him to drive her to Edinburgh, tarting herself up every time he's anywhere in the vicinity. They stayed in the boathouse the other night drinking together until God knows when.'

'But Marie-Claire said . . .'

Julia gives a wry smile. 'Marie-Claire would give Hannibal Lecter the benefit of the doubt.'

'Do you think I should talk to him?'

Julia gives a derisory snort. 'If you want answers, Turner's not the one to talk to. Becky is.'

I head back to my room to brush my teeth and collect my notebook before the masterclass. On the desk sits the green file folder I started six years ago, a few weeks after Michael's death. It contains police and coroner's reports, photos, emails, handwritten notes and action plans, letters, newspaper clippings, research, spreadsheets, and even the weather forecast the night that Michael died. Was all this for nothing? The summer school ends tonight after Cardew's lecture and I have nothing more concrete than I started with. I stare at my pale reflection in the mirror, slowly raise my fist, and begin pounding it against my head.

'Idiot,' I mutter, 'loser,' and from somewhere deep inside comes the word '*sinner*'.

I think of my brief sprint of activism while at university – I joined a protest group for human rights in Darfur, and followed the Italian human rights group 'Non c'è Pace Senza Giustizia' – No Peace Without Justice. I could never have imagined how deeply it would resonate with me fifteen years later.

I grab Michael's diary and make my way to Desra McKinley's office.

The door is open, and I find her sitting at her desk flipping through the proof copy of *Carnation*.

'Kate,' she says brightly, 'how are you?' I pause, uncertain how to step beyond that tainted threshold. 'What can I do for you?'

'I need to speak to you.'

'Of course.' She moves towards the two-seater settee at the back of the room and sits down. 'Come,' she says, patting the cushion beside her, 'sit.'

The diary is soft and sweaty in my hand. I step towards her.

'*Desra!*' I hear a voice behind me. I turn to see a middle-aged man, bearded, dishevelled, and carrying what looks like a ream of loose-leaf paper in his arms. 'I'm having a bloody awful time with my notes.'

She gives a soft, girlish, giggle; nothing like the woman who has been teaching us for the last four days. 'Oh Findlay, you are a sight.' I feel as if I've stepped into an Alan Ayckbourn farce. 'Kate,' she says. 'May I introduce you to Professor Findlay Cardew.'

I attempt a pleasant smile, but Professor Cardew is clearly not interested.

'I can't decide which is the best couplet,' he says, stepping past me.

'No need to worry,' Desra purrs. 'I'm sure they're all wonderful.'

I dig my fingernails into the soft leather of the diary. There is a brief, intimate moment as she moves close to straighten his tie.

'Professor Cardew?' I turn to see the receptionist, Mrs Roe, standing in the doorway. 'The reporter from the *Perth Courier* is here.'

If it's possible for Cardew to look any more flustered, he does. 'You must come, Desi,' he pleads. 'I need you.'

'Sorry, Kate. Duty calls. Can this wait?' Desra says, with a nonchalant air that tells me she doesn't really care whether I say yes or no.

And before I can say another word, they are striding past me and out of the room.

Mrs Roe clears her throat. 'I really must lock up,' she says, indicating for me to leave. As I make my way down the hall, I see Turner approaching.

'Everything all right?'

He gives that 100-watt smile. 'Of course Mrs Hardy, I was just hoping to talk to Desra.'

I'm slightly surprised by his casual use of the teacher's first name, but this is summer school after all, not term time, and maybe Lennoxton has a more casual approach to teacher-student relationships. I hope not.

'She's gone off somewhere with Professor Cardew.' I study him closely. Gone is the bum fluff of a beard he was trying to grow, replaced by a cleanshaven face. He smells of aftershave and expensive cologne. I'm suddenly struck by the fact Michael requested a bottle of expensive eau de toilette for his fifteenth birthday, and try to push away the image of my son splashing Paco Rabanne on his smooth cheeks before meeting her.

I walk in silence to the Ishutin Building, my desperate mood clinging to me like a Highland mist. Why didn't I stop them? *Just a minute, Desra. Professor Cardew, I'd like to speak to Dr McKinley in private please.* And why didn't I ask Turner? *Are you having a relationship with Dr McKinley? Did you know that even though you are over the age of consent for sexual activity, in the eyes of the law you are still considered vulnerable to sexual abuse and exploitation, and it's my duty to report it?*

Nothing. I did nothing. Self-loathing rages through me. I failed. I let Turner down, just like I let Michael down. My courage has evaporated and all that's left is a deep, festering anger.

I make my way down the stairs and into the darkened theatre where my classmates are waiting. I take a seat in the far corner, in the shadows. My mind is scattered, unsettled. I need to regain my self-control. There's the sound of a far door being opened, and then footsteps. Everyone turns to see Desra and Professor Cardew take their places on the stage. I feel my lips curl back in disgust.

'Before we start,' begins McKinley, 'I want to introduce our guest of honour today: Professor Findlay Cardew.' She turns and gazes reverently at the gentleman beside her. 'Many of you know him as an esteemed Scottish poet and recipient of the Saltire Poetry Book Prize, but he is also delivering the final lecture in Lennoxton's prestigious summer lecture series this evening, in this very auditorium.'

'Whoopee!' mutters Julia from behind me, which is followed almost immediately by a swift 'Hush!' from Marie-Claire.

For the next hour, Cardew regales us with anecdotes about his life as a 'distinguished' poet, after-dinner speaker and minor celebrity.

'Shall we begin our feedback session?' Desra eventually asks, interrupting Cardew's account of his liaison with a Croatian glamour model.

The first reading is from Marvin and Roz: a touching piece about how their pets became a substitute for their much-yearned-for children. Caleb's contribution is an extraordinary and highly structured piece about salvation. Sally follows with a hilarious poem about middle-aged libido; and, finally, it's my turn.

I swallow hard and step onto the stage. I clear my throat and try to say the first few words. My voice feels small: unmanageable. I don't think I can do it.

'Remember what I said about reading aloud.' Desra approaches and stepping onto the stage behind me, gently begins rubbing my shoulders. 'Relax, clear your mind. Now a breath, not into your chest, but deeper.' She takes my hand and places it on my lower abdomen. An image of Michael lying naked next to her, his head on her lap, bursts into my mind and makes me snatch my hand away in disgust.

I pick up my notebook. On the page in front of me is an innocuous poem about Celtic myths that I have been working on half-heartedly for the last few days. I find myself flipping to the last page instead: my secret poem. It is a work of fury and spite; an exploration of utter pain, one that I had never imagined reading aloud.

'I'm fine, Desra.' I wait for her to retake her seat, and then I begin.

Moonlight lingers
on the pale abandon
of
your
skin.

Bodies entangle,
contort,
the greedy tendrils
of
your
Sin

Unnatural lovers
Distort
The shifting moonlight
Into slivers
Of sharp-toothed night.

And deep under water
where no fish swim,

351

He
Still
Lives

I am the bone deep, lone keep
custodian of his light.
I am Witiko
Unblinking avenger
Who will not sleep this night.

I am every god and goddess,
Every fate and justice
I am tireless, resolute
A sleeping shark
A pay back in the dark.

I am here. Waiting. I am Diving Fish.

I know my piece is shocking, unexpected, and I think I have failed, but peering into the gloom, I spot Desra, frozen to the spot, her gaping mouth reminding me of my stroke-ridden mother at mealtimes. Then, as if having been shaken by the shoulders, she seems to collect herself and resumes her duties.

'Wonderful, Kate, wonderful.' Her voice sounds far away, ghostlike. 'You really have come a long way.'

Maybe it is the mental image of Desra and Michael together, or maybe the fact that this is the last day of summer school and I haven't achieved half of what I set out to, but there's no time to falter. No more waiting.

'I'll let Findlay offer some feedback,' Desra adds, forcing a smile. She steps back into the shadows and is gone.

'Very interesting use of metaphor and repetition,' begins Cardew, but I'm not listening.

'Did you see the look on her face?' whispers Julia, as I sit down beside her.

I catch the familiar sent of musk and then someone whispers in my ear.

'Was it something you said, chérie?'

38

I wait until after lunch before returning to the Ishutin Building. A banner has been placed across the front with the words *Lennoxton Summer Lecture Series* in large letters. A catering van is parked outside, and a steady stream of workers are transporting boxes of wine glasses, frozen canapés and prosecco into the building. As I step inside, I can hear one of the festival organisers giving instructions to the group of volunteers.

'Make sure you work the room,' the woman says. 'And no more than two glasses of plonk per person. The budget on this event is tight.' I scan the backs of their heads, searching for one in particular. 'Back here at five p.m. precisely, where you'll be given your station for reception drinks and canapés. Attire is black trousers, shoes not trainers, and a clean white shirt or blouse.' The group begins to break up and she is forced to yell above the noise, 'And don't forget to collect your waistcoats from Jeremy on the way out!'

I step back outside and watch as a cluster of people passes. At last, the person I have been waiting for approaches.

'Becky?'

The blonde American looks over in surprise. 'Mrs Hardy,' she says, giving me one of her automatic smiles.

I smile in return. 'May I speak with you for a moment?' We wander over to the water fountain. 'Excited about tonight?'

The teenager shrugs. 'I'm just handing out glasses of cheap prosecco.'

'Nice,' I say, pointing to the gaudy tartan waistcoat she is holding that all the catering staff are forced to wear.

'Atrocious,' scowls Becky. She slips the waistcoat over her t-shirt, where it hangs loosely.

'I think you can adjust it at the back so that it fits better.' I step behind Becky and slide the buckle to the left, pulling the cloth ribbon through to tighten it. 'Better?'

'A little,' says Becky. 'Thanks.'

I take a breath. 'There's something I want to ask you,' and the rest of the words come spilling out, 'and I hope you don't think I'm sticking my nose in where it doesn't belong.'

Becky can't disguise her curiosity. 'Go ahead, Mrs Hardy.'

'I'm not sure if you know that I'm a nurse, and

that I've worked with young people in schools, clinics. Safeguarding. That sort of thing.'

Becky tilts her head sideways as if scrutinising me from a different perspective. 'And what does that have to do with me?'

'Not so much you, as Turner.'

'Turner? What about Turner?'

It's clear I have hit a nerve. 'I really don't know how to put this—'

'Put what?'

This is proving a lot harder than I imagined. 'I'm a little concerned. About Turner. About his relationship with Dr McKinley.'

'What relationship?' She sounds defensive, almost hostile.

'It's just that, well, we've all noticed how close they seem.' I watch as the colour slowly rises from her neck, past her chin and settles on her cheeks. I can't stop now. 'That alone isn't a worry I suppose – I mean what student doesn't like a strong connection with his teacher?'

'A strong connection!' Becky cries. 'What do you mean by that?'

I look around. 'Calm down, Becky. There's nothing to worry about.'

'Nothing to worry about! You've just suggested to me that my boyfriend is having some sort of *relationship* with his teacher!'

'That's not what I said at all.' I employ the slow, easy tone I use with patients. I need to keep things under control, for the moment anyway. 'I was just concerned about what appears to be their unusual closeness. Is this typical, would you say?'

'Turner's friendly with everyone,' snaps Becky, but there is little conviction. 'That's just the way he is.'

'But all these trips to Edinburgh. Does she really need Turner to drive her there?'

Becky gives a tight smile. 'She suffers from car sickness. Has to take tablets that make her drowsy, so she can't drive.'

I feel a sick sensation in the pit of my stomach. 'What kind of tablets?'

Becky shakes her head in exasperation. 'How should I know?'

'But you're sure she takes the kind that make her drowsy?'

'That's what Turner said. That's why she needs him to drive her.'

Suddenly my head seems too heavy for my body and my legs weaken. I perch myself on the stone wall that borders the fountain and think back to the conversation I had with Grace only a few months before.

'You're the nurse. You're the one who told me that cyclizine causes drowsiness.'

'Michael didn't suffer from travel sickness. There's absolutely no reason he should have been taking that sort of medication.'

Becky sits down next to me. 'Are you all right, Mrs Hardy?'

I fight for control, but the knowledge that time is running out threatens to overwhelm me.

Becky takes a long, shaky breath. 'She's always fussing over him, you know? Touching his arm, chatting to him like they're mates or something. I know they were drinking together in the boathouse the other night; I saw them . . .' She absent-mindedly scrapes a speck of moss off the side off the wall with her fingernail. 'But it doesn't mean that they're . . .' she glances at me. 'Well, you know. Does it?'

'I don't know,' I say. 'But if I did know, or even suspect, I would have to do something about it.'

'Because it's not right, is it?' Becky says, almost to herself.

I'm operating on autopilot, still stunned by the realisation that Desra McKinley may have supplied my son with the medication that contributed to his death. 'No, it isn't,' I reply. 'Have you asked Turner about it?'

She gives a bitter laugh. 'Do you really think he'd tell me?'

'Maybe, maybe not. Have you asked *her*?'

Becky's eyes narrow and a fiendish smile plays at the corner of her mouth. 'Now that *would* be interesting, wouldn't it, but maybe *asking* isn't quite the way to put it.'

39

A tangible sense of energy and excitement hangs in the air as the final touches for Findlay Cardew's lecture are put into place. A marquee has been erected and extra staff have been called in to help with security and to direct parking. The mobile catering van is now standing under a large oak, offering food ranging from haggis to vegan curries, and tables and chairs are being set up for early arrivals from Edinburgh or Perth who may require a bite to eat or a gin and tonic. I barely take in the activity as I make my way from my meeting with Becky towards the senior dormitories. Becky's revelation that Desra took travel sickness medication, possibly containing the same chemicals that were found in Michael's blood-stream the night he died, has unnerved me more than I can say. It's time to act. I've dithered long enough.

On my bed the pile of A4 envelopes I bought at a post office in St Andrews yesterday, along with photocopies I made of everything I have on Desra: photos, emails, texts, and also including my own notes on my meeting with Alistair, and Turner's questionable relationship with her. They are addressed to the head teacher and the eleven members of the governing council, including the chair, the Very Reverend James Simpson. All will be attending Cardew's lecture this evening.

'There's nothing like bringing down the mighty,' I whisper, as I seal and address the envelopes. There is a knock at the door, and I hurriedly slip the envelopes under my pillow, next to Michael's diary.

'Yes?'

The door eases open and I'm surprised to see Sally's smiling face.

'I was wondering if you might need a little help getting ready.'

'Getting ready?'

'For tonight, you daft thing.' She sits down on the bed. 'I was a beautician in one of my previous incarnations. I can do your hair if you like?' I stare at her in amazement. 'You want to look your best, don't you?'

Sally has arranged my hair in a messy bun which looks both elegant and informal. I paint my lips a deep, blood red, imagining myself as a fair-haired Lady Macbeth. I had originally planned on wearing a floral summer dress, but instead I opt for a dark maxi dress with a low-cut back. I apply perfume to my wrists, behind my ears and in the groove between my breasts. Finally, as if lifted from a trance, I inhale deeply as I put on the pearl earrings Michael bought me. On the bed next to me is the bag with the envelopes containing the evidence I need to destroy Desra McKinley. All I need to do is find the right moment to hand it over. I imagine standing at the drinks reception, glass in hand, laughing with Marie-Claire and Julia, kissing Caleb on the lips. Desra will be waiting anxiously for the press to arrive. She will be so full of – almost overflowing with – self-importance. There will be the sound of footsteps and a door slamming. The headmaster and the Very Reverend Simpson will storm into the room, followed by a police inspector waving the brown envelopes accusingly. One by one, he will expose her catalogue of sins: her misconduct; her abuse.

'And what about this?' the headmaster will yell, forcing her to read the coroner's report. 'Cyclizine in his bloodstream? And you knew very well, didn't you, that mixed with alcohol it becomes a very dangerous drug indeed. Did you watch as he struggled? As he sank into the water? And then as he surfaced before he went under again? Did you hear his cries for help, the last sound he would ever make, before turning away in cruel abandonment?'

Desra will collapse to the floor, hysterical and remorseful, pleading for forgiveness. All around her the other guests will stare, their mouths open in disbelief; but I will be laughing. I will empty my glass, tip back my head and laugh. I won't stop laughing until the dark blot that is Desra McKinley is nothing more than a tiny black spot on the carpet that can be swept away and forgotten.

My crimson smile twists itself into a grimace of doubt. For that fantasy to come true, I should have gone to the police yesterday immediately after my meeting with Alistair. What's stopping me? Why haven't I been more determined?

I was never one for confrontation, never brave enough to make a scene. That was Grace's gift. I gained my ground in more surreptitious ways. When I was nine, I was bullied by a classmate. The name-calling, pinching and general torment went on for weeks. I bore it bravely, stoically, until one day, fed up with the abuse, I waited until I was alone on the stairwell with my tormentor. When no one was looking, I threw myself down the steps, claiming to have been pushed. Terrified of the bad publicity that would come with an accusation of religious intolerance, the bully was expelled. I didn't mind the fractured wrist. It was worth it.

Now though, sitting on the bed, the brown envelopes beside me, I wonder again if there really is enough evidence to convict that vile woman.

'Sorry, Alistair,' I whisper, knowing full well that once all is revealed, he will be forced to speak to the police.

I politely decline the invitation from Marie-Claire and Julia to join them for a drink before the event. When Caleb knocks and enters at half-past six, I have been sitting on the bed staring at the wall for nearly half an hour.

'Kate?'

He looks handsome in his pale linen suit and tie. His fair hair is slicked back and his tanned skin glowing. He sits down on the bed beside me. 'Kate, what's wrong?' The concern in his voice is poignant.

'I'm not sure.'

'Don't want to go to the lecture?' he asks.

I turn to him and counterfeit my brightest smile. 'Of course I do. I wouldn't miss this evening for the world.'

40

A sizeable crowd has already gathered outside the Ishutin Building. Inside, in a corner near the bar, a table and two chairs have been set up. Piles of Findlay Cardew's most recent poetry collection are stacked on the table, and next to that, a smaller pile of McKinley's Canadian anthology, along with a poster advertising *Carnation: to be released by Epiphany Press in the autumn*.

'Isn't this exciting?' says Caleb. He places his arm around my waist and gently leads me to where Becky is stationed.

'Mrs Hardy,' she says, holding out her tray. Caleb takes two glasses and hands one to me. I down it almost immediately. I watch as Becky scans the room, eyes finally settling on the handsome young man in a tartan waistcoat who is also distributing drinks to the crowd. Turner.

'Are you all right?' I ask. There is a slightly wild

look on her face and her unfocused expression suggests that she has been sampling the merchandise. She opens her mouth to reply when a sudden hush descends upon the room. From outside, the slow wail of a bagpipe commences, the sound growing louder as the piper mounts the steps and emerges into the foyer. Cardew, clad in full Highland dress, enters, accompanied by Desra McKinley. She's wearing what can only be described as a silk tango dress. As she strides confidently into the room, the pipe music stops, replaced by applause and hoots of appreciation. Smiling in delight, Desra does a dramatic swirl, finishing with a kick that exposes the dress's blood-red satin lining. With its strapless back and dramatic side slit, the outfit accentuates every curve of the lecturer's petite frame. She has clearly spent a lot of effort with her hair, slicking it back into shiny curls, and her makeup is flawless.

'She looks stunning.'

I turn to see Julia's normally critical disposition replaced by one of open admiration.

'Down girl,' chuckles Marie-Claire.

'She looks *so* different,' says Caleb, and I can tell that even he is entranced. Turner steps forward with his tray, offering drinks to both poets. McKinley takes a small sip, and then, placing a hand on Turner's arm, leans forward and whispers into his ear. There is a clink of crystal, and I turn to see Becky desperately attempting to steady her tray.

'Careful!' cries the catering manager, who stops to give her a talking to. The music recommences as the piper leads Cardew and McKinley into the auditorium, followed closely behind by the headmaster, the Very Reverend Simpson, and the eleven members of the Board of Governors.

Once everyone is seated, the headmaster takes the stage.

'Good evening everyone,' he says. 'Welcome to the final event in the highly successful summer lecture series hosted at Lennoxton Academy.' He goes on to explain the history of the school and their decision to host the series, ending his introduction with the words, 'But I can't take the credit for the conception and, indeed, delivery of what I hope will be an annual event.' He indicates to where Desra is seated. 'It's all down to Dr Desra McKinley, a sports performance expert who has coached a number of Olympic hopefuls, and as if that isn't enough, is also an internationally recognised poet. Dr McKinley has worked tirelessly to make this series a success. Therefore, and without further ado,' he continues, 'I would like to ask Dr McKinley to introduce our guest speaker, Professor Findlay Cardew.'

A wave of applause floods the theatre and both McKinley and Cardew stand and make their way to the two leather chairs that sit centre stage.

The lecture and subsequent Q&A session seem to go on for hours. All I can think about is the bag under my seat with the thirteen brown envelopes. Three rows ahead of me sits the headmaster and eleven governors, all dressed in their academic robes.

The Q&A finally finishes – now is the moment to hand them the evidence. *'There's something inside that is of the utmost importance to the reputation of the school.'* That's all I will say: any more would make them hesitant. Dubious. I certainly won't mention the words 'grooming' or 'sexual exploitation'.

I place a hand on Caleb's arm.

'Can I meet you in the foyer?' I whisper. 'I've got something I need to do.'

He gives me a quizzical look, and then seeing the seriousness of my expression, nods and kisses me on the cheek. 'Of course.'

I watch as he follows Julia and Marie-Claire out of the auditorium before I make my way along the aisle towards the governors.

'Wasn't that wonderful?' Sally is standing in front of me, blocking the way. 'I can't wait to get a signed copy of their books, can you?'

'What?' Unable to disguise my irritation, I attempt to push past her. 'Excuse me.'

The rest of the crowd are making their way up the stairs to the foyer, and I feel like a Pitlochry salmon swimming against the stream. Someone knocks against me and my bag falls to the ground, scattering the brown envelopes in every direction.

'Oh dear,' says Sally. 'Can I help?'

We spend the next few minutes retrieving the envelopes from under impatient feet and auditorium seats. By the time we have collected them all, the headmaster and the governors are gone. I race up the stairs to find them, hoping it is not too late.

The foyer is teeming with people; bodies shift and merge as guests impatiently make their way forwards for another glass of prosecco or a soggy canapé. Cardew and McKinley are chatting animatedly to a fortyish woman with a heavy gold chain around her neck: the Provost of Perth. Next to her, an attractive young woman records the exchange on her iPhone. Her guest pass reads *PRESS*. Finishing their chat, the two poets make their way towards the table. A small queue has formed, ready to purchase a personally signed copy of their anthologies. The headmaster and board members are nowhere in sight.

'Dammit!' I move through the crowd, desperately seeking out the black-robed governors. Why have I waited so long? I could have posted the envelopes this morning, or even left them with the school secretary. If I've missed this chance, I will never forgive myself.

There is the tinkling sound of metal on crystal and I look to see Desra tapping a spoon against her glass. The headmaster and governors, now free of their dark vestments, emerge from the cloakroom.

'Ladies and gentlemen,' Desra begins. 'Before we carry on with the signings, I would like to make an important announcement.' She leans forward and speaks quietly to Cardew, who responds with a smile. 'I am delighted to announce that Professor Cardew has been offered a prestigious visiting lecturer's post this autumn with The Department of Literary Arts at Brown University in Rhode Island.' There is a round of applause, which Desra silences with a raised hand. 'I am also pleased to say that I have been offered a teaching position in America and will be accompanying Professor Cardew.' She places a hand on his shoulder, which Cardew takes and raises to his lips.

I feel my mouth open, then almost immediately tighten shut in rage. So that was the reason for all those applications to American private schools. Desra is going *with Cardew* to America. Considering the dates on some of the job applications I found in her desk drawer the other day, she must have been planning to do so for months. Will riding on Cardew's coat tails advance her career? Will he be the next professionally useful husband?

I glance towards the headmaster whose face is blank with shock. Clearly he hasn't been informed that she is leaving. Has he been one more pawn in her plan?

I can feel my cheeks burning, and a thin sheen of perspiration glazes my forehead. There's no way I am going to allow Desra McKinley to get away again. I find myself moving forward, pausing only to pick up a cheese knife from the catering table. I make my way towards her, the knife clenched so firmly in my fist I can feel the bone handle cutting into my flesh. Desra is only inches away. Our eyes meet; her smile freezes. I lean forward, but before I can utter the words forming on my lips, there comes the sudden crash of breaking glass from the rear of the hall. All the guests turn to see Becky surrounded by shattered crystal flutes.

'*You screwed her, didn't you, Turner?*' she screams. A clearly drunk Turner, swaying like a puppet in the wind, does not reply. 'Why don't you just admit it?'

The guests stand frozen, engrossed. I think of one of those contemporary theatre experiences where the audience are expected to follow the actors around a performance space, eavesdropping on their lives.

'There's no use in denying it,' continues a now hysterical Becky. 'I saw you coming out of the boat-house with her the other night, and you weren't just drinking, were you?'

The crowded room is pin-drop silent, and there seems to be a sudden suspension of breath.

'So what if I did?' replies Turner, with such casual arrogance that I think Becky will step forward and slap him. She does more than that. Stepping over the broken glass, she propels herself towards Turner, pushing him with all her might. He topples backwards, where he overturns two tables and finally lands prostrate on the floor just inches from the group of governors. The headmaster, his face white with fury, picks Turner up from the floor and guides him firmly towards Becky.

'What on earth is going on here?' he says to the two teenagers, barely managing to contain his anger.

'What's going on here is that *that* woman,' Becky turns, narrows her eyes in unequivocal hatred, and points across the room, 'has been screwing my boyfriend!'

It's like something out of a detective novel. All heads turn to follow the direction in which Becky is pointing, where stands Desra McKinley. The lecturer's eyes are wide, her expression stunned. I feel the warmth of two bodies taking up positions on either side of me.

'*Mon dieu*,' whispers Marie-Claire.

'This is karma in a very big way,' adds Julia.

It takes at least a half hour before the headmaster can calm Becky down. By that time she has already made a call to her father, the CEO of a Fortune 500 company, and her corporate lawyer mother in Upstate New York. Desra, meanwhile, has been ordered to the headmaster's office – 'The Crucible' – where the Board of Governors is waiting.

'And where the offence is,' I whisper, watching as Desra, accompanied by a stern-looking Simpson, leaves the foyer, 'let the great axe fall.'

41

High drama dissolves into banality as broken glass is swept up, explanations are attempted, and the one hundred and fifty guests creep away, as if they in some way were responsible for the discomfiture of the evening.

The summer school students stunned and adrenaline-filled, escape to the boathouse with pilfered bottles of booze, where we drunkenly dissect the events of the evening.

'You don't believe she did it, do you?' asks Sally, her eyes pink.

'It's probably best not to comment until it's looked into properly,' replies Dave, with his usual compassion.

'Where are Marvin and Roz?' asks Caleb, passing a large bag of crisps to the group.

'Packing,' Sally replies, blowing her nose. 'They said they'll not stay another moment more in this *den of iniquity*.'

'I've never seen anything like it,' says a subdued Julia. 'The broken glass, that poor boy toppling over the table, and the *j'accuse* drama of it all.' She drains her tumbler. 'If it wasn't so tragic it could almost be funny.'

'So, you do think she did it?' says Sally, no longer bothering to hold back her tears.

'Yes,' Julia replies, and glancing my way adds, 'and worse.'

I remain silent. I know the full extent of Desra McKinley's wickedness, and I can only hope that at this very moment the Scottish police are escorting her to a holding cell.

The group break up a few minutes later, retiring to their rooms and their own uncomfortable thoughts about the evening.

'Do you want to be alone?' asks Caleb when we stop at my door.

'No,' I reply, and taking his hand I lead him inside.

In the pandemonium that followed Becky's dramatic accusation, I forgot to distribute the envelopes. By the time I remembered, Desra was already in her meeting with the headmaster and the Board of Governors, a *DO NOT DISTURB* sign hanging prominently on the office door and Mrs Roe standing guard nearby.

I wait until Caleb is gently snoring before getting dressed and tiptoeing out of the room. A full moon illuminates the path and I find myself glad to be alone.

373

I enter the keycode for the reception area and ring the bell for the night porter.

'It's important that the headmaster and the Board of Governors receive these first thing tomorrow.' The porter, a gentle middle-aged man named Paulo, nods an acknowledgement. 'It's to do with what happened this evening.'

Tomorrow morning, I will speak to the headmaster in person, then travel to the nearest police station and to the *Perth Courier*, where I will drop off an additional brown envelope each.

'Evidence,' I whisper, as I follow the path to the boathouse, 'of that woman's deeper crimes.'

I stroll along the jetty, the small solar lights casting a soft glow on the weatherworn timber. Now that the awful truth about Desra McKinley has been revealed, I will ensure all the evidence is presented appropriately and clearly, then go home, wherever that may be. Maybe back to Cornwall, maybe not. I hear the soft tip-tap of high heels on wood. I turn. Desra McKinley is standing just a few feet away.

'Kate bloody Hardy.' She sways slightly, and I think she may topple into the water.

'Desra.'

She stumbles forward and now I can see that she has a whisky glass in her hand.

'So, I couldn't figure it out really,' she says, her words garbled. 'This persistent feeling that we had met.' The clouds above shift, and slivers of moonlight ignite the loch. I can see that her dress is torn. Her hair is dishevelled and there are large streaks of mascara on her cheeks. I think of *Jane Eyre's* woman in the attic. She gives a deep chuckle, drains her glass and then, cocking her arm, throws it far into the lake.

'I should go.'

'No, no, no,' says Desra, moving closer. 'Why would you want to leave? I expect you've been waiting for this moment for years.'

'Let me by.'

'So, the thing is,' she continues. 'I was happy to accept the fact that you were from Devon was just an unpleasant coincidence.' I find myself slowly backing away towards the end of the jetty. 'But that poem – and your reference to Diving Fish.' She closes her eyes and raises her face to the night sky. 'Moonlight lingers on the pale abandon of your skin.' I feel my knees weaken. 'He read that to me you know.' Desra is smiling: a wide, demented grin that exposes two prominent incisors. 'After the first time we fucked, he read that to me.'

'Michael,' I whisper. 'His name was Michael.'

'*Michael.*' The way she says it makes it sound dirty. 'Why did you do it?'

At last I have said the words that have polluted my mind for so long.

She feigns an innocent look. 'Do what?'

'Let him go into the water that night. You knew he was drunk. Why did you let him go swimming on his own?'

She gives an indifferent shrug, and not for the first time I understand what it feels like to genuinely want to kill someone.

'I had to be somewhere.' She laughs, an eerie high-pitched cackle that shatters the midnight calm. 'Oh, for Christ's sake, Kate,' she says, and hands on hips in a universal gesture of defiance, adds, 'I wasn't his fucking mother.'

I have been right all along. My darling, trusting boy was betrayed in the most horrendous and evil way imaginable.

'And the travel sickness pills?'

'What about them?'

'You gave him some the night he died, didn't you?'

'He liked the buzz.'

'You killed him.'

'He was a big boy; he knew what he was doing.'

'He was fifteen!' I suddenly feel an odd sense of calm enfold me. As if somewhere within all this astonishing madness, there may be peace. At last I am saying the words that I have only practised in my head for years. I think of my beloved Michael; of Lisa, Alistair, the poor, heartbroken Becky, and all the other unnamed victims. 'Why do you do it, Desra?'

Her eyes are two flat discs. 'I do it because I can.'

There is a sort of perverse tranquillity in her response. At least now I know I am dealing with a madwoman.

'You're finished,' I say, trying to work out some way of getting past her without falling into the water.

'I doubt that.'

'What?'

'Nobody likes a scandal, Kate.' The look of triumph on her face is infuriating. 'At this very moment, both

376

Turner and Becky are *seriously* reconsidering their positions.'

'What do you mean?'

'After all,' she smirks, 'Turner did sneak into my room and sexually assault me.'

'What?'

'I'm sure the headmaster and the Board of Governors will understand that the trauma of it all meant that I couldn't really speak about it until now.'

'You're lying!'

'I really wouldn't want to have to make a formal statement,' says Desra, trying her hardest to look helpless. 'After all, a rape charge will be bound to affect Turner's university applications.'

My eyes widen in disbelief. 'You really *are* crazy.'

Desra gives a little tut. 'I'm not the one who travelled across the country to stalk someone she blames for her idiot son's death!'

I clench my fists ready to punch. 'You won't get away with this.'

'Of course I will. Do you think the headmaster and his little bunch of flunkies want a scandal of this calibre associated with Lennoxton?' She makes an unsuccessful attempt to straighten her ruined dress. 'Do you really think Becky's rich mommy and daddy want a dirty little court case on their daughter's Google profile? Trust me, they won't.' She smiles smugly. 'And I'll be speaking to my solicitor first thing tomorrow morning about little Becky's scene this evening. Slander, defamation of character. I'm sure we can agree on a tidy out-of-court settlement.'

We stand facing each other, only inches apart.

'I don't care what you say. You won't get away with this, I promise you that.'

'Is there something you're not telling me, Kate?'

'On the headmaster's desk right now is an envelope containing copies of the letters of complaint against you from Edgecombe Academy.' *Well, they will be there tomorrow.* 'There's also a taped recording and transcript of my conversation with Lisa Edwards,' I lie – anything to get this arrogant parasite off guard – 'regarding your sexual relationship with Michael.'

Desra stares at me through heavy, drunken eyes. 'Shame both your star witnesses are dead.'

I bend my knees slightly; plant my feet. 'Alistair March isn't.' Even in the half-light I can see Desra's expression change. 'I found him. He's agreed to make a statement to the police.' *Well, he'll agree when he's given a witness summons.* 'That will include, I'm certain, how you groomed, exploited and manipulated him into a sexual relationship. It's called underage rape, Desra; minimum of two years in prison.'

There is a long pause as Desra's inebriated brain attempts to process what I have just said. Then she does something so unexpected that I am completely unprepared. She gives a deep growl of anger that seems to swell up inside her until it emerges as a scream. Her eyes bulge and her lips pull back. She reminds me of a rabid dog.

'You can't do this,' she screams. 'I won't let you!'

'It's too late, Desra. It's done.' I don't feel triumphant, or even pleased with myself. Just very, very tired. I

378

press my palms together and rest them against my lips. 'Susan O'Neill, you are finished.'

My mention of her former name; her former life; seems to tip her over the edge, and suddenly she is running towards me.

'I'm going to kill you!' she screams, and before I know what is happening, she has me around the waist, and both of us are tumbling off the jetty and straight into Loch Haugh.

42

Hitting the water is a shock: not just the intense cold
and darkness, but also the realisation that Desra is
gripping me tightly as we plunge deeper and deeper.
The impact takes my breath away and I force myself
not to breathe. I know from my lifesaving training
that it's one of the most common causes of drowning
– the cold and shock initiate an involuntary breath.
Great when you need a firm supply of oxygen to
your brain to stop passing out after a trauma, but
not so good when you're metres under water.

Water fills my nose, and my lungs are screaming.
My mind races in panic. I need air. I begin twisting
and turning, digging my nails into Desra's exposed
arms. Her grip loosens slightly, and I kick for the
surface. There is a brief, desperate moment when I
suck in a lungful of air before being pulled back
under again.

'Now's not the time to give up, Mum.'

Michael?

'You've come so far; worked so hard to find the truth. You can't give up now.'

But I'm tired Michael. So tired. I just want to go to sleep.

'I can't let you do that, Mum; you know I can't.'

It's too hard, Michael. I can't do it.

'You can, Mum. You must.'

But we could be together again. Just let me sleep, Michael.

'We can't. I won't let you. And besides, if I do, she wins.'

The thought of a gloating, triumphant Desra is too much to bear and I fight back. With precious little oxygen left in my lungs I find myself grappling for Desra's face. I can feel her shoulders, her neck, the back of her head, and then suddenly her jaw line. I slide my hands upwards, past the cheekbones and to the bridge of her nose. With my last ounce of energy, I dig my thumbs deep into Desra's eye sockets. I can feel her body stiffen, then her head twist and turn, but I hold fast. Finally, after what seems like hours, Desra's grip loosens and I struggle free. Fresh air seems miles away, but with one final effort I break the surface and emerge into the night. My first few, desperate gulps of air are intoxicating; then I start choking. Deep, lung-crushing coughs that rattle my body. I'm terrified I will sink down again. Just ahead, I see the jetty with its moss-covered pillars sunk deep into the loch. My arms ache, and my body feels like stone. I am taking my first tentative stroke to safety, when from behind me the water explodes.

'Where are you, you bitch!'

Desra rubs her injured eyes, and then begins swimming blindly towards me. 'When I find you, I am going to kill you!' Desra's fury has imbued her with a renewed energy and she is moving fast. Her vision will clear any second. 'I know you're there, Kate. If you think for one minute you can get away from me . . .'

In the moonlight Desra is a pewter Medusa, her wet hair curling around her forehead like snakes. Her dark eyes narrow and then focus. She spots me and smiles.

'There you are,' she growls, and begins swimming towards me. I am freezing, tired, and running out of strength. I must make it to the jetty before Desra. I turn and begin swimming, forcing my sluggish arms into action, pressing my legs to kick. The jetty is just an arms-length away when I hear a strange sound behind me. I turn to see Desra, her eyes wide with terror.

'Something's got me, something's got me!' Long ribbons of seaweed have twisted their way around her arms and neck and seem to be pulling her down into the depths. I've made it to the jetty and I'm desperately clinging to one of the slippery pillars. 'Help me, Kate! Help me!'

She is only a few metres away. I could swim out, extend my arm, and pull her to safety. I could swim to shore and grab the life ring from the emergency station. I could use the emergency telephone and call for help. I do none of these. Instead I watch silently as Susan O'Neill kicks and splashes; as her tortured, terrified cries are caught by the night breeze and blown southward. I don't move. Don't even blink. Finally, as if pulled under by some unseen force, and with a final, strangled scream of terror, Desra slips into the deep, black water.

With agonising effort, I swim the few metres to the shore and drag myself onto the bank. My legs are cramped, and my left hand is tightly fisted. Something is pressing against my palm. During my attempts to free myself from Desra's grip, I must have inadvertently grabbed something.

I force my fingers open. Nestled in the palm of my hand is a sterling silver necklace with a small blue sea-glass pendant of a fish on the end. The one Michael bought for Susan from the charity shop all those years before.

Moonlight bathes the shore in a ghostly iridescence. The wind howls its mournful cry. Warm tears stream down my freezing cheeks. Tomorrow there will be questions to answer, more lies to tell, but there's only one thing left to say.

'Rest in peace, Michael.'

Epilogue

I wake to the sound of gulls, their high-pitched screams piercing the morning calm. I shiver, pull on my dressing gown, and go downstairs to make some tea. While I wait for the kettle to boil, I wander into the front room and open the curtains. Outside the River Tamar flows onwards, unmoved by human loss or misery, unfeeling in its endless journey to the sea. Tam is basking in a sunny spot on the garden wall. Next to him stands a large estate agent's sign. My mother's house has been sold, its contents divided or given to charity. All that's left is for me to collect my few remaining things and move on. I hear a soft tapping, and, recognising a familiar silhouette through the frosted glass, I smile and open the door.

'Doris, come in.'

The elderly woman shakes her head. 'No, my love, I'll only get all weepy again. I know we said our goodbyes yesterday, but amongst all the hugs and tears I forgot to give you this.' She hands me a large, padded envelope. The postmark is from Scotland. 'Were you expecting it?'

'No,' I reply. 'I wasn't.'

I give Doris one final hug, then wait for her to leave before I tear open the package. Could it be Julia and Marie-Claire's wedding photos? It is, in fact, a book. I turn it over and am stunned to read the title. *Carnation.*

There is a short note from Julia sending best wishes and saying that following Desra McKinley's tragic death, Epiphany Press decided to publish the anthology posthumously, but it has only achieved mediocre sales.

After all, writes Julia, *it was a tragedy, her drowning accidentally like that, wasn't it? It's a shame the Scottish police decided not to investigate Becky's claim any further, but I suppose with the alleged perpetrator dead and the victim back in America, not much they could do, eh?*

Did you know that the Headmaster resigned? Marie-Claire suggested I apply for his post. Can you imagine!

There is another paragraph about the couple's honeymoon in Bali, and a final few sentences.

I always wondered why you didn't go to the police with your niece's story, but I suppose, like you said, she just wanted to put it all behind her. Move on, so to speak.

I can't resist flipping to the original title poem; the poem which Desra has so blatantly plagiarised from

385

Michael. It is just as I had first read it in Michael's diary, word for word. I spot something at the bottom of the page, a notation of some sort, and squint to read the small print.

'Diving Fish' first written 2013 for The Arts Council of England Southwest Artists' Anthology of Poetry

The poem had been Desra's all along.

I slip Julia's letter between the front pages, snap the book shut and then, tying my dressing gown tightly around my waist, slip on a pair of flip-flops and step out into the spring morning. The cool air nips at my ankles, but I still walk the twenty steps from my front door to the riverbank opposite. Raising the small volume to the sky, I fling it as far into the river as possible. It flies through the air, the cream leaves spread wide, then tumbles into the river, where it floats on the surface for a few seconds before disappearing into the wake of a passing motorboat.

Shivering, I hurry back to the warmth of the house and close the door. I hear footsteps behind me.

'What were you doing outside in your dressing gown?'

I feel the warmth of Caleb's body against mine, feel as his hand caresses my swollen, pregnant belly. I raise my hand to my neck and run my fingertips along the silver chain that rests there, and then down to the sea-glass pendant that sits nestled between my breasts.

'Just getting rid of some rubbish,' I whisper.

Acknowledgements

I owe grateful thanks to all the people over the years who supported me on my journey to publication.

My children Danielle and Dominic, who listened, encouraged and offered welcome suggestions, and my husband Nick, who was always there to lend a critical ear, and provide love, support and positive ways forward.

I would also like to thank all the friends and family who looked out for – and after – me: Ce and Dick Sharland; the Johnstons – Heather, Paul, Richard and Fiona; David and Valerie Horspool; Ann Pelletier-Topping, Tre Grey, Sharon Bray, Penny Manios and the lovely Sue Ferry.

To my writer friends, I couldn't have done it without you. Finn Clarke, your unending encouragement and sound advice was, and always is, welcome.

To trusted readers David Horspool and Helena

Boughton, thank you for dotting my i's and crossing my t's.

To my classmates on the UEA MA in Creative Writing – Crime: Denise, Natalie, Femi, Niamh, Mark, Freya, Dimitris, Bob, Niki, Peter, Roe and Matt, and to tutors Henry Sutton, Laura Joyce and Tom Benn, and also my current workshop buddies, Judi Daykin, Wendy Turbin and Karen Taylor for making feedback fun.

Very special thanks goes to *The Big Issue* for creating this opportunity, and the wonderful team at Avon Books: Sabah Khan, Phoebe Morgan, Ellie Pilcher, and especially Molly Walker-Sharp, whose unending support, patience and guidance has allowed me to continue to learn and grow as a writer. Thanks too to copy editor Felicity Radford and proofreader Anne Rieley for their fresh eyes!

A final thanks to my brothers Alan and Bob Michael, my late mother Marielle, and the late, great Roy York who convinced me this story 'had legs'!